THEN THERE WAS YOU

LOVE IN DUNES BAY, BOOK 1

LYNN CRANDALL

UNTITLED

Then There Was You
By Lynn Crandall

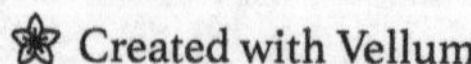 Created with Vellum

To Mike, my one and only.

UNTITLED

Acknowledgment
It takes a team to bring together a book, and I am grateful for the individuals who helped in creating the best book I could: my editors Tamara Eaton and Sue Grimshaw, Lynne McLewin, counselor extraordinaire who helped me write genuine characters, the policemen and journalists who allowed me to pick their brains, Carol Scott, a pharmaceuticals research nurse who provided expert input for the story, Jamie Kurtz, computer genius, Andrew Kurtz, former Chicagoian, my friend and fellow writer and beta reader, HiDee Ekstrom, my husband, one of the best sounding boards in the business, and gifted cover artist Dar Albers. You all mean a lot to me.

1

Cherish Moss grasped Lucy Standish's hand and held her breath, waiting for the verdict. So much was at stake for the elderly woman and her husband Sam.

She laid her free hand on her leg, suddenly noticing it was bouncing. *Confidence, Cherish.*

The hour hand pointed to ten on the clock on the wall, and Cherish watched the second hand slowly, achingly, circle the face. The room was so quiet, as though everyone was holding their breath. She dared a glance at the men and women in the jury box. A few jurors stared at the floor. Others fixed gazes on the judge. She eyed a woman juror who peered at her, but the woman quickly looked away. A chill swept through Cherish, and she tightened her grip on Lucy's hand.

"Has the jury reached a verdict?" The judge's words boomed in the courtroom.

Yes, let's get this over with. Cherish didn't dare smile at her clients for fear of jinxing the outcome.

The jury foreman stood and read from a piece of paper. "The jury finds in favor of the defendant, Dunes Bay Property Management."

Lucy's hand slipped from Cherish's, and she felt the bottom drop from the couple's life. "We'll talk outside of the courtroom," she whispered.

"Thank you, jurors, for your service. You are dismissed. Court is adjourned." The judge pounded his gavel once and moved to his chambers.

Cherish hefted her briefcase off the table and ushered her clients out of the courtroom. Her chest burned in the aftermath of the verdict. She'd wanted a win, not only for the couple, but to prove to her mother and father that her charitable cases *were* worth her time. She could stand quite well on her own two feet in a courtroom, but when it came to holding her own with her parents it was another matter altogether. When they disapproved, it had always been wiser and easier to give in rather than face their sharp tongues. But her charity cases remained worth fighting for.

"Let's go over here." She led Sam and Lucy Standish to an alcove and settled them into open chairs. A plan, that's what she needed. And of course, she had one. Every lawyer worth their trade did.

"Don't lose heart. We're going to appeal. Everything will be okay."

"How could the jury find in favor of the landlord? We told the truth." Mr. Standish's face sagged with wrinkles, but not just from age. Creases in his brow deepened, and Cherish couldn't miss the despair clouding his eyes.

"I know you did. I think the photos the opposition counsel introduced of the burned remains of a space heater in your living room were very compelling for the jurors." She straightened her shoulders, ready to march on her plan to set things right as soon as possible.

But her brain stumbled for words, her attention seized by Mrs. Standish's hand running across the scar that stretched the length of her arm. Her heart clenched. Sam and Lucy needed money. As their lawyer, it had been her job to get it for them.

The case against the Dunes Bay Property Management for negligence had seemed so cut and dry. Where had she gone wrong?

She knelt in front of them both. "Look, when you first told me about losing your home in the fire and the expense of your injuries, I had no doubts we could win against your landlord. I'm really sorry the verdict didn't go our way. The justice system doesn't always seem just. The fire was not your fault, so I have to get the truth across. Meanwhile, I'm going to find a way to get you a home, and money to cover your medical bills."

Mrs. Standish stared out the windows at the front of the Dunes Bay Michigan County Courthouse. "How?"

"I don't know yet. Our first step is an appeal. We know there is a hole in the landlord's story. There has to be because you're telling the truth."

Mrs. Standish took Cherish's hand and smiled a tiny, tired smile. "That is a good point."

"You have been so kind to us, what with finding us a temporary place to live and helping us set up a payment plan at the hospital. You're a good lawyer, and clearly you have a good heart or you wouldn't volunteer your services at Lawyers Can Help. I'll try to focus on hope." Mr. Standish helped his wife stand.

"Thank you. I'll get right into finding grounds for appeal." Cherish moved with them toward the front doors, her brain once again buzzing with questions: What had she missed and how could she set this straight?

"Hey, Cherish." The call reverberated against the stone walls and jerked her to a standstill. "Wait up."

Her pulse leapt like a greyhound bursting from the gate. It was Devin. Her fiancé and opposing counsel was not exactly the man of the hour for the Standishes. She faced them. "I'll be in touch soon. If you have any thoughts, call—"

"C'mon, Cherish," Devin interrupted. "My time is short and I have a last minute question about the wedding."

Cherish shrunk inside. "Just a minute." Her voice sounded loud in the large lobby.

Mrs. Standish's eyes widened. "Go ahead. We understand."

Cherish blew out a breath. Wisps of her bangs lifted, and she ran her hand through them. "I'm sorry. I am not too busy to attend to your needs." Drat Devin. She had worked very hard to assure the Standishes her relationship with opposing counsel and upcoming wedding wouldn't interfere with her devotion to their case. It wasn't like she was doing anything wrong and had tried to keep it a secret from them, but she winced anyway. "I bet Devin is one of the last people you want to see right now."

"You're right. But I'm sure he's not a bad man." Mrs. Standish wrung her hands.

Mr. Standish cleared his throat. "No, he's just doing his job for the other side. Have a good day," he said, walking away with his wife.

"Hey, how's my favorite red head?" Devin's brash confidence clashed loudly with the staid attitude of the courthouse. He planted a kiss on her cheek.

"Well, aren't you pleased with the verdict?" She tried, but she couldn't keep the bitterness out of her voice.

"Whoa, is that sour grapes? I won because I presented a compelling case. Those old people tried to take my client to the cleaners, but I stopped them. That's called justice. Now, can we talk about the wedding?"

"No. I want to talk about how bad I feel for my clients. You snuck that photo in on me. That wasn't fair." She crossed her arms over her midriff and stared up into his face, lips tight. Influential in his career and in his circles, Devon wasn't accustomed to being challenged. She swallowed hard.

"It was up to you to discover all the relevant elements of the case." He took her chin between his thumb and forefinger and lifted it a little. "Don't make me angry. I had a good morning. I'm a more experienced lawyer. Don't take it personally. Especially because I love you. I don't care that you lost."

"Oh, good. Thanks." She could have slapped him. If he weren't Devin. After all, he was a good man. He'd earned a good reputation for being tough but generous. In her personal relationships it was easy for her to let small disturbing things pass. In her powerhouse family, she'd had a lot of practice. Listening to her gut and following her heart only drew impatience and criticism for being overly sensitive. Not worth the attempt to disagree.

"Now, the wedding. I asked my mom to read a poem in the ceremony. You don't mind do you? She really wants to be a part of things."

Cherish stomped on her gut feeling to resist. It was irrational. "Of course I don't mind. What poem?"

He waved his hand. "She hasn't decided yet." He checked his Rolex. "I've got a meeting, so got to run."

Just as briskly as he'd interjected himself into her moments with the Standishes, Devin Raye breezed out the revolving doors.

Cherish stared after him. Sometimes Devin felt like a hit and run, but she liked his zest, his bravado, and—well, his hair. He had really good hair.

Minutes later she climbed into her Jeep Ranger and put aside the loss. It was all she could do for now. On her way to her office, she opened her car window and let the warm summer breeze clear her head. Located on the southern shore of Lake Michigan, Dunes Bay always had a faint scent of the lake. The familiar smell gave her comfort. She loved driving through town and seeing the older homes with front porches, the Farmer's Market on the city plaza, and the shops and small businesses that lined the downtown streets. Tourists wearing beachwear strolled along the streets, heading for the beach. All this gave her a sense of home. And the lake pulled at her. She didn't want to think about the case or her upcoming wedding. When she arrived at work, she would dig in to the case again, later. She needed just to breathe.

At the office of Moss Attorneys at Law, Cherish parked and headed to the door, but stopped when a woman standing near the road holding a sign asking for help caught her attention. She searched through her purse for her wallet as she walked toward the woman and smiled. "How are you today?"

The woman eyed her wallet, then lifted her gaze to meet Cherish's eyes. Lines around her eyes deepened as she squinted in the sunlight. "Fine," she muttered.

Cherish couldn't help but wonder what the woman's story was, and her insides leaned heavily into asking. But she knew better than to pry. She handed the woman a twenty and made eye contact. She wanted to connect, reach her with compassion, but the woman's eyes were guarded. "I hope you have a nice day," Cherish said.

"Thank you," the woman said and tucked the money into a pocket, her gaze darting furtively.

Cherish sighed as she turned to her office building, her heart a little heavy that homelessness exists but a little lighter that she could help out in a small way. A sort of penance for how her family treated her Uncle Peter when he lost his job years ago. Twelve at the time, she didn't have any say in her parents' rejection of him, but she shuddered remembering how her mother had shunned him, her own brother, when he needed financial help, and called him a loser. She couldn't bear it then any more than she could turn a blind eye to the woman outside.

Inside, Cherish took the elevator to the fourth floor and snuck in to her office, relieved to settle alone into her own space.

Soon it all will be over.

She sank into the delicious thought. No more decisions between lace or silk, salmon or pork tenderloin, Tahiti or Switzerland. Poetry or not.

Her wedding, just one day away, would make her Mrs. Devin Raye, emphatically not Moss-Raye.

Cherish slumped deeper into her chair. As with the selection of the dress with a huge bow at her waist capping a long train, she had acquiesced, and agreed to ditch her surname.

She shook off details. They weren't important. She just needed to focus on the man she loved, right? Devin could be sharp, downright explosive at times, but he had his good points too. He could persuade anyone to do anything. He called that charm. When it came to the courtroom or what he wanted in his career trajectory, he was a gladiator. She admired that.

She chewed on her thumbnail, surveying her wedding dress. It stared her down from across the room. She eyed it back. Since the bridal shop delivered the enormous concoction to her office yesterday, she'd kept her distance. The delivery person had given her a strange look and asked how she planned to get it to the church. It was a reasonable question, but Cherish knew what she was doing. She was getting used to the dress. It hung on the lip above the closet, and in its see-through garment bag, she could regard its glossy silk skirt and sleeves dotted with tiny pearls. It was stately, her mother had told her at the bridal shop. It was sophisticated and dramatic.

Cherish began sweating, remembering standing in front of her mother draped in heavy silk.

She had said, "But Mom, it's not me. It's too, umm...stuffy."

"Don't be silly, Cherish. You look elegant. The silk really sets off your copper hair. Devin will have eyes for only you when you walk down the aisle in this dress."

End of discussion. Emma Moss was always right.

She'd learned early it just wasn't worth the fight to stand her ground because one way or another, her mother's way was *the* way. Cherish sighed, as memories wafted over her.

"Cherish, you'll never get into law school if you don't go the extra mile and graduate at the top of your class."

"Don't wait to get in your application for a summer internship with a prominent judge. Summer isn't the time to shirk off, it's the time to further your career. You know I only want what's best for you."

Her mother's guidance didn't have a beginning, it just always had been there, and how could she argue with her mom's insistence? Even when it came to Devin, she supposed Emma Moss was right.

Tap, tap-tap, tap. The sound of her fingers' staccato beat on her desk echoed in her office. Time had flown since she'd said yes to Devin's proposal six months ago and set off a metronome that marked a steady march to the big day. And here she sat, a matter of hours from a new life.

She counted backward in her mind to ten months ago and her first date with Devin. That was the day her parents predicted she and Devin would make a good match.

She hadn't dated in months. After back-to-back betrayals, she had plunged into her work. Then she met Devin at a lawyers' conference when she and her parents sat at the same table as Devin during lunch. He'd given her the full court press, and dazzled her. Her parents admired him right off and didn't hesitate to make him a fixture in the Moss family life, inviting him for dinner at their house and expecting her to show up. Devin had charmed her parents first, then he'd aimed it at her. He charted a flight to New York City and took her to the theater. He booked a room in a fancy Chicago hotel for the weekend and they took a cruise on Lake Michigan. His dynamic personality entranced her. It was so different from hers. With his endorsement from her parents, she hadn't put up much of a struggle to give the relationship more time.

Her mother's words surfaced in her memory. "You're twenty-eight, the perfect age to settle down with someone. Devin is a good catch."

Ugh. Good catch? Really? Her mother had made it seem as though Devin was an object and she was chasing him with throngs of women down streets of the city of Dunes Bay.

Anxiety spiked in her chest. Her parents had better be right about Devin and her belonging together, because as soon as all the fanfare ended, everything about the rest of her life would actually begin. The until-death-do-we-part time.

She breathed in and out deeply and shifted in her chair. Of course, that would be the good part. Waking up in the morning beside Devin, then kissing good-bye as they went their separate ways to work, hers to her family law firm and his to Wellington, Raye, and Black Law Firm.

Oh my God.

The antacids on her desk called to her. So much for being a joyful bride-to-be. Her stomach twisted into knots on a daily basis until two weeks ago. Now, it knotted hourly. Her parents assured her pre-wedding qualms were natural, and she believed them. Yes she did. Her nervous stomach and hair-thin patience didn't mean she was about to get lost in a life she didn't want.

She chewed the fruity tablets that promised relief from her self-created discomfort. She was doing this dance of nerves, inexplicably. Devin was a prominent lawyer in Dunes Bay. He was smart and fun. Who wouldn't want to marry him?

You.

2

"I do!" she hollered. "Devin is everything I could want."

"Cherish, did you call me?" Pansy, her assistant knocked on her office door, then stepped in, her eyebrows arched. Close to her age, Pansy was always the professional, but they shared coffee breaks and some bits about their private lives. Still, Cherish hadn't shared anything about the wedding with her or her misgivings about getting married. There were times she wanted to, but it felt unprofessional and weak. "I thought I heard you calling."

"No, I was just being emphatic with myself. Thank you for checking."

Pansy nodded. "Wedding jitters? That's normal, you know."

"So I've heard."

"Maybe you should go home and see to last-minute details. Everyone would understand, including Adrian and Emma."

The mention of her parents tightened the noose around her neck. They had expectations. Law school had been their idea, but it seemed a good fit to her too; a great way to do good, make a difference. So she'd let them guide her and she'd scraped her way through alongside all the powerhouse students. It took guts and grit and she'd done it, by God, even if she had faked it a bit. Now they expected her to live a "great life," they said. Devin could be a part of that and he loved her. All she had to do was look past his controlling nature. "That's the beauty of my mother taking over wedding planning. I don't have to attend to any details." Cherish ran her tongue over her teeth, still tasting the mango pineapple flavor of the antacid tablet. "She picked the gown, the flowers, the reception menu, all of it."

Pansy's eyes widened. "Without you? You didn't tell me."

"Well, to be fair, she kept me in the loop and asked for my opinions countless times. She freed up my time to attend to my cases." The thing about Pansy was she could see right through her, but she would never press a point. "Planning a wedding is exhausting, you know? I've been very busy with work."

"Right. I understand. That was very nice of her. Okay, well, I'll leave you to your work." Pansy backed out of the room and pulled the door closed.

Cherish leaned backward and surveyed the office she'd been working in since joining her parent's law firm three years ago right out of law school. The dark wood paneling and deep blue sculpted carpeting had surrounded her in warmth since that first day she claimed the office. Pride in accomplishing her dream of becoming a lawyer filled the room as nicely as the ambiance of law books lining the walls. But on this day, as Pansy shut the door, the office stifled her.

Good grief, I'm trapped inside these walls.

She opened a window and inhaled. *Stop it, just stop it. You're fine. Get your head in the game.*

Yes, the work would take care of her. The wedding soon would be over, and her life would go on. *Vow to self—When all around me is making me crazy, I will not get lost.*

She marched across the room and grabbed a folder from a filing cabinet. Her mind took over. The drug company Decidedly Laboratories had been a client at her family's firm for many years, and her father and mother trusted her with its needs. Presently, the company needed to win a lawsuit naming one of the company's new drugs as the cause of liver failure. Shivers tripped through her. It was a terrible assertion. If true, she would be defending the company from gross negligence. Her stomach twisted. *What if the company was guilty?*

Her father strolled into her office, surrounded by his Creed Spice and Wood cologne. Adrian Moss, distinguished lawyer, cool Rock of Gibraltar, slipped into a chair across from her. "Hi, pumpkin. Do you have a few minutes for your father?"

"Of course." She planted her elbows on her desk and balanced her chin on her hands. He had no idea what it was like to suffer from self-doubt. And she would never own up to having any. It was just not allowed.

"Your mother says you're having wedding jitters. Is that true?"

A hard rock formed in her chest. She raised her hands. "Can everybody stop worrying about me? Yes, I'm a bit nervous. That's normal!"

He nodded, his lips pursed. "Okay, then."

"Maybe I said that a little too loudly." She sank back in her chair. "I'm fine, Dad. Thank you for caring."

"You sound stressed." He leaned closer and touched her hand. "Devin will make a good husband. He's not like any of the other guys you've dated. He won't hurt you. Trust me."

"I always have." Her heartbeat pounded in her ears. When it came to love, she had to admit trust was a problem for her.

"Don't think so much, sweetie. Just get on board the great life you're going to have with Devin." He beat a little rhythm on the desk. "Well, I'll let you get back to whatever you were doing."

"I'm working on the Decidedly Laboratories' case. I'm just doing preliminaries." No reason to tell him she'd been in court earlier doing a pro bono case for Lawyers Can Help, and she didn't want to have to defend herself. She clenched her teeth. She shouldn't have to, and that she was hiding her true feelings was really putting her on edge.

He pursed his lips and narrowed his eyes at her. "Devin told me you were in court this morning as counselor for some charity group. You know our priority isn't pro bono, it's billable hours. Your mother and I have entrusted the Decidedly Laboratories case to you. That's where the money is."

She didn't know whether to stomp her foot in protest of his attitude or apologize for letting down her parents.

"I'm on top of the big case, Dad. Like I said, I'm working on it right now."

"That's my girl." He beamed at her. "A wedding tomorrow and a honeymoon, but you're digging into a complex case. You're made of good stuff."

"Thanks." In his wake, Cherish sighed. *Why is everything annoying me?* Her father's praise chafed under her skin. He wasn't saying she was great of her own accord, only that she was like him and her mom —a workaholic willing to sacrifice almost anything in service of clients. But his opinion about her pro bono work not measuring up to the firm's needs was a serious blow. She did the work under the radar. She didn't need her parents' constant reminder to prioritize billable hours. How could she have been so nearsighted about the Standishes' case coming to light? She hadn't counted on Devin exposing her. He was so like her parents, always focusing on money. She wanted to scream, *how could you betray me?* But of course the three of them talked. Sometimes she wondered if her parents considered him a better lawyer than her. Other times she questioned if he was the son they never had.

"Cherish?" It was Pansy on the intercom. "You have a call on line one. It's Devin."

"Got it." She ran her hands down her pants and collected her nerves. "Hi, why didn't you call my cellphone?"

Devin's laughter rumbled in her ear. "Well, hi to you too."

Irritation fired like tiny rockets in her body. "Sorry. I'm fine. How are you, Devin," she said, emphasizing his name.

"Don't get twitchy, I'm just being polite. Besides, you never answer your cellphone."

"That's not true." She ran her gaze over the papers on her desk, noting the age of the petitioner, Henry Pole—thirty-four, self-employed father of two. She gritted her teeth. It would be hard not to sympathize with this man. It would be her job to make him unsympathetic to the jury. *Crap.*

"Cherish, are you listening?" Devin's voice was prickly.

"Yes."

"Well, can you meet me for lunch?"

Oops. "Oh, sorry. I got distracted for a minute. You know, a case in front of me. Yes, sure. Where and when?"

"How about Miguel's at one?"

Acid in her belly boiled just thinking of a burrito. "Umm...I don't feel like Mexican. How about we meet at Soup and Salad? We could sit in the sunshine on the patio."

"Oh, well, sure. I could really get into a plate of steak fajitas. But if you want something else, that's fine."

Was it fine? It didn't sound like it. Disappointment in his voice was too much for her to ignore. "No, Mexican is fine. If I leave now I can make it by one."

"If you're sure, that would be great." His voice softened. "I can't wait to see you, beautiful."

"You saw me just an hour ago."

"You don't want me to miss you?"

His petulance set her teeth on edge. "Of course. It's sweet of you."

"Pretty soon I'll see you every day and every night."

She bit her lip hard. "It's going to be...nice." *Stop acting ridiculous!*

3

Cherish swished through the glass doors at Miguel's and searched the room for Devin. She spotted his raised hand at the back of the dining area and sped to his table. "I'm sorry I'm late."

Devin chuckled. "I know you. You lost track of time. It's okay. I've already ordered for you, to save time."

Her chest tightened. "How did you know what I want?"

He grinned. "I know you're a salad girl. I ordered a fajita taco salad."

Her insides became a discordant head-banger song. "Nice. Thank you." It wasn't the time to quibble over small things, like salad or soup. Cherish settled her gaze on Devin, trying to center her focus. His black hair was a neatly trimmed cut that complemented the sharp lines of his face. From his dark gray suit, crisp, pale blue shirt, and midnight blue tie, to the upward tilt of his chin, he exuded confidence. Suddenly aware he was watching her, she looked in his brown eyes. They invited her in.

"Hi, Cherish."

She just smiled.

"Only twenty-nine hours and," he checked his watch, "about thirty minutes until I can call you all mine."

She nodded, sure her skin blanched. "Who's counting, right?"

He shook his head, his eyes glittering. "That's one thing I love about you. You are always calm. You balance my crazy-hectic life." He rested his hand palm up on the table, and she responded, laying her hand in his. "It's going to be good, you and me. We like the same things."

"We do." She swallowed a lump in her throat. "What do we like?"

"You nut. We like the house we both paid for. Our house on the hill. We picked out the interiors without one argument."

"Right." She shrugged. "We like the brown leather couch."

"We understand our work and careers are a high priority," Devin said.

"We agree on that."

The waiter set their food in front of them, and Cherish shoved the romaine lettuce and plum tomatoes around the bowl. She couldn't stop herself from sniffing the salad.

Devin paused his fork between bites. "Is something wrong with your salad?"

"No, it's good. Just a bit peppery."

"You like pepper." He stuffed his bite into his mouth and smirked around his chewing.

"No, I don't."

"I could swear at last Sunday's dinner your dad passed you the pepper and commented your family puts pepper on everything." He narrowed his eyes as though picturing the scene in his mind was proof.

"My mother likes pepper, my sister likes pepper, and my dad likes pepper, but I'm not them. Eating pepper makes me feel weird. I'm going to ask the waiter for water."

Devin put down his fork and stared at her. "This," he gestured between them, "is about wedding day nerves, isn't it?"

"Everyone is declaring me a nervous wreck, but—"

"That is it. You're not normally so flustered." He rolled his eyes. "So demanding."

"I'm demanding?" Her heart sank. How could he dismiss her so easily? Had he been dismissive all along? Maybe so and she'd been misinterpreting it as, oh, *caring for her*. A hard jolt shook her insides.

She steepled her fingers and pressed her lips tightly together. The lively Mexican music playing in the background got louder in her head, and she weighed the possibility she was overreacting. Her highly sensitive nature, her parents had always called it, was showing. Funny the little things she'd overlooked earlier in this relationship — Devin's tendency to override her, his flash of a temper, his self-centeredness — were growing in annoyance as the wedding neared. Racing thoughts scrambling for answers dizzied her brain.

"Not normally. You're easygoing, agreeable, when you're not having wedding jitters."

"Are you nervous about tomorrow?" It would somehow ease her anxiety if she knew he was anxious too.

He slammed his fist on the table, and his drink splashed. She sucked in a breath.

"What is going on? Are you having second thoughts, because if you are, it's kind of late for that." He gritted his teeth.

She hadn't expected he would have one of his outbursts. Not here, in public. "No, no second thoughts."

His phone vibrated against the table and he checked it. "It's the office. I have to go." He thrust his credit card at her. "Finish your lunch. Pay with my card, and don't fret." He pulled her into a stiff hug.

"Thank you for lunch, but I'll pay. Take your card." Bitterness was developing a bad taste in her mouth.

"Suit yourself. I'll call you tonight, babe. One more day and you'll see. Everything is going to be great. Trust me."

A slow boil rolled in her gut as she watched Devin through a window stride down the sidewalk toward his firm's downtown office.

She shoved the salad aside. What was wrong with her? Her throat was sandpaper, and she downed the contents of her water glass in rapid gulps.

Devin was a good man, the man she was going to marry. Maybe everything was moving too fast. The wedding had snuck up on her and now it was going off in her head like a gong. He was right. Her nerves were frazzled.

I could use a drink.

She settled onto a stool at the bar and beckoned the bartender.

"Hi there. What can I get you?"

"I'd like a merlot, please."

A minute later, the jovial bartender set her wine in front of her. She took a sip, closing her eyes and centering on the smooth way it slipped down her throat.

"You like your wine."

Cherish startled. "You're still here." The young man hardly looked of age to serve liquor. She peered at his nametag. "Leo, are you in college?"

"Yes, I'm a freshman, studying to be a lawyer. What's your name?"

"Too-old-for-you." Yes, she was being glib, but his flirting was the last thing she wanted.

"C'mon. Really, let's be friendly." His gaze drifted down her body and back up.

"Cherish. I'm a Libra. I know you're going to ask me what I do for a living so I'll just tell you. I'm a lawyer."

His eyes brightened. "No kidding? What firm?"

She took another sip, ignoring his question. Devin was right about her being surly. "I work at—"

"Hey, Leo. Sorry to interrupt but could I get an IPA?"

Cherish checked out the man who dropped onto a stool next to her, and tuned out his conversation with Leo. His golden brown hair was in need of a trim, but the shaggy around his ears and above his collar at the back of his neck softened his rugged features.

"I haven't seen you at the beach lately, Grayson. The water is actually warm, for Lake Michigan."

"I'm not twenty-two anymore, you know? I have to make a living."

"Hey, so do I, dude. What do you call bartending?" Leo laughed.

"It looked more like flirting just a minute ago. How about that beer?"

"Sure."

The man faced Cherish and her thoughts vaporized. His crystal-blue eyes glinted clear and direct. "Leo is harmless, but sometimes he comes on strong," he said.

Words stuck in her throat. He'd caught her staring at his profile, sizing up the strong, straight sweep of his nose, his solid jawline. His voice was low and richly baritone. The sound of it drifted through her like a rolling, deep wave. "I wasn't offended. He's young. I take it you know him well."

The corners of his eyes crinkled and his smile lit his face. "I'm a regular customer."

"Oh, you're an alcoholic?" His statement demanded teasing, and his open demeanor made saying it easy.

He thanked Leo for the beer and took a slow series of gulps of his pale ale. Cherish watched, unabashed, and marveled. She was engaging in a casual conversation with a strange man, free of strain, defensiveness, and annoyance.

"You're a funny girl, I see. No, I am not a heavy drinker. I just like this place. I'm a local small business owner and I want to support other independents."

She didn't want to know anything more about him. By tomorrow, she'd be married. "My name is Cherish." She offered a handshake.

"Nice to meet you." He took her hand and held it without shaking. "I'm Grayson Steele, but everyone calls me Gray."

His hand enclosed hers in warmth, but she shivered. "You don't really want to get to know me. I'm a mess. I'm a workaholic just like my parents, and I don't like pepper." She put her fingers to her temples. "My temper is presently combustible, and I'm afraid I'm making some big mistakes with my life."

She glanced down, noticing he still held her hand. She lifted her gaze to find his expression calm, thoughtful.

She pulled her hand away. "I'm sorry, I just spilled my anxiety all over you, and I don't even know you."

His phone rang. "I'm sorry. I need to take this. Hello."

His eyes narrowed and she caught a glimpse of something serious in his face, just before he hung up.

"Wrong number?"

"Nobody there."

"I hate when that happens. Really, how did you get my number, I always want to ask?"

Gray chewed on the inside of his cheek, his eyes seemingly appraising her. "No matter. The number was blocked so I should have known better than to pick up. I've sort of been expecting a call. Back to what we were talking about. I don't think it's wrong to work hard. You probably care a lot about your work, maybe you even love it. It would be weird if you didn't immerse in something you love." He rubbed his thumb over his chin. "Maybe you're passionate, maybe even intense. That's okay. You can be more than one thing, so you probably are calm too. As for being unsure of what you're doing, at least you're paying attention to what your heart is saying."

Slowly, deliberately, Cherish exhaled. "Are you a psychiatrist?"

His eyes crinkled again. "Far from it. Look, I don't mean to sound like I have answers. I don't." He swallowed the last bit of beer in his mug and made to leave.

Her heart stuttered, and she had to stomp on an urge to grab his arm to keep him from going. "Do you charge for your advice?"

"There's that humor again. I should mind my own business."

She cringed. "I didn't mean to sound flippant. Thank you. Thank you for listening. I'm truly not a hysterical woman."

Gray placed a hand on her shoulder and she didn't jerk away. Quite the opposite. Parts of her leaned in to his touch.

"I don't think you are. Hang in there."

Again, thoughts bombarded her. *You should be aghast at what you're feeling. You're essentially a married woman. What would Devin think if he knew you "leaned in?"*

Cherish sipped the last of her wine, ignoring the voice. Gray had seen her, despite her hysterics. And all the pent up tension she had been holding drifted away.

An insidious question reared in her chest, cracking it open and letting in light. Shouldn't Devin have been the one to see her, to frame her in a way that didn't make her feel restrained and ready to burst?

"Can I pour you another glass of wine, Cherish?" Leo took her empty glass and wiped off the bar.

A quick look at her phone told her it was time to get back to the office. The afternoon was still early, but she needed to spend it productively. "No thanks. I have to go." She paid her bill, and left him a nice tip.

Outside, the sunlight on her skin made her wistful for a relaxing mid-day in the summer sun. The Lake Michigan beaches outside of Dunes Bay were some of the most beautiful in the country. But she was too busy working to spend much time enjoying them.

The six blocks to her office passed in a blur of teasing apart conflicting emotions. Echoes of the morning's conversations reverberated in her gut, pushing anxiety to a high-pitched whine. *It's just jitters. You're thinking too much. Trust me.*

Inside the elevator, she recited to herself. *I'm a lawyer. I can present a thoughtful argument with skill.*

She dropped her purse on her desk, and breathed in a full breath, let it out slowly, then headed toward her mother's office.

Emma Moss was a force—a talented lawyer and a commanding leader. The problem with having a strong woman for a mother was that she tended to direct and expect compliance.

Butterflies flitted in Cherish's stomach as she knocked once on her mother's office door, then charged inside.

4

"Just a minute." Her mother held up a finger without looking away from her computer screen.

Cherish crossed her arms and tapped her foot.

Her mother waved her to sit, so she slid in to the chair opposite her mother's desk. The room was an oven, and Cherish found it difficult to breathe.

"Okay, I'm sorry to keep you waiting." Her mother gave her a sweet smile. "Your father told me he talked to you. He said you're on edge."

"Guilty." There was no sense in denying the truth. Sheepish, but resolved, Cherish seized the direction of the conversation. "Mom, I'm having second thoughts."

Her mother's mouth dropped open. She closed it, and rolled her eyes. "What do you mean?"

Cherish looked down at her hands, neatly folded in her lap. "I'm not sure about marrying Devin." She cleared her throat, trying to cover the tremble in her voice.

"Honey, second thoughts are normal. You don't know how much I questioned marrying your father, but I went through with it because it was the right thing to do. And look around." Her mother spread her arms and leaned back in her chair. "Everything worked out fine. We've had gratifying careers, raised two wonderful daughters, and lived a good life."

Cherish winced. Her mother hadn't mentioned loving her father. "What are you saying? You didn't love Dad and I don't have to love the man I marry?"

Her mom's lips tightened and she sat silent as seconds ticked by. "Cherish Elena Moss, I'm only saying when we're young we don't know as much as we think we do, but everything works out fine."

"You're not helping, Mom." If it weren't for the God-awful heat in the room, she would have laughed, hysterically.

Her mom circled the desk and kneeled in front of Cherish. "You have to trust me. It's just wedding nerves. Tomorrow you'll say your vows and feel blessed. You'll dance at your wedding with your father and your new husband, and your nerves will be fine."

"You think so?" Her voice was small, pinched. She couldn't get enough air.

"Don't you love Devin? Hasn't he been good to you?"

Her mother's eyes could be so piercing and, well, demanding. Cherish fiddled with her diamond engagement ring, twirling it on her finger.

"Well?" Her mother stretched upright and stared down at her. "Put these disturbing thoughts out of your mind. Do you think we'd allow you to marry a man we didn't trust to take care of you?"

"Allow me to marry?" Her mother's words made her cringe. They gave away her mother's true feelings .

Her mother waved her hand. "Oh, you know what I mean. Don't overthink it."

Take care of? Did she need taking care of?

"It's pretty late in the process to take these jitters seriously, but don't you love Devin?"

Cherish searched the ceiling for a response. What did she know about true love? Her history reminded her of past boyfriends. She'd been convinced each one was her forever love, then got gut-smacked, twice, by betrayal.

"Well, do you?" Her mom's voice rose.

"Of course."

"Then you need to do the right thing and marry him. I mean, everything is planned."

"You make a good point, Mom. I need to honor my commitment. It's settled. I'll get back to work."

Her mother hugged her, and it felt right to have it decided, and to please her.

"I'm so happy for you. I'm glad we had this talk."

Cherish headed to the door, acceptance sifting through her.

"Oh, Cherish, I see you had your gown delivered here. Why? You know you'll have to find a way to get it to the church."

"I wanted to look at it. I didn't think past that. I'll figure it out." She hadn't actually lied.

"I'll call the bridal shop and ask them to deliver it to church tomorrow. You don't need to worry about one more thing."

"Thanks." Her mom meant well, and Cherish didn't want to be a thorn in her side by protesting she didn't need the help.

Back at her desk, Cherish summoned her legal assistant over the intercom and riffled through court documents for the Decidedly Lab's case. She didn't lift her head when she heard footsteps in her office.

"Pansy, sit down. I have some things I'd like you to research."

"I'll sit, but I'd rather not do research for you, sis."

Cherish jerked her head up at the sound of the voice. "Oh, Rachel. I didn't know it was you. You're sneaky."

"Correction. I'm stealthy." The corners of Rachel's mouth lifted into a smile.

"Yes, I'm having what's called wedding jitters. No, I don't need any help with them." Cherish sighed. "I. Am. Fine."

"Good. I wasn't planning to give you a pep talk."

Cherish rubbed her forehead. "Oh."

Her sister was older by two years, so she'd joined the family firm a few years before her. From Cherish's first day, Rachel had made herself available but never hovered. She eyed her across the desk, suspicious of her smile anyway.

Rachel scrunched up her nose and opened her mouth to talk, then quickly closed it.

Cherish bounced her pen between her fingers, waiting.

"Just a minute," Rachel said, closing the door and sitting back down. "I need to talk to you."

"Shoot. Is this work-related or wedding-related?"

Rachel tucked locks of her long auburn hair behind her ears. "Neither, um, both. Well, not specifically."

"Just say it. You're making me uncomfortable."

Her sister's expression crumpled. "Oh, I'm so sorry. Well, I have started following a blog. No, I follow lots of blogs, all kinds of blogs, but one I follow—the reason I want to talk to you is I read something this morning on this one blog. I have to tell you about what I read." Rachel blew out a sigh.

"Geez, Rachel. Just tell me. The suspense is killing me." Cherish laughed, but she wasn't kidding.

"The blog is called Eyes On. The blogger writes about social justice issues and gets specific about his concerns."

Cherish rolled her eyes. "That's a pretty vague description." She checked the time, feeling her work hours slip away. "Can you get right to your point?"

"Devin is the subject of today's blog post. And not in a good way."

"Oh crap."

"Yeah. According to this post. Well, here, let me show you." Rachel turned her laptop for Cherish to read out loud.

"'Local defense attorney Devin Raye is sitting pretty on his bank account now that the case of Sam and Lucy Standish versus Dunes Bay Property Management is over. It's too bad the property management company was found innocent of negligence as asserted by Mr. and Mrs. Standish, when Raye knows better.'"

Cherish couldn't breathe.

She lifted her eyes to meet Rachel's. "Oh my God."

"I know." Her sister bit her thumbnail.

Cherish's shoulders tensed, but she couldn't stop reading. "'The elderly Standishes' rental house was destroyed in a fire and they were hospitalized with severe smoke inhalation. Treated for heat, second degree burns, and severe chemical injury to their upper airways, the couple has accrued exorbitant medical bills in addition to losing all of their possessions.'"

"This part is true." Cherish squinted at the text. "Sam and Lucy barely survived. They have nothing." She directed her attention back to the blog.

"'According to court documents, Dunes Bay Property Management claimed to have recently updated wiring in the rental house and had supporting documents—requisitions and invoices for the work—to prove it. Their story was that Mr. and Mrs. Standish had used a space heater that overloaded the circuits in the house and caused the fire.

"'*While the fire investigator attributed the cause of the fire to overloaded circuits in his report and his testimony, his opinion is suspect. Hired by the defendant's insurance company, he testified that he is required to perform an unbiased investigation. However, it did not come out in the trial that Raye influenced his testimony with a threat.*

"'*Why would Raye tamper with a witness? This blogger looked into that and speculates that it's SOP for Raye. He's a find-any-way kind of lawyer to get the verdict he wants for his client. There is precedence for this blogger's speculation.*

"'*In this case, Raye introduced into evidence photos of a burned space heater. Court documents detail testimony from firefighters purporting they never saw a heater when they entered the home already engulfed with flames.*'"

Stunned. Weak. How could this be true? "Where did this guy get his information? The firefighters were my best witnesses, but Devin discredited their accounts. The jury bought Devin's version of what happened because of the photos and the investigator's report."

"The blogger is anonymous." Rachel pursed her lips. "This is the kind of thing he brings out into the open. His posts have even prompted investigations into child and animal neglect and abuse, spousal abuse, political corruption."

"How do you know the blogger is a man?"

Rachel hmmphed. "I guess I don't know that."

Cherish scrolled through the piece. "Does this article end pretty soon?" Anxiety spiked in her gut again, only this time the bottom dropped from her heart.

"'How did this travesty of justice happen? Let's ask Raye. In calls to his office, this blogger tried to do just that, but his comment was no comment.

"'An investigative reporter would persist. All this blogger has is the word of a compromised investigator and Raye's previous actions.

"'Now, my question is not what happened, Raye, it is why did you witness tamper and falsify evidence?

"'This inquiring blogger wants to know.'"

Rachel touched her shoulder. "I thought you should know. I'm not sure what I would do in this situation, and I'm not going to tell you what's best."

Numbness crept through Cherish, suppressing thoughts and screams aching inside her. "It can't be true. Devin wouldn't do something illegal." Her voice screeched. "He wouldn't cheat in court, not against me."

"We don't know anything about this blogger, other than that he or she writes really well. Don't worry about it."

Cherish scrolled back to the top. "He's got twenty-five thousand subscribers! I need a rock."

"A rock? What for?"

"To hide under."

"I see. What about Devin's side of the story? Before you go hiding, don't you want to talk to him?"

"I'm going to see him at the rehearsal tonight. How can I face him? There will be people there." She stared at Rachel, and couldn't stop trembling. "Have I done it again? Have I trusted a man who is untrustworthy?"

"C'mere."

She propped herself up in her sister's hug, but Rachel could not hug away despair. "I have to talk to Devin, but first I need to give a close look to the Standish file. Oh my God. If Devin falsified evidence, he's going to face not just me, but, oh my God."

5

$\mathcal{C}$herish turned down her street, ruminating on how she would get through the rehearsal. At least she would be able to leave whenever she needed to because she and Devin planned to drive separately to the church. She'd wanted to come home alone and have the night to herself.

Her house in sight, her shoulders tensed. Devin's car sat in her driveway. *Crap! Why is here?* She sat in her car, a loss for words. If she brought up what she'd learned, Devin might get volatile. *I'll wait until after the rehearsal dinner.*

She headed inside, assuming a façade.

"Cherish? You're home," Devin said from the kitchen.

Her pulse pounded in her ears. She eyed the boxes sitting randomly around the room waiting for the movers to relocate her things to the home she would live in with Devin. Dreams and plans melted in her heavy heart.

"I know I'm early, but I wanted to see you before the rehearsal." He came in to the living room and gave her a sheepish grin. "It's going to be a long evening, so if I drive, I can bring you home and spend the night."

She met his smile with a frown. "I thought we agreed I would drive myself, and that we'd spend the night apart, a sort of goodbye to our singleness."

"I know, but I thought we could celebrate together. Maybe watch a movie and eat popcorn. Have a simple, light-hearted evening before our big day."

She stared at him, silent.

His grin dropped. "Is something wrong?"

"I'm frankly surprised you can even think of celebrating." She dropped her briefcase and purse to the floor, along with her plan not to bring up the Standish case.

"I don't know what you're talking about. Did you have a bad afternoon at work?" He opened his arms to her. "Let me make it better."

She shook her head and stood in place. "I wish you could make it better, but Devin, what have you done? Tell me you didn't tamper with a witness and plant a heater as proof the Standishes were responsible for the fire."

He narrowed his eyes and worked his jaw. "Where did you hear that?"

"Answer my question."

He ran his hand through his black hair. "I didn't hear a question. What's the question?"

She balled and unclenched her fingers. "Devin. Stop playing games. Did you plant evidence? Did you threaten the fire investigator?" Her heart raced so fast she was sure it verged on exploding.

"Why do you always do this?" A muscle in Devin's cheek clenched.

"Do what?" Aghast at his reaction, she peered at his eyes, searching for a clue of the man she thought she knew, planned to marry. The dark look on his face stole her breath.

"You always make a big deal about something and make me feel like a rat. Why can't we ever just have a normal, happy relationship?"

Had she encountered this side of Devin and ignored it? He was using a tactic to distract away from her accusation and make her question herself, not him.

"You aren't denying it." She swallowed hard.

"Of course I am." He stomped his foot. "I don't know why you think I would do such a thing. Who said that about me? Tell me," he hollered and stepped closer.

She backed up. "Stop yelling. You're making me nervous. You still haven't denied it."

He gave her sad eyes. "You have to believe me, baby," he said softly.

Tears misted her eyes. His words softened her fears. "I want to believe you. I don't want to think that you would betray me and my clients for the win, the paycheck."

"Oh, man. That's a terrible thought. Can I hug you now?"

She nodded. His instantaneous mood shift made her head spin. But when his arms surrounded her, his familiarity somehow comforted her. Maybe he was innocent. He was right, she did look for things that might be a problem. She'd missed signs of trouble too many times to trust herself. Besides, had the blogger offered any proof or simply speculation?

"Better?" He brushed a lock of hair off her face. "Whoever told you I'd done those things was a troublemaker. It was terrible that the Standishes were injured and lost their domicile. But it wasn't the fault of Dunes Bay Property Management. Believe me?"

Cherish strained to see something, anything, in Devin's eyes that would verify he wasn't lying. *I'm doing it again. I'm scrutinizing my fiancé for deceit.*

"I do."

"I like the sound of that. I'll like it better when you say I do tomorrow at our wedding."

"Thank you for putting up with me."

He kissed her head. "Once we're married, everything will settle down. Can I get you a drink? Or water?"

"I'm going to stick to water." She gulped the ice water he handed her, an attempt to douse the irksome misgivings insisting he was glossing over something important.

He didn't notice. Nor did he notice her silence. His enthusiasm for their honeymoon at a chalet in the Swiss Alps droned against her ears.

"The snow and cold will be a fun getaway from summer heat. You're going to love the scenic view of the chalet," he said.

"From what you've described, it sounds lovely. Remind me, when you went before did you go there with your family?"

He lowered his gaze and shrugged. "I don't remember. It doesn't matter who I went with. It will be like going the first time when we go together."

Cherish hadn't forgotten his story. He'd gone with Alicia Piper, his former girlfriend. It made her feel kind of creepy that he was taking her to the same place, but there was no reason to pretend he didn't recall.

Pretend? Is that what she was going to call it?

"Right. It will be my first time. You know what? I need to get ready for the rehearsal. And as we agreed, I'm driving myself and spending my last night alone."

He rolled his eyes. "I can't convince you otherwise?"

"No, I want to indulge in my beauty ritual." Actually, she only planned to take a long bath and sleep. "You understand?"

"Of course. A girl needs her night-before, right?" He pulled her close. "You do what you have to, and I'll see you at the church." He chuckled.

"Thank you." His chuckle sort of made her sick. He was preening, like a Cheshire cat, and it made her squeamish. Her instincts took over and she dodged his kiss as artfully as possible. She pressed her fingers to his lips. "Until tomorrow."

"Ah, I get it. Building sexual tension. Grrr. Nice."

Cherish closed the door after he left and sank to the floor. The thought of dinner and conversation drained her energy. She had to rally. She was making everything harder and she had to stop it.

CHERISH OPENED the church door and strode into the lobby, her confidence high. Sure, she knew that confidence was held together by a thread, or, many threads. Her dress, actually. Its slim lines hugged her contours comfortably. She needed comfortable. The sage linen fabric took her heart immediately when she saw it in the store. It looked cool, calm, with a hint of wise. *Wise?* Sure, it was right there in the color's name. From the dress to her silver linen strappy shoes and matching bag, every bit of her look had been selected to present a flawless image. Her insides were a mash of conflicting emotions, but her appearance protected her from detection.

"Cherish, sweetie, you look lovely," her mom gushed. She hugged her and pulled at her arm. "You're almost late. The pastor has been pacing."

"It's only six-twenty-eight. I wouldn't call that late," she said.

Her mom swept her along, oblivious of Cherish's silence. Didn't notice, didn't care. Emma was a queen, in charge of a grand event. Cherish lifted her chin and forced herself to think about her outfit. *My dress is calm, collected, just like me?*

Inside the sanctuary, Rachel stood alone just inside the door, a welcome sight. She shot her mom a warning look. "Mother, Cherish is the bride. It's her prerogative to arrive when she's ready and not a minute before. Cut her some slack."

Her mother waved a hand. "Rachel, stop being so sensitive. I just want to take care of Cherish, make sure she's the perfect hostess." Loud laughter grabbed her attention. "Oh, I wonder what's so funny," she said, and marched toward the laughter.

Rachel took Cherish by the hand and led her to the bathroom. "Devin isn't here yet."

"I'm okay. I confronted him."

Rachel's eyes widened. "How did that go?"

"Honestly, he got angry." She chewed on her lower lip. "But he said he didn't do anything wrong."

"He got mad at you? For talking to him about it?" Rachel lifted her brows.

"Yeah, but it wasn't a big deal." Cherish checked out her shoes.

She couldn't pull anything over Rachel. "Well, it was kind of scary and disappointing, but you know him. He's passionate. And I understand his anger if he's been wrongly accused."

"Do you believe him? You think he has been wrongly accused?" Rachel asked.

"I believe him." She faced Rachel, assuming her best I-am-woman-hear-me-roar expression.

Rachel nodded. "Okay. That's good."

A woman opened the door. "Oh, excuse me."

Rachel laughed. "No problem. Come on in. We were just talking."

"Yes, just talking." Cherish surveyed her reflection in the mirror. Lipstick, check. Hair, check. Smile. Smile. *Cherish, smile, for Pete's sake. This is your night.*

Rachel rested an arm over her shoulders. "Looking for something, like answers? You are beautiful, sis."

Her sister was the best. "Thank you. So are you. I'm unsure what my questions are, much less the answers."

"Aww. The answers will come to you. Shall we join the rest of the wedding party?"

"Yes." Cherish reached for the door handle, but Rachel stopped her.

"Here, My Lady, let me open the door for you. You're the bride of the hour, sis." With a flourish she shoved the door open and they stepped out.

"Cherish, Cherish. We're all ready to begin." Her mother bustled out of the sanctuary. "Where have you been?"

"Checking my face, Mom."

Her mother glared at her. "Devin is here. He's been asking about you. He needs you up at the altar."

At the doorway, Cherish gazed up the aisle and locked eyes with Devin. She searched for a clue. Was he still upset? What if he was? Would he make a scene?

Her grip on her purse tightened and she smoothed her dress.

Devin shot her a tight smile and beckoned her. "We're all waiting, babe," he said.

"Sorry, I'm ready," she said, and made her way to his side.

"Hey gorgeous. Hey everyone, this is my soon-to-be wife, my beautiful wife. I know you guys are jealous, but I got her."

Cherish shivered. She went through the motions of rehearsing the ceremony, smiling and standing in the right places. It was normal to feel uptight, she told herself, even to question if Devin was talking too loud or was she just being overly sensitive again?

An hour later, they all walked into the room set up for the dinner, and she sat at the head of the bridal party table with Devon.

The plain white china dishes were simple, just the way Cherish would have wanted if her mom had asked. She admired the small silver bags filled with chocolates and tiny scrolls with sayings. She read her scroll. "Once in a while, right in the middle of an ordinary life, love gives us a fairy tale." A beautiful thought, but it only made her feel more confused.

She watched her bridesmaids sip wine and dip sushi in soy sauce with chopsticks. These were some of her friends since high school, the lifelong kind made possible by living in the same town all her life. But still, she felt removed from the festivities. It wasn't them or the catered sushi, spring rolls, or seaweed miso soup. It was her, and she wondered if this sense of being separate from life had always been inside her, she just hadn't noticed.

"Toast!" Her dad stood up at the end of the long table and raised his glass. "To my darling daughter, Cherish, and her amazing fiancé. You make a very A-list couple and I am excited about all the things you'll accomplish and the happiness you'll have together. May you always make memorable moments as man and wife starting tomorrow."

Clinking glasses and chatter filled the room, and gratitude filled her for this moment with friends and family surrounding her. "Thank you, Dad. But that would be husband and wife. Devin doesn't have to be declared a man."

The room exploded in uneasy laughter.

"That's my Cherish, a stickler for details. That's why she is such a good lawyer," her father said.

Cherish's heart reached toward him. A longing to feel his love and acceptance ached inside her. Hadn't he always told her he loved her? Yes, so why didn't she feel it?

Devin raised his glass. "Here's to my soon-to-be wife and her quick wit."

She clinked glasses with Devin, and he kissed her.

A ruckus of spoons against wine glasses and cheers rang out. She pulled back from the kiss and smiled up at him. His eyes gleamed.

"That's my girl." He turned away. "Thank you, Adrian. Our marriage can't help but be epic."

Her smile disappeared. His? Girl? At least he hadn't said it to anyone else. How humiliating, even between just them. She guzzled more wine.

Dinner started to wind down and people said their goodbyes, slowly drifting toward the door. She spotted Devin with her mom and dad chatting in a group on the other side of the large room and decided to join them. As she got closer, she overheard her mother say something about "creative accounting" for clients. She froze. The phrase sent a chill through her. Maybe she misunderstood.

"Hey babe, we were just talking shop." Devin grinned and squeezed her shoulders.

"I heard," she tried to keep emotion out of her voice. "Exactly what were you referring to, Mom? I mean, I can assume creative accounting means padding statements or something worse, but I would like to know what you mean."

"I didn't mean I am doing those things. Don't trouble your thoughts." Her mother gave Devin a pointed look.

"We were talking about billable hours and I was saying, it's all about billable hours," he said. "Clients need to be educated that a lawyer's time is valuable. They can't call and chat without expecting a bill. It's business."

Her father slapped Devin's back. "Absolutely. The minute I answer a call or an email, the clock is running."

"Of course, we have good software for tracking time," her mother said. "But I remember back in the day, when a client came into my office I turned on a timer. It gave a succinct message."

The hairs on Cherish's neck stood up. A sneaking suspicion tightened her chest, but she kept it to herself. "You guys, this is our wedding rehearsal. Geez, could you possibly not talk about work?"

Laughter jarred her nerves.

"There it is again, that Cherish sensitivity," her father said, nodding toward her. "Okay, how about a joke? A lawyer dies and goes to Heaven. 'There must be some mistake,' the lawyer argues. 'I'm too young to die. I'm only fifty-five.' 'Fifty-five?' says Saint Peter. 'No, according to our calculations, you're eighty-two.' 'How'd you get that?' the lawyer asks. Answers St. Peter, 'We added up your time sheets.'"

"Good one. Let that be a warning to you." Cherish would have thought it funny if it weren't so true. "Money isn't everything."

This time her mother chortled. "This from a lawyer, mind you, who does pro bono, which takes time away from our firm's billable hours."

More laughter slithered through her body. Her values weren't a joke. "I'm doing my share at the firm." She pivoted and headed toward the door.

6

"Cherish, wait up," Devin called, catching up with her as she stepped outside. "We were just having some fun. Lighten up."

She checked her watch. Eight-thirty. "I'm leaving. I need to get my sleep."

"It's still early. How about I come over for a while? You know..." He lifted his eyebrows.

"I told you, I want to be alone tonight. As you said, the night is young. Go back inside and enjoy the party."

He yanked her close. "You won't change your mind?"

Her body got rigid. The yank was forceful, not romantic, and it made her question his feelings. "Are you upset about what I said in there about money?"

He nuzzled her neck and she felt him harden against her. She stepped back, her guard going up.

He shrugged. "No. I know you. You don't care very much about billable hours. But that's only because you have the luxury of your father's money."

Ice water flowed through her veins. "You really think that?"

"Forget it. I was out of line. Maybe I've had too much wine. Take me home?"

Anger boiled inside her. "No, Devin. I'll see you tomorrow." She got behind the wheel of her car and left him behind.

After her day, she needed relief. No, she needed to escape. She quickly stopped at home to change into shorts and a tank top, then made the two-mile drive to Dunes Bay Beach just in time to catch the beginning of a setting sun.

A warm breeze embraced her when she touched her feet to the pavement in the parking lot. She looked up as cries from seagulls above her head filled the air. She left her shoes on the car seat and savored the warm sand between her toes while making her way across the wide expanse of beach toward the water.

Peace sifted through her with the rhythmic gentle rushing of waves to shore and then receding. *Shush, murmur. Shush, murmur.*

At the shore, she lowered to the sand. She had grown up taking in sunsets over the lake, but they still awed her with majestic beauty. Wonder did amazing things for her soul, and her nerves settled with the pastel pinks and blues of the evening sky that stretched above the lake.

Fading sunlight sparkled a path on the surface, beckoning her. She stepped to the water's edge and waded to just above her knees. The brisk water temperature raised goosebumps on her skin. She closed her eyes and stood still, simply listening to waves.

"It's beautiful, isn't it?"

Cherish sucked in a breath and turned to the man's voice.

"I'm sorry. I didn't mean to scare you," he called.

In the low light, she could barely make out his face, but the voice she knew. It was Grayson's.

"I didn't hear you coming. I thought I was alone."

He came closer but remained on the beach. "Remember me? I'm Gray."

"Yeah, the alcoholic from the bar."

"The funny woman, Cherish." He shot her a half-grin. "You picked a good spot to be alone. Most people gravitate to the beach farther north. Sorry I intruded on your solitude. I usually walk the beach this time of day if I can. Have a good evening." He waved and turned away.

"You don't have to leave." The words popped out all by themselves.

He stopped and pivoted in the sand. "You sure?"

"Yes, I wouldn't mind some company for—" A large wave snuck up behind her and knocked her off balance. Somehow, she managed to go under in the little more than two feet of water she had been standing in. The next wave hit too quickly for her to get her footing and pushed her deeper into the water.

Hands grabbed under her arms and pulled her out. Through her blurry eyes, Grayson's smile was reassuring. She sputtered, catching her breath. Warmth spread from her neck up across her face, and she was grateful for the dim light of almost sundown. She couldn't feel more sheepish.

"Are you all right? Those waves came at you. Must have been a large boat out there somewhere stirring up the water."

She stood still, deeply aware of his hands on her shoulders. His firm grip steadied her. His hands, warm and calloused, sent shivers up and down her spine.

"Oh, you're cold. I have a blanket back at my house. It's not far. I'll go fetch it. You can come with me. I promise I won't—"

"No, I'm fine." She really was, wasn't she? "The air is summery. I have a blanket in my car if I need it."

He scanned the parking lot. "That must be your Jeep. Is it locked?"

"No. I was afraid I might lose my keys in the sand." A giggle bubbled out. "Who knew I was going to almost drown in shallow water? And me a born and raised Lake Michigan native. How embarrassing."

He chuckled, an easy sonorous sound that bounced around her.

"There's that humor again. I'll be right back."

She caught herself watching him sprinting to her car, and turned away. The whole idea of coming to the beach was to get away where she could not think, just for a while. But with Gray showing up, she hadn't thought even once about Devin or the Standishes. The peace she didn't have internally surrounded her.

"Here you go." Gray draped the blanket over her shoulders, and Cherish caught a whiff of sawdust from him. *Mmm, subtle, but pleasant.*

"That was fast. Thank you."

"So, born and raised Michigander, have you always lived in Dunes Bay?" He bent and picked up a dark, flat stone. He turned it between his fingers, then sent it skipping across the tranquil water. His follow through was smooth. It had a simple grace.

He waited for her answer.

"All my life. What about you?"

"I grew up here too. I went to Southside High School. Go Mustangs!" He pumped the air with his fists.

"I'm a North Central High grad. Rah, rah, Huskies."

His gaze dropped on her, and his shuttered eyes confused her. "I'm class of 2002, what are you?"

"2008. Dune's Bay is not a huge town, but big enough that we never crossed paths. Not that I know of anyway." The conversation didn't feel probing. It had no endgame, but rather was more like two people just getting acquainted. It relaxed her.

It also came to a stop, but she didn't mind the silence.

Gray picked up another stone and flung it farther out in the rolling swells. "Do you like a good sunset? I do. Sometimes when I sail I stay out late enough to be with them." He scratched his head. "Oh, man. That sounded weird."

"I didn't think it was weird. I want to know more. I have never sailed. You must have a boat," she said, watching him purse his lips and go inward, obviously searching for a way to answer her question. She couldn't wait to hear it.

His expressive eyes peered at the now crimson and brilliant oranges spreading from the sun balancing on the horizon. "Yes, I have two, actually. A fishing boat and a sailboat. Alone on the lake in the evening, I can sit with the quiet and let all my senses open. The moments are sacred out there with the sunset in my face."

Speechless. If Devin had just said those same words she would wonder if he had drank too much. From Gray, they seemed perfectly in tune with nature.

"Wow, that didn't help redeem me from sounding odd at all. I can get really caught up, sorry."

"No, I liked what you said. It makes sense. I'm jealous of your experiences."

"You're just being nice."

"I learned some things today that upset me. I came to the beach tonight to get away, to think. Then I ran into you, and I haven't thought about my troubles."

With the waves washing in and out, Cherish appreciated the hush she stood in with Gray. He didn't say a word, and he didn't have to. His presence wasn't grabby or proddy, it didn't demand or restrain. Did she dare tell him?

"I'm getting married tomorrow."

"Oh, congratulations. Tomorrow, wow."

"I don't know if I can go through with it. I'm not sure I want to." There. She'd said the words no one wanted to hear.

Gray swallowed the exclamation that flew into his throat. But that left him with nothing.

"What do you say to that? I hardly know you and then I drop a bomb like that." Cherish shifted from one foot to the other.

His instinct was to hug her. Discomfort was all over her face. He had to say something. Her big green eyes looked up at him, all lost and searching.

"I don't know what to say. I didn't know you were engaged. But if there is anyone you can say anything to, it's me. I'm an impartial observer." He zeroed in on her eyes, drawn to help her. Guilt squiggled in his gut. He hadn't lied. He didn't know she was engaged, but he did know who she was. He knew all about her court cases for Lawyers Can Help. Was it wrong not to tell her? Would she die inside if she knew he had blogged about Devin? "It must be terrifying to think of facing the man you're engaged to with misgivings and telling your family there isn't going to be a wedding, much less a marriage. Is the thing you learned today the reason for having doubts?"

Waves sizzled and hissed onto shore and retreated, over and over until Gray wanted to prod Cherish to answer.

"I don't know for sure. It's probably more than just one thing."

She trembled, and he couldn't stop himself. He opened his arms wide. "C'mere." She didn't hesitate to close the space between them. "I'm sorry this is happening to you." He shut his eyes to her delicate, peachy scent. His pulse perked up, against all his wishes.

"Thank you." She sniffed, and his heart skipped a beat.

He pulled back before she noticed her effect on him. He balled his fingers. *What a heartless bastard I am, getting aroused when she's in real trouble.*

She lifted her chin. "I'll be all right. The wedding isn't until six tomorrow evening. I-I-I have some time yet."

"Right. It's a big decision and you don't want to make it under pressure." He lifted his little finger to her. "I pinky swear I won't tell anyone."

A half-chuckle came off her lips, and she linked her finger with his. "Thank you for that. Friends?"

How could he not befriend such an interesting woman? He winced inside. He had good reason not to, but her problems were real and it wasn't in him to leave her in the deep end all alone. "Friends." *Just friends, Gray. Nothing more.* "I'll walk you to your car, okay? It's going to be completely dark soon."

At her Jeep, she tossed in the blanket and slid behind the wheel, closing the door between them.

He rested his hand on the open window. "I understand you're not in the best of circumstances, but I enjoyed the evening with you. I hope you can find peace."

She rolled her eyes. "Peace would be nice. Thank you for listening to me. I really will be okay. And who knows? Maybe I will walk down the aisle tomorrow as planned and say my vows."

He waved back at her as she drove away, ignoring her peach scent lingering on his clothes. Cherish was nearly a married woman, and besides, nothing had changed for him just because a beautiful and fascinating woman had captured his attention. He couldn't put her in the danger that accompanied him. Not ever.

Loneliness crept back into his heart. It was simply a cause and effect he had to live with since Chicago, and he knew it as well as he knew the way back to his beach house. The sound of his feet against the wooden steps punctuated the aloneness inside him. Aching imagined a different life, one in which he would open his door to lights on and a family welcoming him.

He unlocked his door and flipped on the light. Stop feeling sorry for yourself. What is, is. Cause and effect.

Cherish. Her name tumbled around inside his brain, like rocks and shells caught up in the tide. Without pretention or thought of consequences, she'd emptied her troubled soul to him, and he'd been unable to let her sink.

Great metaphors, Gray. Don't take yourself so seriously.

He knew all about awkward metaphors, silly similes, and improper sentence structure. Not that it mattered. His journalism days were over, left behind in a cloud of death threats in Chicago. Also at an end, the possibility he could ever have a relationship with a woman. He refused to have anyone placed in danger because of him.

"Enough wallowing." He grabbed a beer from the fridge and dropped into a chair in his living room for a night of Major League ball on his 65-inch television. When he moved back to Dune's Bay he decided that if he had to live alone, he would give himself the pleasure of a big screen. "Okay boys, let's play some baseball."

His cellphone rang before he'd had one swallow of beer. It was his brother. "You always know the worst time to call, Jasper."

"I try."

"Well, don't try so hard. I've just settled in for some TV. What do you want?"

"Tomorrow's forecast is sunny and hot. It's a Saturday. How about you, me, and Rhys go fishing?"

"Oh, man," Gray shouted at his TV. "The game is baseball, not hot potato."

"Let me guess. The Cubs aren't playing well."

"Aww, the guy dropped the ball and the Tigers got a run in."

"Tragedy. Now, what about fishing tomorrow with your brothers?"

"Have you asked Rhys already?"

"Yes, he wants to go. The plan is to meet at your shop around seven and head out before the sun gets high. I'll even bring coffee."

"Oh, so you want my boat, not me per se." The easy back and forth with his brothers had always meant something to him, especially when he returned to Dunes Bay for sanctuary.

"Well, I don't mind if you come along." Jasper chuckled. "You're okay company, but we do need your boat."

"You did say you'd bring coffee. Bring sandwiches too and it's a deal. I'll see you at my shop tomorrow. Don't be late."

"Thanks, Gray."

He settled back into watching the game, but in minutes, his thoughts wandered. He wouldn't change places with Cherish tomorrow morning, but her indecision really got under his skin. How could she be in such a bad place? She was a lawyer, not to mention a grown woman. How had she gotten so lost?

The devil on his shoulder goaded him. You're not one to judge her. He swallowed a sip of his beer, nodding. "You got that right. I've made some rash decisions myself."

If he could go back in time and change his actions, would he? He had been such a hot newspaper reporter and his work had exhilarated him. He had not hesitated to investigate and report on suspicious activity at the Chicago Police Department. It had been his job to hold public figures' feet to the fire. And now he had to live with the consequences of his decision.

Boy, he wouldn't wish that fate on Cherish. He didn't want to think about it or her wedding, so much *not* that the fishing tomorrow sounded like an excellent escape from a reality.

Sounds of the game brought him back, but he didn't have the interest in such mundane stuff. He turned off the TV and stared unfocused across the room. Waves outside on the beach slowed his pulse, and he sank into the hush of his home. His gaze landed randomly on a picture sitting on his fireplace mantle of him and his brothers, all smiles and fun times. The oldest of the three, Rhys was a kid at heart at thirty-four, and Jasper, the youngest, was twenty-six, just a kid. They didn't know, because he hadn't told any of his family, that he had fled Chicago a man wanted by the Gang of Four. That's what he and his editor had called the four dirty detectives at CPD. He had wanted to keep his brothers from changing, from turning into scared and protective people. His family and the anchor they were for each other meant too much to his survival. He just hoped the decision to return home didn't turn out to be a fatal one.

The thought sent him out to his deck to peer into the darkness. He slammed his fist on the railing at the edge of his deck. "That will not happen. I will make sure of it."

He looked up into the security camera hanging from under the roof near his door. It hardly made him feel secure. Professional killers wouldn't even flinch at such a system. Which was why he had an alarm system also installed when he moved in. When set, the alarm would sound and notify the security company of an intruder at his perimeter.

In the dark, Gray strained to see out beyond his property. Despite his measures for safety, someone lethal could be out there in the darkness, undetected.

He strolled inside the lighted living room, closed the door, and locked it. He set the alarm system and headed to bed. He put away in the back of his mind, thoughts of looming danger nearby that could snuff out his life while he slept.

GRAY SQUINTED at the sunlight streaming in the east window in his bedroom. The sunrise made a great alarm clock, especially on mornings when lake-effect clouds abstained from covering the sky.

He peeked over the blanket at his clock. Almost six. He had an hour to shower, eat, and get to his shop in time to meet Jasper and Rhys.

He settled back under the covers and closed his eyes. It was as if he had never left the beach last night. Right there in front of his brain stood Cherish, her eyes quietly pleading for help.

He lay in the stillness, his heart flinching. Today she would become Mrs. Raye. Anything Devin Raye did made it into the Dunes Bay newspaper, so anyone in town who read knew Cherish and Devin were a couple, including him. But he had not known they were engaged. He picked at his lower lip, loss expanding inside him until he couldn't catch his breath. Before meeting Cherish, he had nearly accepted loneliness as a norm. He hardly knew her, but he wanted to know her. Really know her. Like did she prefer the toilet paper roll over or under? Was she a moon-watcher or was that too silly for her? And why did she smell so good?

Gray didn't have a chance to learn all about her. She already belonged to another man.

He kicked off the covers and crawled out of bed. *Who am I kidding? I lost the possibility of Cherish back in Chicago.*

He focused more than he needed to on preparing for a few hours on the lake. Hat, check. Sunscreen, check. Sunglasses, check. Last but not least, sandwiches and munchies. He didn't fish, so he didn't need poles and such. Jasper and Rhys would bring their own gear. But, a little time on the water with his brothers would be a good distraction from the pestering gnats in his brain disguised at thoughts.

He made the short trek across the sand from his house to his shop and up the wooden ramp to the front door. The thud, thud of his deck shoes mixed with the soft whisper of waves lapping against his boat moored at the slip and eased the self-pity tensing his shoulders. The weathered paint on his shop's sign reminded him of his workload. It used to read Thomas Steele Boat Renovation and Repair. Now it just read Dunes Bay Boat Repair.

The view from outside his shop stopped him. The lake glittered in the early morning sun and a cool breeze refreshed the summer heat. He sat on the railing and soaked in the sunlight. He couldn't ask for a better view. Nature was in his bones. It exhilarated and rested him. The Lake Michigan water stretched to the horizon, a grand spaciousness that clarified things in his head. Sometimes the lake was a glorious blue, and sometimes it was a stormy gray, but right now, its cool green reminded him of sparkling green eyes. Those eyes were quick and intelligent in a way that kindled his imagination of a spirited conversation. But last night, they were soulful and sad.

He had wanted to help Cherish. That was the only excuse he could give himself for offering such Buddha-like advice to a stranger.

He jumped down from the railing and unlocked the door. Inside his shop, the earthy scent of sawdust and hard work welcomed him. This place was as much home as his beach house. The work he did here kept him engaged with life and community as much as he dared.

He surveyed the wooden hull of a boat elevated from the rafters. A restoration project, the boat was a classic. Repairing and restoring boats was his profession now, along with fixing motorcycles and snowmobiles. It didn't give him the thrills of his former job. He missed doing interviews, especially face-to-face when he could detect a source wasn't forthright. He had liked the challenge of zeroing in on the kernel of a story and filling in the details readers needed to know.

He shrugged. Changing careers probably was not easy for anyone. Now, he accepted it was his job to make sure outdoor enthusiasts could enjoy all the summer and winter pleasures of the Lake Michigan area. Yeah, right.

Footsteps on the deck gave him goosebumps. Everything in him prepared for self-defense. He didn't hide behind a desk, or grab a heavy object, but his muscles tensed and he clenched his teeth.

The doorknob twisted. He'd been through this vigilance so many times in the year since he'd given up journalism, and nothing terrible had ever happened to him.

But he couldn't let down his guard, not even once. The death threats made against him and his family because of his investigative reporting had changed his life, but he sure as hell didn't want to lose it or see anyone else killed because of him.

GRAY BRACED HIMSELF FOR AN INTRUDER, his muscles tight, his breath still.

The door opened and his dad walked in. "Hey, son. Brought you some coffee."

Gray exhaled and took the cup. "Thanks, Dad." His father didn't know about the death threats. As far as anyone knew, he'd bought his dad's business to help him out after his heart attack.

His dad slapped the hull of the boat and smiled. "I thought I'd put in some work on this today. Are you okay with that?"

"Of course. I'd appreciate your help."

"She's a beauty." His dad ran his hand over the wood, his gaze soft as though he were admiring a beautiful face. "You've done a great job with this project."

"Thanks. It's going to take time to get it back to its original glory, but it will be worth it. She sat in the weather without protection or proper care too long, longer than she deserved." Gray couldn't keep the sentiment out of his voice either. His dad was the Thomas in the former sign. Memories of standing on a chair to watch his dad slide his plane across a wooden surface on a boat project flooded him. He had been mesmerized, and inhaled a lasting appreciation of the craftsmanship of classic wooden boats.

"Point me to what you want me to work on, son."

Gray scratched his head, a little guilt pricking. "Uh, well, I should tell you, I'm going fishing this morning, so you just make yourself at home."

His dad laughed. "Oh, I see how it is. Are you going out with your brothers?"

"Yes. Jasper asked me last night and Rhys wanted in too. I'm really sorry to leave you here alone, working on my project, no less."

"Oh, don't worry about me. I love working here. Kind of miss it. Retirement is great, don't get me wrong. Your mother and I are living the life."

"Hey Dad! Hey Gray?" Jasper busted through the door with his usual irrepressible enthusiasm and Rhys followed. "Are we going to have a Steele men's fishing day?"

"Hi Dad." Rhys wrapped a hug around their father. "It looks to me like Gray is putting you to work." He turned to Gray. "That doesn't seem right."

Gray frowned. "You know working is his idea." He ruffled Rhys's brown hair and lifted his hand above Jasper's, but held it there. "I see you've already tousled your hair, or is that your bed-head look?"

"Okay, old man." Jasper raised his fists and bounced a couple of steps. "You're messing with the kid here. I have power and speed."

Gray faked a punch. "If I'm an old man, you must be a baby."

Rhys shoved his hand against Jasper's forehead. "I may be older but I can take you if I want to, little brother. Both of you, in fact."

Gray stepped back. "Oh, sure, and probably at the same time."

"I've got all three of you beat in the age bracket, so I'll just stand here and watch." Gray's dad leaned against a counter and crossed his arms.

"Or, we could get going." Gray grabbed his things and motioned to the door. "I hope you didn't forget the coffee and sandwiches, Jas."

"Course not. But I know you, and you've got sandwiches in your bag."

"Just get in the boat." Gray set the food in the galley and dropped into the captain's seat. "Somebody better cast off or we're not going anywhere."

"Got it." Jasper dropped the line onto the boat deck and leaped on board. He struck a pose, pointing out toward the open lake. "The fish await, men. But first, where's that coffee?"

The boat motor purred to life and Gray pointed the boat out onto the big lake. A change of pace this morning would be good for his soul. Still, his insides churned. He couldn't have complete peace knowing what Cherish was about to do, no matter the serenity surrounding him.

8

Somewhere in the church, Devin dressed in his dark tux and crisp white shirt. One of his groomsmen would help him with his bow tie. No, probably his mother would tie his tie. Cherish nodded. Yes, his mother certainly would do that.

Cherish stood in her underwear, staring at her reflection in the full-length mirror in the church changing room. Her heartbeat pulsed in her throat. Jitters. That's what she had. It wasn't a sign of misgivings or a change of heart. She pulled in a deep breath and let it out. In the mirror, she saw the dress hanging behind her. She bit at her thumbnail and recited to herself. *It all will be over soon.*

"Cherish, honey. Marcy is ready to do your hair and makeup." Her mother flitted around her shoulders.

"I thought Rachel was going to do that." Her heart raced.

"We changed that. Rachel is with the florist in the auditorium. Marcy is my stylist and she's wonderful. Nothing to worry about, sweetheart. Just sit over there and relax. It's your wedding day, enjoy a little pampering."

Obedient, that was her. Cherish sat in the designated chair and closed her eyes while Marcy draped her with a cape.

Anyone would expect that her night had been restless. Wasn't it that way for every bride? There was more to her sleepless night, though. Thoughts kept playing of her conversation with Devin about his claim of innocence of any wrong-doing in the Standish case. Turmoil burned all night in her gut, struggling with his statement that she had failed her clients through inexperience. How could she stomach his pompous attitude? *I mean, this is nothing new for Devin — right?* Didn't she admire his, what did she call it? Confidence? But why now, of all weeks, days, hours, minutes was it driving her nuts? *Did I just wake up?*

"Cherish, can you please sit still?" Marcy's voice was all sugar. "I don't want to pull on your hair."

"Sorry, I hadn't realized I was bouncing my foot so hard."

"Oh, it's okay," Marcy said. "It's normal to have wedding jitters."

Cherish rubbed her forehead. Gah — Shouting a warning that she couldn't be held accountable for her actions if one more person said the word *jitters* probably wouldn't be right.

Her teeth chattered.

"Oh, baby, are you cold?" Her mother bustled toward her with a robe. "Slip this on." She lifted the cape and helped Cherish with the robe.

"Thanks Mom." The problem wasn't a chill, though. Cherish tightened her cheeks.

"You have lovely red hair. It's a nice length too," Marcy said, twisting loose curls of her shoulder-length hair into a large knot at the nape of her neck and adding small, white blossoms of stephanotis.

Rachel stepped in and shared a sister-smile with her. "Everything is squared away with the flowers. People are arriving."

"Wonderful." Her mother was giddy with Rachel's update.

Cherish sat still for everything. The hair, the makeup, and her mother's flittering. Then it was time for the dress.

"Okay, last step." Rachel took the dress out of the bag.

"Here, let me help." Her mother grabbed part of the white silk mass and between the two of them, managed to raise it above her head.

Cherish lifted her arms and shivered. Her arms slid into the long sleeves first. Then the dress slipped over her head, down her shoulders, and settled at her waist, engulfing her. She held her breath.

"Oh, you look lovely, dear." Aunt Patty stuck her head in the door. "Sorry to barge in but I want to wish you well." She came up to Cherish and hugged her delicately. Her bare arms were warm and friendly, so much so all Cherish wanted to do was cry on her shoulder.

"I'm so glad to see you," she mumbled into her aunt's embrace. "Thank you for coming." A belligerent tear trickled down her cheek.

"Aww...my amazing niece. Don't cry."

Aunt Patty's plump body was a soft place where Cherish had always found solace from her crazy parents' pressure. She rocked slightly, back and forth, in Aunt Patty's arms. "I have jitters," Cherish whispered to her.

"You're going to be all right," her aunt said, and let her go with a smile.

"Breathe, Cherish," Rachel whispered. "You look beautiful." She took her hand and squeezed it.

Cherish released her breath. "It shouldn't be so hard."

Aunt Patty touched her shoulder. "Change is always hard." She put her hand on the door. "I've got to go but I'll be in the auditorium sending you good thoughts."

"What shouldn't be hard, dear?" Her mom brushed tears away from her cheeks. "You make a gorgeous bride. You and Devin are perfect for each other. You have been from the start."

Rachel eyed her and she wanted to shrink down to the size of a violet. "Thank you, Mom, Rachel." Her voice cracked.

"What is hard?" Rachel asked. "Tell me, sis."

Certain everyone could see her heart pound, Cherish blinked hard. "Umm..." What could she say? She'd made her decision. Devin was right about her. She made a big deal about things. But not this time. She emptied her mind of doubts, grateful in her jitters to have people just point her in the right direction. "Nothing. I'm um, happy."

Her mother lunged toward her, then stopped. "Oh, I want to give you a hug, but I can't mess up your hair and make-up. You look perfect. I'm so glad you're happy."

"Yes, me too." Rachel set her lips and Cherish offered a smile. "If not today, then when, huh sis?" Her sister laughed, too loud.

"Right." Cherish didn't see anything funny.

Andrea, a close friend and one of her bridesmaids, cracked open the door. "We're ready to start. You look so pretty. Are you ready?"

Strands from trumpets in the small orchestra playing Henry Purcell's "Trumpet Voluntary" wafted in, and sounds of activity in the foyer told Cherish the other bridesmaids had begun their procession in the sanctuary.

Rachel touched her shoulder. "Ready?"

Am I?

"Here you go." Her mom handed her the bouquet of lavender and white stephanotis surrounded by English ivy and baby's breath. "Your father is just outside."

Cherish inhaled. "Okay, I'm ready."

Rachel took her place at the end of the bridesmaids' lineup. She looked over her shoulder at Cherish. "Smile," she mouthed.

"You are so beautiful. My daughter, I'm so proud of you." Her father kissed her forehead.

The beaming in her dad's eyes struck her with such sincerity she couldn't stop her eyes from misting. "Thanks, Dad."

He offered her his arm and she took hold of it. The trumpets stopped playing and the orchestra began playing Handel's "Occasional Oratorio" and she hung on tight to her father.

"Our turn, sweetie," he whispered.

She stared at the floor and moved with him to under the arched entrance to the sanctuary. Her heart wasn't singing. She could barely hear the orchestra over the blood rushing in her ears.

"Let's go." Her father nudged her.

She took a step, then another. *I can do this.* Her eyes trained on the flowers in her bouncing bouquet. *Why is it bouncing?*

Her father put his hand over hers. Oh. She was trembling, that's why.

Everyone rose to their feet as she entered, and heat crawled up her neck. *I'm going to faint. No, I can't do that. Breathe, Cherish.*

What would Devin think if she fainted? She looked down the long aisle at Devin, standing at the altar so handsome, so tall and, and, satisfied, that was the expression on his face. He smiled and she narrowed her eyes.

She glanced around at the people, everyone smiling her way. She'd made it almost halfway. It soon would be over.

Would it? Her feet hesitated. Would her misgivings ever be over? Her gaze went to Devin again, searching for confirmation that he was the one. Her one and only to share all the ups and downs of married life. Why did he want to marry her? He loved her, that was it. Her feet slowed. Did he? Love her? Her sensitive nature? Her tendency to overreact? Did he love that she didn't like pepper? That creative accounting made her sick at heart?

"Cherish," her dad whispered. "We're almost there. Let's not stop walking yet." His voice was strained, but emphatic.

She took another step, then stopped. Devin's face slipped into a frown. *What is he thinking? That I make a big deal about little things?*

Would she ever know the truth about the Standish case, whether or not he had betrayed her?

She stepped backward, slowly. The march continued, and she took another step toward the back of the sanctuary. Her mother's stricken face cut into her heart. Devin reached out his hand, coaxing.

So now she had to be coaxed to start her so-called dream life? Yesterday she vowed to herself she would not get lost in someone's idea of her life. Was she going to renege on her promise to please herself before others?

"No."

"What do you mean, no?" Panic in her dad's voice scared her.

"I mean, no." Cherish's heart went out to her parents, the friends, and family gathered. She took one long look at Devin. The room hushed as she stared at him. "I'm sorry, Devin."

"You're dumping me?" Rage filled his voice. His features hardened. "If you leave me..."

9

Cherish grabbed the folds of her dress and sprinted back up the aisle. She heard some of Devin's threats, but she had the wind at her back and nothing could stop her.

She shoved open the front doors of the church and raced down the street as fast as her feet would go, tossing the beautiful flowers to the ground and tearing her wedding do loose.

"Oh my God, what have I done?" Running in her heels and dragging her long train behind, she knew she made a spectacle to anyone on the street. Some stopped and stared as though she was a ghost. Others pointed her out and asked her where she was going.

Some smiled, and she smiled back. For those, she was grateful. Her flight was reckless. No doubt, there would be consequences to face. But the moment in the church when everything got small and tight, the path down the aisle came to a dead end. It would have been wrong to go through with her vow to love, respect, and cherish a man she didn't trust.

"Hey there, need a ride?" Rachel pulled her car up beside her, matching Cherish's pace.

Cherish crumpled to the pavement, sobbing. In a second, Rachel stopped her car in the middle of the street and ran to her side.

"Oh, sis. I'm here. What can I do?"

"I couldn't go through with it." Tears wouldn't stop. "I didn't want to upset everyone. I didn't want to hurt Devin."

Rachel hugged her and rocked her. "I know. I know. Don't think about Dad or Mom, or even Devin."

A car stopped and a man yelled through his window. "Get out of the road. You're blocking traffic."

"Oh, I'm sorry." She was messing up everything.

"Let's get out of here. I'll take you home."

With Rachel's arms still around her, Cherish let her usher her to the car. She rested her head against the seat, deflated. "I can't go home. That would be the first place Devin would go to find me, and I can't face him. Not yet. I don't have any place to go." Expressions on her mom and dad's faces burned in her eyelids. She couldn't escape their shock. And Devin, well, his angry explosion reverberated through her still. Not that she could blame him.

"I can take you to my place."

"Yeah, like no one will think of that." She clamped her lips closed. Drat. Her sister didn't deserve that. "I'm sorry. I didn't mean to sound flippant. I appreciate your help so much." New tears meandered down her cheeks.

"No worries, sis. I'll be your guard. We can go straight to my place, then I'll snag clothes and stuff from your house later." Rachel glanced at her and their eyes held for a split second. "We could stop for a meal at Darcy's but we might be a little overdressed."

Cherish couldn't help it, she broke out laughing, and Rachel joined in. Tension in her chest eased, and she pulled in a deep breath and released it. "I don't know, do you think we'll ever get another chance to eat dinner at a burger joint dressed as a bride and maid of honor?"

"We should do it once a month. Why not?" Rachel shrugged, glints shining in her eyes.

Cherish ran her hands over her full silk skirt. The long train bunched around her feet. "I don't like this dress. I can't wait to take it off. I never want to see it again."

"Why did you pick it out?" Rachel turned down the street where she lived.

Cherish fingered the pearl beads on one of her sleeves. "I'm ashamed to say it, but I let Mom pressure me. God, she even cried when I tried it on. I told her it wasn't my style, but you know Mom. She insisted it was perfect. I thought her tears were a sign it was the right dress. You were always better than me at standing up for to her."

"Well, maybe I am more headstrong, but I paid for that, remember? I was always getting in trouble. You were the younger daughter, four years younger than me. You learned by my example how to avoid 'the glare'."

Cherish couldn't help but share a chuckle. "Oh God, Mom's glare."

Rachel sobered. "I'm sorry about the dress. I didn't know that was happening. I wish I'd been there for you. It is a nice dress, but it was only perfect for Mom's needs, it sounds like."

"She is a force. It doesn't seem worth it to me sometimes to resist her. I mean, she has good taste, she has certain needs, and I can make her happy by doing what she wants. It doesn't matter what I want. Not enough, anyway, to make Dad and Mom unhappy."

"It does matter, though," Rachel said.

Before Cherish mustered the energy to disagree, Rachel pulled the car in to her driveway and ran around to the passenger side to help her out.

"Here, I'll grab the train. It's heavy."

"No, just let it drag." She grabbed Rachel's hand and they walked slowly up the front steps and into the house. As soon as Rachel closed the front door, Cherish dropped her guard.

The urge to run still beat inside her like a rapid cadence on a snare drum. Was this what it felt like to escape prison, or was this new life charging up and down her spine?

She looped her train over her arm and opened the glass doors at the back of Rachel's living room. Summer evening breezed in her face, buoying her spirits. She stepped barefoot onto the stone patio.

Warmth radiating off the surface was real, solid. It streamed up her legs and spread throughout her body.

Suddenly everything, her arms, her torso, her skin, wanted out of the dress. Now. She reached around for the bow where the open back met her waist, and clawed at the clasp. Too much dress got in her way, and panic burned up her throat. She struggled, trying to shrug the dress off her shoulders, but the long sleeves were too tight. *I'm being eaten by a mountain of a dress.* "I can't get out!"

Rachel bolted to her. "I'll help. Hang on."

Cherish stared at her, frozen. Seeing her sister in the periwinkle knee-length silk dress reminded her of the celebration she had ruined.

Rachel's fingers made quick work of unhooking the dress at the waist and pulling off the choking sleeves.

Cherish shoved the whole mess to the ground and stepped out, glee bubbling. "Thanks. I can breathe."

"Awww, sis, I wish I'd known you were feeling so pressured." She dipped her head. "I'm sorry I left you alone in that. I shouldn't have told you about Devin. I shouldn't have shown you the blog post. I'm sorry for that most of all. It wasn't fair. I destroyed your happily ever after. It's my fault you're here in my backyard in your underwear, not in your glorious gown at your reception."

"No." Cherish shook her head. "None of this mess is your doing. I got lost in a whirlwind, someone else's dream."

"I get that. You got knocked off your center with those other guys you dated. People rushed in to rescue you. Dad and Mom had good intentions, but they took over, which is so like them. Our parents are always sure their way is best." Rachel hugged her again. "I'm proud of you for standing up for yourself."

"I didn't have a back-up plan for not marrying Devin. The decision had been made and I meant to become Mrs. Raye. Now what?"

"I don't know, but you don't have to figure that out tonight. What do you feel like doing right now?"

Rachel's eyes glittered. If her energy wasn't flat, her sister's excitement would be contagious.

Coneflowers and Black-eyed Susans in Rachel's backyard swayed in the breeze. Velvety grass carpeted the ground, and rows of trees bordered the space. It reminded Cherish of a secret garden, and that her sister did everything perfectly. *Geez! Just call me Eeyore.*

Rachel rested her hand on one hip. "Well, what do you want to do? Don't think too much."

"The truth is, I don't know what I want to do."

"Okay, I understand. But I'm not going to make suggestions. Take your time, and when you come up with something you want, let me know. In the meantime, you can look through my clothes for something to put on, unless you prefer just the very lacy underwear you're wearing. Did Mom buy you that?"

Cherish scanned her underwear. "Yes, she did." She couldn't get out of the stuff fast enough. Everything down to her underwear had been done for her. "Which drawer is your underwear drawer?"

Rhys pulled a large trout from the cooler sitting on Gray's deck and raised it in the air. "Anyone in the mood for fresh trout for dinner? I just happened to have made the best catch of the day."

Jasper reached for Rhys's cap and pulled it down over his eyes. "Yes, that's a nice fish. But how about this?" He pulled a larger fish from the cooler. "*This* is a trout."

Gray stepped toward his kitchen inside. "Okay, you two. Dad and Mom will be here soon. Let's get busy on preparing these fish. Oh, and don't plan on me cleaning these guys. You caught them, you clean them. I'll cut vegetables to grill for dinner."

"I'm not afraid of a little fish-cleaning," Jasper said, cutting into the fish with a kitchen knife.

"Me either. Hand me a knife, will you?" Rhys pointed to the knife drawer.

"More power to you guys," Gray said, handing over a knife. He leaned against the counter and watched in silence.

"I smell fish. Hi boys," his dad said, walking inside with his mom.

"You three must have had a successful fishing trip," his mom said. "Good."

His parents smiled at him and made themselves at home. It was a nice feeling to know they felt comfortable at his house.

He checked the time and a melancholy swept over him. He grabbed discarded pieces of fish and walked outside on the deck to get air.

Hungry gulls swarmed above his head, crying and chirping.

"Here you go." He tossed up small pieces of fish to the colony of gulls. He focused on their distinct cries back-dropped by sounds of rolling waves.

Two great brothers. Wonderful parents. A thriving boat business. A house that would make any beach bum happy. A house that sat on a bluff, with stairs that led directly down to the beach. He had so much. Yet, he was unhappy.

He pounded his fist on the railing surrounding his deck. He wanted more. He wanted to write news for a newspaper, and he wanted to get to know Cherish. She would be married now. He didn't expect she would have canceled her wedding.

God, why did I have to meet her? I'm so damn tired of this aching for more and knowing I can never have it.

"Gray, are you all right?" His mom stepped up beside him and rubbed his back.

He hugged her. "Yes, I'm fine. Just enjoying the view."

She stared out to the lake. "It's an awesome sight."

He watched her shoulders relax and draped his arm across them, standing quietly with her at his side. He got his height from his dad, not his mom. She was short and petite, but so much larger than life. She inspired him. Sometimes the gusto that came out of her was the only thing he had to go on. And sometimes her kindness and accepting ways were what protected him from hopelessness.

"I appreciate the sacrifice you made when you moved back and took over Dad's business." Her eyes searched his soul. "Sometimes I wonder if it was right for you, if you're happy here."

He couldn't hide anything from her. But he had to keep up the lie that gave her peace of mind.

"Mom, you don't have to keep thanking me. I'm carrying on the family business. I'm close to people I love, you, Dad, and my brothers." He swept his hand out over the view. "And I have all this."

"But is it enough, son? Are you happy?"

"How could I not be?"

"Your brothers are grilling a mean meal," his dad said. "Nice day of fishing, it seems."

His dad joining them gave Gray an easy way to ignore his mom's question. But he felt her eyes on him still. "It was a good way to spend the day." He grinned at his parents, and led them around the house to the other end of the deck where the food was grilling.

Gray sniffed the air. "The food smells good. I see you took care of the vegetables."

Jasper poked him. "Yes, we did. You disappeared."

"You could have called me, I would've fixed them."

"No, it's okay." Rhys chuckled. "Just giving you crap. We got it figured out. We cook and you clean up."

His mom walked inside and started opening kitchen cupboards. "Are these plates all right?"

"No." He scooped his mother and carried her to a chair at the table. "You are not lifting a finger. You and Dad are my guests."

"Oh, you goof." She smiled up at him. "I would rather be busy."

"Too bad. Tonight, you relax."

"That's right, Mom," Jasper confirmed. "But this dinner is ready, so somebody better make themselves useful." Jasper pointed the grill tongs at Gray.

Quickly he set the table and before long everyone was seated.

"Dig in." Rhys passed a plate of impressive grilled trout to his mom. "Don't be shy. There's plenty."

Gray took a bite of the seasoned tomatoes, onions, peppers, and potatoes. "Mmm. This is good. My compliments, Jas, Rhys."

Conversation about Jasper's work as an EMT and Rhys's technology start-up flowed easily, and Grayson sat on the edge, taking all of it in. Guilt chased down echoes of his hopes and dreams. He had so much to be grateful for.

Dinner wound down and he sent his family to the living room to relax while he cleaned up. Laughter interspersed with serious tones spilled into the kitchen.

The last dish put away, Gray made his rounds, checking security camera input on his bedroom television. He scrutinized the feed from the exterior of his house. His regular routine of checking made him very familiar with the perimeter, so he would catch the tiniest difference easily.

Next, he focused on feed from discreetly placed interior cameras. God, if he ever saw a prowler or anything suspicious he would attack like a mad dog to keep his family safe.

He let out a long breath. Nothing appeared out of the ordinary, but the ever present possibility that one day or night someone would be sneaking around weighed around his neck like a ball and chain.

"Gray, come join us before we have to leave," his dad called.

"I'll be right there." One more thing to check and he could relax for a while. He checked the newsfeed on his laptop, scrolling through various headlines.

He sucked in a breath, and read a headline.

Prominent Dunes Bay Lawyer Left at the Altar.

He speed-read the first lines, holding his breath. Could this unlucky groom be Cherish's? Everything in the article blurred until he saw the bride's name, Cherish Moss.

His heart flipped and flopped, and he wasn't sure he was sad for her or happy. He stood and turned one way, then another, like a vacuum robot caught in a corner.

He slumped into a chair. Nothing. He could do nothing. This was Cherish's business, not his. But oh, how he wanted to know what she was doing, how she was feeling. In less than a day he'd become completely caught up in presence.

"Gray, we're leaving," his mom called.

"Yeah, Mr. Poor Host, your family has things to do. See you later." The sarcasm in Jasper's voice stung.

He strode to the other room. "I'm very sorry I got distracted. Please, stay. I want to be with you."

"Oh you doofus," Rhys said, punching his arm slightly. "We're just joking with you."

"Yeah, we joke," Jasper said. "But, we are leaving."

His mom hugged him. "No hard feelings. Love you," she added leaving.

With everyone gone, Gray raced back to his computer. He reread the article. More details registered in his brain, and his pulse raced.

Words jumped out at him, reminding him of what he'd done. He blinked hard. This was bad, so bad. He'd outed Devin about bribery and evidence tampering. Cherish said she'd learned bad news. Had she read his post? Had it changed her mind about the marriage? It was like him to get so engrossed in writing a post that he didn't make connections to real people. He never meant to hurt her.

If she had read that post could she have read others? His mind whirled, and he pulled up other posts on his blog, searching for the one he never wanted her to read. The one he wrote about her firm. He hadn't known her when he'd written it. The post questioned her firm's choice of clientele, suggesting the firm was only interested in making money and catering to big name companies. He squirmed, just reading the heading.

Decidedly Laboratories Pits Moss Attorneys at Law Against Ill Man.

He swallowed hard, and read on.

In another sorry case of Big Business exerting its right to care less about the people it hurts than its large bank accounts, Decidedly Laboratories tilts the scale in their favor with Moss Attorneys at Law powerhouse.

Well, this blogger will be watching the case, but not holding my breath that Moss will display good judgment and high ideals in defending the indefensible damage done to Henry Pole, a victim of loose protection from harm in a drug trial in which he participated.

A lot is at stake for both parties of Henry Pole versus Decidedly Laboratories. Doctors have already maintained Pole's liver failure is a side effect of the drug administered to him in the trial. Isn't that enough to make a giant corporation open its coffers and own up to its missteps?

Apparently not. But Pole's losses are grave, and he needs money to pay medical bills. Though this blogger is no lawyer, it seems he is also due a large damage award for pain and suffering.

Come on Moss Attorneys, can you really help a corporation willing to ignore its responsibilities and still look yourselves in the mirror?

This blogger hopes not.

Yup, he had written that piece. It needed to be written. He wasn't a journalist anymore but his instinct told him to hold public figures' and businesses' feet to the fire. Public documents were readily available, and he used them to find post ideas. When he read the court's database of upcoming cases, he knew the Pole case needed fire and feet holding and a fair resolution.

He shoved back from his laptop, balancing between the high road and belief that Cherish would not be the kind of lawyer he wrote about.

He scrubbed his hand through his hair. He could delete the post before Cherish saw it. She had enough to deal with, and he didn't want to give her something else. He wasn't even sure she'd read his post about Devin. His gut eased, and ameliorating his jab at her firm stood out as his next goal. He didn't want to take down his post. Victims of Decidedly Lab's negligence needed help. But if he could, he would rescue her from the aftermath of leaving Devin at the altar.

He glanced out the window. It wasn't dark out yet. It was only eight. If he left right now, he could drive to her place and just check on her. Yeah, that would be the friendly thing to do.

He didn't know where she lived, but he used to be an investigative reporter. He could damn well find anyone or anything.

CHERISH HUDDLED on the bed in Rachel's guestroom, at her wits' end. Texts and voice messages stacked up in her phone's recent calls. Devin, Devin, Devin, Mom, Dad, Devin. The pastor who was to marry them. Devin. Calls coming in all evening were her penance for running out on her wedding, her fiancé, and her friends, but most of all, her parents.

She'd failed, she'd failed, she'd failed.

Broken a commitment.

Cherish had committed the cardinal sin in her parents' eyes because their embarrassment was more important than her life. If only she could have a conversation with them, a true heart-to-heart, where they would understand her not marrying Devin. But heart-to-hearts were not done in her family. And how could she explain her actions when even she didn't understand completely. So every time she ignored a call, guilt pricked her heart. She knew she had to talk to people, but not yet.

Rachel had been fending off calls, which helped so much, and she would be forever grateful. Still, she longed for distance from the chaos she had created. Her eyes glued to her screen for the next call, and slowly, deliberately, she slid the volume button on her phone to silent. She grabbed the bed pillow and pulled it over her head.

Her sister's footsteps coming up the stairs made her go rigid. Who was on the other end of Rachel's phone this time?

"It's Mom calling again. What do you want me to say?" Rachel crinkled her nose, as though a lie would make her sick.

"I don't want to talk to anyone, not just her," Cherish whispered. "Tell her not to worry, I'm just not yet ready to talk."

Rachel gave a thumbs-up and walked away, speaking to Mom. "Don't worry. Cherish is going to talk to you, it's too soon, that's all."

Cherish held her breath while Rachel tuned her attention to their mom. This was one of those times it would be so much easier for her to acquiesce and talk to her mom, rather than hold her own and allow herself time.

She listened in on Rachel's side of the conversation, fidgeting with buttons on the shirt Rachel loaned her.

"Cherish knows you love her, Mom. And she loves you. We'll deal with all of that later. Of course you can call me for updates. Okay, I love you too."

Sounds of Rachel loading the dishwasher floated up to her. The least she could do was help out in the kitchen. This whole runaway bride gig had affected her sister too, and she hadn't meant for that to happen.

In the kitchen she hugged Rachel so hard it was as much to hold herself up as to show her love for all she'd done.

"Oh, what's this? You know I'd do anything for you." Rachel asked. Hugging her back with as much enthusiasm as Cherish gave.

"Thank you for being here for me. You are my rock." She slid onto a kitchen stool. "But it's not fair to you. You've taken me in, shared your clothes, and put yourself between me and well-meaning people."

Rachel smirked. "It's the least I can do after telling you about the unfavorable blog post about he-we-won't-mention." Rachel shot her a rueful smile. "Can you forgive me?"

"There's nothing to forgive. I'm grateful. You know, a new acquaintance asked me if bad news was why I was uncertain about marrying Devin. I told him, and now I'm admitting to you, it wasn't just bad news, it wasn't just one thing. Things had piled up until I couldn't go through with it."

"I'm still sorry your perfect day turned sour, but if running away was right for other reasons as well, then I'm glad you did it. No looking back." Rachel raised her fist and grinned.

"Onward and upward." Gusto behind her words perked her mood, but the emptiness and not-knowing what to do next persisted. "At the rehearsal, I heard Mom talking about doing creative accounting. She wouldn't explain, and I didn't press. Do you know anything about that?"

"Hmm, I don't. That's a little scary to hear," Rachel said, rolling her eyes. "Though it wouldn't surprise me — don't get me wrong Cherish, I know nothing. But mom and dad have a ruthless side to the business. I've seen a consistent pattern of disregarding genuine wrong-doing in preference for wins for big clients. I've never wanted you to know. You know, me big sister you little sister. But we both should find out the whole story, don't you think?"

"We should go into the accounting program." Cherish watched Rachel's eyes widen.

Rachel hesitated for a moment then nodded. "Yes. Let's do that." She retrieved her laptop from her bedroom and they sat down at the island in the center of the kitchen. Rachel logged into the firm's private server and clicked on accounting. "Since all key executives have access to the main files we probably should be able to log in without a problem. I don't ever go into accounting, do you?"

Cherish shrugged. "No. I never have."

"Okay, we're in."

Cherish chewed on her thumbnail and perused files with Rachel, minutes ticking by.

"I don't see anything alarming." Rachel arched her eyebrows.

"Let's try Mom's email address. EmmaMoss.MossAAL@Moss-AAL.com. Oh, the account is password protected. That's interesting," Cherish said, her brain running possibilities. "What would Dad and Mom use for a password?"

She looked at Rachel and Rachel looked back.

"Any ideas?" Rachel finally asked.

Cherish peered at the password box. "What is this little question mark about?"

"Do we dare click on it?" Rachel asked, scrunching up her face.

"Here, let me do it. That way if we're found out you can say I did it."

"What? No," Rachel protested.

Cherish quickly tapped the box and a question popped up. "Oh, this is a security question."

"Geez, really? Thank you Google. Name of Rachel's first boyfriend?" Rachel read. "That's weird. It's personalized."

"It's also a question we can answer, right?" Cherish tapped her chin. "I think I remember a Colin."

"Yes, it was fifth grade and his name was Colin something. Let's try it."

Cherish started to tap in the name, then stopped, nerves jangling. "What if it's case sensitive?"

"Mom likes uppercase." Rachel giggled.

"This isn't funny. But I think you're right. She always capitalizes everything. Mom thinks in emphatic terms." Cherish tapped in all upper case C-O-L-I-N. She hovered her finger over the touchpad. It trembled. "Are we doing this?"

"Yes," Rachel stated. "We are big girls and this is our firm too. If Mom and Dad are doing something shady, we have the right to know."

"Absolutely. It could reflect badly on our careers." Cherish entered the answer and stared.

Rachel threw up her hands. "Unbelievable. We're in."

"I feel like co-conspirators. This account is private, not the firm's accounting pages," Cherish said.

After about fifteen minutes of searching, Cherish clicked on a button labeled 'Specials.' It opened up accounting of payments and withdrawals in the millions. "What the heck?" She exchanged a worried look with her sister.

"These accounts look like what I would call creative accounting," Rachel said, biting a fingernail.

Cherish scrolled down one company page. "Do you know anything about this Tantorum Inc.?"

"Never heard of it. We could double-check it on the clients list, but that could take time. There are a lot of clients." Rachel didn't take her eyes off the Tantorum transactions column. "A lot of money is flowing with just this one client." She grabbed Cherish's arm.

"Yeah, this appears to be—"

"Money laundering, but we don't *know* that," Rachel said.

"Yes. But what if it is, what are we going to do?" Cherish's heart pounded in her chest. "We have to talk to Mom and Dad, let them explain."

"We will. But not tonight. We need to think about this and make sure we're not misjudging what we've found." Rachel took hold of her shoulders. "You have enough to deal with already."

Cherish ran her fingers through her hair. Her thoughts reeled. "Could this be why Devin pushed so hard to date me, propose to me, marry quickly? And why Dad and Mom were so in favor of it? If they're laundering money for clients, they're committing crimes. My brain is melting. I should never have gotten engaged."

Rachel pinned her gaze. "You're going to be fine, Cherish Elena Moss. We'll find out the truth about Mom and Dad. I'm sure or at least hope there's an explanation that's not illegal. Just know you have done nothing wrong, sis. Do what you need to do to get your bearings back first, okay?"

Like a robot, Cherish nodded. "Thank you for the pep talk. I don't know what to think anymore."

"It was as much for myself as you." Rachel looked rueful. "And now, if you think you can spare me for a bit, I'll go get your things from your place. Okay?"

"You don't mind me staying here?"

"Stay as long as you like. Actually, it's fun having you here."

"Then yes, I would appreciate having my things. If anyone comes to the door, I won't answer."

With Rachel gone, Cherish stood in the middle of the living room, shivering. It wasn't cold in the house, but for the first time since she'd run back up the aisle and out of the church, she felt alone. Her world had collapsed, in many directions, and with the absence of anyone to keep up a stiff front for, shock took over, creeping like heavy frost through every cell.

She, good old reliable Cherish Moss, ran.

It was as if someone had pulled the plug on her life and now she swirled round and round, empty of any self-direction.

She paced through the house, searching for distraction. Rachel's décor was House Beautiful itself. She had been here hundreds of times, but just now noticed the striking contrast of midnight blue painted walls, and black overstuffed couch and chairs softened by a warm distressed wooden table and cabinets. Eclectic collections of art pieces filled surfaces with interest, but not clutter.

Her sister's life was well-ordered and had all the right elements: a successful career, a busy social life, a mind of her own. Well, two out of three for herself wasn't bad. But how had she lost her sense of self-determination? It was becoming clearer and clearer. She'd always been wobbly in that department. She'd tried to keep the peace. She had believed the family story: her parents were perfect and so was her family. In the big picture of families, she had nothing to complain about. But it wasn't true. Oh, she didn't doubt her parents loved her. But they, her parents, in particular her mother, had squashed her with manipulation and conditional love.

She sniffed. *I have spunk. I made it through law school. I can litigate with the best of them, can't I?*

So what had happened?

She dragged her gaze across the room, shying from phone calls she needed to make. Her shoulders hunched at the weight of what was to come. Then she saw it. The dress, rolled into a white ball of silk, lay in a corner past the end of the couch. The room got dizzy, but she kept peering at the dress. Tears welled again.

"Oh my God. What have I done?"

It wasn't that she felt like she made the wrong decision for herself. She worried for everyone else. Her mind filled with wedding flowers, the towering cake, centerpieces for the reception, dancing with her dad. And gifts. All the gifts had been sent to the house she and Devin bought, furnished, and planned to live in.

She shuddered. At one time Devin was the perfect guy, wasn't he? Or was she caught up once again in doing what's right, not making an issue, rather than looking out for herself. Her toes never tingled at his kisses, her heart never swelled seeing him after being apart, maybe she never did love him. And maybe he never loved her.

Then why did he want to marry her? Was it truly all some plot to secure his wealth and status?

She grabbed her head in both hands. "What do I do now?"

Everything raced at her, demanding immediate attention before anything else went bad or anyone got hurt. It was up to her to fix this mess.

And then what to do about her parents, the business — ugh, first things first.

She ran upstairs to the guestroom and pulled open a drawer in a nightstand. The box was still there. The box she had put her engagement ring in when Rachel brought her here. She lifted the lid and shook her head. The ring was beautiful. Devin had told her to pick anything she wanted and she'd chosen a half-carat white diamond set between two elegant platinum sloping curves.

Devin needed for her to have more, so he'd upgraded the stone to a two-carat setting. If it were not so gaudy, it would be the perfect ring.

She swiped away a tear that escaped down her cheek. The manipulation of his actions started to weigh on her. He always had to do better, have the last say, control her. "Enough." The ring went back in the drawer and Cherish went to the kitchen to find something to make for dinner. Keep herself occupied and distracted. She would deal with the what-nexts later.

In the refrigerator she found makings for an omelet, all very nice and orderly.

Her attention drifted to the living room again, and the pile of wedding dress. An evening sun filled the room with a golden radiance. Cherish grabbed the cord and slammed the drapes closed at each window, closed to the sun, closed to the outside world.

"Yup, this is the right house." Grayson double-checked the address, and pulled his pick-up to the curb in front of what he believed was Cherish's house. He sat inside his Dodge RAM surveying the small white cottage with a green door located in a tree-lined cul-de-sac. The area looked bright and fresh, just like Cherish.

Now don't go thinking all mushy about Cherish. This is a non-mushy visit.

A car in the driveway clued him someone, maybe Cherish, was inside.

Hustling out of the truck and up the front steps he knocked on the front door, waited for a response, then knocked again, harder. Did he dare peek in the window? He looked over one shoulder across the cul-de-sac, and then the other. Peace, quiet, and no noticeable curious neighbors anywhere. Maybe he could check around back.

Right, that wouldn't be awkward if he did find her back there.

He raised his hand to try another knock, but the door opened.

"Can I help you?"

"Umm... You're not Cherish."

The young woman standing on the other side of the storm door frowned. "No, I'm not. What do you want with Cherish?"

Gray had rehearsed what he would say when he got here—what he would say to Cherish. *Hi. I don't mean to intrude, but are you okay? I read the newspaper article about your day.*

He had no back-up plan for someone else at the door. "I'm Grayson Steele, I'm a friend of Cherish. I just wanted to check on her. I mean, I imagine her day has been kind of rough."

The woman still frowned and kept the storm door between them closed. "So you're a friend. Well, if you're any kind of friend of Cherish's you would understand she doesn't want to talk to people, not tonight."

Except for her auburn hair, the young woman didn't look like Cherish. This woman had brown eyes and a round face. Cherish had an oval face, and definitely different coloration.

"Oh." He realized his smile hadn't faded, thinking of Cherish. "I understand that. I do know her and only want to talk to her. I don't have her phone number. I don't suppose you'd give it to me? I am not a stalker or a serial killer, I promise."

The woman shoved her hand onto her hip and glared. "I'm going to shut this door now, so just be on your way."

He held up his index finger. "It's just that she told me last night she was getting married today. But she was scared. Then when I read she hadn't gone through with it, I, well, I just want to tell her I'm here if she needs to talk, about anything."

The young woman's face softened. Her shoulders relaxed, and she dropped her hand to her side. "What did you say your name is?"

"Grayson Steele, but almost everyone calls me Gray." He pulled one of his business cards from his wallet. "Here's my phone number and my shop's address. Could you please give it to her and tell her I hope she's okay?"

The woman opened the door and took his card. "Grayson," she said, and lifted her gaze to his. "That's a nice name. I appreciate your concern. I'll tell her you asked about her."

The sound of a car squealing into the cul-de-sac and racing into the driveway interrupted them. The driver jumped out and marched up the lawn.

"Now Devin, don't come charging at me like that." The woman's voice was sharp.

Gray recognized the lawyer-socialite trying to bully his way inside.

The woman's order didn't stop him from reaching the door. Gray stood still but his muscles tightened, prepared for whatever may happen.

"Where is she, Rachel? I know you know. Is she inside?" He tried to see around Rachel and into the house. "Cherish, Cherish, I know you're in there. Either let me in or I'm coming inside." He banged on the storm door.

Devin eyed Gray, still standing on the front porch. Gray stared at him and remained quiet.

"Rachel, who is this guy? What's he doing here?" He paced a couple steps on the porch. "Cherish, come out here right now. We need to talk."

"Just leave," Rachel said. "She'll call you when she's ready to talk. I told you that already on the phone, six times."

Devin balled his fist and raised it in Rachel's face. "Just because you're her sister doesn't mean you can keep me away. Where is she?"

Gray took one long step across the porch and snapped Devin's fist behind his back. "You were asked to leave. I won't get physical with you unless you touch that woman or insist on making a pest of yourself."

"Ow. Let me go, you bastard. This is none of your damn business. I'll leave when I want. My wife is in there."

Gray's teeth ached he gritted them so hard. He had acted without thought to protect the woman, who apparently was Cherish's sister. He didn't need to argue that Cherish was not his wife. The man was a cheat and a liar, but he did just get left at the altar. "Calm down. I'll let go but you do as Rachel says or I'll hurt you worse. I'm a man of peace, but you're way out of line."

Devin spat on the ground, surveyed Grayson up and down, then stepped down the stairs. "I'll find her. You can't keep her from me."

Rachel groaned. "Give her some time, and all the space she needs before you pressure her to do something she's not ready for."

Devin grunted and climbed in his sporty Lexus. He backed out into the street and drove away as though the speed limit wasn't meant for him.

Rachel blew out a long breath. "I'm sorry you saw that. That is the man Cherish did not marry today."

"I gathered that. I can understand he'd be upset, but we're not savages. He had no right to threaten you."

"No he didn't. You're right. Do you want to come in? I'm here picking up a few things for Cherish. She's really not here."

"No, I'm going to give you your space." Worry sprouted in his mind like kudzu. "I'm just wondering, will he be able to find Cherish?"

Rachel's eyes widened and her hand went to her throat. "Oh, oh, I need to get back home." She opened the door wide and gestured him inside. "Please, could you help me with some of these boxes?"

"Sure. Just stack some up here." He held his arms out. "Can you warn Cherish?"

"She's at my house and she's not answering her phone," she said, stacking three boxes in his arms.

Grayson's heart jumped into his throat. "I see. Are there any more boxes?"

Rachel paused. "Is that too heavy? I've probably packed too much but I don't know how long she's staying."

"No." It really wasn't. Imagination took over and filled his head with silky intimate clothing on top of more lacey, frilly things packed in the boxes. "You can add another one." Uncomfortable urges responded to the idea of Cherish wearing the imaginary nightwear.

"No, that's all of it." Rachel peeked around two smaller boxes in her arms. She led him out the front door, locked it, and nearly sprinted to her car, bottles inside the boxes rattling. "You can follow me. And please keep up."

The only way not to lose sight of Rachel's BMW was to ride her bumper. She sped around curves hugging the road like a racecar driver. Reckless, in fact, darting in and out of traffic. Fortunately, her car was orange, and his truck was fast.

CHERISH SHRANK into a corner in the kitchen at the sound of the doorbell chime. If she ignored it, the person at the door would go away. If she had to talk to someone about the wedding, she'd, well, she couldn't.

Coward.

The doorbell rang again. She covered her face with her hands. Whoever it was deserved an explanation, but not now.

Bam, bam, bam. The person was persistent, knocking hard on the door. "Go away," she whispered.

The pounding continued. "Cherish, I know you're in there. Let me in, baby. I need to talk to you."

Oh God. It was Devin. Of course he would find her. She had nothing inside—no strength, fortitude, or instinct—and she needed all of them in order to stand up to him. *Geez! Why can't everyone just wait?*

"Please, Cherish, let me in. I love you." His voice got to her. It was gentle and pleading.

Didn't she owe him a conversation at least? She stayed in the corner and chewed her thumbnail. Her heart raced. She couldn't let him in, she just couldn't. He would flash his confident charm and she would give in. She had to stop being such a pushover, so limp. She knew what she wanted in the courtroom and could hold her own. Where was that Cherish when she needed her?

He got quiet and she breathed out slowly. Maybe she had missed the bullet this time. Indecision loaded onto guilt in her gut. Hiding only postponed facing Devin.

She snuck into the living room to peek out a window, hoping he had left. Her body froze. Devin stared into the living room through the front door window. He dipped his head and smiled, clearly expecting her to open the door. There was no escaping him now.

Well, it must be the moment to talk.

She opened the door and he charged past her to the middle of the room.

"What are you doing here?" He shook his head. "What happened at the church?"

So no nice gentle Devin after all. Her breaths came in short shallow pulls. She hid behind her arms wrapped around her body and said nothing.

"You're going to stonewall me? Me? I'm your husband, or should be by now. Talk to me."

"No, I'm not stonewalling. But I don't like you storming in here and grilling me." Whoa. How did she do that?

"Excuse me. I deserve an explanation for why you left me in the church."

"I know you do. But you have to stop yelling at me." Her insides trembled, but she gave him a stern look. Would he buy her attempt at bravado? She had to make him. She would never hit anyone but she had to stand up to this pushy, demanding Devin.

He sighed. "I'm sorry. I'm sorry. If I say it three times will you tell me what's wrong? Do you not love me? No, I know that's not it. You're making a big deal about something. Tell me what it is?"

Something inside her broke. "Okay, I'll tell you," she yelled. "You betrayed me. I don't know if I love you."

His gaze dropped. "I never betrayed you. Who have you been talking to? Did Alicia call you?"

"What are you talking about? Why would Alicia call me?" Stunned realization tripped in her brain. He had a reason to think of Alicia. "I'm talking about court."

"I know," he said. "I didn't betray you."

How odd. He wouldn't look at her. "You did. You suppressed evidence. That was wrong. You may pay serious consequences for that. But you did it to me. You cheated, on me."

"I thought we talked through that. I thought you understood I bested you in court, that's all."

"You talked about it. You tried to make the whole thing about me and—"

"It is about you." His eyes flamed and some spit flew out of the corner of his mouth.

She flinched and took a step backward. Now she just wanted him the hell out of here. "Okay, it's about me. It's my doing, you're completely without blame. Now go." She pointed to the door.

His lids dropped and held for a half-second. He blew out a sigh and opened his eyes. "Listen, I love you. Let's go right now to the minister and get married. Tonight. We could still leave tomorrow morning for Switzerland." He held out his arms. "What do you say? It's just a tiny misunderstanding of something, I'm sure. I can fix this."

She put her hand to her heart. It began collapsing inward. It pained her to watch him make his case. He was such a lawyer, dispassionate while impassioned. Even now.

"Why do you want to marry me?"

He spread his arms wide? "How can ask you me that? I just told you I love you."

He dropped his arms to his sides. "Please, come with me to talk to the minister and let's get married, as we'd planned today. As you agreed to six months ago. I won't leave until you say yes."

"Why the rush? You've been pushing for marriage from our first date. Why? And don't say because you love me." She didn't raise her voice, but she crossed her arms over her chest and waited for satisfaction. Something sincere and from his heart.

His mouth dropped open. "That sounds like an accusation. I'm not going to dignify that with a response."

"That's funny. I thought it was a simple question?" He was too quick to raise defenses. Uneasiness squirmed through her, prompting more suspicion of ulterior motives.

Noises in the driveway caught her attention. Behind her back, she crossed her fingers on both hands, hoping for Rachel to walk through the kitchen entrance from the garage.

Devin narrowed his eyes. "Are you expecting someone?"

The entry door opened and Rachel walked inside. She put boxes down on the table and stopped. "Devin. I told you stay away." She marched briskly to Cherish. "Are you okay?"

"Of course, she's all right. I'm not going to hurt the woman I love."

"Did you let him in? I'm sorry I didn't get back sooner."

"Hey, I'm not a blank wall. I can hear you talking, and I don't like your insinuation." Devin opened his mouth to continue, but stopped, his mouth gaping.

"Hi Cherish. Where do you want these boxes?" Gray asked.

Cherish inhaled a sharp breath at the sight of him. "Just put them down anywhere. Thank you for bringing them. But why, how?"

"He stopped by your house to check on you." Rachel said, then nodded toward Devin. "We can talk more later."

"Who are you?" Devin rolled his eyes and glared. "You're the same guy who gave me a hard time at Cherish's house, aren't you? Well, you can leave. You don't belong here, either."

"Sorry, bud, I'm just helping out. No need to get up in my face again."

Astonishment quivered in Cherish. "You two know each other?"

"No. He's meddling where he doesn't belong," Devin quickly charged.

"Yes, I know him, but only technically through his media coverage." Gray gave her a steady smile, the one that lit up his eyes.

When he spoke, it was as though he saw only her. He made her feel like someone worth noticing.

"I had wanted to see if you were okay, that's why I went to your house." Gray glanced at Devin's tapping foot and up at Rachel, glued to the conversation. "Mind if I hang around for a while?"

Cherish smiled. "Thank you. That would be fine. I guess you've met my sister."

"Did you hear me? I asked you something," Devin asked, his voice louder.

She rubbed her forehead, searching for any clue about his question. When had she started going on autopilot whenever Devin talked?

"Cherish." His voice was crisp.

Oops. Did it again. "I heard you talking, I just didn't catch your question. Do you want to ask me again?"

He took her elbow and started toward the kitchen. Out of the corner of her eye she saw Gray move closer, but she shook her head.

His voice went low again. "Will you marry me, tonight?"

Her nerves walked on tiptoe on the top of a fence, and she didn't look down or she might disappear. She looked him directly in his eyes. "No."

She eyed Gray. He nodded and reached out his hand as he approached. "Here's my contact info. Call me if you want to. I'm not far."

"Get out of here," Devin demanded.

"No, I think you should go." Cherish pointed to the door, trembling inside.

"This isn't over." Devin blew out a sigh and brushed past her and out the door.

She took hold of one end of Gray's card and smiled. "Thank you for thinking of me. And for understanding."

He held onto the card for several long seconds before releasing his end. Kindness in his face matched his friendliness. She could use a friend, a neutral one with no agenda for her life.

"Any time." Gray left out the front door without a backward glance. But she watched him until he closed the door.

12
_____

Gray headed to his bedroom, a soldier walking the wall, ensuring all was well. He dropped in the chair at his desk and began his nightly online search. He had to clear, just like a cop cleared a suspect's hideout. Even now, a year since the death threats, the possibility of being caught off guard niggled inside him when he hit the sack at night if he didn't first search the net.

He circled his shoulders and tried to relax at his computer. He plugged the same words as always into his search engine and scrolled through results: Gang of Four, police corruption, Chicago Police Department, Kane Hastings.

His belly tightened and the minutes passed. Staying on top of the news wasn't just about him. It was about his brothers, his mom, and his dad. He fisted his hands, trying to tame the ache he carried of losing any one of them.

He squeezed his eyes shut to rest for a minute, then continued staring at his screen. He jumped at the sound of his phone, and nearly fell backward. Who could be calling at this hour? He didn't recognize the number, but at least there was one. He pressed the accept button, leery.

"Hello?"

"Hi, Gray."

The voice on the other end was soft, uncertain, but he recognized it. "Cherish. Are you okay?"

She sighed heavily, but said nothing. Her breath in his ear closed the distance between them. "I don't know. I didn't wake you did I?"

"No, I'm always awake, not a heavy sleeper – what's up?"

"I did something really radical today, or yesterday now. It's midnight." Cherish told him why she called.

"I guess so. But you had your reasons."

"I can't think about what explanation I'll give to the people expecting one. It's too complex and I have to stop the churning in my brain. But I was lying here in bed thinking about a line from a movie. It's something like, 'Of all the gin joints in the towns, in all the world.' And then I called you."

Gray pictured her green eyes, her copper hair, her fidgety mouth. He smiled inside. "Ah, Casa Blanca. Like you and me at the bar? I remember you at the restaurant. You, the funny woman. The mess, you called yourself."

She breathed softly. "You the alcoholic. We keep running into each other, and I wondered why, why you, why do you say the right words?"

She sounded tired. He couldn't resist continuing the game she'd started. "I hear a line in my head. 'What in heaven's name brought you to Casablanca?'" He hoped the line would cheer her up.

Cherish laughed, and lulled him into wondering the same things. What brought her into his life and why couldn't he escape her, or want to?

"See, that's what you do. You see me, the real me." She sniffed, twice.

"What are you crying about, specifically? I know the day has been hard, you're tired, and your dream fell apart. Is there something else?"

"My tears are not sad. I'm touched by your words. I could use a friend right now. A friend like you. Could we be friends?"

He held that idea close, as if it were a fragile, precious thing. He didn't know what to say.

"Well, I understand if you don't want to. I am a mess, after all, and you have your own life." Her words tumbled out fast.

"Shh. I would like to be friends. I didn't hesitate in answering you, I just wanted to be still for minute and appreciate your offer."

"Thank you. I don't know what to do now."

A distant ship's foghorn sounded out on the lake, and he waited for Cherish to say something more.

"I had my life planned out and now I don't."

"What do you want to do?" Her voice relaxed his mind.

"I thought I wanted to get married, have a family, work at my mom and dad's firm, you know, live happily ever after."

"I mean if you could do something you want, say, tomorrow, what would it be?"

"Umm...escape to a desert island where no one would be able to reach me. I know, I know. I should be giving people explanations."

Gray ignored her self-flaying. She needed a break. "I could provide that escape for you, at least a short one."

"What? I can't leave town right now. I have work and everyone would think I ran away." Her voice dropped off into silence.

"Didn't you have plans for a honeymoon?"

"Oh, well, yes. I do have time off, two weeks," she said with a little more spark.

"I'm not talking about a long getaway, just a day or even hours. You don't even have to leave town." He swore he heard her gasp. "Would you like to go out in my boat later this morning?"

"What? Your boat? On Lake Michigan? Today?"

"It's Sunday. The forecast is for sunny and hot. It's not the Caribbean, but it's a big inland sea. No one will bother you." He couldn't believe he asked her, but he had, and eagerness urged him on. "I'll bring everything we need. You just come to my shop. You have my address, and you probably have a phone with a GPS."

"You have no idea how perfect that sounds. I'm in. What time?"

"I need to get some sleep and so do you. How about nine?"

"How about seven? I can't wait to escape."

"Who needs sleep, right? I'll be waiting."

"Gray?"

"Yes?"

"Am I crazy to do this, escape with you?"

"No, I don't think so. You've had a rough time for a while and everyone needs respite from hard times."

"I don't really know you."

"You know I'm a local resident and I own a business. That's not nothing."

"You're right. Good night."

He hung up the phone and relaxed into the idea of spending time with Cherish in a few hours. His mind went to work listing the things he needed to do before seven. Casually, his gaze dropped to his laptop. He refreshed the search one last time, half-rising out of his chair.

"Oh my God." He sank back down, his muscles rigid.

There it was. The thing he had hoped would never happen. The headline on yesterday's *Chicago Daily Banner*.

"Former Chicago Police Detective Released After Serving One Year of His Sentence." This was not good. This was so not good. He scanned the short article, knots twisting his gut.

A spokesman for the Illinois Department of Corrections said Kane Hastings, convicted of framing innocent people for crimes and taking part in a burglary ring, has been released from prison after serving only one year of his twenty-year sentence.

HE PACED in front of his desk. Back and forth, back and forth, his head pounding.

His phone rang, and a rock jumped into his throat. He grabbed up his phone, trembling, and heaved a sigh. He knew the number. It was his former editor at *The Chicago Daily Banner*.

"It's Eric. I shouldn't be contacting you like this."

"I saw it." They both knew the unspoken thing. "Are you all right?"

"Yeah, sure. I have things to discuss."

"Email me. It's safe."

"And how is that? I know you told me, but is it really untraceable?"

"It is. My brother helped me hide behind layers of security. It's okay."

The line went silent and almost immediately, Eric's email popped in to his inbox.

GRAY, WATCH YOUR BACK. Kane Hastings' early release is a sure sign dirty business is afoot. Considering his crimes, it's irregular that he would be released so early. Probably got some kind of under the table deal, which would mean the Gang of Four is up to no good. I know you, and you'll want to investigate what's up, but don't. Stay where you are, wherever that is, and stay vigilant. Kane meant it when he threatened to kill you. And he's probably more determined after time in prison. Keep in touch and I'll let you know if I learn anything important.

Gray stretched back in his chair and rubbed his eyes. It didn't surprise him that Eric was up so late, probably working. Thank God he was working late. Eric was his only connection to that business from his past and he knew he could count on him to feed him Kane's next address, job location, maybe even make of car. But it would take time to gather that info.

Fire burned in his chest, and he closed his laptop harder than it needed. This was the last thing he wanted on his mind while out with Cherish. All he wanted was to be there for her.

Were the no-name phone calls Hastings? Was he being selfish by not telling his family about the danger? Worse, was he being reckless with their lives? Should he cancel plans with Cherish? No, no. This is not what he wanted his life to be about, running and hiding and not really living. And he would not flake on Cherish.

13

Cherish got up early and quietly went about getting ready for her day on the lake with Gray. She left a note on the kitchen table for Rachel to find when she woke up. *Rachel, I'm going boating with my new friend. You know, Gray. Don't worry. He's a reputable local businessman. But just to be safe, I'm taking my pepper spray. If you don't hear from me by bedtime, here's his phone number and address.*

She left his card beside the note, then carried her things to her car in the driveway and drove out onto the street following her phone's directions to Grayson's shop.

It was early enough that the air was clear and warm but not suffocating. Dunes Bay was just waking up, so few cars were on the roads.

For the first time since she left the church without Devin, her heart wasn't in her feet. Gray's offer was a literal godsend, and glimpses of joy filled her head.

Her pulse was high. She could feel it. The run-in with Devin still churned inside her. She shoved the pedal down to pick up speed. Was she racing away from Devin even still? Or were the flutters in her heart for escaping with Gray?

"Head east onto Canterberry Trail and proceed two miles." Her phone recited directions and the scenery around her—trees arching over the roads making a natural tunnel, the neighborhood homes all fresh and inviting turning to the city scape—delighted her senses.

"At Sunset Drive, turn left."

"Thanks Gladys." She couldn't be the only one who gave her GPS a name.

Gladys told her Sunset Drive was yards away. She turned and passed by a sandwich shop, a coffee shop, a hardware store, and picked up the moist scent of the lake.

"The destination is on your left."

Cherish parked in the small parking lot outside of Dunes Bay Boat Repair and grabbed her bag, full of more things than she needed, no doubt.

Nerves scrambling, she opened the door to the shop and stepped inside. A bell on the door announced her entrance, but Gray was just across the room standing in sawdust and turned to see her.

"Good morning," he called, and brushed off his clothes.

"Hi. Am I too early? I left home before I needed to. You look like you're in the middle of a project."

He chuckled and walked toward her. "Your timing is fine. I'm always mid-project. I hope you're not allergic to dust. There's plenty here."

"No, I'm not very allergic." She couldn't pull her gaze away from the spine of a large wooden boat he had been sanding. "This is beautiful. Is this yours? Can I touch it?"

"Be my guest. It is a thing of beauty, but it's not mine. I'm renovating it for a client. He bought it from an estate. It's got some years on it, but a little spit and polish and she'll be glorious."

His eyes shone, and they got to her. It was refreshing to see a man who didn't censor his emotions.

"Do you love your work?" she asked.

Something dark flitted across his face, then was gone. She held her breath. Had she pushed a button?

"My work is satisfying, and that I like. Shall we get going?"

Cherish filed that answer under what is he hiding, and couldn't fathom Gray hiding anything. "I'm ready." She shielded her eyes and looked out across the water. It glistened blue and bright under the early morning sunlight.

Gray carried some things down the ramp to the dock and she followed. Without missing a beat, he jumped on his boat's deck and offered her a hand. "Come on board. Get acquainted."

"Hey, hey, Grayson."

An older man flagged him from the boardwalk around his shop. "Hi Dad. You just caught me. I'm about to cast off."

His dad's smile stretched wide and he rested one foot on the edge of the boat. "Are you going to introduce me to your guest?" He didn't wait for Gray. He reached out a hand to Cherish. "I'm Thomas, Grayson's dad."

Cherish took his hand and shook. His handshake was hearty and she couldn't help but smile back. "My name is Cherish. It's nice to meet you."

"I'd invite you to join us, Dad, but I have food for only two."

"For goodness sake, son. I don't want to intrude. I'm here to spend some time working. Are you okay with that?"

The ease with which the two men interacted gleamed in Cherish's heart. How nice it would be if her parents were as casual and unassuming in their relationship with her as Gray's dad appeared to be.

"I'll always say yes to extra help. I don't know when we'll be back."

Two younger men sauntered up the boardwalk in the direction of Gray's boat, and Cherish couldn't help but notice similarities to Gray in their faces and the way they walked—direct and fast paced, as though on a mission. The breeze tossed her hair across her face and she wanted to stay hidden behind it. How many people were going out in the boat? She had thought it was going to be just Gray and her. A sinking feeling dampened her excitement. Even two more people to pay attention to, to make nice with, was more than she could face. Maybe since he didn't know her very well Gray didn't understand her need for escape.

The two men stepped up to the boat, and Gray moved in front of her. "What brings you here? Don't tell me you're volunteering to work on the boat."

"As a matter of fact, we are. Dad mentioned he was going to be here today, so we decided to pay you back for taking us fishing." The man was muscled, just like Gray, but his eyes were a different shade of blue and he looked younger.

Sheepish at her unfriendliness, she moved closer. "Hi, I'm Cherish."

"Nice to meet you. I'm Jasper."

"He is my little brother, and that one there is my older brother, Rhys."

Jasper frowned. "Who you calling little? Do I need to remind you that I work out regularly as part of my EMT training?" He flexed his bicep. "This is rock hard."

"Okay, Jasper. Quit showing off for the pretty lady." Rhys shoved Jasper aside and took off his cap. "I am Rhys, the oldest, but also the smartest. I run my own company."

"Geesh, you two. Is this your first day in ninth grade?" Gray turned to Cherish and winked. "I'm sorry for this display of masculine weirdness. I didn't know they were going to be here."

The wind dumped strands of her hair across her face again, but she brushed it away without thought. "It's been nice meeting your family. Are there any sisters, a mother, a couple aunts and uncles on their way here?" She shielded her eyes from the sun and pretended to look for others.

"She's funny," Jasper said.

"She is. Just my mom is missing." Gray grinned and her spirits lifted. "Now, will one of you cast off for me and then we'll leave you to your work. Cherish, you can sit wherever you're comfortable."

"Here you go." Rhys untied the line tying the boat to the dock and tossed it onto the deck. "Have a good one."

Cherish perched on a seat at Gray's side and watched his brothers and father step into the shop.

"Are you comfortable?" Gray glanced over his shoulder at her.

She nodded, and he headed the boat out onto the lake. She put her hands to her stomach. She didn't know if the giddiness there was excitement for an adventure or fears of the unknown.

The boat's sails flapped and filled with wind, propelling them across the rolling waves. She sat stiffly, resisting the movement of the boat as it rose and fell in the swells.

Gray climbed with steady feet around the cabin and across the deck to let out more sail. His effortless skill with the boat assured her. He probably knew sailing the lake like he knew his A,B,Cs.

He ducked under the boom, one of the few things she knew about a sailboat, and slipped behind the wheel. He eyed her, then rested his hand on her shoulder. "Relax into the movement. It won't feel so jerky." He put both hands back on the wheel and his foot on a cabinet beside him.

"I haven't been sailing before." Cherish looked at her hands sitting in her lap, and noticed her breathing was tight.

"Oh, a family like yours, I would have guessed owns a large yawl, goes sailing all the time."

"My parents have a yacht, but it's not a sail boat. I don't even know what a yawl is." The bow lifted high off the water and she braced for the drop.

"It's a two-masted sailing, large watercraft. It's okay." Gray's smile made her heart race. Or was that fear? "I'll keep you safe. Try slow breathing."

Her eyes closed, Cherish let out a long, slow breath. Tension in her shoulders eased, and she drew in a deep breath, then let it out. The sun warmed her skin. Her eyes still closed, she heard waves lap against the hull and she relaxed into the boat's movements.

Up, then down. Rising, dipping. She accepted the rhythm as a natural part of her, and freedom, a quality she ached for, filled her lungs.

She opened her eyes and couldn't believe the beauty of nothing but water and sky all around. And the quiet.

Neither of them had spoken for about twenty minutes, yet it hadn't been awkward, only serene.

She touched his shoulder to get his attention. "This is something I could definitely get used to."

"You're more relaxed. I'm glad." He turned back to the wheel, and steered the boat in a slow circle, lowering her close to the surface of the water.

She laughed, and dropped her fingers into the small waves beside the hull. God, she hadn't laughed with such pleasure in eons.

Gray gave her a mischievous grin, then turned the boat in an opposite circle and leaned into it. The boat lifted out of the water on her side, and Cherish hung on the side as she rose with it.

Exhilaration drove through her body and tickled her stomach as the boat sliced through the water on its side. Cherish raised her hands above her head and savored the moment.

"Woohoo!" she hollered. "I love this!"

Gray laughed, and their eyes met. She held her breath, unable to look away. There was so much intensity in that one minute, it gripped her hard. What was he seeing when he looked at her?

"There you are." The mellow roll of the words off his tongue was the kind of thing about him that coaxed her to believe he was real. But it probably was just a line.

The boat lowered into the water. Gulls cried and circled overhead, making a good distraction from the lump forming in her gut. "What did you mean?"

He slid into the seat beside her, urgency in his eyes. "I only meant you looked carefree. I'm glad to see it after what you've been through."

She couldn't stop the tears from brimming her eyes. She had no words, only emotions. And those were hard to explain.

"I'm sorry. I didn't mean to make you cry."

"You didn't." If only she could stay collected this time.

He slowly raised a finger to her cheek and gently brushed away her tears. "You don't have to explain anything."

Wind dragged her hair over her face, and she pushed at it in the instant that Gray lifted it off her eyes. Their hands touched and she melted in the warmth of his skin.

The back of his hand remained pressed to hers, and she let the moment stretch, her heart thudding.

"Wait, what am I doing?" Gray jerked his hand away as if her skin had prickers. "I'm sorry. That was out of line. You're so fresh off your relationship with Devin. I-I'm sorry."

She watched him retreat, torn between what didn't just happen and the startling mention of Devin. "No, you don't need to apologize. Geez, I haven't let myself think about Devin and what I did to him."

"Of course."

Gray was all business now. It was probably for the best.

She stretched out on the deck and let her thoughts do their usual thing. I hope Pansy is gathering what I need for an appeal. Oh, it's Sunday. She's not working. I should have gone into the office and prepared to submit it. But Pansy can prepare quite a bit of it while I work on the drug company case. Time is passing so fast. Of course, I would be on my honeymoon now anyway. Skiing and climbing as Devin wanted. She shivered. Too much thinking.

"It's such a warm sunny day. I like it," she hollered at Gray.

He nodded. "I'm going to teach you a little bit about sailing."

"Why?"

"Because it's fun. Who knows, maybe you have an inner sailor waiting to take sail."

"Well, that was a bad play on words, but okay. That sounds interesting. We've got all day, right?"

"We do."

"I'm all in." She turned her attention upward, and watched the sails billowing.

"You probably know some basic boat terms." Gray pointed to the front. "That's the bow. The back is called the stern. Beneath the stern is the rudder. The rudder and the keel under the boat help keep it upright and help me sail in the direction I want."

"Got it. Bow, stern, rudder, keel. I know starboard is on the right when I'm facing the bow and port is on the left."

"Correct. Did you learn that on your father's yacht?" His eyes teased her.

"Yes, in fact I did."

"So you do know about boating."

"Not really." She spread her arms and arched her back. "This is an experience. It feels hands-on. A day on my parents' yacht wasn't that different from spending a day at a garden party."

He laughed again, and she was quite sure it was in delight, not mockery.

"I get it, I think. This is an in-your-face, one-with-the-elements kind of thing."

She laid flat on her back. The sunshine-warmed deck was better than a spa treatment. "Yes, and I'm queen of the inland sea." She couldn't believe she just said that. What was she, twelve?

"I'm having a great day too." He walked to her side and stood over her, his expression somber. She didn't know how to decipher it.

That threw her. Deciphering was useful for her. She'd always needed it to know what people were really thinking, rather than what they were saying. *No, Cherish. I don't care if you wear that dress to the Stensons' dinner party. If that's the look you want, it's fine.* She could still feel the displeasure leaking out from her mother, despite her seeming approval.

God, it was exhausting living like that. All the trying to mold herself to please her parents was becoming more and more uncomfortable as she saw them for who they really were, and the parts of her that had chosen to be an individual—the part that chose to do charity work—wanted to express.

Gray held out a hand to her. "Let's get you deeper into this experience. We've gone as far as we can in this tack, so I have to turn the boat through the wind, called tacking, then release the jib sheet. I'm going to show you how to work the lines." He pulled her to her feet. "We're getting close to our destination."

He held her hand as they walked the deck to what looked like a looped rope and some hardware.

"These are sheets. They change the angle of the sail, which is what we need to do." He crouched and took hold of a crank. "This is a winch. Go ahead, take hold of it and start turning it."

She chuckled. "You're putting me to work?"

"It's not work, it's fun." He beamed at her, and goosebumps popped up on her skin. To her horror. Strains of the wedding march taunted her inside her head. *I can't be having goosebumps for another man, not yet.*

She yanked at her shirt collar. "It's getting really windy out here."

Gray wrapped her hand around the crank and held it there, his covering hers. "You can do this. It's not hard. If something goes wrong I'm right here. Watch out for the boom. You don't want it to hit your head."

So, he could see right through her. But he'd deduced the wrong reason for her nerves. Thankfully. "Right." The pressure of his hand led her to move the crank in the correct direction. The sail responded and her heart tripped. He was right, this was fun. "Let go and let me do it myself."

14

"Keep that up until I yell stop. Don't dilly dally." Gray took hold of the wheel and steered the boat to fill the mainsail. "You're looking good. You're a natural."

Hopefully Cherish had no way of knowing the battle raging inside him. Giving her a day to put all tensions aside had become his mission when he'd heard the desperation in her voice. The gusto she was giving to working the lines gave him a smile. Friendship would be nice, as long as he remained careful.

"Stop! We're in good shape."

"You mean I did it right?"

Lights in her eyes clued him in this moment she was happy. Keeping a woman like Cherish happy was something he could devote his life to. He gave her a thumbs-up. "Gold star. We're heading to a special place I want to show you."

"What else can I do?" Cherish bounced on her toes, carefree.

He stepped back and gestured her in. "Come take the wheel."

"You're kidding me. I—"

"It's easy and I'm right here."

She bobbled her head but she couldn't hide her interest. "Don't leave."

"I won't."

Cherish slid past him and her hands hovered over the wheel. "Is it like driving a car? Hands at ten and two?"

"Here." He took both her hands and gently massaged them. "Loosen up. Now put them where they feel comfortable." His stomach clenched at the touch of her skin and whiff of her summery scent. "Remember, you're the queen of the world."

"Queen of the sea," she corrected, grinning.

"Just keep it steady. The wind will take us to our destination, you just have to keep the boat on course."

"I can feel the water under my feet. Not literally, of course. It's an amazing feeling."

"Yeah, I know what you mean. That connection to the lake is what makes a sailor great."

The wind gusted and she shrieked as she lost control of the wheel. The boat listed enough to almost topple her over, but Grayson caught her. He stopped the wheel from spinning and nodded to her. "You're okay. See, I got you."

"I wasn't prepared for that."

His breathing deepened. Her body didn't move away from his. He stamped on his urge to nuzzle her neck, it was so tempting. "Put your hands back on the wheel. That wasn't fatal. You've got this, remember."

He guided her hands onto the wheel and stepped away, putting the brakes on his thoughts.

She shrugged and tightened her grip. "Where is this place you're taking me? Why is it special?" Her voice brimmed with excitement.

He pointed in the direction of the shoreline coming into view. "We're going to anchor over there. And when we get to shore you'll see for yourself why it's special."

He watched over her, making sure she didn't have any more incidents. Yeah, that was one reason he kept his eyes on her. Really, he simply wanted to savor the way her face looked, all absorbed and delighted. It mesmerized him. He wanted to commit it to memory to remind him of this wonderful day when loneliness crept in.

He did what he needed to do to slow the boat. He waited to take over until he couldn't any longer. "Cherish, I need the wheel now. You can relax, while I bring the boat into the cove."

She scanned the shore. "I don't see any cove."

He rounded a point reaching out into the water, and heard her quietly gasp.

"Gray, I see what you mean. It's beautiful. The trees, the sand, the water. It's perfect."

"It's also hidden, so you'll have your private escape." He made a quick turn into the wind and luffed the sails. Can you keep your hands on the wheel while I drop anchor?"

Her eyes darted around the interior of the cove as she stood with the wheel. He kept an eye on her while he slowly lowered the anchor off the bow and tied it off. The boat straightened and he let out a sigh. "Thanks. We're set. We can swim off the boat and just hang around here or swim to shore."

"Both sound lovely. I've lost track of time."

"We've been sailing for around two hours. It's about nine. Do you have a schedule to keep?"

Cherish laughed and it was contagious. He laughed with her, not knowing what the joke was.

"I lost track of time. I never do that."

"Oh, cool!"

"No. I do not have a schedule. Thank you for reminding me. I want to do both but I didn't know if we have time."

"I understand the grindstone and all that. I have no plans for today other than providing your escape." The grin insisted on coming out, inexplicably. She made him happy. "How about we start with coffee and something to eat?"

"Oh, just sit on the deck? Love that idea." She raised her brows. "Do we have those items?"

"They come with the escape. Join me in the galley and you can see what I have."

He showed her around the galley and pointed to the bathroom where she could change. He carried a tray with a coffee carafe, cups, and a plate of cheeses and fruits to the deck where he'd place chairs and a small table. He scratched his head, realizing he had never made such a fuss before with anyone on his boat. But he didn't have time to ponder any implication. Cherish walked onto the deck and he lost his speech. Her two-piece swimsuit was covered by a filmy beach cover-up, but he got a very good idea of her curvy beauty. This was so unfair.

"Is something wrong?" She looked at him with those emerald eyes and he had to think of something to explain his gawking.

"Oh, I saw something, but it's gone."

"What was it?"

Really? You want specifics? "Maybe a bird."

She slanted her head. "For a minute I thought maybe you were looking at me."

"You caught me. I was. Not in an ogling way, but you are striking. And I am a guy. Sorry. I was out of line."

"I didn't feel uncomfortable. If we're going to be friends, we can't get caught up in taking things too personally."

"Good thought. Have a seat and help yourself." He grabbed the carafe and poured her a cup. Her words were kind but they didn't change anything about his attraction to her.

She took a sip and sighed. "This is so good. Hits the spot." She took a slice of gouda and a handful of strawberries. "My gosh, Gray, this is all so wonderful."

"It was easy." The small talk was getting to him. It wasn't his thing. He wanted to know so much more depth: what drove her away from Devin; what about her work satisfied her; why did she spill her story to him that day at the bar?

But she sat there breathing in the quiet, he guessed. She'd told him she didn't want to talk to anybody, so he sat in the silence and let her just be.

"The sounds of the waves are relaxing." Her voice was soft. "I can see why you like this spot. The water is so clear I can see down to the sandy bottom. The trees at the back of the beach swaying in the wind are intoxicating. Do you come here often?"

"Not a lot. But it's a good place to clear my mind and ponder life. I didn't go looking for it, I simply noticed it one time when I was taking a project I'd completed on a test run. At the time I thought about how nice it would be to share with, well, the right person. I mean, someone who would appreciate it as I do." The words rolled off his tongue. Maybe it was the setting or something more, something specific about Cherish, but opening up was getting easy.

His brain slammed down a door on the thought. Probably too easy. It wouldn't be good for her.

"It's so funny that you've lived here all your life and so have I and we've never met."

He picked at crumbs on his plate. "I moved to Chicago out of college."

Her eyes widened. "Oh, why?"

"I wanted to be a big city newspaper reporter. Chicago can get in your blood very quickly. I didn't miss this place. I loved my work and the opportunities to write substantive stories, stories that would make a difference in the world."

"Of course. Did you get to do that?"

His guard went up, but still he kept talking. "I did. I ruffled feathers. It was a different kind of exhilaration than nature."

Cherish warmed up his coffee and hers. "Then why did you come back?"

The sordid truth of it all pricked under his skin like sandpaper, but he could hold that back. "My dad had a heart attack. I came back to help him out and ended up buying the business."

"Oh, I'm so sorry about your dad. He seemed pretty perky today. Is he doing okay?"

"He will never have the strength and endurance he had before the heart thing. But my brothers and I want to help out our parents. They deserve the help."

Cherish looked down, nodding. "You're a tight knit bunch, I guess."

Her wistful look and sigh didn't escape his notice, but he kept his observation to himself, for now at least. "You could say that."

"My family is...different. My parents are very hands on, to put it kindly." She immediately twisted to face him. "But they've always wanted what's best for me."

"Of course. Now that you're an adult?" He left the question hanging for her to respond or ignore because it was none of his business.

"Yeah, I'm twenty-eight and things need to change. You don't have that problem, do you? Your parents trust you."

His heart went out to her. "They haven't had a little girl to protect, like your parents have. But I don't know what it would be like to have parents who managed me."

Cherish sat quietly, staring into the horizon.

"But too much talking about myself," he said. "How about a brisk Lake Michigan swim? I'll put down the ladder and we can swim right here for a while. Sound good?"

"Ooo, so good."

"You do swim, don't you?"

"Of course. I live in Dunes Bay. How could I not swim?"

She let her beach cover fall to the deck and climbed down a few steps on the ladder and dropped into the water, shrieking.

"I warned you."

He watched her submerge and swim several yards before her head popped up. "Come on in and see for yourself."

He pulled off his T-shirt and leaped off the side and plunged in over his head, then swam in her direction until he saw her legs treading under water before he came up for air.

"Boy, that will clear your head. Typical Lake Michigan water temperature in June."

"I still love it." Cherish lay back into the water and backstroked closer to shore.

Sunlight glistened in water droplets on her skin. Her shoulder-length hair floated around her head like a halo.

Gray shook his head hard and water flung into the air. *Get your head out of the stars.*

His breaststroke cut through the water to catch up to her side.

"The water is going to get shallow soon, so you can walk to the beach. I'm going back to the boat to get towels and things."

"Mmm, stay in the water. It's so delicious." She kicked her feet in his face, splashing him vigorously.

He couldn't resist. "You asked for it." He leaned on her and she sank below him.

He watched her, his heart racing, as she swam to the surface. Laughter spilled out of her and she feigned ramming him with her arms. Caught up in her delight, he paddled directly in front of her, treading water just like her. Cherish squinted and got very quiet. The smile dropped from her lips. He stared and she stared back, just the sound of waves lapping around them breaking the silence.

"Cherish." He dropped her name and couldn't speak the words sitting there at the tip of his tongue.

She let out a heavy sigh. "I almost kissed you, Gray. I'm sorry. I know we're just friends. Yesterday and my family and Devin, lord, Devin. I haven't thought of any of that all morning. But I still have to deal with what I did."

"But not today. No harm, no foul. We're relaxing and having fun, that's all. Continue to swim or do whatever. I'm going to take some things to the beach."

Gray stretched into his breaststroke heading to the boat. He couldn't get away from the tense moment with Cherish fast enough. Each strike of his arms into the water helped clear the shame of letting go with Cherish.

15

Cherish floated on her back not far off the shore and absorbed the peace of the lake's motion and the blue sky. Time was passing, but she had no sense of it. She'd heard Gray paddle his dingy to the beach, but otherwise the only sounds she was aware of were the wind, water, and gulls chirping nearby. Would it be so wrong to remain suspended in time in this peace?

She rolled over with the next wave and treaded water, her eyes just above the surface, and watched Gray spread a blanket under the shade of the trees lining the cove. His muscles defined with each movement, drawing her in. Water droplets glistened on his skin. Mmm. It was her turn to ogle. Parts of her warned her, this is wrong. Other parts got giddy. She lingered, enjoying her view.

Embarrassment registered in the center of her chest like a blast of frigid water. Ogling, really? Not strictly-friend behavior.

She dove under, clearing her head, and surfaced closer to shore.

If she and Gray stayed, living a life in seclusion from all her problems, what would that be like? She liked learning more about him, but he was holding back. She had no right to force him to knock down his walls, but she wanted to know more.

He waved at her as she dragged herself out of the water when it was knee deep. "Here's a towel." He held up a blue and white striped beach towel and waited.

"Thanks." She reached for the towel, but he wrapped it around her shoulders and she nuzzled into it. The gesture wasn't invasive or anything but kind. It gave her a sense of being cared for.

"How was your swim?" He sat cross-legged and patted the blanket he had spread on the ground. "I think the swimming here is wonderful."

Cherish relaxed onto the blanket, sinking into the way the breeze whispered through the pines in the cove. "I'll say. Thank you for bringing me here."

"Did swimming give you an appetite? I have sandwiches and veggies with my mother's homemade dill dip."

"That sounds delicious. Is it lunch time?" She eyed his spread and her stomach growled.

"There is no time here. If we're hungry, let's eat." He lifted his brows.

"That sounds right." His thinking refreshed her. No rules, no regimen. It was so not what she was accustomed to.

He passed her a sandwich and a bottle of water, then set the dip and veggies between them, and she helped herself.

"Mmm...this is good."

Chitchat filled the space while they ate, but the distance between them frustrated her. She'd never had a male friend. She was on shaky, unfamiliar ground. He probably had plenty of other parts of his life to attend to, and lord knew she did. "Ugh."

Gray tilted his head at her. "Have your thoughts caught up with you?"

"Have we established whether or not you're a mind reader?" She frowned. "I'm sorry. They crept into the quiet. I'm working on submitting an appeal for one of my cases and putting together arguments for another."

He nodded. "Right. Work goes on, doesn't it? There is nothing you can do right now. Can you let your brain rest a little longer?"

"I can try." She twisted her fingers. "It's just that the case I'm putting together an appeal for is—" What could she say that would fit her emotions? "The people are in real trouble and it's not their fault. Yet, the jury didn't find in their favor. I need to help them get their life back." Anxiety knotted in her chest.

"Do you want to talk about it?"

She couldn't keep her hands still. "My clients needed to win. Their lives were destroyed in a fire and they deserve justice. That's my job, but I failed."

"I see. I bet you didn't fail. Didn't I read that the opposing lawyer bribed the fire investigator? Is that true? That would have changed the outcome, you know."

Her hands started to tremble. "Yeah, that was Devin. He swore to me he didn't do that. Whether he did or didn't, I have to set things right for my clients. It's what the law is all about."

She looked into his face, feeling exposed. Aspects of the case were hard to think about. His eyes gleamed at her. What was that about? Was he mocking her? Her nerves jittered at the possibility he could see through her and know how hard the failure hit her.

"You love the law, don't you?"

She melted into a puddle on the blanket. He'd done it again. He had peered inside her and seen her. He had listened and heard her. "I do. When I'm representing my clients, I consider myself the great equalizer."

"That sounds grand? Do you have arm bands, a shield, and some kind of symbol for that moniker?" he teased.

She punched his arm. "No. But I'm serious. The law ensures justice is applied consistently to all people. It stands guard against injustice. Being a lawyer is about helping people who need help. It's meant to equalize the playing field, and give people peace of mind and security."

"I feel your passion. You've convinced me the law is a noble thing, but not that lawyers are trustworthy."

"You're talking about Devin, aren't you? I've believed in him. Now, I feel I barely know him." Again, she sought answers in Gray's eyes. "Do you think he could have done what he's accused of?"

Gray turned away and stared out over the lake. "I read that a reporter at the community newspaper found evidence I don't know him. Do you think he's innocent?"

He clearly was avoiding answering. "I asked him. He told me he was innocent. I believed him. But..."

"But when you listen to your intuition you have suspicions. Is that right?"

"I'm not good with my intuition. I need facts. I don't have enough facts yet."

"I think you have instincts and intuition. Why did you run away from the wedding?"

His questions were turning into a list of points. Resistance built insider her and she clenched her jaw.

"You don't have to answer that," he said. "I'm sorry. We weren't going to talk seriously today."

"Right. No serious talk." She dug her toes into the sand. "Yet, the truth is, all the serious is right there, like someone standing just outside of my peripheral vision."

"I get that. It takes effort not to turn and look, face what's there." Gray lay back on the blanket, resting against his arms crossed under his head.

"It sounds like you know what it's like." Cherish faced him on her side and leaned on her arm. "Is that true?"

"Sort of. I had a problem in Chicago that haunts me. I would tell you about it if I could." He knitted his brow, sending chills up and down her spine.

"You can trust me, Gray." He had helped her so much, she wanted to be there for him.

"It's not about trust. The thing is much more complicated than that." He rolled to his side. "I do trust you, Cherish."

There it was again. That temptation to kiss him. "Maybe it's impossible to be friends with Gray."

"What?" He sat up, his eyes wide.

"Oh, did I say that out loud? I have to stop doing that."

"You don't want to be friends? Have I done something to upset you?"

"No, I mean, yes. That's not what I meant. See this is what I do. I mess things up. That's why my parents have always guided me and why I let them. It's why Devin disregards me."

He shook his head and touched her hand briefly, but said nothing. He listened. No interruptions. The touch of his hand slowed her whirling thoughts.

"I'm not as scattered-brained or helpless as I seem. I can't be." She didn't dare look at Gray. In her voice was a plea for reassurance, and she didn't want that. Not need that. "Everything is falling apart. I'm letting down my parents, and I've always looked up to them. They only want what's best for me. And so do Rachel, and Devin. Of course Devin wants me to be happy and successful. But something isn't right. I don't feel so good." Finally, her heart stopped spilling. She looked at Gray, and saw his calm expression.

"I've seen you at work at the courthouse—"

"When? You were in the courtroom?" What was he talking about?

"Yes, it was before we met. You're a very solid, strong attorney. You are highly skilled at representing your client. You were very cool and collected."

"Thank you." Her breath froze, trying to process that Gray had seen her litigating a case. Had she really been collected?

"As for letting everyone down, that's not your problem. Get back to work when you're ready. But in the meantime know that you're a good attorney, and you'll make it right with your clients. That's what's in your heart, right?"

"The only way through is through, kind of thing. I will have to talk to my parents, and to Devin."

"But not today."

"Not today." She wasn't done. There was more to say, and the more gave her comfort because she had no confusion about it. "Gray, I'm embarrassed to say that what I blurted out about being friends pertained to my thought in that moment of wanting to kiss you. I'm so grateful for our new friendship. I don't want to muddy up our intention to be just friends. I do want that very much. You didn't do anything inappropriate. That was all me. I'm sorry for that and for the confusion."

He PULLED her to her feet and gave her a half-grin. "I can't say I'm offended by the idea of kissing. I enjoy the way your brain works, so no apology, please. Friends." He dropped a kiss to her forehead. "Do you want to swim some more? We have time before we should head back."

Gray's graciousness spread through her. This was crazy. He couldn't be so, so, understanding.

She ran toward the water's edge and splashed in up to her ankles. "Does this answer your question?" She shot him a glance over her shoulder, and caught him narrowing his eyes. She wanted to know what brought on that slight frown. There was more to know, but Cherish didn't have it in her to spoil the day with more speculation.

His face bloomed into a smile. "Good decision."

GRAY PACKED up the leftover food and drink with the blankets, towels, and sunscreen and paddled back to the boat watching Cherish take one more swim in the cove. He hoped the long after-noon of swimming, snacking, and napping had given her what she needed to pick up life where she left it in the early morning. This friendship thing was giving him hope, and he wanted it to do the same for her.

"I don't want to leave," she said as she climbed up the ladder into the boat.

He watched her towel dry her strawberry blond locks, biting his tongue. *I should have told her.* What kind of a friend keeps a deadly secret? "We can come again, if you want to."

"I'd love to. Next time I'll bring the food and drink."

"I'll take you up on that." She'd said the magic words: next time.

"You can teach me more about sailing. We'll become sailing buddies, get very tan, and talk about everything."

His heart turned over, relishing the spontaneous joy on her face. "To learn to sail you'll have to spend hours and hours on the boat."

Cherish laughed. "Okay, chief."

"That would be captain."

"Aye, aye." She saluted him.

He pulled up anchor and set sail for home. As lighthearted as their banter was, it didn't tell the whole story. This was some way to live. Falling for a woman he could never have, hiding from danger, and trying to protect her and his family from that danger.

Cherish sat near him, eyeing the slowly setting sun. Her features were peaceful and she didn't bother with conversation. Gray took in the shushing sounds of water and wind, and the beautiful crimson and gold streaking the sky. It was enough to be present with nature and to share it with Cherish.

The boat creaked occasionally, and swayed in the wind and roll of the waves. Gray kept busy enough with steering and tending to the sails. The sun told him they'd been out for a while, but time flowed slow and easy.

"This might be my favorite part of the day," she said. "You make everything seem so effortless, I'm hardly aware of anything but the beauty."

He nodded. "I'm glad. But I enjoy the actual sailing process too. You will too, eventually."

"Will we be back before the sun goes down?"

"Yes. We're not far now. You'll see the marina soon."

"Okay." But she continued to face away toward the sunset. "I wish I could sustain this peace when I face what's waiting for me at home."

"I know. It can be hard to find a sense of calm in tough moments. But you do it all the time, Cherish. It's the life of a lawyer."

She turned her face to him, her eyes glistening in the low light. "Thank you for that reminder. You have no idea..." Her gaze dipped.

He turned the wheel and gave her time to finish her sentence. It seemed important.

"I'm trying to say, thank you for the day and for what you see in me. I don't know when I've had someone who cared without an agenda. It means a lot to me, friend." She pulled her cellphone from her bag. "I should check in with Rachel. She might be sinking under tons of questions from Dad and Mom. It looks like I have a decent connection." She turned away from him and he focused on sailing, but he could overhear her side of the conversation.

"Yes, everything is all right. I'm fine. Don't worry, Rachel. Yeah. Uh huh."

He surmised Cherish was saying little in response to Rachel's question because they pertained to him.

"How many times did Mom call? None? You're joking. Oh. Don't tell anyone anything, especially not Devin. It's none of anyone's business." She sighed heavily. "I'll let you know when I'm back on land. Bye."

She disconnected and turned her face back toward the setting sun. Silent. Gray tried to give her space, but after a few minutes he had to say something.

"Listen," he said. "I don't know why our paths never crossed before. Maybe it's a timing thing. I understand the timing isn't right for you to get involved with me. I just know I can use a friend right now, with no ties or expectations."

"Okay. I'll try to keep my lips off you."

He laughed with her. "Okay, that's a relief," he teased.

She got quiet again, and the simple sounds around them kept him company. Lights from shore glowed warmly. "Do you want to stay for dinner when we get back? You must be hungry. It's going to be a late dinner."

"Umm...maybe. Are you offering to cook?"

"I am."

He began preparations to ease the boat into the marina.

A SHRILL ALARM blared out across the water, and Gray froze. It continued to ring out, clanging against his nerves.

"Hang on. I have to put in and get to my house pronto."

Cherish gripped his arm. "Is that alarm at your house?"

"Yes."

"What do we do?"

"You get down in the cabin. I'm going to take care of the boat and check out my house. The alarm company will have called the police so everything should be safe, but I don't want to take any chances."

His body strained to get docked. At the same time he secured his boat, his mind tackled his predicament. He poked his head into the cabin. Cherish sat hunkered down on the end of a bunk. Her eyes blinked at him. He didn't mince words. "Stay put until I come for you."

16

Gray raced up the dock past his shop and ran the short distance to his beach house. The police were nowhere around and he could hardly hear himself think with the alarm sounding loud and clear.

The front door stood ajar. He swallowed hard and stepped in to the darkness of his empty home. At least he hoped it was empty. That was the point of the alarm, to scare off intruders.

Quickly, he entered the passcode in the keypad just inside his door to silence the blasted alarm. He flipped on a light and trod through his house. The living room looked undisrupted, as did the kitchen. There were no doors hanging open or drawers pulled out. Every room looked as he had left it.

Sirens alerted him the police were close. His muscles tensed. He wanted to find evidence of the intruder before the cops took over. If there was anything to find, he suspected it would be something he'd want to keep to himself. He couldn't trust anyone in the police department, not even here in Dunes Bay.

He walked upstairs to his bedroom and stepped quietly to his desk. He'd have to check his computer, but he didn't have enough time right now. He turned in circles, surveying the entire room. Nothing out of place.

He walked into his bathroom and ran headlong into Jasper. "Whoa! What the hell are you doing here, lurking in my bathroom?"

Jasper gave him a sheepish smile. "I had to pee. I left my coat here in your house. I needed it and you wouldn't answer your phone all day. I didn't know breaking into your house would alert the whole town. Why do you have that system? Geez Gray."

"Well, you hear those sirens? Those are cops and they're going to be here any minute. You scared the shit out of me. I have Cherish hiding in my boat. I didn't know what the heck was happening."

Gray breathed in and out, trying to quiet the rage that set off with the alarm. It could have been Hastings or one of his men.

"I'm sorry, Gray. I really upset you."

"I'm not so mad at you, it's just that I didn't know if something was wrong."

"Dunes Bay PD. Is anyone here?"

"I'll be right down. I'm the owner." He grabbed Jasper's arm. "You're coming downstairs to explain."

"Hello, Officer. I'm Grayson Steele. I'm sorry to have bothered you. There is no problem here."

The officer eyed him. "I need to see some ID, Mr. Steele."

Gray handed him his driver's license and the officer studied him for a long minute, while a second officer looked around the door.

"What do you mean there is no problem? Your alarm went off on its own?"

"It looks like this lock is broken, so somebody tried to break in." The second officer took up studying him.

"Right. I did that. I needed my coat. I left it here last night."

"He forgot the lock code so he just broke in, not thinking about an alarm system."

"And who are you?" the first officer asked.

"Jasper, Jasper Steele." He pointed to Gray. "His brother."

"Have any ID on you? I'll need to see it." The officer gave him a smirk.

Gray shrugged, going for casual. "I was sailing and he had no way to reach me."

"That's the story you two are going to stick with?" The first officer gave them the once over.

"I'm telling you there is no problem. Other than my brother making himself at home and causing this disruption. But he's like that." Gray offered a big grin.

"Okay, I'll fill out a report. If you need a copy for insurance purposes call the department."

Both officers walked out the door, but the first officer stopped. "Do I need to remind you, Mr. Steele, the police have better things to do than clean up a mess you made?"

"I'm sorry, Officer. It won't happen again." Jasper's lips were a straight line, but Gray suspected the reprimand didn't mean much to him.

"Thank you for your services, officers." Grey leaned against the doorframe, waiting for the men. *Just go.* He couldn't get the police out of the way fast enough. All he could think of was Cherish huddled, scared, in the cabin.

He watched through a window as the police drove off, then sprinted down the beach toward his dock. In minutes he knocked on the cabin door. "It's me, Cherish. Gray. Everything is fine. There's no danger."

He opened the door and found an empty cabin. Oh my God, what happened to her? Had Hastings or one of his men been watching when he'd docked the boat? Had they seen Cherish?

"I'm here." A floor cabinet opened and Cherish extricated herself from the small space. "I was scared, so I hid. Are you all right?"

Relief flooded Gray. He pulled her into a hug. His heart sank feeling her tremble. "Everything is fine. Jasper accidently set off the alarm. He's the intruder. Are you okay now?"

"Oh thank goodness nothing terrible happened. I'm fine."

"Why don't you come in, at least until your nerves settle. It was scary to hear that alarm warning."

"Okay, I'd like that."

They walked side by side to his home, and he ushered her into the living room.

"Hi Cherish. Sorry I ruined your evening. Boy, that alarm is loud." Jasper shook his head.

"So you're the culprit. I wasn't sure Gray was coming back. My imagination went wild waiting. Luckily, I had pepper spray in my beach bag so I wasn't completely defenseless."

Jasper ran his hand through his hair and opened his mouth, but closed it again.

Gray had to work hard at suppressing a smile. Cherish had really gotten him.

"You, you, you had pepper spray?" He stared at her, then turned to Gray. "Good thinking. Especially since you were out on the water with this guy all day. You wouldn't want to take any chances."

Gray shrugged. "No, you wouldn't. Not that I would do anything threatening." He had to admit he was impressed with Cherish. "We haven't known each other very long."

"Well, I've had enough excitement for a while." Jasper sank into a chair, feigning exhaustion.

"Don't make yourself too comfortable." Gray crossed his arms over his chest.

"Oh."

"I'm going to make dinner for Cherish." Gray gestured toward the door for his brother to leave.

"I probably should give Rachel a call." Her eyes looked tired at that thought.

"No dinner? Then maybe just stay a little longer, just to get your bearings."

She glanced around the room. "Yes, that would be nice." She sank into the couch and dropped her head against the plush back.

"I'm sorry about what happened. I hope it hasn't ruined your escape day."

"It is unsettling, but no, it hasn't ruined the wonderful day."

"Good. Would you like some coffee? I can brew it right now. It wouldn't take long."

"I would," Jasper spoke up.

"I wasn't asking you." Gray's cell phone chirped. "It's Mom. Cherish do you mind if I take this?"

"No, of course not. In fact, I'm going to make that call to Rachel."

"I'll give you privacy." Gray headed into the kitchen, gesturing for Jasper to follow. "Hi Mom, what's up?"

"Have you had dinner? It's eight-thirty, but your dad and I would like to make dinner for you. I know you've been out on the lake all day with Cherish. I'd love to treat you. And meet her, if you think it would be okay."

"Umm, Cherish and I are friends, only friends, Mom. Besides, she's tired and may want to go home. Jasper is here too."

"Okay, I'll call Rhys and see if he would like to join us, then be over soon."

"You're coming here to make dinner? That would be even better. Thanks Mom."

When he heard Cherish telling Rachel good-bye, Gray walked into the living room. He didn't want to pry, but her face looked drawn. "Is everything okay?"

Cherish looked up from the couch. "Not really. I should go home, but I don't want to. Stepping into the fire after such a lovely day feels beyond me."

"The offer for dinner still stands. In fact, my mom is going to make dinner for us. She's a good cook. Feel free to stay."

The corners of her lips lifted. "I'd love to."

"I'm staying too," Jasper called from the kitchen.

"Good, while you're waiting for the meal you can fix my front door."

17

Cherish sat at the table savoring the delicious aroma of Portobello fajitas, sweet potato fries, and a spicy oriental slaw, helping herself to dishes as they passed around the oval wooden table. Her heart was stirred by Gray's family.

Susan, Gray's mother, had walked in the door and directly to her, offering a hug and warm smile. His dad shook her hand, then made a joke about how Gray had failed to introduce her to him the first time they met. Now, surrounded by them all, she was content to sit on the periphery and enjoy the food and the easy camaraderie among them that spilled over her like honey.

"Be sure to take plenty of the slaw. These men will eat it out from under you if you don't." Susan gave her a knowing look.

"Dinner is scrumptious. Gray was right, you're a good cook."

"Thank you, dear. Now that I'm retired from my real estate business, I have time and energy to expand my repertoire of menus."

"You're outdoing your specialties from our childhood," Jasper said. "Remember goulash and—"

"Oh, man, I remember goulash, and the corn dogs," Jasper interrupted. "Straight from the freezer to the frying pan."

"Yeah, growing up it was all boxed mac and cheese, cans of soup, and frozen pizza for meals." Rhys winked at his mom. "My favorite was—"

"Don't say it," Gray said, chuckling. "We all know your favorite was Mom's Leftovers Surprise Soup."

"Oh, don't remind me." Rhys rubbed his stomach and moaned.

Cherish knew the kidding was all in fun, and laughed along.

"Oh, it wasn't that bad. Your Dad cooked occasionally too," Susan shot back.

"I'll say I did. I made a mean bunch of hamburgers and hot dogs on the grill."

Jasper clanged his fork against his water glass while chewing a mouthful of fries. "Obviously we grew up fine. And nowadays it's wonderful to eat from your exploration of foods, Mom."

Conversation drifted from food to work on the boat hanging in Gray's shop, but Cherish heard it as music playing. Gray's family clearly were engaged with each other and cared for one another. Their teasing was kind hearted, not biting. Their interest in each other was genuine. Guilt stung in her gut for wishing her family had such grace. She loved her family and her parents loved her and Rachel, in their own way. But remnants of her mother's cold-shoulder if she ever spoke of enjoying the company of a friend still got triggered. Admitting a stark contrast between her family relationships and the warmth of Gray's made her cringe inside, as if her mother could hear her thoughts.

"How about your work, Cherish?" Gray's mom asked. "I know you're an attorney. I've seen articles in the newspaper about one of your trials. Can you tell us a bit about what you're working on?"

Cherish exchanged a glance with Gray. It spoke to her. In the brief seconds, he gave her assurance. It was up to her to say whatever she wanted.

"My caseload is intense right now. I'm representing a company accused of neglect. I'm in discovery stage, and honestly, it's challenging."

All eyes on her, Cherish took a drink of water.

Rhys studied her. "Challenging how?"

"I'm letting myself feel for the plaintiff. I can't allow that to happen. It could reflect on my defense strategy."

Jasper leaned on one elbow, tuned in. "It's like me when I arrive on the scene of an accident caused by a drunk driver and see a fatality of an innocent party. It's my job to administer aid to the drunk, but it's hard to have compassion."

Oh my gosh, insight and sensitivity run in the family. "That's it exactly, Jasper."

Tom leaned back in his chair. "I don't think you've ever mentioned that predicament as something you wrestle with, son."

Jasper shrugged "It happens."

"It's a common situation for lawyers. I'll work it out."

"Cherish also volunteers her services at a nonprofit agency." Gray's glance roved around the table. "She is working on an appeal for one of those cases."

"That's wonderful, Cherish." Gray's mom passed the slaw again and smiled. "You have a big heart."

A blush crept up her neck and she searched for words. "You're making too much of it. I simply like to help people and feel strongly that everyone has the right to quality representation."

"Excuse us for admiring your work." Tom laughed. "It's not every day we talk to a lawyer, especially one with an altruistic bent. We don't mean to put you on the spot."

Rhys swiped a napkin across his lips and tossed it on his empty plate. "You'll get used to us. We're weird, but we don't mean to make you feel uncomfortable."

The tone in the room lifted, and Cherish relaxed. "I appreciate your admiration. I'm probably not used to it. I'm not the top lawyer in town or even in my parents' firm. Go ahead, admire me some more."

Laughter filled the room and she couldn't help but lap it up.

"Great dinner, Mom." Gray patted her shoulder and carried his dishes to the sink.

Cherish picked up hers and reached for Tom's plate, but Jasper grabbed it away from her. "I've got this. You can relax in the living room or on the deck if you want."

"I can help clean up. It's the least I can do."

"We're not cleaning up. That's Gray's job," Rhys said, clearing off the table.

"Oh, then what are you doing?" Cherish rested one hand on her hip.

"Trying to get you to go into the living room and take it easy." Rhys stood in front her, an immovable object. "Really, it's okay."

Gray put his hands on her shoulders and escorted her to an upholstered chair. "Your day of escape isn't quite over." His low voice was for her ears only. "After I'm done in the kitchen we can go out on the deck and you can catch your breath if you need to. I know my family can be intense."

"I'd like that." Cherish slipped into the soft cushions and rested her head against the back. She closed her eyes and sat with the present moment. It was funny how Gray's family's graciousness stirred up anxiety. Her muscles resisted relaxation, but stiff and tight felt familiar. How had she gotten this way?

Tom and Jasper walked in and plopped down on the couch. "Isn't there a game on, Dad?"

"Probably. Are you a Tigers fan, Cherish?" Tom picked up the television remote and bounced it in his hand nonchalantly.

"I'm not really a sports fan at all." It was relaxing to chat with the family. "My parents were never into sports, so I guess I didn't have that influence."

"What?" Jasper slapped his knee. "Unheard of. We here are staunch Tigers fans, Lions fans, and Michigan State basketball fans."

Cherish laughed. "So year-round sports fans, I get it. I'm happy for you."

"Let's introduce her, Dad."

"What are we introducing Cherish to?" Rhys dropped onto the couch, all interest.

"Sports. She needs a team. Her sports education is lacking." Jasper clicked on the TV.

"Oh, she does?" Rhys turned to her. "We don't miss many games of our favorite teams."

Gray picked up a baseball bat sitting in a basket near the front door along with mitts, a basketball, and a soccer ball, and wrapped his fingers around it, giving a casual swing. "We're die-hard fans, too, not simply fair weather. A healthy appreciation for the glory of sports makes life worth living."

"Or so you say." Cherish played along with their exuberance because it made her heart smile. She tuned to the television screen while Jasper flipped through stations in search of a game.

Gray's mom came into the room from upstairs. "Don't listen to these fanatics, Cherish. You don't need anyone telling you what to do."

Oh really? Tell my mother, father, and Devin that. "Thank you, Susan. Maybe it's something I should be open to. Maybe that's what's missing in my life."

Susan laughed. "I doubt it."

Jasper's flipping paused on a newsbreak just long enough to freeze Cherish's blood. She wanted to disappear through the floor.

"Jasper, can you flip back a channel," Tom asked.

"This one?"

"Yes. Is this about your case, Cherish?"

She bit her lip and said nothing. Her nightmare played across the screen as a man in a suit stood on the courthouse steps, talking into a microphone to a group of reporters.

"The State Bar Association of Michigan has been asked to investigate the ethics practices of the firm of Wellington, Raye, and Black. Through an anonymous tip, we have learned of alleged violations of ethics rules of our organization in regards to a client of Devin Raye. Mind you, we've as yet received no complaint against Mr. Raye or any attorneys in the firm."

Jasper muted the sound. "So I guess we don't know if this is about one of your cases, right, Cherish?"

"Shh...turn on the sound." Rhys shook his head. "The guy is answering questions."

Cherish didn't have to hear any more. She knew very well the case in question was hers for Sam and Lucy Standish. Chills twisted through her. Devin's claim of innocence of any wrongdoing echoed in her mind. Who was the anonymous source? Was it the blogger of Eyes On, or someone who followed the blog?

"Can you tell us who gave the association the tip?"

"I told you, it was anonymous. The individual who reported the potential violation directed us to a blog post on *Eyes On*. The blog owner is anonymous as well. I can't tell you who we got the tip from, but I can tell you the source was reliable and we verified information in the blog post. That's all I have to report for now."

With a thank you to the crowd, the man stepped away, and the reporter assured viewers she would be following the emerging story.

"I'm sorry about Devin, Cherish." Gray was the first to speak in the quiet aftermath of the news report.

"Me too," Rhys added.

"Yeah, what a tough situation." Jasper grimaced.

"Thanks everyone." Cherish shrugged. "I'm fine." Wasn't she always fine? That's what was expected, right? "I should be getting home. I've had a wonderful time with all of you tonight. Thank you for including me in your family time."

Gray held up one finger. "Could you stay a little longer? I want to talk to you about something."

She checked her watch. Ten o'clock. Why not delay the confrontation? "Okay."

"Let's go out on the deck." Gray led her through the kitchen and out into the darkness outside.

Her breath caught. "It's so dark out on the lake. But the moonlit path against the fluid black of the water is striking. I've always loved the lake, but I'm seeing it with fresh appreciation." She looked up at Gray, expecting agreement, but it startled her to see his brow furrowed.

"That news report, my family pressing, I'm sorry that happened in there. What a crappy way to end the day."

"That's bothering you?" She touched his cheek, briefly. She couldn't stop herself, he'd moved her. "Thank you for noticing. I wish the news about Devin had come to me from the bar association directly, not in the nightly news. I wish the anonymous blogger hadn't strongly suggested Devin's wrongdoing with unsubstantiated evidence, but regardless your family is wonderful. I appreciate their concern."

"I'm glad you're taking it so well."

The way Gray eyed her she wasn't convinced he believed what she said. "I told you, I'm fine."

"You don't have to be fine. I don't expect you to be anything other than honest with yourself." He shuffled his feet on the deck and turned to face the beach. "Could it be the blogger cares about injustice enough to bring out perceived wrongdoing into the open so truth is shared?"

"I don't know enough about this anonymous blogger to know his or her intentions. Maybe the person is a troublemaker or likes to promote sensationalism for his or her own benefit."

The wind tossed Gray's hair across his face and he hunched his shoulders. "I guess anything is possible. But what if it's true about Devin?"

Cherish pulled her arms tightly over her chest. "Frankly, I don't want to think about it tonight. But if he did something wrong, as the blogger alleged, it could help my clients eventually."

She continued to lean on the railing beside him in the quiet sounds of the lake. Her mind was still and it felt good for a change. Maybe she would stand here all night, just being.

"Gray, Cherish, sorry to intrude, but we're all going home. Have a good evening." Tom took a backward step toward the door.

"You don't have to go. I have to leave anyway. I have some consequences to address at my sister's house."

Gray saw Cherish to her car and waved good-bye to his family, then raced up to his bedroom. No one but Eric knew he wrote the Eyes On blog, and he trusted Eric.

18

Quickly checking his security cameras on the way to his office Gray couldn't move fast enough. He swiped at the sweat beaded on his forehead and opened his email account, the one that was well protected. The only person he could talk to was Eric. He would know how far the news of the bar's investigation had reached.

Eric, read anything about the Michigan Bar Association's investigation into Devin Raye? I need to know how far this story has spread. Get back to me ASAP, please.

It was Sunday evening. Eric worked Sundays but it was later than he usually worked. Still, Gray stared at his inbox, tapping his fingers on his desk.

Just because his blog article had gotten attention for outing Devin's crime didn't mean Hastings and his "associates" would make a connection to him.

He leaned back in his chair and closed his eyes. Maybe he was overreacting. The bar's spokesperson had said he'd gotten a tip from someone about the contents of his post. It would be natural for the investigation to pursue the owner of the blog, but Rhys had made sure his identity was untraceable.

He blew out a long breath. Yes, he was safe and so was his family —and Cherish.

Ping.

Gray jumped at the sound of an email landing in his inbox. It was Eric.

Hey Grayson, I hope this isn't bad news, but one of the Chicago papers followed up with an article after the press conference and mentioned your blog. That article got picked up by the AP, so it potentially went national. Why?

"Well, shit, shit, shit." Gray's pulse raced. Even though no one knew *he* wrote the post, he felt exposed, cringing as imaginary heavy footsteps walked up to his front door.

Seriously? Get a grip, man. Letting his mind create worst-case scenarios wouldn't help him a bit. A clear head and focus would be the way to get through this thing with Hastings and his buddies.

Hastings. I don't want to be in the public eye and draw him or any of his cohorts here to where my family lives. I should have thought of that when I started the blog.

He stepped onto the balcony off his bedroom and looked out over the lake. Reflections of stars on the rolling waves reminded him of the awesomeness of simple things. The scents and sounds of the lake were a part of him. Tuning into them never failed to slow his pulse and quiet his mind.

He walked back inside and checked his email. Yup, Eric had already responded. *Yes, you should have. But of course you wouldn't have been able to stay silent. Holding responsible parties' feet to the fire is in your nature. And you're damn good at it. It's probable the Associated Press tried to discover who wrote the post on your blog. If they couldn't connect you, maybe the Bar won't either. Keep in touch.*

Gray stared a full minute at the email. Eric was not only his former editor, he was a confidant. He needed his input. But the thing with Hastings and his gang was his own doing and Eric was one more person he wanted to keep safe.

It's better if you don't know any more.

Instantly, Eric's response popped up.

Don't even think that. I mean it. Stay in touch or I'll come drag your ass back to Chicago.

Gray closed his laptop and allowed his reality to form inside him, not some dream or hope or wish he'd been protecting. He didn't know how to proceed but he was certain it would come to him.

He grabbed his keys, walked downstairs and outside, heading to his shop, where his mind could get into a slow, steady rhythm and let pieces of his life forward fall into place.

Unlocking his shop door, Gray's body tensed, always wary for some form of violence to jump out at him. But stepping inside, the scent of sawdust and wood and the familiarity of his workspace absorbed his full attention. He surveyed the boat hanging from the ceiling and mentally thanked his dad and brothers for the progress they'd made on the project. He took in its bones. Within the framework, the boat held tradition, integrity, and sound structure, aspects found only in a quality ship. Those aspects filled him, renewing his hope for a better world.

He chuckled. "All that from a boat? I'm truly a romantic."

Holding his smoothing plane, he leaned into the work. His hands felt the connection between his tools and the boat. Every move of his arms, his body, his hands, was in flow. The work was deliberate, caring. He could work through the night and begin the morning refreshed from the effects of the labor.

And while his body performed the tasks, his mind wrapped in instinct and intuition, and a plan developed to set his life in order. It would take courage, strength, and vision, but he had those things inside him.

Right now, Cherish faced something worse — a family determined to control her and her future.

❧

CHERISH ENTERED the back door to Rachel's house. Two cars lined up in the driveway were enough warning alone.

She hugged a wall on the other side of Rachel's living room, listening.

"When did you say Cherish would be here?" The voice was her mother's, and the pinched tone was another warning flag.

"I didn't say." Rachel's answer made love swell inside her.

A lump formed in her throat.

"It's getting really late. Where is she?"

Devin. His voice sent her back two steps toward the door. *This is cowardly. I'm leaving all the hard work to my sister. It's just another courtroom.*

"Hi Rachel. I didn't know you invited company over." She leaned against a wall. "Mom, Dad—Devin."

A secret glance between Rachel and her confirmed what she'd suspected. The trio had descended on her without invitation or warning.

"Darling, where have you been? I've been so worried about you. "You look so, tanned." Her mother sniffed. "And what is that smell, suntan lotion?" Her mom's eyes were sharp, her signature look when she was about to explode.

Cherish took a perch on an upholstered chair. "I know you have questions," she regarded her mother and father, then paused on Devin. "I don't know when I'll be able to answer them."

Devin jumped to his feet. "What? You can't tell me especially why you left me standing alone at the altar, the one where I was supposed to make you my wife? You owe me an explanation."

She refused to break eye contact. "I do. And Mom, Dad, I know I need to explain to you what happened too. It's not completely worked out in my brain yet. I wish you could give me a little more time."

"Pumpkin, it's been more than twenty-four hours since we watched in shock as our beautiful, sensible daughter ran out of the church." Her father's eyes pleaded with her. "Friends are clamoring for answers. Can you understand how awkward and sad the situation is for us?"

Her mother shook her head. "Really, sweetheart. You should be on your honeymoon."

Cherish stiffened, trying to keep the shaking inside from bursting outward. Even though this outrage and lack of understanding was exactly what she expected, the shock of it drained warmth from her fingers. She didn't dare stand or she might fall over, so she continued to stare at them from the chair. "So you want me to marry Devin, knowing he has committed a crime and betrayed me in the courtroom?"

"I told you I did nothing wrong." Devin's expression was glacial. "I read the post on that blog. The blogger is a coward, hiding behind anonymity. I'm going to find out who he is and out him for the fraud he is."

"How do you know the blogger is a him?" Cherish just felt like being difficult.

"What? It doesn't matter. Him, her, them. There is no evidence to back up the blogger's accusations and I'm going to make him, her, them pay."

"The bar association believes there is reason to investigate." She could crumble or she could remain firmly in charge of her story.

Her mother shot a sweet smile at her. "Never mind all that. It is incumbent upon a lawyer to take care of the client. That is a lawyer's job."

"Mother, what are you saying? That what Devin is accused of is acceptable?"

Her father cleared his throat. "What your mother is trying to say, dear, is that in the context of serving the needs of a client, lawyers may have to go the extra mile. It's the way it is. When you've been a lawyer for as long as I have you understand these things." He shifted on the couch.

Oh my God. He's telling me he's okay with doing something illegal.

She exchanged glances with her sister, thinking of the files they happened upon worth millions of dollars.

"It's not personal. It's business." Devin crouched in front her and took her hand. "I want to be able to give you the life you deserve. That requires I represent big clients who invest a lot of money in my services. As my wife, you'll understand it's a trade-off sometimes. I have to do things, cut corners, in order to provide the life we both want."

Not personal. Just business. As his wife she'd understand. The words prompted a quiet scream in her head. She pulled away her hand and Devin sat back on the couch.

"He's right, sweetie. It doesn't mean he is a terrible person, he's just a good lawyer." Her mother's eyes were soft, coaxing.

Cherish so wanted her parents' approval. Pleasing them had always been so important. Tears brimmed her eyelids. Not anymore.

"So Dad, Mom, you're good lawyers." She looked at Rachel. "You're a good lawyer, sis." A sob choked back her words.

"We've done what was required to fulfill our promises to our clients." Her mother's eyes were pins and needles. "Just as Devin has. You love him, don't you? Stick by him."

"It's that simple?" Numbness crept through her. Her parents took liberties with the law, just as she and Rachel had suspected. Admiration for them that was such a part of her shattered in heavy piles in her heart.

"Yes, Cherish, it's that simple." Devin frowned. "You don't have to make this a big complicated deal."

She couldn't speak. Disbelief and disillusion hardened her muscles. And seconds passed without anyone talking.

"I cannot believe you're telling us lawyers breaking laws is standard operating procedure," Rachel said, her foot bouncing up and down. "I don't break laws."

"I don't either," Cherish chimed in. "I'm not just some goody two shoes, as you imply. I'm a lawyer and I uphold the law."

Her father stood. "I'm sorry you feel you can judge us." His expression was impenetrable. "Well, Emma, we've said what we wanted her to hear. Let's leave her to think about it all."

"Okay. Well, I hope you can at least grasp the importance of supporting Devin." Her mother rose and smiled tightly. "We love you and only want the best for you. That's all we've ever wanted for both you and your sister." Her mother took two steps. "I know you've been out having fun today while we've been left in the dark to wonder what on earth is wrong with you. I hope you enjoyed your vacation day." Her mother spit the words, then marched out the door, her father following, closing the door behind them.

But Devin remained on the couch, rubbing his hands across the fabric. "Rachel, could I speak to Cherish alone?"

"Are you okay with that, sis?"

"I'm fine." She would not cry or shrink.

"I'm sensing you're not buying what your parents said." Devin studied her. "Do you think they would lead you astray, or that I would for that matter?"

"I don't know what to think right now. When I obtained my law degree and passed the bar that kind of thinking was deemed unethical, so based on that...I need to think about it." She focused on centering herself. It didn't help.

"Then trust me. Trust me, babe. And if you can't just do that, then I'll make it easier for you." He stared at the floor while the kitchen clock ticked off minutes in the background. "I know things about your parents that you don't."

"Oh really?" Her heart raced and she could have put her fist in his face, but he would probably sue her.

"They help clients launder money using offshore trusts."

"How would you know?" She fisted her hands. What else did he know?

"They talk to me. They acted as trustees of the accounts to protect the client's privacy."

"Why would they talk to you about such things? Unless you're all working with clients who break the law. Is that what you're doing?" She could have screamed the question in his face.

"I'm talking only about your parents. Check the firm's records for Tantorum Inc." Devin sighed.

He hadn't answered her question, but then, she probably already knew the answer. It was a logical conclusion.

"Look, I don't want to hurt your parents. What they have done was service their clients. That is what they're supposed to do. It's what I did. If you can see your way to stand up for me during the bar's investigation, I'll never speak of what your parents have done, not to you or anyone else again."

"So now you're blackmailing me? Devin, who are you?"

"I'm the man who wants to marry you. I know you love me still and I am the man who can make you happy."

"Devin, I don't know what to say."

"Say you'll marry me. You know you just had cold feet."

"You think that." She couldn't keep the wry tone out of her voice.

"Okay, marry me and I'll make the Standishes whole."

She chewed on her fingernails like they were her last meal. This was too much.

A thick, heavy sob lodged in her chest. She suppressed the urge to run. Was it not bad enough he'd offered her a bribe, a freaking bribe? He also had to confirm her parents were not the shining stars she believed them to be and make her responsible for an investigation that could only turn out bad?

"You can think it over. I understand I've said some things that are hard to hear. It's time to know the truth, and go one from here, baby." He headed to the door, and turned toward her.

Cherish felt his eyes roaming over her and measured her words. "Do you think I would marry you to help my client? To protect my parents?"

"I think you want to marry me. I just gave you more, compelling reasons." He pulled her up to face him. "I love you. We'll talk later."

Her arms dropped to her side and silently she watched him leave.

"Is he gone?" Rachel whispered from the kitchen.

"He is. I didn't realize you were in the kitchen." Cherish dropped into a chair.

Rachel walked in and wedged herself into the same chair. "I'm so sorry you went through all that." She pulled her into a hug. "Oh, my poor little sister. I should never have let them in."

"I knew I had to face them. I didn't expect to have to talk to all three at once." She leaned against Rachel's shoulder and warmth spread throughout her body. Even though their parents had developed different, dysfunctional relationships with both of them, she and Rachel had leaned on each other for support, even as young children, and she was grateful now for that connection.

"They gave you the hard press. But you stood up to them, all of them."

Cherish sat up straight. "I feel like a putz for not knowing what has been going on."

Rachel got out of the chair and stood above her. "I didn't know either. Of course Devin seized the opportunity to distract you from his wrongdoing. He's the putz." She put her hand to her mouth. "Oh, sorry. If you still love him, I shouldn't call him names."

"Did you know Mom essentially told me she didn't love Dad when they married?"

The look on Rachel's face wrenched Cherish's heart. "I'm sorry. You didn't know. I probably should not have said anything — then again, we're learning a lot about our family lately."

"No, I didn't know. When did she tell you that?"

"The day before the wedding, trying to convince me I should marry Devin."

"Boy, you have had your eyes opened. Shock, shock, shock."

"I have really done a number on this family. And I left my trail of tears for you to deal with. I apologize and thank you."

Rachel hugged her again and she soaked up all the love they shared. It steadied her, but it did not delete the shock and sorrow of her evening.

"I had a wonderful day with Gray." She stepped back and followed Rachel upstairs to her bedroom.

"I'm so glad. I was on pins and needles after I read your note. Geez, Cherish, you barely know the guy and you go way out on the lake alone with him?"

"I'm not going to apologize. I told you not to worry. Gray is trustworthy. He owns a business."

"Oh, he owns a business. Like that means the guy wouldn't gut you out on the lake."

Cherish stuck out her tongue. "Are you trying to ruin my perfect day?"

"No. I get it. I'm glad you're safe. You needed to have some peace and happiness to get through all that's happened. From what I could tell, he seems nice."

"I've been so boggled I didn't tell you about him. Gray is ... unexpected. I met him and immediately poured out my life to him. He didn't even flinch. I haven't known him but a few days, but I feel comfortable alone with him. He has no agenda for me. We're becoming good friends."

"That's perfect. Is he someone special?" She winked.

"The timing isn't right for us to be anything romantic. I'm barely unengaged."

"It's a good idea to take things slow right now." She cocked her head and gave Cherish a funny look.

"What?"

"Are you really considering marrying Devin?" Rachel asked.

"Oh, you heard that." She grabbed her head and shook it back and forth. "I don't know if I can turn him down. But I can't say yes either. There has to be a way out of this, I just have to think on it. I don't want anything terrible to happen to Dad and Mom. And my clients, Sam and Lucy, are in dire straits. I could barely think before everyone showed up here tonight and blew my life away. Sort of like pulling open the curtain on the Wizard of Oz and I'm still watching the big and powerful head."

"I've got the perfect idea. Do you want to get ready for bed and watch a silly movie on TV? I can make popcorn. And during the commercials we can talk more about options — heck sis, we're two fabulous lawyers, we ought to be able to figure this all out and get rid of Devin too."

Rachel could always put a smile on her face. "Maybe relaxing a bit with a movie would clear our heads enough to think up a plan. Just like old times when we were kids When Mom and Dad forbid one of us from seeing a friend they thought was a bad influence."

"Yeah, like Uncle Peter when he was having financial problems." Rachel shook her head. "Do you remember when they told him to stay away?"

"I could never forget. Remember how we sent him money from our allowances?"

"You did that, not me." Rachel's eyes teared. "You have always been the one with the soft heart."

"Aww, thanks, sis. I wonder how he is? I lost track of his whereabouts a couple years ago."

"Me too." Cherish suddenly wished she'd made more effort to keep track of her ailing uncle.

"So how about it? Movie and popcorn?"

"I don't think I can get back to that time when we were kids, not even in my heart. I'm just going to go to bed."

"It's early. Want a book to read? I bet you haven't read a book for pleasure in a long time. It would be good for you to occupy your brain with something else."

"Tempting, but no thanks." Cherish walked across the hall to the guest room, her home away from home since the wedding that wasn't, and called back to Rachel. "Thank you for being a good lawyer who abides by the laws."

Rachel threw a bed pillow across the hall. "You goof. I believe in the law and its values and ethics. I always will, just like you. Sleep well."

Cherish shut the door and dropped her clothes to the floor. She didn't have enough substance to do much more. She pulled on pajama pants and a cropped camisole and slid under the blankets. Her thoughts were a swarm of bees. Could she really sacrifice her life to save her parents from at best, disbarment, and at worst, criminal prosecution? People sacrifice for love all the time. It could be considered fucking noble.

No more thinking. She wrapped herself in memories of sailing and swimming with Gray, and enjoying his family's dinner. She couldn't help but laugh when she remembered Jasper, Rhys, and Gray all trying to convert her to a Detroit Tigers fan.

19

Gray unlocked the deadbolt on his front door and tapped in the security code, relieved that this time there were no signs of entry. He smirked, thinking of Jasper and his unabashed acceptance of himself. He was such a bro.

He reset the security system and slid onto the couch. His muscles burned from his night's work on the boat, but calm permeated his body and mind.

He flipped on the TV to see if he could catch the end of the Tiger's home game. "Oh man," Gray grumbled. At the top of the ninth inning against the Red Sox, the Tigers were down by three. "Let's have a rally guys, just four runs for a win. You're baseball players aren't you? Play baseball."

His shop phone, the second he installed in his house, rang. He checked the screen and saw a blocked number. "Crap. I hate this. Is the caller a client or killer?"

Ring, ring, ring. If he held off answering another two rings the call would go to voicemail. After all, it was late.

The answering machine started talking. "You have reached Dunes Bay Boat Repair. Please leave your name, phone number, and brief message. I'll call you back during regular hours."

He held his breath, waiting for the message to begin. The line wasn't silent, but no one spoke. He could hear breathing and chewing, as though the caller had gum in his or her mouth. Then silence.

Gray's stomach twisted. There wasn't any way to confirm the call was from Hastings or one of his cronies, but it still sent anxiety spiking through him.

He checked the security camera feeds. Nothing. "I swear I'm going to put myself in an early grave all by myself."

So much for watching the game. He turned off the TV and picked up his flashlight from the coffee table. He never let it sit very far from him in case the lights went out in a storm coming off the lake.

He grabbed his bat from the basket at the door. Maybe the call didn't mean anything, it was nothing but he still wanted to be prepared for whatever happened. He slipped into the darkness outside his home and headed down the beach to his shop. He didn't want to find anything amiss but he knew his imagination would run wild while he tried to get some sleep if he didn't check it out.

A sliver of a moon hung high above the lake. He hated that such serenity could be interrupted by the thought of a killer nearby. He clenched his teeth. He hadn't done anything wrong, and the hell if he would let a bad ex-cop steal his life. It was improbable Hastings would show up here so soon after being released from prison, but Gray knew nothing was impossible when it came to the criminal and his men. If Hastings showed up, Gray was ready to give him a fight.

Boats moored at the nearby marina jostled on the choppy water. He liked that for cover sound as he walked up the ramp to his shop. His pace was deliberate and cautious, and his steps were as quiet as he could make them. He shone his flashlight around the perimeter of his building, watchful for anything that didn't belong there.

He stepped around a corner away from the parking lot and deeper into darkness and stopped. The scent of tobacco wafted to him. No one in his family smoked, so he couldn't attribute the smell to any of them. His muscles tensed, ready to react to danger.

He turned another corner up the side of his shop and back around to the front. He surveyed the door with his flashlight. He shrugged, feeling silly. Security alarms and cameras were installed here too, but he couldn't put all his trust in them. It could be a fatal mistake.

He stopped cold and bent low a few feet down the ramp from his door. Lying on the wooden planks was a cigarette butt, flattened but still smoking.

At the same time he heard footsteps, someone jumped on his back and his bat dropped from his hand. The mugger punched his head, once, twice. It was a man, that much Gray could tell.

"Get off me." He head-slammed backward and the man groaned.

Gray swiftly jumped away and reached the bat, facing the man. "Harvey Smith. You here to do Hastings dirty work?"

"I don't know what you mean. I'm here to talk to you." He kicked away the bat and pulled a knife from his pocket, stabbing the air. "Yeah. I've been waiting for this night for too long." Smith laughed at Gray as he dodged the knife. "I'm not going to kill you. I need you. Hastings wants you to write a new article for the newspaper retracting your accusations."

"Never."

Gray shifted on his feet, to the left, to the right, ready to dodge the blade. He bided his time, letting Smith get comfortable. "Hasting and I have been thinking about you, Gray. We've had plenty of time to think. How many ways could we kill you for writing that article that put Hastings in prison. Then it came to us. If you wrote a new story exonerating Hastings, me, and the guys you would be the laughing stock of Chicago. We liked that idea. A lot."

"Then put down the knife and let's talk." All he had to do was distract Smith enough to overpower him, then call the FBI.

"First I'm going to give you a good ass kicking."

"I see. Hastings was a good prisoner. I can't think of another reason why he got released early. Or can I?"

Smith lunged at him, and Gray kicked his feet out from under him. The man landed on his ass, and hollered, "You bastard."

Gray ignored the taunt, and stomped on his foot, just out of reach of the knife. The man grabbed for him with his muscular scarred hands and flashed the knife while climbing to his feet. Gray jumped at Smith and twisted his arm hard against his back, then slammed the knife against the railing until his hand bled and the knife dropped. He picked up his bat and waved it at Hastings.

His chest heaving, Smith clawed his way toward the knife, but Grayson reached it first. "Looking for this?"

Smith took off down the dock and dove into the dark water. Gray ran, searching for a sign of Smith, but he'd disappeared.

He leaned on the railing behind him and tried to catch his breath. So this was what a death threat looked like in action. A large man with shoulder-length dark hair and thick thighs who smoked too much.

Back inside his house, Gray stood in the dark living room, staring outside. He didn't dare assume Smith was gone. He had driven to Dunes Bay just to beat him up, thinking he could force him to write a retraction. Why would he give up? And how had he found him? Had Hastings read the article about Devin and then found a way through his blog's security?

He needed to shower, get the stink off him from Smith. The vile man carried a cloud of hatred around with him.

But Gray couldn't stop pacing from one window to another, his focus watchful for any movement and his ears tuned to any suspicious sounds. Worse, he had no way of knowing if Smith would go after someone Gray cared about. He stared at his cellphone, contemplating. Should he check on his family? He tossed the phone on the couch and decided not to alarm any of them. After more than hour passed, he let go of the expectation of another attack.

But his guard remained alert, even as he poured a beer and guzzled in the dark of his living room. Hastings and his thugs had found him, so probably more of his kind would be next. He had himself to blame, and his drive to advocate for justice. If he had never set up his blog and posted with regularity, maybe his family would have always been safe and he, well, he could live.

He carried his bat up the stairs to his room. He couldn't call the police. For all he knew, Chicago cops had connections in the Dunes

Bay PD. Now that Hastings knew where he lived, no one around him was safe.

Gray slid into bed, his bat beside him, and stared at the ceiling. He could disappear again. No, he couldn't leave everyone to become useful objects for the Gang to force him out of hiding. More pieces of the plan that began coming together while he worked on the boat fell into place. Tomorrow, he would do the right thing.

20

Cherish was supposed to be on her honeymoon, but she was glad to be working the Monday after she skipped out on her wedding. This room at her client's place of business felt more in her element than she would have on a ski run in the Swiss Alps. She shuddered, thinking about how close she came to being married to Devin.

The faces of the men and women from research and development at Decidedly Laboratories and the company's lawyers sitting across from Cherish at the table reminded her of four chipmunks, busily chomping up seeds and nuts. No, chipmunks were cute, and these people were chewing up and swallowing decency as though it was a morning snack.

She surveyed the company's conference room and couldn't drop her critical point of view. The company's emphasis on success and its large assets were plastered on the walls in posters and graphs and smiling faces, presumably of people taking their drugs.

The representatives of the company reported glowing results and happy drug trial participants. The words they used set her teeth on edge. Words such as cost effective, dividends rates, and pleasing shareholders filled her ears with muck. Still, the company was her client. She didn't have to like it, but it was her job to protect them from losses.

"So you've shared with me the positive outcomes of the study on Ceedadelphine 62. Your records support your claim that you follow FDA protocol drug trials."

"Yes, it's all outlined right in front of you." One lawyer gestured to a file of papers he'd brought for the deposition.

"Yes, I see. Everything appears to be above board. How do you explain what happened to Henry Pole?"

All of them gave her tells—looking up at the ceiling, pursing lips, throat clearing, and shifting in the seat.

"We had Mr. Pole checked out—" the lawyer began.

"By the company doctor, right?"

"Yes, that's our policy, and it's at no cost to the patient. But, as I was saying, we told Mr. Pole the doctor concluded he had a severe reaction because he had another medication in his system."

"I see that in the doctor's report," she said.

"Listen," spoke up one of the chipmunks, the registered nurse who was the clinical supervisor. "We care about the individuals who participate in trials and take every precaution we are obliged to by law."

"Of course. Because if you didn't, your drug wouldn't pass FDA's requirements for acceptance."

"Indeed." The lawyer gave her an impatient and condescending snarl, but it didn't make her flinch.

"You know, this is the information I need from you in order to make a good case in court. You want that, right?" Cherish knew they did, but the group's defensive attitude disturbed her.

"Of course." The researcher relaxed. "You're doing your job and we thank you." The woman chewed her lower lip, and Cherish's suspicion grew.

"Mr. Pole disregarded our policies and rules," the lawyer said. "He wanted to participate for the money, but he brought his liver failure on himself. Decidedly Laboratories can't jeopardize our drug's FDA acceptance and release to the public because one man tried to work the system and it backfired." The lawyer gathered up his files and briefcase. "So if you're done, I have another appointment I must make."

"Sure."

The others followed him out and Cherish needed a shower. She couldn't leave Decidedly Laboratories fast enough.

CHERISH PICKED up a take-out cup of soup for lunch on her way to her office. She sat it on her desk and opened a window, then breathed in outside air. The attitude of her clients sickened her. Their presence was a green fog that threatened to choke her lungs.

So this was what it was like for her mother and father. Facing a client of questionable integrity and knowing that meeting their expectations would take her into new territory where lines of right and wrong blurred.

Dizziness spun the room around her and she sat down at her desk. She had to get beyond this need to please her parents. Being driven to comply with their ideas was no way to live her life.

Her cellphone chirped and she saw it was Devin calling. *My gosh, is he pressuring me already?* She pressed the ignore button. "Not now, Devin."

Agitation sparked in her, making her restless. Her mind was a broken record, nagging about her cases, her parents' expectations, Devin's proposal.

"God, I need Grayson." She imagined picking up a phone call from him right now and enjoying waves of peace at the sound of his voice. His sparkly clear eyes rose in her memories, and her heart skipped a beat.

This won't help me with my problems. She shook her head, attempting to shake out the turmoil in her mind and focus on her options for Decidedly Laboratories.

The wallpaper on her computer desktop revolved to a natural vista, and Gray's face popped right back into her mind. She ran her thumbnail over her teeth. She didn't know much about him. She could do a search and see what came up.

Another idea took over. She wriggled her mouse and punched the address for Eyes On blog, curious if she could miraculously discover the name of the blogger.

Minutes later she knew nothing more about the blogger. She paged to past posts and time suspended. The blogger's posts appeared well researched. The topics were fascinating and important, covering local politics, school issues, influential residents, and the courts. The tone was articulate and biting. She couldn't stop reading, and continued to check out past posts.

A subject line made her gasp.

Decidedly Laboratories Hires Moss Attorneys at Law.

She perused the post. The writing was so articulate it pulled her along even as it made her hurt all over. Cherish couldn't breathe. The blogger's accusations against her client and her parents' law firm were too close to reality. It hurt to be publicly chastised. What was the value of it? She tightened her fingers into a ball until her nails cut into her palms. She had to find out the name of the blogger.

A knock at the door startled her, she was so deep into figuring out the blog owner. "Yes?"

Pansy walked in. "There is a Mr. Steele here to see you. He doesn't have an appointment. Do you want me schedule one for another time?"

"No, send him in. Thanks, Pansy."

Cherish shoved the Decidedly Laboratories files under a pile of other files and gathered her thoughts.

Gray walked in, looking tall, dark, and handsome—more than he should be allowed. "Good morning, Cherish."

"Hi." She gestured to a chair. "Have a seat. It's nice to see you." She noticed a quiver in her voice and cleared her throat.

"Did you survive the inquisition?" He leaned forward, tightening the space between them.

Cherish tried to sit still, but it was a challenge. Why was he here?

She chuckled. "I don't know yet. Ask me later. Are you here to check on me?"

"Yes and no. I did wonder last night if your family would go easy on you."

A heavy rock dropped in her stomach. "I really disappointed my parents. Devin was there too."

"Really? Why?"

"They all wanted answers to my actions, but mostly they wanted to convince me to stick with the original plan."

"The plan to marry Devin? That's not any of their say-so, but I'm sure you'll do what is right for you." He looked around her office, a somber expression on his face. His gaze noted the files on her desk. "You're working."

"I have to get back into the swing of things. People depend on me."

"Right." He stared at the desk.

"What's on your mind? What is the other reason you're here?"

He pulled in a long breath and sat up tall in the chair. Ominous invisible clouds filled the room, just hanging in the air. She crossed her arms.

"I have to tell you something, something that might affect our friendship."

"Okay. I'm listening."

"I did something before I knew you. What I did might hurt your feelings. But I didn't know you, so it wasn't personal."

Cherish pulled her arms closer. "Just tell me. Spit it out. I trust you and I believe you wouldn't deliberately hurt me."

"I own a blog. I write about a range of topics, but mostly my blog informs the community of what's going on that I feel should get notice."

"What does that have to do with me?" Alarms went off in her head. Was he the blogger she'd been looking for?

"I blogged about your firm's relationship with Decidedly Laboratories. It wasn't a complimentary post."

Cherish couldn't sit still any longer. She stood up and faced him. "You wrote that post? Gray, how could you?"

"I didn't intend to hurt you or your family. I didn't know you, as I said."

"I heard you." She spun away toward the outside wall. Her heart pounded in her ears. He'd betrayed her. Just like Devin, and justified it as doing his job. "You're just like all the others. You don't care about our friendship, you used me." Her heart shattered into shards of glass.

"Don't say that. I'm not at all like Devin. How do you figure I used you?"

"You wanted to write a sensational piece about a sympathetic victim, just to stir up trouble and gain attention." She turned back to him and her muscles clenched. His eyes drooped and shoulders slumped, but she had to harden herself to his feelings.

"So you've read the post, I'm guessing."

"I just saw it. All this time you were the blogger and you never said anything to me."

"I came here to tell you face to face before you learned about my post in the news, what with Devin's problems with the bar and the public interest in Henry Pole's lawsuit."

"You broke up my wedding. Do you understand that? I read your post about Devin suppressing evidence. I couldn't go through with it knowing he may have done something criminal." She could so use his listening ear, but she couldn't trust him now. He might post her words.

"You know that's not true. I did not break up your wedding. You were already having doubts the day we met in the bar." He turned away and took two steps toward the door. "But if that's how you see it, that's your decision."

"Devin wants to marry me still." The words blurted out.

Gray gave her a frown. "Of course he does. Are you considering it? Cherish, does he make you happy? Do you love him?"

She couldn't look him in the eye. "There are extenuating circumstances you don't know about. I'm still thinking."

"I wish you well. Whatever decision you make."

It sounded like good-bye. Her muscles contracted independent of her wishes. "Gray, why does it sound like you're going somewhere?"

"I'm going back to Chicago."

"Because of me?" Incredulity beat in her chest.

His eyes held hers. Crystalline in clarity, yet she couldn't read them.

"Partly. If you're going to marry Devin, our friendship is going to be out of the question. You know that."

"You said partly. What is the other reason?"

"I have some work to finish. I've been avoiding it, thinking it was the right thing to do. But it's landed on my doorstep and I see that I was wrong." He offered her his hand.

She looked at it, noting its powerful strength, knowing its warm and gentle touch. She grasped it and he shook her hand softly, without letting go. She stared, knowing this was probably the last time she'd feel his touch.

He let go and walked out the door.

Cherish closed it and leaned against its hard surface. Her brain was a scramble. It was so tempting to slip back into the role she had always known: a compliant daughter, a second-rate lawyer, fiancée to a man who didn't really even know her.

All of it sounded life-sucking. And on top of everything, she was pretty sure she'd just lost the best friend she would ever have.

21

Gray knew he was doing the right thing, yet his feet wanted to walk back to Cherish's office and just be in her presence. But he continued on his way to his car. He couldn't keep her from going back to Devin, nor would he try. It was her life.

He slipped behind the wheel and wrestled his emotions. Cherish was special. He admitted it to himself while lying in bed last night. Alone. In the year after leaving Chicago, he had grappled with being alone for the rest of his life. Last night it had become so clear that it wasn't merely his choice, he had no other option. But in the moment of acceptance, another fact crystalized. He could see being with Cherish. In his case, that was not an option with Hastings on the run.

He tipped his head back and looked at the clear sky through his sunroof. The future was unknown. He could deal with that for now.

He pulled out his cellphone and texted his family. *Can we meet? My house. Now?*

He pulled out of his parking space at the Moss firm and drove toward home, prematurely missing the downtown restaurants and homey feel. Dunes Bay was his childhood home. As much as he loved Chicago, after returning home, his appreciation for the town, the lake, and the Michigan outdoor sports had blossomed. The friends he had enjoyed in Chicago were great, but his brothers and parents meant more now.

His phone chirped several times, but he waited to check. He drove into his garage with last night's attack still fresh. He could see Smith's glaring eyes and gritted teeth as though he were leering at the door.

Inside, he checked the locks and windows, and looked for signs of Smith around his property. Satisfied everything was clear, he looked at his texts. They all were coming, as he'd asked. That was what his family was about. He could always count on each one of them to be there when he needed them.

His phone rang. It was Jasper.

"Hey Jas."

"What's going on? Why didn't you answer your phone? It's a work day. I'm on. I know something is going on or you wouldn't have called a family meeting right now."

"Yeah, sorry about that. It's nothing siren-worthy, but it's important. I'll tell you when you get here."

"I'll be there in a few minutes. I'm on my way."

Gray couldn't just sit and wait. In the kitchen he ground coffee beans and started brewing coffee. Out on the deck he gazed across the lake. Dark bundles of clouds rolled in the sky. Waves of steel gray swelled and charged into shore, crashing on the beach. The drama fired all his senses. At least in Chicago he would still have access to Lake Michigan and all its grandeur.

"Gray, it's Mom and Dad," his mother called from inside.

He went in and gave them each a hug, just like always. Only he held on a little longer.

"I'm making coffee. Thanks for coming on a moment's notice. I know Jasper is almost here. Rhys had some things to tie up at work, but he'll be here soon."

"Should I be scared, son?" His mom sat down and crossed her legs, holding her body rigid.

"I don't want to say anything until you're all here. I know that's not reassuring, Mom, Dad."

"It's okay, we can wait." His dad sat beside her and rested his arm over her shoulders.

"I think the coffee is done." In the kitchen, Gray took out mugs from the cupboard and lined them up on the counter. He held the coffee pot above one mug, but froze. The magnitude of what he had to tell them made him want to barf. In this moment they had no awareness of the danger that surrounded him. He was about to drop that in their life and change everything.

It hurt, but he had to do it.

He heard Jasper and Rhys arrive, but couldn't bring himself to leave the kitchen.

"Gray, what are you doing out here in the kitchen?" Rhys patted his shoulder. "Your family awaits you in the other room. You're keeping us on pins and needles."

Of course, he couldn't hide forever. Of course they would come to him. "Grab yourself some coffee, I'm taking these cups to Dad and Mom."

His movements were jerky, unnatural. He almost spilled coffee as he handed it to his parents. "I know you like it black but I have cream and sugar if you want."

"Thank you. This smells good." His mom smiled at him, a little upward curve that was as much a question as anything.

"Help yourself, Jasper if you want coffee."

He sat with his coffee and sipped it deliberately. *Why am I making such a big deal about this news?* Oh yeah, the possibility of dying and thugs showing up on their doorsteps.

"Spill, bro." Jasper leaned back into the couch and eyed him.

"When I moved back to Dunes Bay to help out at the shop, I had another reason to leave Chicago. I never said anything because I didn't want to worry any of you or change our relationships."

His voice was shaky and he tried to gain control. They all sat waiting for him to go on.

"I wrote a series of articles for *The Chicago Daily Banner* about some corrupt detectives. It was an investigative series that revealed the crimes and led to arrests. Prison time for one dirty cop in particular."

"Oh, Gray. That is amazing. Why didn't you tell us about those stories?" his mom asked.

"The bad guys didn't appreciate my work, Mom. I got death threats."

Her hand went to her mouth.

Rhys sat on the edge of his chair. "Holy shit. You should have told us. You shouldn't have been alone in that stuff."

"I didn't want that, the danger, to infiltrate my family. You have been with me. You just didn't know I was hiding here." His head got too heavy to hold up. He stared at the floor, trying to breathe.

"Why tell us now?" His dad nodded as though he already knew the answer.

"The cop that went to prison must have worked an under the table deal. He was sentenced to twenty years, but he was just released. That means others in the prison system or police department are conspiring with him. He couldn't have gotten a release after only one year served unless several someones made it happen."

"Wouldn't that take prison authorities, judges, to make happen?" His dad scrubbed his hand through his hair.

"It would. So that gives you an idea of how bad the situation is. I angered some really bad dudes. I've wanted to keep you all safe, but instead I've brought the danger here."

Rhys uncrossed his legs and dropped his feet to the floor. "So this is why you were insistent your identity be hidden with your blog and your email address. It's making more sense now. I thought when you asked me to make that happen you just wanted privacy. So how would they find you? Does anyone in Chicago know you're here?"

"Only my former editor and he would never tell. This discussion is irrelevant. They've found me. Last night one of the former cops in that group jumped me outside my shop. He had a knife. He wanted to force me to write an updated article exonerating the men."

"Oh my God, son." Color drained from his mom's face. "Are you all right?"

"We fought, I got a couple bumps and bruises on my head, but I'm okay. He escaped. That's why … " His words stumbled in his brain.

"Let me guess. There's more." Jasper pursed his lips and studied him.

"I have to go back to Chicago."

Rhys jumped up. "No, Gray, no. You have to stay here, with us. We can keep you and each other safe."

"He's right," Jasper said. "Coming back was the absolute right thing to do. Going back would be a mistake. We wouldn't be there to protect you."

"My mind is made up. I'm going to write more articles, at least one. There is more to tell the public, bring out into the light. That is my job. I've been avoiding it for too long. I'm not a quitter."

"You're too stubborn. Listen to your brothers." His dad's eyes misted.

"I wouldn't be able to look any of you in the face if I stayed and one of you got hurt. I'm going to finish the job. Please don't tell anyone what I've just shared. Especially don't tell Cherish. She has a lot on her plate and I don't want to be responsible for something terrible happening to her if she tried to get involved. This is my problem and I'm going to take care of it. Promise me." Everything he cared about relied on their promises. He had to make them understand. "Please."

"Of course." His mom spoke up first. "I don't want you to leave, but I respect your decision." She looked around at the others. "We all do, right?"

"I guess so." Jasper hung his head and kicked at the carpeting.

"Rhys?" Gray needed Rhys to agree. As his older brother, Rhys tended to try to take charge. "I can count on you, right?"

"Oh, yeah. I'll keep quiet. But I don't like you tackling this alone."

"None one of us wants anything to happen to you, son." His dad held his gaze. "But we'll honor your wishes. Promise us you'll do everything conceivable to stay safe."

"I don't want to die, you know."

"Promise!" Jasper demanded.

"I will. Thank you all for everything. It's meant so much to be in this family. I never expected to put you in danger." His voice broke and he looked away.

"You didn't do anything wrong." Jasper pointed a finger at him. "We'll hold down the fort and you stay in touch. I mean daily. I'll keep an eye on Cherish."

"We both will," Rhys added.

"Can you be discreet? She is very smart and aware. If you give her suspicions, she'll demand answers. That cannot happen."

"So when are you leaving?" his mom asked.

"This afternoon. I'm going to get a hotel room for as long as I need to be in Chicago. You have my email address, so if you want to contact me use it. As Rhys just said, it's safe."

"So you are coming back?" A sob punctuated the end of his mom's question.

"I'm not quitting the shop or closing the business. I'm hoping I can get help with the work while I'm gone." He raised his eyebrows.

His dad nodded his head. "I could use more time at the shop. I'm trying to keep busy and stay out of your mom's hair."

"Of course Jasper and I will help out."

"Thanks, guys. It means a lot to me."

"I'm going to set the alarm when I leave, so nobody needs to check on my house. Please stay alert to anyone showing up you don't know. Call the police if you're suspicious of someone, but don't tell them anything. We can't trust anyone. I really don't want to get a creepy phone call about one of you being kidnapped or worse."

They said goodbyes all around with lots of hugging, and then Gray was alone. He racked his brain for anything he could have left out or be missing in his admonitions to keep safe. When he was certain he had done everything possible, he packed his clothes, toiletries, and his laptop, set the alarm, and drove away.

Leaving now at two, he would face the light side of five o'clock traffic and get to his hotel in time for a Lou Malnatis Chicago deep-dish pizza.

22

"I've prepared a task list for the Decidedly Laboratories case. Do you want to go over it?" Pansy stood just inside Cherish's office, holding a file.

Cherish smiled at her, grateful for a paralegal who could hold up her end without direction from her and manage the team. "Come in. Perfect timing. Let's work at the table."

Pansy joined her then laid documents and files across the table. "The trial was scheduled for six weeks out, but it's been moved up to next Monday because the plaintiff is sick. Here I've outlined a timeline for all tasks and delegated responsible team members. Here's a list of potential interviews. I know you'll want some of these for yourself."

Cherish looked over Pansy's work. As usual, it was thorough and comprehensive. "I'd like to get depositions from two of these researchers at the lab and the RN in charge of the study of Ceedadelphine 62, so please schedule those as soon as possible. The first thing I want, though, is to talk to the plaintiff."

"Consider it done. I'll add them to your schedule as I secure the interviews."

"What do we know about the judge?" Cherish knew a judge could make or break a case.

Pansy sighed. "We have Judge Georgana York."

"Oh. Well, make sure everyone on the team is informed of her preferences and follows them completely. She is tough, but fair. Anything else?"

"When you have enough information, you can discuss trial strategy with me if you want. I'll be getting knee deep in gathering information."

"Thank you. This is good."

Pansy eyed her and remained seated. "Do you mind if I ask you something personal?"

"Of course not." Cherish busied her anxiety by fingering her pendant of mother of pearl. She could the guess the question coming.

"How are you? I can't imagine how hard it was to do what you did and to deal with the aftermath."

"You mean leaving Devin at the altar? I'm fine. Thank you for asking." She gripped her pendant tighter. "I should have kept in touch with you, but honestly, I've been a mess. I have many things to sort out. But for now I'm finding focus in my work." She gave her a smile she hoped looked strong.

"I understand. I admit I was surprised to see you come in today, but it makes sense."

A quiet knock on the door interrupted the conversation. She wondered if the person at the door was a save from having to talk more or just another with questions about the non-wedding. "Come in."

She nearly choked on her saliva. "Devin. What are you doing here?"

"If you're busy I can come back later." His pursed lips made her wonder if Devin was for once unsure of himself.

"Pansy, is there more to discuss?" She didn't willfully telegraph "save me" to her, but it was there on her face, she was certain.

"No, that's it for now." She gathered her things and walked to the door. "Hi Devin."

Pansy apparently missed her "save me" face or chose to ignore the request.

Devin nodded at her assistant as she passed him and closed the door behind her.

"So you're busy?"

"What do you want?" She wasn't in the mood for small talk, and wanted him to get to the point.

"Can I sit down?" The unsure notes in his voice made her uneasy.

She pointed to a chair at her desk.

He pulled in a long breath and exhaled. "I don't want to lose you. I love you."

"You say that, but I don't believe you." She couldn't help but think of Gray and the way he listened to her.

"How can you say that. We have differences, but all couples do."

"Our problem goes beyond mere differences. What you've done is serious, not just to me but to the legal community." She tapped her finger against her knee.

"Can you appreciate that what I did wasn't strictly illegal?" His gaze dipped at her sputter. "You loved me. Can you love me again?"

She didn't respond. If he hadn't threatened to hurt her family, maybe he could have persuaded the old Cherish to say yes. That Cherish would have considered his request, but only because if she did, everything she'd known would fall back in to place. Her life would go on as planned, according to what her parents and Devin had set in motion. But he had made too many mistakes. "I can't trust you. I don't see any way our relationship can work."

"Cherish, were you really that unhappy? Didn't we have a good thing going? Whatever I did that made you unhappy in our relation-ship, I can fix. I can change."

This did not sound like Devin, the king of the world. Her thoughts tumbled. Why was he acting like this? Did she owe him a second chance? Confusion and fear of making a mistake muddied her resolve. The familiar questioning of her decisions reared.

"I'm sorry I broke up with you so publicly. It just happened. But getting back together would be a bad idea."

His lips formed a tight line and he crossed his legs. "What about our plans, our house? Do they mean nothing to you?" His voice rose in volume and pitch. "My firm isn't happy with me. I need you to come back or I won't survive."

"You won't survive? What are you talking about? Your work? How can I help you there?" Deep down Cherish knew it wasn't just about her.

"I mean I'm not eating. I can't think, can't sleep. Please, give me a chance to show you I can make you happy." He sat on the edge of the chair.

It hurt her insides to hear him plead. It wasn't like him. She couldn't be his reason for falling apart. She steadied her breath, and her questions about herself fell away. It was too unbelievable, something else was going on. And with her relationship with her parents and their legal vulnerability there was too much at stake. But she needed to figure all that out first, keep him believing he was in control "Maybe."

Instantly his presence filled the room. "Thank you. Would you go out to dinner with me tonight?"

Whoa, slow down, Mr. Manipulator. "I can't tonight. Maybe next week?"

"How about tomorrow night? We could discuss ways of getting your parents out of trouble."

"What? How about next month?" Her ears started ringing.

He shook his head. "I don't think it's wise to put off your parents' legal problems," he said.

Oh God, he wasn't giving up on making threats. Is he going to force my hand? He is leaving me no choice. "Do you know something? Is the Bar onto my parents? Did you talk to authorities? You're equally involved in all this too."

"Let's talk about it later. I'll pick you up at seven tomorrow night. Where I'll take you will be a surprise." He got up and took steps toward the door, but stopped and turned back. "At Rachel's?"

"No, my house."

"Hi Rachel."

Cherish looked up and saw her sister coming into the office, closing the door when she strode in.

"What is Devin doing here? Stalking you?" Her sister's eyes flashed.

"He asked me to give him another chance."

"I know it's your business, but didn't he already burn those bridges when he destroyed evidence?" Rachel dropped into a chair and plopped her feet on Cherish's desk.

"I think everyone deserves a second chance, right?" Her thoughts wobbled.

"Are we still talking about you taking him back, or are referring to his crime?"

"Don't confuse me further. I'm going out with him for dinner. That's all I'm doing. I want to find out everything that is going on. I'm suspicious but I don't want him to know I doubt him. Not yet."

"I get it." Rachel twisted strands of her long auburn hair. "Did he say something that incriminating or just blow smoke?"

"He thinks I can save him from being fired and charged with something I think. But the problem for me is that he seemed to be implying Mom and Dad are already in jeopardy and that our relationship has something to do with their future. I had to say yes."

"Oh." Rachel frowned. "Well, be careful. I don't like the idea of it but I can see why you gave in, though. It's probably a ploy."

"I promised myself I wouldn't succumb to falling back into old patterns. This is me taking control, just not letting on."

"Of course."

"Thanks. I know I've been a burden to you since I ran out of the wedding. You've been a genuine life saver."

"Aww...you're not a burden, at least not a huge one." Rachel flashed her a big smile. "It's what sisters do. Take care of each other. Even though I didn't protect you very well from the truth of our family or trust you enough to keep you informed, I had good intentions."

"I know that. It's time for me to take control of my life, and part of that is discovering truths. I'm still shaky about where I go from here. But one thing I'm ready for is moving back home soon."

"Oh. You're welcome to stay longer. I like having you around."

"I appreciate that but I need to settle back in to my own home."

Rachel stared at her shoes, red, strappy Prada mules with pointy black patent leather toes. Rachel did like shoes, especially expensive ones. But staring at them gave Cherish suspicions. Was Rachel avoiding looking at her because she had something on her mind she was afraid to say?

"What? Tell me what you're thinking." Cherish leaned her elbows on her desk.

"What about Grayson? Your new good friend? Is he not someone you're interested in, you know, romantically?"

"He betrayed me, Rachel. He blogged about our firm representing Decidedly Laboratories in the court case. He made us sound elitist."

"So you don't want to give Gray a second chance? Strictly speaking, he didn't betray *you*. I know the post you're referring to. The post was targeting Decidedly for hiring our firm instead of owning up to their responsibility. He wasn't laying blame for doing harm on our firm, he was fingering Decidedly."

"Are you saying I shouldn't be going to court for our client? It's my job. I have to do a good job."

"I'm not saying you should or shouldn't. Didn't Dad give that case to you? Did you think about not taking it? Probably not, because we're not given the choice. But maybe we should be. Especially if people are sick because of Decidedly's negligence or worse."

Cherish's head resisted Rachel's line of thought. "Pick and choose clients? That's easy for you to say. You're a top lawyer in the firm. I have to prove myself yet. This is a complex case. I could prove to Mom and Dad that I'm a good lawyer. Can you imagine if I refused to take the case?"

"I'm not criticizing you, sis. I don't think you had choice in representing Decidedly Laboratories."

"So you're suggesting Gray made a valid point in his blog post.

Well I don't need him undermining my work. I'm so tired of people deciding what I should do."

"I understand. But Gray didn't even know you when he wrote that post."

All her arguments against Gray deflated and she sank into her chair. "Right. It was an older post. I've been so used to believing Dad and Mom know best, I just went to defending them. But who decides what is right?"

"It is a complex question."

Cherish couldn't stop herself from coming undone. Tears blurred her vision. "I thought I was getting clear, learning how to be strong and express my values. Now I'm confused again. Things are not black and white. What's good for me might not be good for the firm. Or Devin."

"You're underestimating yourself, which is understandable considering what you've been through."

She closed her eyes to center herself. "Maybe I should have been easier on Gray. But it doesn't matter. He left town. He and I were just friends. He didn't want a romantic relationship with me. Our timing just wasn't there, I guess." She rocked back and forth in her chair. Misery at her missteps, combined with the end of something so good, curled her shoulders.

Rachel was at her side instantly, wrapping her arms around her. "I'm sorry I pushed you so hard. You've made huge life choices in the last few days. It probably feels as if you've fallen over a cliff and are free falling into a bottomless pit."

"That's one way to put it. I don't know if I'll ever be normal again. I guess I make a new normal." She gave Rachel a wry smile. "One that is a better fit."

"If anyone can do it, it's you. Gray saw that in you. So do I. I was wrong to try to protect you. You don't need protection."

Cherish wiped her eyes and blew her nose. "Thank you. I'm going to reserve judgment on Devin. I'm going to find out if Decidedly Laboratories is guilty and figure out what to do from there."

"Onward and upward." Rachel stood up and paused, checking her shoes again.

"Great shoes, sis. Are they for a special occasion?"

"Who needs a special occasion to wear shoes like these?" She kicked up one foot, then disappeared down the hall.

23

When the Twin Anchors Restaurant and Tavern came into sight, Gray's stomach started growling. He hadn't eaten lunch, and breakfast was hours ago. Besides, the ribs at Twin Anchors were legendary. So were many of the patrons, who over the years were the likes of Frank Sinatra, Conan O'Brien, and many other celebrities and professional athletes.

But he drove on by. There was no telling who he might run into there. He headed toward the Lincoln Hotel, where he could settle in and get a hamburger at The J. Parker on the roof. The pizza he'd thought of was out of the question since the place was so popular.

After parking, he carried his bags to the front desk. A young woman with dark brown almond eyes smiled at him.

"Hello sir, do you have a reservation?" Her Japanese accent was slight.

"I do." He gave her his name and identification, warily watching over her while keeping an eye on his surroundings. He couldn't help it. Even though he doubted Hastings or any of the others in the gang knew he was in town. He had been living cautiously with his guard always up for more than a year. It was second nature. He needed that vigilance now more than ever.

He took the elevator to his third floor room, let himself in, then relaxed his shoulders when he locked the door. He dropped his things on the king-size bed and surveyed the room. A desk, a refrigerator, a couch and small upholstered chair, a coffee table. Plenty of workspace. This was going to be home for a while.

The three-hour drive had been dull and tiring, but now that he was in Chicago, he felt its energy pulsing through him. Good. That would keep his mind sharp. If he were honest, he couldn't wait to get into his work. He could convince himself he could breathe in the aroma of newsprint just by summoning it. His nerves fired. Where to start was the question.

He set up his laptop on the desk and sent a quick email to Eric.

I'm in town. Hotel Lincoln, room 224. Come talk, but be careful.

Eric would show up, but Gray was in full-on work mode. The sooner he learned what the Gang of Four was up to, the sooner he could find the kernel of his story.

He opened files of his original story and research. The names of the families were there. If it weren't for them, the young mostly black men Hastings and his Gang of Four had falsely accused of serious crimes may never have been exonerated. It was the families who had brought the criminal activity to his attention and pleaded for his help.

Anguish-filled faces of the aunts and uncles, mothers and fathers rose in his mind. He would never forget sitting across the table in the kitchen in Pearl Nevaro's home, getting stories from each one, especially Pearl's.

"Mr. Steele, it's been three years since the jury read the verdict, guilty, and sent my nephew Luther to prison for murder, a crime he did not commit. I know he didn't do it. He was with me buying groceries when the real gunman killed a shopkeeper down the street."

The Latino woman sniffed and wiped tears from her cheeks, and Gray gritted his teeth. He knew Luther was only one of the young men in the neighborhood who had been given life sentences based on jailhouse testimony and the testimony of people of questionable character.

"It's probably been a long, frustrating three years, Mrs. Nevaro. But I

commend you for organizing a support group for other families who are going through the same thing. The work you, your sisters, and other members in the group have done—the database, the court transcripts and police reports—will expedite my investigation." Gingerly, he placed his hand on hers, and got angrier by her trembling.

"We have done a lot of work. When you read over our information, you'll see patterns and cracks in the arresting officers' reports." Pearl paused, trying to compose herself. "Mr. Steele—"

"Please," Gray interrupted. "Call me Gray."

Pearl nodded, her eyes closed as though the weight of her circumstances was more than she could bear. "Gray, if you could hear my nephew when he calls me. His voice is full of despair. He's giving up, but his imprisonment is all wrong. I need to bring him home."

"I'm sure it is very hard to have hope, but you need to. Luther needs you to and I need you to."

Pearl sat staring down at the kitchen table, her shoulders slumped. The others stood around the table, quiet, as if afraid to have hope. A drip, drip of the kitchen faucet punctuated the collective anguish.

He knew their cases: Azra and Eli Butler's son was beaten into admitting to a double-murder; Fayth and Brailin Holmes' two sons charged and found guilty based on a suspicious eye witness account; Dajon and Capria Hall's grandson interrogated for hours without water or food; Malik and Treat Powell's nephews found dead in their cells, apparent suicide victims.

"Things are going to be different this time," Gray said, He had to say something. "I've been talking to some members of the Chicago City Council. They were not aware of your cases. I'm going to keep digging and then I'm going to expose all the corruption and false convictions to all of Chicago. Hastings and his men won't be able to hide anywhere."

"You're giving us a glimmer of hope," Pearl said slowly, deliberately, her voice rising. "My Luther is a good boy, a good young man. And he is just one of many of our neighborhood's young men who need help to fight the system that unjustly took away their lives, put them in jail when they're innocent."

Gray pulled his thoughts back to the present, wincing from the memories of what the families and their loved ones had gone through. But his reporting had succeeded in holding Hastings accountable. At least until he'd gotten released.

A knock at the door startled him. He crept across the room to peer through the peephole in the door.

"It's me, Gray." Eric's voice was low and his face familiar.

"Come in, it's great to see you." Gray breathed a sigh and closed the door as Eric bustled in.

"Great to see you too. It's been awhile."

Eric surveyed the room. "I see you've been working already."

"Yeah, I've been reliving those days and thinking about how bad it was for the families before Hastings went to trial," Gray said. "Through the cooked up charges, fixed trials, and prison time, they never gave up on their children."

Eric eyed the names on the screen. "They all were courageous and dedicated people. They were fortunate to get you on board. You pulled together a phenomenal series of articles exposing the Gang of Four's crimes."

"I had a good editor."

Eric chuckled. "Yes you did. How is it to re-familiarize yourself with the stories? What those four white cops did is still unbelievable. But your work was good."

Gray let out a long breath. "It was gratifying to be able to get the truth out there for the families and the men. When I think about being in the courtroom and listening to the civil rights lawyer fire questions at Hastings about racially motivated beatings, murders, and arrests, I get sick inside as well as gratified."

"That's why your series of articles were so important. You were able to prove a river of racism-fueled greed. Thousands of dollars passed to them in exchange for fixing just a single investigation. I don't think anyone could have believed what was going on unless you showed them the truth. The real culprit paid and the Gang tagged an innocent person. The dirty collaborating lawyer made sure the wrong person went to prison."

Gray balled and flexed his fingers. "I'll never forget that forty-five innocent people were framed."

In his mind, Gray could still see Hastings standing for the jury's verdict, then turning toward him, his face a rocky cliff, his eyes full of rage. "That day in court when Hastings was sentenced was the last time I saw him. He managed to lunge for me and yell at me, 'I'm going to kill you!'"

"I know. I was there." Eric shivered. "It still makes me shudder. You took it so chill. I had to talk you into leaving town."

"Still, Hastings found me."

Eric punched his arm. "You didn't tell me. I was afraid of that. I think I know how." He pulled a flyer from his pocket and handed it to Gray. "I saw this in the newsroom along with a press release."

Gray's pulse raced. "I didn't know about this."

"Yeah, it seems you're a very good boatwright."

Speechless, Gray read the flyer again. It announced an event celebrating a boat he'd restored returning to the water. "It gives my name, the name of my business, and my phone number. Cripes! So this is how Hastings found my number and my shop."

"It's possible. You didn't know you and your project were being highlighted in the Chicago papers and at the Lake?"

"No. Weird. Here I've taken all the precautions I could to protect my privacy online and then here it gets broken with an old school promo."

"So what happened with Hastings?" Eric asked.

"He sent Harvey Smith to Dunes Bay. He jumped me in the dark outside my house, but I introduced him to my bat." Gray fake swung a bat through the air. "He wanted to coerce me into agreeing to write a story for the paper exonerating the Gang."

Eric frowned. "Oh wow. I take it you declined."

"Wholeheartedly."

"So which one of you won the fight? Since you're here, I take it he got away. Those men are still a threat."

"That is why I am back here again. Hastings is a little older but he and the Gang are still very dangerous. I should have stayed to make sure the whole story came out about who all was involved."

"No, you did the right thing. Your articles helped. The crimes brought to light in your articles even prompted the CPD to change policies, though the old ways are endemic. But Gray, I don't understand why you're here. There is nothing you can do about Hastings' early release. The other members of our Gang of Four are no longer police officers, at least not here in town, and I don't know their whereabouts."

Gray smirked. "But?" He knew his editor well enough to know there was more to say.

"If you're determined to write a story, an update, so to speak, I have a couple leads. I have the name of a judge who is suffering remorse for turning a blind eye to the corruption. He could be a break."

"He was involved? Is he a member of the Gang?"

"I don't know anything further. Supposedly he confessed to his wife, the wife told a friend at lunch, the friend had a friend who was a friend of one of the families involved, you know how these things can go. The family emailed me."

Adrenaline sizzled in Gray's blood vessels. "Who emailed you? Which judge?"

"It was Pearl Navaro. The judge she named was Judge Jeffrey Tesslon."

Gray scribbled the names in his notebook. "This is a good start, thanks." His brain whirred, and a strategy cascaded into questions. "I'm going to be working late tonight."

"Of course you are. You've got that glazed look in your eyes. You're barely seeing me right now, right? Your plans are unfolding."

"You got me. I'm picturing the Gang: Abner Cross, Brock Cross, Harvey Smith, and of course, their brash leader, Kane Hastings. All white men, all dirty cops out on the street not behind bars."

"Can you put all that thought on hold and head up to the restaurant and have a nonbusiness dinner with me? We can catch up."

Gray leaned back in his seat. It did sound good. "I'd like that, old friend."

"Well, I don't know about the old part, but friend, yes. You can catch me up on your boat business and your love life. You do have one, don't you?" Eric teased.

Gray pulled the door closed to his room and headed to the elevator, weighing his words. Gray had always kept his private life to himself for business purposes. Thoughts of Cherish softened his mind. "Not really. There is one woman, though, who is a good friend."

"Aww, you're getting all squishy about her aren't you?" Eric sauntered into the elevator. "Top floor you said?"

Gray pressed the button and leaned against the wall, watching the floors go by. "Her name is Cherish. She's just a friend."

"Sure." Eric chuckled.

Who was he kidding? He had picked up his phone to call her more than once since he checked in. He just wanted to talk to her, hear her voice.

"Here we are, top floor," Eric said.

The elevator door opened and Gray closed his thoughts to her, wishing things could be different.

"I'll make breakfast," Cherish called upstairs to Rachel. "Then can you take me home?"

Rachel ran down into the kitchen. "You're going home today? Why?"

"It's time. I'm ready, I think." Cherish whipped the pancake batter and spooned pools on the griddle. "Hungry?"

Rachel nodded and sniffed. "They smell good. Want me to help you pack while you're cooking?"

"No, this will be ready quickly." She flipped them over. "Very quickly. They're already getting dark."

"You always cook so hot," Rachel said and laughed.

"Here, get a plate." Cherish shoved a spatula under a pancake and dropped it onto Rachel's plate.

"Remember Mom's menus? I don't think I ever saw her cook, but Iris was great," Rachel said over a mouthful of pancake. "Guess that's why Mom hired her. Maybe Mom can't cook at all."

"How did you learn to cook? I didn't learn until out of college, and then it was mainly frozen pizza and packaged meals." Cherish relished this long overdue moment with her sister.

"Same for me," Rachel said, chuckling. She slanted her head.

"You know, what you've been through was terrible. But in a tiny sort of way, I'm almost grateful. It's given us a chance to reconnect."

"My pleasure," Cherish teased. "I know what you mean, though. Life's been pretty hectic. And speaking of hectic, let's get going."

She loaded up her few boxes in Rachel's car, torn between eagerness to get into her own routine and reluctance to fall back. Things had changed.

"All set?" Rachel asked.

Cherish closed the trunk. "Yup."

Small talk filled the short distance to her home. Everything had been so intense and heavy for so long, a lighthearted interval was nice.

Inside her house, they split up to put things away and it went fast.

"Thank you for your help." Cherish hung some tops and a couple of dresses back in her own closet.

"I'm sort of sad you're back here. I was so comfortable having you at my place." Rachel emptied a box of shoes on the floor.

"You made my stay a wonderful haven. I owe you."

Rachel pulled her into a sisterly hug and remained quiet. "It's the least I could do for my little sister, all things considered."

Cherish pulled away, and her mouth dropped open. "What do you mean?"

Rachel played with her shirt collar. "I let you down, and I didn't even realize I was doing it." Her voice cracked.

Cherish pulled her down to sit beside her on the couch. "What's going on? I don't know what you're talking about." She had to make Rachel feel better.

Rachel pursed her lips and gave Cherish a nervous smile. "I didn't notice, I freakin didn't notice that you and your happiness were being ignored. Where was I? Why didn't I go with you and Mom to find your wedding dress?" One tear meandered down her cheek.

"Don't," Cherish whispered. "Don't berate yourself. I didn't let anyone know how I felt."

Rachel clenched her hands and held them to her lips. She blinked rapidly. "Yes you did." She rolled her eyes. "When I think about it, I missed all your clues. I saw you were unhappy but I just thought it was anxiety and rushed in to take over like Mom always does."

A lump in Cherish's throat made it hard to speak, but she had to. "Rachel, Rachel. It's okay. You didn't do anything wrong."

Rachel's eyes were saucers. "Yes I did," she yelled. "I left you alone. My head was in my work, the damned work. Always pushing myself to keep focused on my career. Meanwhile, you were falling into a deep hole and I didn't even notice." Her shoulders shook and she buried her face in her hands.

Cherish was coming apart at the seams. This outburst from Rachel was unexpected, startling. "Shh," she said, running her hand over Rachel's back. "I didn't expect you to take care of me or rescue me. I didn't really think at all. Don't cry. I love you." Her breaths came fast.

Rachel sat back. "You're selling yourself short. I know you didn't confide in me, but that's because I was unavailable." She exhaled slowly. "We believe we're close, but actually, we're not, not as close as we think. We can't be because I've been engrossed in my own life."

"You're perfect. You've done everything right and your career is spectacular," Cherish said.

"It's a myth. You don't see what's underneath it." Rachel eyed her. "I have insecurities."

"We can talk about this. I want you to tell me how you really feel," Cherish said, fully knowing their shared belief that it wasn't safe to speak their truths.

"I want to tell you all about it, but I can't. Everything I've known about my family is coming apart. What we need to discuss is how we're going to address Mom and Dad's illegal activities. God, this is bad." Rachel pulled up straight and left the room. Cherish followed her down the stairs.

"Wait, we can talk. Where are you going?" Desperation filled the air and stirred up fierce anxiety in Cherish's gut.

"I better get out of your hair so you can get ready for your date. Don't worry, I'll figure out what to do with Dad and Mom."

Cherish stopped her just short of walking out the front door. "We're in this together. We'll figure things out. *Together.* We can do it differently this time."

"I'd like that, sis."

With Rachel gone, the silence in her house echoed. "I'm home," she announced to the living room furniture. "Maybe I'll get a cat. Cats are nice companions. Who needs a man?" Her voice trailed off into wondering. What is Gray doing in Chicago tonight? Maybe he's reuniting with his Chicago friends at the favorite bar and grill. Or maybe they were making it a night at Navy Pier. She gritted her teeth. Maybe a female friend was special, and they were dining on a romantic cruise on Lake Michigan.

She shook the thoughts out of her mind. Since she knew very little about him, she had no grounds for speculating him a love life or for being jealous. He had his life in Chicago as a big city investigative reporter and she had her staid life here in Dunes Bay. And she loved her life here.

Upstairs in her bedroom she picked an outfit for the evening out. Her orange sherbet off-the-shoulder sack dress would be comfortable, especially teamed with a pair of pale tapioca, low, block heels with an ankle strap.

She checked herself in the full-length mirror and liked the way her dress brought out the vivid copper of her hair.

Not that she was trying to impress Devin. She wanted to be comfortable, that was all.

Her phone rang. It was her mom and though she hesitated to answer, she did. "Hi Mom."

"Hi sweetie. I won't keep you. I imagine you're getting dressed for your dinner date."

"Oh, you know about that?" Weird.

"Devin stopped into my office today and told me he had just asked you out. I'm so pleased you're giving him a second chance. That's why I called."

"We're just going to dinner." Cherish chewed her fingernails, while familiar walls starting closing in.

"I understand, but it must mean your feelings for him are still there. It's good to try to rekindle your relationship."

Cherish's voice stuck in her throat. She loved her mother very much, but her mother couldn't tolerate her having her own mind. That hurt.

"Cherish, did you hear me?"

"I heard you, Mom. I know you like Devin and would like to see us together again."

"Well, it's your life." Her mother cleared her throat. "I'm not trying to tell you what to do."

The hell you're not. "Thank you for caring. I do need to finish getting ready."

"Of course. Love you. I hope you enjoy your evening."

Cherish stared at the phone. Her mother's good intentions exhausted her.

At the sound of her doorbell, she took one last look and headed downstairs.

Devin stood on the stoop when she opened the door. An awkward moment of nothing to say hit her. "Hi, you're right on time."

"I always am, aren't I?" He stepped back to let her close and lock the door.

The question was rhetorical. He was always punctual for everything and damn arrogant about it, as though it somehow made him a better person. She turned her face upward and breathed in the summer evening air. Relax. "It's so nice out tonight."

Devin opened the car door for her and she dropped into the low seat in his convertible BMW as he closed the door and went around to the driver's side.

"How does Flash sound?" he asked.

"Do you feel like sushi?" This didn't sound like Devin.

"I know you like it. Flash serves very good sushi, or so I'm told."

"That's right. When we ate there once, you didn't eat sushi. It's my favorite Japanese restaurant."

"I ordered the salmon. It was exquisite. But if you feel like a Kobe beef hamburger or steak, you can have it there."

"Hmm." That was the best response she could come up with. Devin's rule about don't make a big deal over things was hard to abide by. She had opinions, after all. With the top down, Cherish could sink into the warm evening breeze, let it toss her hair and not worry about it.

"I want to take you there because you like the sushi." He gave knowing smile. "I know what you like."

Oh, so this was part of the new Devin he promised he could be. "Thank you for thinking of me." Her words sounded stilted, flat, but he didn't notice. "Do you know where Kobe beef comes from?"

"I don't need to know where it comes from. What I know is it is delicious and crazy tender." He eyed her. "Why?"

"I just wondered." Whether the restaurant served genuine Kobe beef or a different strain of Japanese cattle shouldn't matter to her. It didn't sit well with her to pay more than one hundred dollars for a slab of meat if it didn't come from the Japanese Black breed? *But why am I nitpicking?*

Inside the restaurant Cherish's enthusiasm lifted with the pounding beat of the synthesized music. The décor fit the restaurant's name. A revolving palette of colors lit a waterfall on one wall at the back. The concrete floor sparkled with tiny bits of embedded glitter. The sushi chefs worked their magic at an open grill against another wall, lending drama to the flamboyant atmosphere of the room.

The waiter seated them at a booth near the waterfall, and suddenly she was staring face to face with Devin, with so much and yet so little between them.

"I'm glad you've been going into work. It's probably important to stay focused on your clients. It's hard for me not to be able to see you."

She rolled her eyes. "You've seen me every day."

"That's not what I mean." He frowned. "I mean be with you as we were, a couple."

"Wait a minute. How did you learn I was at the office?" She crossed her legs and bounced one leg up and down.

"Uh, your mother called me." Pink blush crept up his neck,

which never happened. "She, um, well, I can't remember exactly why she called, but she mentioned you were in your office. Probably just in passing." The blush turned his cheeks into round red apples.

The blush was a dead give-away he was fudging the truth. It was more likely her mom had encouraged him to drop in to see her. It wouldn't surprise her if they had even talked strategy. "So then you drove right over and asked me for a date." She could only imagine her eyes flaming because she couldn't see them, but Devin pulled back from the table, his eyes wide.

"So shoot me. I wanted to see you. We were engaged, remember. I love you. Is that so terrible?"

"Okay, I get it. What are we doing here? Because I don't want to jump right back into the place we were. Things have changed." Regrets were piling up. His reaction was her doing. She was giving him mixed signals because of her own confusion. The question was, why was *she* here? It wasn't just to give him a second chance, she needed to know what he planned for her parents.

"I know, and I know they needed to change. That's why I wanted to treat you to your favorite meal and we can just talk."

"I'm listening. I'm not trying to make things hard for you. Go ahead and say what you want to say."

The waiter brought water glasses and set them on the table, quelling conversation. He listed the specials and took their drink orders while the interrupted conversation hung in the air like smoke.

"I'll be right back with your drinks." The older man walked away leaving Cherish alone with Devin again.

He twisted his lips. It looked as though he was having difficulty getting started. She sipped her water and waited, hoping for the right moment to come up when she could redirect the conversation to her parents.

"I'd like to take a vacation with you. We already planned time off." He dipped his eyes. "We are supposed to be on our honeymoon." He held up his palm to her. "Now before you dismiss the idea, think about it."

Think and listen was all she could do. Shocked, words failed her. He couldn't be serious.

"I know I need to change, and I'm willing to hear what you need from me." He leaned closer, his face pained. "I'm the same man you fell in love with. If we get away from all the pressures, maybe you could love me again."

"What about the investigation into your work? Could you even leave town?"

His face dropped. "You had to bring that up. I thought we had a deal. You're going to vouch for me and I'm going to keep quiet about your parents' indiscretions."

Her heart froze. There was her opening, but she was speechless. "You're asking me to put my career on the line for something you did wrong? You really want me to do that?"

"I would think it would be something you would want to do, save the guy you promised to marry and the parents you love from disbarment."

She shook her head slowly. "You think I would lie and give false testimony? If you believe that, you don't even know me." Discouragement twisted her heart. Of course he didn't know her or care to know who she really was, that was part of the problem. But the realization went deeper and took her breath away.

"Yes I do. I know you get confused and need guidance. I'm here for you during those times. I know you want to do what is right." He pounded his fist on the tabletop just as their drinks were being delivered.

"Oh, I'm sorry sir. Is there a problem?" The waiter eyed Devin suspiciously. "Miss, is everything okay?"

"Of course everything is fine," Devin growled.

Cherish nodded, not fearing Devin, but finding it interesting that the waiter was concerned for her.

"Your meals will be ready soon." He pivoted and marched to another table.

"As I was saying, if we could get away to the Swiss Alps as we planned—"

"What are you going to do about my parents?" she interrupted.

Devin jerked. "What do you mean? In what context?"

She leaned across the table. "You know things, what they've done. Are you going to report them?"

His lips twisted from a frown to a tight smile. "My concern is us. If we took some time off, we could probably fix this relationship. We have already started building our life together. It would be so easy to go on from here. Our house is ready to move into."

She leveled her gaze at him. "You didn't answer my question."

"Are you going to help me get back into good graces with my boss?" One of his eyes twitched. "C'mon Cherish, give me another chance.

"That is what I thought I was doing by going to dinner with you. But I can see this was a massive mistake."

"What? It's a mistake to try to mend our relationship? Our relationship is important. I need you in my life. You need me."

For a tiny moment, her heart went out to him. It was hard to be firm when his eyes were so intense. He didn't know how right he was that she had needed him. If she acquiesced, she would please her parents, and Devin would stop crying.

The moment froze and her perspective shifted. She didn't respond and Devin didn't notice.

"Your dinners," the waiter said. "A variety of sushi and sushi rolls served with saffron rice and an assortment of greens, Miss. And for you, sir, filet mignon served with bacon, shiitake mushrooms, potatoes, and bok choy in a balsamic glaze. Enjoy your meals."

Devin dug into his steak, cutting off a big chunk and stuffing it in his mouth. "This is very good," he managed to say out of the corner of his mouth.

Cherish moved as though she were underwater. Slowly she squeezed a California roll between chopsticks, dipped it in soy sauce, and gradually ate it. Devin's words stopped her in place. Was easy what she wanted? If it meant having the same-same, being mocked, lied to, made to adhere to certain rules? Probably not. She knew clearly why she had been impatient with his arrogance and nitpicky about his ignorance about Kobe. She didn't like him.

"How is your meal?" Devin continued eating with gusto.

"Good." She swallowed and chased the food down with a gulp of wine. Her hands trembled just enough for her to know but not Devin.

The wonderful food became paste in her mouth. There were things to say, but here? Now?

No. She wracked her brain for something benign to say.

"You're rather quiet tonight. Are you tired? I know you've been preparing the case for Decidedly Laboratories. See, that's another reason we should take a vacation. You've been working too hard for too long."

"I can handle the workload. I'm fine." Quick, Cherish, change the subject. "What about those Tigers, huh?"

"Tigers? What are you talking about? What tigers?"

"The Detroit Tigers. They've been on a run. Have you caught any of the games?"

"No, I'm not a Tigers fan, not even a fan of baseball. You could have been talking tigers in the zoo for all I know. Since when are you a sports fan?"

Well, that did the job, even though it was short lived. How could she explain this sudden interest in sports?

"Oh, someone I know follows the team. It may have spawned a new interest for me. Do you think you could become a fan?" Things were getting more inane by the second.

"Of baseball?" His expression was incredulous enough she had to stifle a laugh. "Do you want me to? Is that something you could see us getting into?"

Before she could concoct a reason to bring up baseball that didn't include the name Grayson Steele, Devin glared at her.

"Does this new interest have anything to do with your friend Gray? That's it, isn't it? He's why you're reluctant to agree to a vacation with me." He slammed his napkin on the table. "That bastard. He moved in on you when you ran out on our wedding. That's it."

"Gray moved back to Chicago."

"Oh. When? Why?"

"Did you know he's an important newspaper reporter? He missed the life. He said he had unfinished stories he wanted to complete." She strove to maintain a casual, little-do-I-care tone to her words. Nothing to reveal how much she missed her good friend.

Devin's face beamed, but he was wrong to deduce Gray was no longer someone important to her.

"I don't know anything about him. All I know is that he intruded on my access to you on The Day. It was clear he knew you."

"We met a day before The Day, as you refer to it. Just small talk, nothing serious." This was not the time to tell him Gray helped her escape everything and everyone bearing down on her, including him. Or that in their first encounter, he'd seen who she really was.

"You haven't answered my question. Is he the reason you won't go away with me?" His eyes dared her to look away.

She blinked twice. "He isn't in my life."

Still staring, Devin's lip twitched. "I can tell when someone is lying to me, Cherish."

That was rich. He was almost, almost calling her a liar. He, the great and powerful liar of all liars. Did he really believe she had forgotten about Alicia Piper, his former girlfriend? Did he really think she didn't catch his slip the other day when he asked if Alicia had called her? Did he really believe she wouldn't remember he traveled with her to the Swiss Alps before they met? It was so tacky of him to plan a honeymoon at the same place. "Then you know I'm telling you the truth." She glanced at her uneaten plate of food. No matter that she loved the meal, she couldn't stomach another bite. "Do you mind if we leave? If you want to talk some more, we could do so at my house."

The drive to her house was quiet. Devin commented on the weather, the rising temperatures of Lake Michigan, and how any day now they could go to the beach and not turn into ice cubes in the water, which was completely untrue. Any genuine lake-lover knew water temps didn't warm until at least July.

While he held up his end of the conversation, Devin didn't act like he noticed she wasn't. She replayed the dinner conversation, and out of nowhere she remembered Gray the day they met and that she'd vomited her life story on his lap. He hadn't cared. What was the advice he offered? *I believe in taking time to listen to your gut and trust your instincts.* The words had stuck because they posed a huge contrast with what she'd experienced with anyone else.

Devin pulled his car into her driveway and she jumped out, trying to contain the situation. "Let's sit on the stoop. It's so nice out."

He sauntered across the grass and sat beside her. In her peripheral vision she saw him move his hand closer to her. But he stopped short of touching her.

Her mouth went dry. It was past time for a heart-to-heart with him. When she just opened her mouth, he cut off her.

"This is so pleasant, sitting here with you. It's like it is natural, perfect." He turned and touched her chin. "I love you, Cherish. You love me. I know, and you know it too."

Then he licked his lips, and she pulled away, dodging an impending kiss.

"Devin," she started slowly. She didn't want to hurt him, not at all. "I've put you through hell and you say you still love me and you know I love you." Cherish bit her lip. She didn't have tears to shed, but full awareness of his possible reaction and that of her parents stirred a quiet panic inside her body. He opened his mouth and she put her fingers to his mouth. "Let me finish. Earlier you told me I loved you before and asked if I could love you again. The thing is, I thought I loved you, but I was a different person. I can't go back to being that person."

"You think you've changed?" He spit the question. "You're just the same. You're making a big deal about things I've done, blowing them all out of proportion. You've always done that. It got worse just before the wedding, but I thought it was your nerves."

The storm he made tore at her resolve. It was so unnecessary.

"It was nerves, Devin. But not in the way you thought. I was having second, third, and fourth thoughts about marrying you. Whether you believe I blew things out of proportion is irrelevant."

"Irrelevant! How can you say that? You're being so selfish. That's okay," he said, simmering. "We can work on that."

"There's no need. I'm simply stating matter-of-factly what is real for me." Cherish stood and moved toward the front door. "I'm not going on any vacation or make-up trip with you. I know I do not love you, nor will I ever."

He grabbed her arm and pulled her close. "You don't mean what you're saying. Let me help you come to your senses." The intensity that was Devin popped out of his eyes.

Cherish yanked her arm away and unlocked the front door before he could stop her. "Thank you for dinner, Devin. I hope you have a good life and survive the bar's investigation."

He stuck his foot in the doorway, preventing her from closing the door. He narrowed his eyes and spoke menacingly. "The deal for your parents is off. Don't be surprised if they come under investigation."

Cherish smiled inside. This outburst and threat wasn't unexpected. "There never was any deal."

She slammed the door closed with his foot still in the way, but he pulled it out when she applied pressure.

Her pulse racing, she flew to her bedroom and flopped on her bed. A small smile crept onto her face. "I'm breaking old patterns and old bridges right and left. I'd say I'm changed."

25

Full of scrambled eggs, bacon, and a toasted English muffin from the hotel's continental breakfast and armed with coffee, Gray doubled-down on getting an interview with Judge Jeffrey Tesslon. He hoped a call to his office wouldn't set off alarms. He had absence in his favor. Since he'd been out of town for more than a year, it was possible the judge would have forgotten about him.

He called the judge's office, gathering up his rusty, reporter persona.

"Judge Tesslon's office," the receptionist answered.

"Hello, this is Grayson Steele. I'm an old friend of the judge. Can you tell me, does he have a busy morning? I'd like to drop by and see him if possible."

"His schedule is pretty full. I could ask him, but he's in a meeting right now, and after that ends he'll go for a quick lunch."

"Oh," Gray faked disappointment as a former friend would. "Thank you. I'll try to catch him later."

He hung up, knowing where he'd look for the judge later.

Things were humming in his gut. He drew deeper into his thoughts. Did he have any friends in the department he could tap into? Dumb idea, Gray. If any cops in Chicago know where the Gang is, best stay away from them.

He bounced the eraser end of his pencil against his desk. A sense of spinning his wheels already hardened in his shoulders. This time things were different than they used to be when he wrote regularly for *The Chicago Daily Banner*. He wasn't hiding then.

He paced the room from corner to corner. Go back to the beginning, he told himself. The crux of the original story was that Detective Hastings ran his unit like a mad dog, and the other detectives got caught up in his schemes and were either too dumb or too scared to stop him. This time, the story was about putting Hastings back in jail and bringing out the culpability of Smith, the Cross brothers, and the collaborating network of judges, lawyers, and police administrators.

With that all squared away in his mind, Gray's sense of purpose dislodged any cobwebs, and clarity took over. He couldn't stay hunkered down in the hotel. Just as in his beat days, he had to go to the streets and stir the pot.

Outside of the hotel, he hailed a cab and directed the driver to take him to Lou Malnatis Pizza restaurant. It took minutes for the driver to weave through traffic and stop outside of the pizza place.

"Thanks." Gray paid his fare and headed into the café. He knew directly where to go. The judge ate here every day and always took the corner booth. The lunch crowd was heavy and noisy. Gray sank into it as though it were an old chair and headed to where he saw the judge in his usual spot. He was not easily missed. The judge was short and roundish, like a panda bear. Baggy eyes and multiple chins suggested he was in his mid-seventies.

"Hello, mind of I join you for lunch, Judge?" Gray slid into the booth across from him.

Judge Tesslon looked up from his Chicago-style pizza and frowned. Immediately he shuffled a pile of papers into a semi-neat pile and shoved them in his briefcase. "It looks like you already have. Where have you been, Grayson? I haven't seen your byline or you for quite a while."

A waitress stepped up to the booth. "Can I get you something, sir?"

"Just black coffee. Thank you." He gave his full attention to the judge, ignoring his question. "I want to help ease your conscious."

The judge's expression got very sober. "What does that mean?"

"You know and I know that you have regrets over the many innocent people you sentenced, fully aware Hastings and his cop buddies were running a ring of corruption. I'm giving you a chance to square your conscious before they decide your knowledge threatens their freedom."

"You also know talking to you wouldn't be good for my health or my career. What makes you think I would do such a thing?" The judge gulped from his coffee cup and looked over each shoulder.

Gray waited to respond until the waitress sat his coffee in front of him. "Thanks," he said to the young blonde and smiled.

He leaned close across the table and spoke in a low voice. "Because basically you're not a terrible person. What you did is eating you from the inside out. You want to confess. You need to confess. And as the saying goes, confession is good for the soul. Besides, the justice department would look more kindly on you at sentencing if you cooperate."

The judge stared into space, and chewed on the tip of a toothpick.

Gray pulled at one earlobe, then scratched his head, waiting for the judge to speak. He peered over the edge of his coffee cup, maintaining eye contact on the judge. The judge likely knew Gray was taking a long shot, leading him to believe confessing was his best option forward.

"All that business is over. I'm not involved in any criminal activity now, and those cops are gone."

"You do understand I know the full story. What you did was wrong, no question about that. It went on for a long time. Many people suffered." The judge stared at him, his eyes old-man watery. "As for the ex-cops no longer a threat, well, one of them attacked me two days ago."

"I suppose it was Hastings. He just got out of prison." The judge dipped his gaze.

Gray narrowed his eyes. "You know anything about that outlandishly early release?" When the judge didn't say anything, Gray went on. "You could continue to pretend you never did anything wrong and hope for the best. But if your plan to escape justice includes protection from the Gang of Four, consider it from their point of view. What do you have to offer them now? As you said, the business is over. You're now only a liability."

The judge sighed heavily and aged ten years right before Gray. "You're right about my remorse. But it's not that I've grown a conscious. Two months ago I was diagnosed with pancreatic cancer. I don't have long to live." He eyed Gray. "My family doesn't know what I've done. I don't want them to get hurt by learning about me. But I can't leave this earth without owning up. What do you want to know?"

Gray pulled out his recorder and turned it on. "Are you still in touch with the Gang?"

The judge shifted in his seat. "They check in with me once in a while. All of them still live in Chicago, but they keep to themselves, or so I'm told."

"Do you have contact information?"

The judge quirked one eyebrow.

"I want last known addresses. You can get that for me, I'm guessing."

The judge ran his thumb over his chin and nodded. "I'll get it to you."

"Good. I also want to know your involvement." Gray held the judge's gaze.

The judge checked the time and released another long sigh. "Where do you want to start?"

Excitement fluttered in Gray's gut. "How did it begin?

. . .

GRAY PUSHED OPEN the diner's door and typical Chicago winds ripped it from his hands. It slammed against the window, but no harm done.

He strode down the pavement feeling every hour of sitting in his stiff legs. The judge spilled everything he knew, or at least he gave Gray a lot of useful information. Pearl's tip was solid; the judge's soul was riddled with guilt and the timing was right to hear him out.

Gray's gaze swept upward to take in the skyscrapers that lined the streets. White fluffy clouds slowly drifted above the buildings in a blue sky. All around him the city hummed with its frenetic activity. His heart suddenly longed to share it all with Cherish. He could imagine her bright smile and excitement for a street concert or a walk along the Lake Front trail.

"Hey Gray!" called a man down the street. Korean American Yoo Jin Kang hailed him from in front of his food stand.

Yoo Jin had been a good source for street-level information when Gray worked in the city. Before leaving for the diner earlier, his plans included stopping by to mine Yoo if he was still around.

He held out his hand and Yoo grabbed it. His accent was a sweet sound to Gray. "Hey! Long time no see, Gray. You back now? Chicago miss you?"

"I'm here now, that's all I know. It's good to see you. How's business? I see you're not selling hot dogs."

"Business good. Hot dogs not so popular. Everybody want Kim chi with spicy noodles, bolgogi, and tteokbokki. What you have?"

The aromas rising from the foods taunted Gray. "I'll have the tteokbokki. I like rice cakes and fish cakes, and supporting local businessmen."

He chatted with Yoo for a few minutes, getting a survey of city politics from his point of view. Four young men dressed in slim jeans and polo shirts ordered lunch from Yoo, then stood eating and talking.

Gray heard them chatting about boat races and liquor licenses and restaurant and bar outdoor seating. It interested him because these were concerns of Chicagoans. But when a young woman with shoulder length red hair and slim hips caught his eye up the block, all he could think of was Cherish. What was she doing? How were things with Devin?

He balled his fingers and tightened them, willing away the longing in his gut to just get a glimpse of her.

"Hey, I know you." A young police officer in uniform strolled up with his partner, another equally young cop. "Yeah, you're that reporter, what's your name?"

"Grayson Steele," the other officer added. "You're the one who got those dirty cops kicked off the force."

"Yes, I am Grayson and I was a *Chicago Daily Banner* reporter."

"It's nice to meet you in person. I'm Jason, this is Austin."

"Grayson," Austin muttered.

"Man, those cops were mad." Jason shook his head. "Scary, too. Those guys really did damage to the department. Thanks to you, they're gone and administrators are working on improving the system."

"Well, I did some investigative reporting, but I'd say the civil rights lawyer, Nathan Orlando, was responsible for stopping those crimes. You know, I would like to talk to you two and get an update on your experience with Chicago policing. Would you be willing?"

"I would," Jason said. "Would you?" He turned to Austin.

"Maybe.

Jason scrunched his face. "Though, I'm not sure it's safe. Could we be anonymous sources?"

"I'll see how it goes. Just give me a few minutes and then I'll buy you lunch. You know you want some spicy noodles." He shot them a smile and pulled out his cellphone to record the interview.

"All right," Jason said.

"I'm going to pass," Austin said, nudging Jason. "Catch up with me later." Briskly, he pounded down the street and turned a corner.

Gray shrugged. "So, you said the detectives from the Gang of Four were scary. Did you have any personal experiences with any of them?"

"Gang of Four? That's what you call them? That's a good description. I didn't work in the district with them very long before the trial that put Hastings away, but everyone knew their reputation, Hastings especially."

"What do you mean?"

Jason cast his gaze around, then turned back to Gray. "Their interrogations were brutal and they got away with it." He checked the streets again.

So, Jason was on edge. He didn't want to be standing here with a reporter. "Right. Since the trial, have things in the district changed?"

"They are changing. But cops stick together, you know that. No one wants to be the one who stands out."

"Is there fear that city officials might not protect officers who abide by the laws?"

"I'll just reiterate what I said," Jason said, getting jumpy. "Things are changing, but past influences are still prevalent. Hey man, I've got to go. How about those noodles?"

"Sure. Thanks for your time." He didn't blame Jason for his reluctance.

He finished with Jason and told Yoo goodbye just as his phone rang. He pulled it from his pocket and stared. "Cherish?"

"Yes, it's me."

Her voice over the phone lifted his heart and dropped it back down.

Panic lit up his nerves. Someone could tap into this call. She didn't even know the danger she could be in now. "Why are you calling?"

"I-I-I don't know what to say? I want to talk to you. You sound upset that I've called."

He gripped the phone tightly, willing for a safety web. "No, it's not that."

"Good, because I'm on the train to Chicago. I need you to pick me up at Union Station. The train will arrive at four." Her voice shrunk. "Can you do that?"

"Of course. I'll be there."

"Thank you. I'll see you soon?"

"Yes. Please, Cherish, be careful."

26

*C*herish bit at her bottom lip.

Okay, maybe she didn't think things through completely. She should have made the call to Gray before buying a train ticket and boarding for Chicago. But he told her he cared about her. And she'd awoken this morning feeling very much the conqueror of her own life. All that burning bridges and letting go. Sudden clarity told her Devin had been right about one thing; she could get away from her work, thanks to Pansy. It also had compelled her to get to Gray as soon as possible and talk to him face-to-face.

She closed her eyes and replayed what she knew. His immediate disconnect and the distant tone in his voice was unexpected.

Had she misinterpreted the signs? Gray had vacillated between getting close and comfortable and pulling back and keeping things to himself. What was the last thing he'd said? Be careful? What was that about?

Well, she would soon find out if she had misjudged her options. The train slowly maneuvered into Union Station. The process strained her last nerve, it took so long.

Finally, the doors opened and she grabbed her purse and bag and followed the line of passengers to the steps off the train. Butterflies fluttered in her stomach, not knowing what was coming on the other side of the doors into the station. She was relieved Gray had agreed to meet her, but she hadn't given him much choice. Would he be there waiting as he had promised? Would he smile at her or demand she get back on the train?

She stopped in the middle of the mash of exiting passengers and scanned for a familiar face. Her heartbeat drummed in her chest. She saw Gray among the groups of people.

He raised his arm over his head and motioned her in his direction. He shoved through people until they reached other.

"Hi, Cherish."

Instantly, Gray wrapped his arm around her shoulders and began moving toward the way out. His smile didn't ease her mind. It didn't reach his eyes.

"Gray, is something wrong?" She turned her head to look left, then right, searching for why he was acting so strange.

He continued toward the door, his grip tight on her, and said nothing.

Outside, he grabbed a cab and she climbed in first with Gray right behind her. He told the cab driver to head to Hotel Lincoln, but directed him to take a roundabout route. That done, he looked down into her face. "Hi there."

Cherish melted. The corner of his eyes crinkled. Those eyes, the familiar bright blue that penetrated her soul. "Hi."

"I apologize for being abrupt and not answering your question." He frowned and rubbed his forehead. "The answer is yes, there is something terribly wrong. You're not safe here, not with me especially. I had to get you out of the crowded, public location."

Her heart pounded harder and louder in her ears. "Not safe? What's going on?" She grimaced. "Although, I admit I'm the last person to ask that question. You're probably wondering what the hell I'm doing here? I'm sorry I didn't call you—"

"Shh." He touched his fingers to her lips. "I want to know all about it. I'm happy, so happy to see you."

She glowed in the sparkle in his eyes, knowing he was telling her the truth. "But?" There was a but coming, she could tell.

"Not right now. When we get to the hotel we can talk. I'll tell you things I should've told you sooner."

What could she do but wait? But questions jangled through her. Why the secrecy? Was this Gray's way of keeping his distance? Maybe she shouldn't have come. History should tell her she didn't possess good instincts. Former boyfriend disasters and her near miss with Devin were proof of that.

Downtown Chicago whirred past the cab's window. In the "scenic" route Gray had instructed the cabbie to take they passed by Willis Tower. She tried to, but couldn't see all the way to the top of the 110-story building.

"Pretty impressive, isn't it?" Gray scooched closer to her and cranked his head to look up at the tower. "Have you been to the Skydeck?"

"Years ago. I haven't been on The Ledge, have you?"

"Of course. It's a must-do in Chicago, especially since I lived here."

He stared up, inches from her face, and she couldn't miss the awe in his expression.

She shivered, not sure whether it was his closeness or the idea of The Ledge that affected her. "You like heights, then, right?"

Gray slid back to his side of the seat. "You picked up on that." He chuckled. "I don't mind heights. The view is worth pushing through the fears."

"I'm a feet-on-the-ground type of person. The Skydeck is one thing, but the glass Ledge is quite another thing." Would they ever get to the hotel? This chitchat simply filled time. Eagerness bubbled inside her like a geyser, straining to say what she came here for. "Maybe while I'm here we could take in Navy Pier. My memories of it are exhilarating, if for no other reason than the way it stretches into the lake."

Gray didn't look at her. He checked out the back window and knitted his brow. "Yeah, maybe." He touched the driver's shoulder. "Let us out here, please."

"This not Hotel Lincoln," the driver protested.

"I know. Change of plans."

Gray paid the driver and took her arm, ushering her to the sidewalk heading east.

"Is something wrong?" Urgency in him was palpable.

"We're going to walk a few blocks, then take the Brown Line up to the Sedgwick stop. I'll explain later."

Cherish kept quiet beside Gray's long strides. He glanced frequently over his shoulder and peered down alleys. She practically had to run to keep up with his pace. All of the intrigue and Gray's troubled expression overloaded her senses, and the noise of the city shrieked in her head.

They reached the station and quickly climbed on the train, dashing for seats. Gray slipped his arm across the back of the seat behind her back, as though protecting her.

"Should I be watchful?" she asked.

He closed his eyes and sighed heavily. "No, I'm taking care of things."

He didn't have to tell her something was wrong. It was on his face, in his voice. She had to believe him, trust him, that he knew what he was doing. The situation coiling around Gray didn't make her feel all warm and cozy, but his arm around her imbued her with faith, or was it courage?

She sunk into the moment, sitting beside guarded Gray and bouncing around on the train, bracing for its stops—nine times—and watching passengers come and go, distracted and in a hurry. Fifteen minutes later, Gray stood.

"This is our stop." His arm still around her, he led her off the train, again picking up his pace. "It's about a half-mile to the hotel. Just stick close to me and keep your eyes open."

"What would I be looking for?"

"A man or men coming fast for us." He stopped mid-step and grabbed her shoulders. "I'm sorry. I shouldn't have said that."

"You're in trouble?"

"Sadly, that's sort of true." He took her hand and continued marching down Wells Street. Only about ten minutes more and they pushed through the glass doors on Clark Street into Hotel Lincoln.

They hurried through the lobby toward the elevators and took one to the tenth floor. As the only two occupants in the elevator, Cherish stood opposite of Gray, leaning against the wall.

"Do you think someone is following us?" Cherish spoke just above a whisper even though they were alone.

"Someone was following us. I'm fairly certain we ditched them when we changed our course." He crossed his arms over his chest and rested his head against the wall. "I don't want you involved in my problems."

"So my coming to Chicago now isn't good timing." She shrugged. "I'm sorry. I had an impulse and followed up on it. I was only thinking of wanting to see you and share some things."

The elevator slowed. Gray stepped across the elevator and put himself between Cherish and the door. His lack of response and his position cinched her lungs and a grave sensation sunk to the pit of her stomach. *What have I gotten into?*

27

$\mathcal{G}$ray was a muscled soldier preparing for an enemy invasion, as the elevator door started to slide open. Cherish held her breath, on alert for some man or men to drag them off to places unknown.

The doorway fully open, a small group of people loaded down with suitcases and fanny packs stood aside to let them out, smiling like happy tourists.

She giggled. "Thank you." Cherish nodded to each one as she stepped into the hallway.

Gray again pulled her in close to his side and hurried to his room, quickly sliding his key card through the lock, sending her inside, and slamming the arm to the interior lock across the door.

Cherish stood, her feet together, unmoving just inside the door. Now what?

The drapes were closed across both windows in the room, but Gray pulled one aside a little and surveyed the street below. He dropped it closed again and checked his phone, then his email on his laptop.

His vigilance chilled her blood. It told her danger was serious, so serious he couldn't rest. He walked past her to double-check the locked door. Finally, he blew out a deep breath.

He pointed to a couch. "Please, have a seat."

She dropped into the couch, not very relieved, while he planted a straight-back chair in front of her.

"Why are you here?" His eyes searched her face.

"What is going on? Why are people following you? I take it they mean you harm."

He crossed his legs and leaned forward, propping one arm on the other. "I'll explain, but first, can you please tell me why you're here? You told me you were going back with Devin. Frankly, I didn't expect to see you ever again."

Cherish had to calm her heartbeat. Gray's stern attitude at pick up, his reserve, his alarm raced through her bloodstream. "I had to talk to you."

"You had to talk to me? What's going on that you came to Chicago to talk to me? Is something wrong? What about Devin?"

"Well, I'm not back with Devin. I told him I couldn't be with him. I'm sorry I told you that. I got confused. Your post about my court case with Decidedly Laboratories shocked me. It triggered my fears of betrayal. I doubted myself again. If you were not the trustworthy person I believed you to be, what other things had I misjudged, like maybe Devin, his guilt or innocence?"

Gray nodded, but kept his gaze on her, saying nothing. It was up to her to speak.

"I learned my parents are doing unethical things in their law practice. Devin is blackmailing me. But my parents dismissed their activities as how it is to be a lawyer, the kind of lawyer who will do anything for their clients, and informed me that's how they practice law and I should accept it as normal." The words spilled, like water pouring out of an open dam. "They strongly suggested Devin hadn't done anything wrong."

Gray straightened in his chair and uncrossed his legs, then crossed the opposite leg over the other. "I see."

"You have to understand that for all of my life my parents have guided my decisions. I understood I needed their input, after all, several boyfriends hurt me badly. My judgment was questioned and corrected." Blush warmed her cheeks. "As I'm telling you this, it sounds so childish and dysfunctional."

"No, it doesn't, not on your part. Your parents have undermined your confidence. You want to please them. That's normal. You loved them, wanted them to love you. They taught you to do what they told you to do, for your own good. I saw that, Cherish."

"I didn't. It was hard for me to see that when they wanted me to change my attitude, go back with Devin, they simply didn't want me to rock the boat. Their plans for my marriage to Devin fit their strategy to keep me submissive and quiet. But when I learned Devin was the same kind of person, I knew I was through with him. Still, I had to play along with him. He was pressuring me to marry him or he would get my parents in trouble." She ran her hands through her hair. It all sounded so messed up as she tried to explain to Gray.

His gaze tightened on her. "You really considered marrying him under those circumstances? Cherish, a part of you really needs to take care of your parents, huh."

She dropped her lids, fighting gathering tears. "Yes." He understood that she could be strong and lawyerly at the same time she feared for her parents and wanted to protect them. "But you've given me freedom in the short time I've known you. Freedom to be myself. So when I cleared my thoughts, I knew I couldn't continue as I have in the past, going along with my parents' idea of how I should live. I had to accept that I had gone along with them and now I have to accept responsibility." She drew in a deep breath and exhaled.

"I had to talk to you and tell you how I feel. Only now I see I've made a mistake again. I should have called and asked if would be okay to visit." Relief threaded through her. So many words had been balled up inside her. Weighing what to say, what to keep quiet. But she'd said them and now she could breathe. "I didn't run away from anything in Dunes Bay. I came to the place where I could talk to my best friend. But if you want me to leave, I'll go right now."

Gray slanted his head and pursed his lips, eyeing her. He nodded.

"Well, you don't say. I'm so happy for you. There's nothing like claiming your own life, in my opinion. It's hard but so worth it."

A smile started in her heart and ended up on her face. "It's like standing on the ledge; scary but worth doing."

His smile widened. "Hey, that sounds familiar."

"I'm not done with settling everything. There are things I need to do, but I'm figuring it out on my own." Cherish started counting the stripes in the drapes. There was more she wanted from him—assurances, truth—but her throat went dry. Maybe the timing wasn't right yet.

Gray took a seat next to her on the couch, not meeting her gaze. "I'm sorry I left you the way I did. I didn't want to walk away from you, but I had to."

"Because I told you I was going back to Devin." Her stomach lurched.

"Not just that." He stared into space and uncertainty wafted around him. "I had to come to Chicago to keep you safe. You and my family."

"Safe from what?"

"A year ago, I went back to Dunes Bay to avoid the consequences of a series of stories I wrote. Some very bad people had done terrible things and I brought out in the open what they'd done. There were four men and one, Kane Hastings, was imprisoned for his crimes. The others somehow escaped prosecution. I thought I had taken all measures to keep death threats from following me. I thought the right thing to do was to protect my family, and then you, from having any knowledge of my past. I was wrong about that. Hastings got early release and set a plan in motion for me. He sent a guy to Dunes Bay who threatened to hurt me if I didn't comply with that plan. I realized I had to go back to Chicago and do a follow-up story or none of us would ever be completely safe."

Cherish covered her mouth, speechless. Distress hammered all over Gray's body. His expression drooped. Her arms ached to hold him, hug him, until his pain dissolved.

He chuckled, sarcasm dripping. "I know. What do you say to that?

There's nothing to say. I screwed up badly. I don't regret writing the stories. They needed to be written."

"No, no. You shouldn't have regrets. How could you not write the story?"

He leaned a tiny bit closer. "I had to. I'm an investigative reporter. The crimes were horrific. But I should have stayed. I should have dealt with the criminals."

"It's not too late?" She lifted the last word in her question, not sure if it was too late or not. She couldn't look away, his expression was so earnest, questioning, self-condemning. Her hand moved, as though caught up in a beam, inching toward his cheek. She cupped it and he closed the small space between them.

His lips a breath from hers, he paused. "Friends?"

She shut her eyes. "Friends."

Her heart lilted as Gray's lips touched hers. His kiss was soft, tentative, and brief.

Still so near his breath brushed her face, Cherish hung there, suspended in the idea of letting go, giving in and letting the flutter in her chest blossom. She bit her lower lip and peered into Gray's eyes. They were soft, tender, questioning.

She stepped back without dropping her gaze. "Friends." Was their timing ever going to be right?

He slanted his head and sighed. "Friends. Very good friends. Let's not mess that up." He searched the room and she waited for his uncertainty to coalesce into a next move. "Do you need a room?"

"Yes, I suppose I do. I didn't plan ahead." She scuffed her shoe on the rug.

"You can stay here. In fact, if you're comfortable with it, I wish you would." He started pacing the floor. "I don't want you alone, not in this town with Hastings and his gang free and roaming."

"Thank you. I would be fine here with you." The tension of minutes ago still stirred in the air and a little sadness crept over her. But she put it out of her mind. Gray was in trouble and that was all that needed attention now.

"Then it's settled. Hungry?"

She rubbed her stomach. "I'm getting hungry."

"Me too.

"The café in the hotel is still open. I'll quick get us some coffee and something to eat." He pointed his finger at her. "Stay there. I'll be right back. Lock the door-latch. Don't open for anyone but me."

"Yes sir."

He stuffed the keycard in his pocket, put his shoes on and blew her a kiss as he stepped watchfully into the hall.

She surveyed the room and found a place to set her things. She'd packed so quickly, she needed to make sure she had everything she needed.

A sharp knock—knock at the door startled her. She crept on tiptoe to the door. Gray wouldn't be back already and he wouldn't have knocked. He would have said it was him. But what if something had happened on the way to get coffee?

She put her eye close to the peephole. She jumped back. A uniformed cop stood on the other side of the door. As though he could see her behind the door, the officer held up his badge.

"Chicago PD. I need to talk with you." The cop wasn't asking, he was demanding.

What would happen if she simply ignored him?

He rapped again, harder this time. "Miss, I need to talk to you. Open up."

What? Did he say Miss, as in he knew she was alone in the room? Something must have happened to Gray, that was the only explanation.

Bam, bam, bam. "Open up now," the officer yelled.

She unlatched and opened the door a crack. Her throat closed. Another man stood beside the officer, and before she could slam the door closed the officer shoved his foot between it and the doorframe.

She opened her mouth to scream, but the other man slapped his hand over her mouth.

"Don't even think about screaming." He twisted her arm behind her back and pushed her toward the stairway.

Her heart pounding in her ears, Cherish struggled to escape his hold on her, she bit down on the man's fingers, and back-kicked his shin.

"You bitch," he hollered stumbling.

Frantic, she sprinted away from the men. "Help, help," she hollered. The cop immediately outran her and grabbed her around the waist and hit her over the head with his baton. Her knees went weak and she struggled to stay on her feet.

"Settle down," he commanded, his teeth gritted. "I don't want to hurt you, but you're coming with us."

28

*Y*es, there were problems, deadly problems in fact. Still, Gray's steps had snap. Cherish's visit had fast-tracked their friendship to something so big he couldn't contain his happiness.

Juggling a bag of blueberry muffins and two coffees, he took the elevator back to his floor, more eager than vigilant.

He stepped into the hall and turned the corner, images of Cherish waiting for him, filled his thoughts. He picked up his pace and took the bag of muffins in his teeth to pull out his keycard.

"Cherish, it's me. Unlatch the door."

No response. No noise from the other side of the door.

"Cherish?" Maybe she was in the shower. His heart clenched.

She could have forgotten to latch the door, he told himself. He swiped his card, lifted the handle, and shoved the door open.

"Cherish?" He checked the bathroom. Empty. His ears started ringing. He set the coffees and muffins on a table, nearly dropping them. He froze at the sight of a note.

We have her. You know who. We'll be in touch.

A tornado swept him into a state of chaos. He dropped on the couch, his head in his hands. Think. Think.

He started for his laptop, then dropped back to the couch. Walls closed in. How had they found him? He had tried so hard to maintain privacy. He stared at his laptop on the desk. Did he dare email Eric? Had the men hacked his brother's security measures? He rubbed his temples. Was it the judge? Had the judge burned him?

He jumped up. Duh! It was the phone. Somehow the Gang had been monitoring his cell. Probably they were hooked up with another dirty cop who could access records for them. Maybe Smith had put a lowjack on his truck when he found him in Dunes Bay and tracked him to the hotel. There were possibilities.

He splayed his fingers, yelling inside, pacing. "Oh my God, Cherish. I'm so sorry." Every muscle in his body ached. Silently, he vowed. *I'm not going to let them hurt you, Cherish. No matter what it takes, I'll take care of you.*

What was he supposed to do? Sit and wait for a phone call, a knock on the door? Would calling the police make matters worse? He had to be smart. He couldn't trust the police, so he was on his own,

Too many questions swarmed in his mind. Waiting was out of the question. He shoved his phone in his pocket and took off for the hotel desk. As crazy as it sounded, he was tempted to take the stairs. All ten flights, two at a time. At least the action would relieve pent up angst.

On the ground floor, he got off the elevator and sped to the desk.

"I'd like to speak to the manager." Gray furiously tapped his fingers on the counter.

"Of course, sir. May I tell him what this is in regards to?" The mild-mannered clerk smiled.

Gray wanted to lunge over the counter and shake her. "It's private."

Minutes passed like sludge, but finally he was summoned to the manager's office.

The short, middle-aged man offered his hand. "How can I help you?"

The niceties crawled under Gray's skin. He didn't have time for such things. "I need to see the videos from the tenth floor of this afternoon. Pronto. A woman is missing."

The man's eyes flinched. "Are you a police officer?"

Gray fisted his fingers. "No, I'm a reporter. I'm working on a piece. I can't give you the details of my investigations, but I can assure you seeing the video is a matter of life and death, and right now, you're wasting vital time."

The man stared at him, narrowing his eyes. "Do you have some credentials you can show me?"

"You can talk to my editor at *The Chicago Daily Banner*. But why? Are you hiding something? My editor would be interested in knowing what?" Gray gave him his best I-mean-business stare.

"This is irregular, but I guess there would be no harm. I assure you I'm not hiding anything. Follow me."

Gray followed him to a nearby room with a sign that read, Security. The manager instructed one of the security guards to play the footage from cameras on the tenth floor and then left.

It didn't take long before he saw the worst. He saw it all. The young cop he'd met yesterday, Austin Mayer, and Hastings walking up the hall to his room, pounding on the door, and Cherish opening the door.

"There. Slow the tape." His stomach twisted into knots. The scene played out in slow motion. Austin hit Cherish. Then they grabbed her and dragged her down the hall and into an elevator.

"Geez," the security guy exclaimed. "This just happened. Where were you?"

Gray stomped on his rage. "The question is where were you?"

"I've been here all along."

"You couldn't have been or you're an accomplice."

"Hell no! Don't tell my boss, please, but I stepped away for a smoke. I was gone only minutes. It must have happened then. Geez! I'll call the police." He picked up the phone, but Gray grabbed it from him and slammed it back down.

"No! You've done enough. Your excuse for leaving your post is very lame. You really expect me to believe you're not an accomplice?"

"No, I mean yes! I'm not an accomplice. I messed up, but I need this job. What can I do to help?" The man's face was blank.

"I'll find out if you're lying," Gray threatened. "I want to see that tape again. I'll talk to the authorities." As terrible as it was that the security guard missed what happened to Cherish, it did give Gray an upper hand for getting the tape and actually worked in his favor. Clearly corruption in the CPD still existed, even if only in Austin. The security guard's screw up presented possibilities of losing Cherish at the hands of not only the Gang of Four, but other cops, like Austin, aiming to keep secrets. Jason's strong implication that corruption in the department hadn't died out gave him shivers. Was there more he didn't know? Was Jason being truthful or giving him a song and dance to distract or trap him?

"Well?" Gray clenched his teeth and scowled.

"Settle down, settle down. I'll run it back for you." Sweat wetting his brow broke the guard's cool cucumber façade. "Here, you said you were gone from the room at seven, so right around here we might see something more."

He had to see the video again, make sure he hadn't missed something.

Right in front of his eyes as he watched, aching to make it stop, the cop hit Cherish and the other guy walked into the room. Sickened, he watched her wobble and wanted to catch her.

"The other guy seems to care about the cameras. He's facing away." The guard turned to Gray. "Do you know who these two are, or at least the cop?"

"I do. And by the hairstyle and color and body build I can guess the identity of the other guy." Anger spun, a rotary saw blade ripping at his heart. The other man stepped back into the hall and Gray got a glimpse of his profile. "Hastings." As the two practically dragged Cherish down the hall and out of sight, he moaned. "I just missed them."

∿

CHERISH ROLLED over on the musty so-called mattress and tried to see her surroundings. After she'd been yanked from the hotel room, two men had shoved her in a car, blindfolded her, and brought her here. A long, noisy night dragged by as her thoughts raced. Upmost on her mind was how to escape, right along with why did she end up here? She didn't know what time it was or long she'd been lying here in this vacuum.

The door opened and a man gruffly wrapped the blindfold over her eyes before they adjusted to the light.

"Let's go," the man ordered, pulling her to her feet. He shoved her into a chair and wrapped tape over her mouth. "There. Behave."

Okay, now what? The tape hurt every time she swallowed. Everything was black under the blindfold. Her wrists and ankles were secured to a hard chair, that much she knew. She wriggled, testing her bounds.

A hand cracked across her face. "Sit still," a voice demanded.

She hollered but she couldn't open her mouth and it just sounded like a sick cat. Her throat was dry and miserable. Helpless, there was nothing to do. An odd calm settled over her. Was it calm, though, or was she dissociated? Either way, she felt next to nothing, which was a whole lot easier to manage than panic and tears.

Muttering somewhere in the room echoed as though she were inside a tunnel. No, the sounds weren't sharp, they bounced off hard walls. That was it. She'd already determined the floor was cement. Considering the place smelled of must and damp, she put two and two together to get basement. She also deduced she was still in Chicago, thanks to the rumbling EL that roared nearby.

"Hey, Abner, bring a beer. The cooler is in the corner."

"Shut up, you asshole."

Cherish shivered. Sounds of the second man getting rough made her want to disappear.

"Brock, who you calling an asshole? Get me a beer."

Footsteps thudded across the floor. She heard the cooler open and someone catching what she presumed was a bottle or can.

"Now will you shut up? Or would you rather just give her all our names?"

One of them nudged her foot. "Oh, she doesn't know anything." It was the first voice. Brock was wrong. She now knew a few things.

So these were some of the Gang Gray told her about. The dirty cops who wanted to hurt him. The ones Gray tried to shield his family from. The reasons he kept her at a distance. Her heart sank. She wished she could reach out right now and caress his brow, tell him she understood his secrets, his reticence, and apologize for stuffing him inside the same box as all her failed relationships and accusing him of betrayal.

The men spoke in low conversation she could barely make out, but in the darkness she tuned out all other sounds but the words they spoke.

"Do you think it's about time to make the call?" This voice came from a third man. It was higher-pitched than the other two. But it wasn't the voice of the man at the hotel room door with the cop.

Someone blew out a puff of cigarette smoke. It filled the air and she tried to hold her breath.

"Let's make him squirm a little longer." That was the voice. The other man, all gravely and coarse.

A guy chuckled. "Yeah, we've taken his prize possession. Let's let him wonder what's happening." This was yet another voice, from what sounded like an older man.

Scuffling headed along the cement floor toward her, and she braced herself for the unknown. She hollered inside her head while the tape was ripped off her mouth. "Hey, you thirsty?"

"Yes," she squeaked out.

Next the blindfold came off and she winced at the light from a lamp across the small room.

"Why did you do that, Smith?" The man from the hotel room lunged at the guy in front her and plowed his fist into the guy's face.

"Stop it!" Smith yelled. "It doesn't matter."

Cherish's pulse staggered. She knew what that meant. The plan didn't include letting her or Gray live.

"Excuse me, why am I here? It can't be to pressure Gray into doing what you want. You could have just killed him."

"Shut up," the man from the hotel said.

"Who are you? Like Smith said, you might as well tell me." Cherish managed to keep her voice calm, somehow.

"I'm the one in charge here. That's all you need to know."

"Oh, so you're Hastings." Hastings' eyes narrowed, but she continued. "I mean, really, why did you drag me into this? I didn't do anything."

Hastings leaned close enough she almost gagged on his smoky breath. "Shut up or I'll let you lick your dry lips all day and listen to your empty stomach grumble. Isn't it obvious? We want him to write the truth."

"Oh, you need him to exonerate you." She stared into his steely eyes and saw false bravado. Menace. Cunning. Yes. But mostly grave concern.

A smile slipped out. Gray knew something. They couldn't kill him without getting that something out of him.

29

$\mathcal{H}$eat rose in shimmering waves off the cement at AT&T Plaza in Millennium Park. When Hastings called to demand a rewrite of the article and threatened to harm Cherish, Gray insisted on a proof-of-life meeting at the Cloud Gate, aka the Bean. A popular tourist attraction in the skyscraper-lined Loop, the Bean's popularity and public location offered some protection. Hastings wouldn't dare pull anything violent amongst the crowds.

Still, Gray's confidence squirmed. As long as the thugs had their hands on Cherish, tension would twist in his body.

He kept up a steady scan of his surroundings. Hastings would not sneak up on him. He noticed a figure walk out of the Grant Park North parking garage into the sunlight, and light a cigarette. Gray swallowed hard. It was Hastings.

"Don't think because you're the only one I see, doesn't mean I believe for a minute that you came alone as I instructed." Gray glared at Hastings as he stopped in front of him.

"You're not making the rules, buddy." Hastings flicked ash off the end of his cigarette. "Here's how it's going to be. You write a piece that takes the blame for those murders and such off me and my men. You tell me who your informant is."

"I don't have any informants. I use sources."

"I consider anyone who would talk to you about me and my men informants. I want a name. That's it. You and your girl walk away."

"Just like that."

"Yes. Give me a name. Then the day that story I want comes out, we'll meet again and you get the girl."

Gray watched Hastings take a long deep pull of his cigarette and blow out a cloud of smoke. "I want to see Cherish." He decided against protesting whether or not she was his "girl." No point in getting nitpicky.

"Follow me." Hastings turned toward the garage across South Columbus Drive.

"Bring her here." What did Hastings take him for? The last place he'd go alone was into a huge parking structure where anyone could be hiding anywhere, ready to grab him.

Waiting a little longer in the bright sun was a safe choice. It wouldn't do Cherish any good if he were taken.

Minutes later, Hastings marched Cherish across traffic, his hand tight on her arm, and up to Gray.

His fist balled. Red marks glistened across her face, indicating they'd gagged her with tape, then peeled off skin in tearing it off. One cheek was red and swollen. Anger warred with regret. Reaching for Cherish's face and cupping it in his hands won out over punching Hastings in the gut.

"Hold on, not too close," Hastings warned under his breath. "You can see she is fine."

Gray ignored him and continued to caress her face, gently touching her bright red cheek. "You're okay?"

"Don't worry about me." Her eyes wide, she looked steadily into his face.

She meant it. He saw it in her eyes. She had courage and strength. Her words were composed, confident.

"I'm going to take care of things." He nodded, and hoped she understood he wouldn't let her down.

"That's enough." Hastings jerked her away from him. "When

you're done with your article, leave a message for me with Officer Mayer at the sixteenth district. You got that?"

"Then you'll let Cherish go and get off my back?" Gray pinned him with his gaze. There was a chance, he supposed, that Hastings wasn't lying, but not much of one.

"Nice try, Steele. You'll get the girl when you give me the name of your informant. I know you have one. That's the only reason you'd be in town again." Hastings smiled, exposing his cracked and tobacco-stained teeth. He pulled Cherish alongside him and strode into the parking structure. "Don't keep me waiting," he tossed over his shoulder.

Hastings' words played in Gray's head as he took a bus back to the hotel. Don't keep me waiting. What kind of game were Hastings and his gang playing?

In his room, Gray sat down to email Eric, let him know where he was at with the story, but mostly to talk to a friendly face, so to speak. His fingers rested on his laptop keys, hesitating. This was his problem, not Eric's.

Wait. I'm doing it again, keeping secrets that would leave Eric vulnerable.

HASTINGS AND HIS GANG KIDNAPPED MY FRIEND CHERISH. NO COPS, PLEASE. I'M WORKING IT OUT. WATCH YOUR BACK. I SHOULD HAVE THE STORY TO YOU SOON.

Sure, he'd finish the story ASAP. Under normal circumstances, he would hunker down with his notes and pound out the story. The process would release his anxieties. This time was different. Cherish's life was at stake, and that was all he could think of.

He shook his head, trying to erase the image of her sore cheek.

Eric's email response popped in and with effort Gray switched his focus.

OH MY GOD! WHAT CAN I DO?

"Thanks," Gray said to the walls. The truth was, the danger Cherish was in was his doing. He wasn't alone, though.

He found Rachel's phone number and called. She should know

about her sister and now was the right time to assure her Cherish was alive. He dialed. This was not something to tell through text.

"Hi Gray. This is unexpected."

"I know. I'm afraid I have bad news." He paused. How do you tell someone their sister was kidnapped? "There is a long version, but I don't have time for that now. Cherish has been kidnapped."

"Oh my God!" Rachel shrieked.

"I've seen her and she's okay. I'm working on her rescue right now. Rachel, I'm not going to let anything terrible happen, I promise."

"Something terrible already has happened. Why on earth?"

"I know. I know. But I can't talk now. I'll be in touch. And, Rachel, please don't talk about this to anyone, not your parents, not even the authorities."

"What? Where are you? I have to call the police. This is awful. Tell me what happened, where she is." Rachel's fear colored her voice. "I don't understand. I'm coming wherever you are."

"I wish I could tell you more, but it's not safe. I'm in Chicago, but please do not come here. It's too dangerous and there isn't anything you can do." How could he make her stay away?

"I can be there when you find her. She's my sister."

Rachel was crying, he could tell. "I'm sorry. I can't imagine how you must feel. But the best thing you can do for Cherish is to stay in Dunes Bay, safe. The people we're dealing with are desperate and I don't want anyone else in harm's way. Cherish will be fine, I'll make sure of it but if more people come into the picture I can't make sure anyone will be safe."

She exhaled a trembling breath. "Okay. But please, please, stay in touch."

"I will."

That was hard. It couldn't be any other way. But he drew in deep breaths and let them out. He had to clear his thoughts and attack the story. Thoughts expanded. Hastings was not an unknown factor. He got off on inflicting pain, known throughout his crappy career — the guy had so many complaints over the years it was mind boggling how he stayed a cop for as long as he did.

And he had a grudge against Gray. Hastings wouldn't be satisfied with Gray's compliance, not that he intended to meet the demands. Hastings wanted blood. And he especially wanted to satisfy that craving slowly and painfully.

The story was key to ending the Gang's criminal activity. He couldn't write it and rescue Cherish without cloning himself. The beauty of it was he didn't have to. He had brothers.

"Rhys, I need you." Gray didn't have to say more over the phone, his brother would deduce something serious was up.

"You'll give me details later?"

"Yes. We can't stay on this line. Bring Jasper too if you can."

"We're on our way."

ANGER CHARGED like a herd of bulls through Cherish. Hastings hadn't even blindfolded her on the ride to and from The Bean. He had kept her close in an elevator that took them to the same basement she had been held captive in. Only now she knew it was in an insignificant empty apartment building near the Damen Station for the Brown Line.

Hastings jerked her along through the basement to the same room at the back and shoved her into the same hard chair.

"Be a good girl and I won't blindfold, gag you, or restrict you to the chair."

She glanced around the empty room. "Where is everyone else?" She might as well try to learn something. Hastings seemed in a good mood, probably because he thought his plan was coming together. His arrogant swagger, his full-of-himself attitude told her he probably felt in control of the situation and her, and reminded Cherish of the man she'd almost married. A shiver slid up and down her spine. *Ack!* She clenched her teeth. Knocking Hastings down a few notches would be fun.

"They went to eat. Don't worry. They'll be back. Besides, I can handle a little snip of a thing like you."

She disregarded his remark. "Do I get to eat?"

Hastings grunted. But he picked up his cellphone from a shelf on a nearby wall and turned his back on her, as if trying to have a private conversation in the basement was possible. "Hey, Austin. Bring me some dogs from Portillo's. What? With chilies. No, no ketchup, you moron. But first check on Gray. See if he's still in the hotel." He hung up and turned back to her.

"Your food will be here soon. Meanwhile, shut up." Hastings set his phone on the shelf and launched into a mini convulsive coughing fit, then lit up another cigarette.

Cherish covered her nose and shook her head.

"What? You don't like the smoke?" Laughter the sound of tires on gravel came out of him. "You think it will kill you?" He laughed again.

Cold shivers tremored through her. "What, you think they won't kill you?" She grinned.

The smoke was bad, but her own smell was disgusting. The mat she slept on was filthy, and of course she hadn't showered. The mat alone made her itch. Worse, she couldn't stop thinking. Wondering what Gray was doing. Where her parents were. If she'd ever see Rachel again. But she had not shed any tears, by God, she was too angry. She had to get out. Had to. Here she finally was taking complete charge of her life and before she even got a chance to, she might get killed.

"Isn't it bad enough you put so many innocent people in jail? Why would you bring in a young officer like Austin?"

"It's a family business. Why would I feel bad about it?" He sunk in a chair and propped his feet up on the shaky wooden table.

The others straggled in, Austin among them carrying two cans of pop and a bag that announced itself with the smell of hot dogs.

"What's this about family business?" Abner asked.

"She said I should feel guilty that Austin has been corrupted." Hastings's cigarette bounced in the corner of his lips.

The others broke out laughing. "Did you tell her Abner and me are brothers?" Brock laughed. "And that Harvey Smith there is Austin's uncle?"

Hastings chugged his can of cola and wiped his mouth on his shirt. "Besides, Austin has skills. He knows technology. Don't you?"

"I know where I belong," Austin said, his eyes narrowed. "Don't you worry about me."

"Wow, aren't you so proud of your family business?" She didn't bother to keep the contempt out of her voice. "I wonder how you'll feel, Austin, about your family's business when you sit in a cell inside a penitentiary. No one has been hurt yet. You haven't shot anyone. If you let me go, I'll do my best to see to it that the DA goes easy on you. Right now you wouldn't be looking at a long prison sentence. Let me go now before someone gets hurt and life changes permanently."

"Haven't I told you to shut up enough?" Hastings leered at her. "I'll slap that tape across your mouth again, if you don't mind your words."

Hastings tossed her one bag of food and a can of some generic cola. He pulled a chair to the table and slid in, taking a big bite out of his dog while the others took places around him.

Henry leaned his elbows on the table. "How long do you suppose we'll have to wait? I'm getting sick of babysitting."

Cherish ate a few bites and sipped her pop, weighing the moment. "Hey, I need to pee."

"Then do it." Abner smirked. "You know where the room is."

She walked around the table and swerved breezily past the shelf, palming the cellphone still sitting there. She held her breath, assuming one of them would notice, but kept heading in the direction of the tiny room near the elevator.

"I told you to check on Gray before getting food."

She closed the bathroom door on Hastings scolding Austin. The creepy room made her gag. Filth was everywhere. But one dirty window looked like heaven to her. She crossed her fingers that a shove or two would open the ancient thing. She slowly unlatched the lock. It creaked, loud and obnoxious.

"What's going on in there?" Hastings pounded on the door. "Open this door."

Shit. She placed her palms on the edge, gathering all her strength. She had so little time. She pushed hard. The hinge groaned.

Hastings banged hard on the door. "I'm going to bust down this door if you don't open it right now."

She had no choice. She pulled the window down, leaving it open a slit and prayed it wouldn't be detected. "Okay, okay," she said, turning the knob and pulling the door open. "I wasn't finished yet."

Hastings yanked her out of the room and deposited her back in the chair. He shoved her hands on the arms and wrapped tape tightly around them. "I don't care. You'll have to pee your pants."

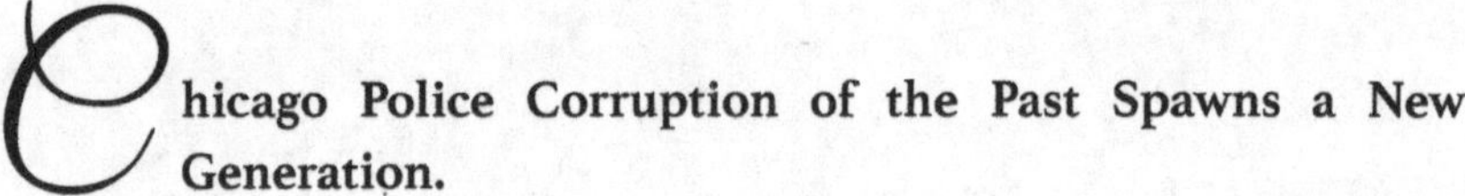

Chicago Police Corruption of the Past Spawns a New Generation.

There, he had the headline, anyway, and the framework for the lede. Gray reread the article he was working on.

In the year since corrupt former Chicago Police Detective Kane Hastings was convicted of racketeering and framing innocent people for crimes, the Chicago Police Department has made strides in eliminating endemic criminal activity among its police force. The justice system has addressed the importance of releasing wrongly imprisoned individuals. Yet, the ugly wreaked upon the citizens of Chicago by Hastings and his Gang of Four didn't go away, and now is recruiting a new generation of police officers in the Sixteenth District.

Though changes have been made, a young district officer who wanted to remain anonymous for fear of retaliation, said change is resisted by some.

"Cops stick together, you know that," the anonymous source said. "No one wants to be the one who stands out."

As long as he kept his focus on the story, Gray could put words, sentences, paragraphs, and facts together. But it wasn't coming easily. His heart was somewhere else. It pleaded with his sanity to search for

Cherish. He was an investigative reporter, for Christ sake. Surely he knew someone who could offer a clue.

He gulped from his paper coffee cup, and frowned. The coffee was hours old and cold. He checked the time and groaned.

Cherish, where are you?

He jumped at a hard rap on the door. "Gray, it's us, Rhys and Jasper."

Gray peered through the peephole, then tore open the door. "Get in here you two." He hugged Rhys, then Jasper. "Thank you for coming." He checked the time again. "You made good time." He blew out a long breath.

Jasper opened the mini fridge. "Do you have anything good in here? Where's your john? I need to pee. It was a long drive."

"Umm...just water. There's a café and restaurant in the hotel." Gray's mind dizzied. "I don't have time to eat. Cherish is in trouble and I don't know where she is." He heard his voice rise higher, but couldn't stop it. He pointed. "The bathroom is there."

Rhys sat on the edge of the couch. "Pay no attention to the man at the fridge. What's going on?"

Jasper finished guzzling a bottle of water. "Yeah, tell us what you need from us," he said.

"Just being here is helping me." He dropped his head in his hands and told them about Cherish's visit, the danger it put her in, and the kidnapping.

"So Hastings says he'll let her go and leave you alone if you write the story according to his invention and give him the name of a presumed source who would rat on him if given the chance. But you suspect it's a trap."

Jasper tipped his Tiger's cap up and scratched his head. "You, bro, need to finish that story pronto."

Gray's mouth was dry. "I need to find Cherish."

"Yes you do, and it's a job for the Steele brothers." Rhys squared his jaw.

Jasper grabbed them both and yanked them in line. "The Steele brothers."

CHERISH'S MUSCLES ached to move. She'd been confined to the chair for what felt like days, but only three hours had passed since she'd tried to get out the bathroom window. She really did have to pee now. Hastings had gone outside for fresh air, he'd said. Any minute she expected him to notice his phone was missing. It lay in her pocket, weighty and conspicuous. Nerves in her stomach lurched. This might be her moment to try again to get away.

"Hey, I need to use the restroom again," she hollered at Abner Cross.

He ignored her.

"Hey, you, Abner. I don't want to urinate all over the floor. Do you want that?"

"Shut up," Abner said, but he got out his chair. "You really think I care if you piss yourself?"

"Fine. I will. But I really have to go bad, so don't say I didn't warn you when Hastings gets angry that the whole room smells." If whining didn't get him to let her out of the chair, maybe the threat of Hastings' temper would.

"Hold your panties," Abner said, and shuffled lazily to her. "This is going to hurt."

She bit her lower lip as he ripped off the duct tape on her hands and feet. "Go ahead. You know the way."

This time she turned on the faucet and let the water pour out fast, hoping the sound would mask her escape.

She reached up to the window and pressed slowly and steadily until it moved a little. The hinge complained, but she started singing an impromptu tune. "I love the trees at my house. I even have bees and an occasional mouse."

"What are you doing, singing like that?" Abner yelled through the door.

"Sorry, I am tense. It helps me go."

"Well hurry up."

Again, she pushed with all her might and the window opened a crack. She grabbed the window frame and hefted one foot up, and kicked at it just hard enough to open it wide while belting out the song. "We had some flowers at the edge of the fence. Along came spring showers and gave it a drench."

Her pulse raced, her blood made a high-pitched wringing in her ears. She slid through the window and dropped to the other side just at the moment an L train rumbled by.

She took off running without a glance behind her, her breaths heaving. But she didn't stop, couldn't stop even when she had no more breath. Racing down the sidewalk, she didn't cry for help, she just kept running, her sneakers pounding out a beat on the pavement.

A side stitch doubled her over and she leaned against a tree, she didn't know where. She had to stop and get her bearings. But first, she called Gray.

THE LANDLINE on the desk rang, startling him. He exchanged eye contact with his brothers, frozen.

Jasper shrugged. "Answer it."

"Hello?"

"Gray, it's me, Cherish."

His grip on the phone tightened. He could barely hear her. "Cherish, oh my God, where are you?"

"I don't have much time. I got away from Hastings. I don't know where I am, but I think I'm somewhere east of Damen Station. I hope I did the right thing by calling the hotel phone. You said your cell wasn't safe."

"Good move. Stay out in the open. Stay away from the cops. Mingle in crowds. You'll be a little safer that way. I'm coming now. My brothers are with me."

"Okay." Her voice shook and he wanted to reach through the phone and hold her close.

"We're not far from you. I'll be right there."

"Ask her if she knows where they had her," Rhys whispered.

"I'm sorry, I have just one question before I hang up. Do you know where Hastings was keeping you?"

"At a vacant apartment building near here, west of Damen Station."

"Got it." Silence stretched between him and Cherish. There was so much to say but no time. "Did they hurt you?"

"I'm okay. Be careful. Gray, they mean to hurt us both, you know."

"I'm not going to give them the opportunity."

He hung up and stared out the window. "Cherish is safe. For now." A rolling boil bubbled in his gut. He pounded his fist once on the desk. "I am so sick of these criminals. I've had their threat hounding me too long." He faced Rhys and Jasper.

"Then let's end this." Jasper nodded. "We know where their hideout is. We have an idea where Cherish is. What are we waiting for?"

"Hold on, little brother." Rhys slapped Jasper on his back. "What are you thinking, going in that basement guns blazing? We don't have guns and these are some majorly bad guys with guns."

"We don't have time to debate this." Gray stuffed his cellphone in his jeans' pocket and pulled his Tiger's cap low over his eyes. "Are you coming?"

Rhys stepped in front of Gray. "Wait. We don't all need to go to Cherish."

"Right. You go find her. Bring her here, then finish your damn story. Rhys and I will track down Hastings and his buddies and call the cops."

"That's the problem. We can't call the police. They can't be trusted." Gray drummed his fingers, rat-ta-tat-tat, on the desk, clawing at the roadblock that was police corruption.

"There has to be someone we can get help from, even just temporarily." Rhys scrubbed the back of his neck.

A thought sparked in Gray's memory. "There is. Nathan Orlando, the civil rights lawyer who prosecuted Hastings." He quickly scrolled through his cellphone. "Here's his number. Call him, tell him I gave you his number, fill him in. Maybe he can call the FBI."

"Got it. You go get Cherish," Jasper said. "We'll go get the bad guys."

Gray opened the door. "Keep me informed," he called, heading out. Dangerous thugs, uncertainty of where to find them, and corrupt cops. It seemed an impossible feat ahead of him and his brothers. But he had to believe the odds were in their favor, somehow.

UNFAMILIAR FACES all around her kept Cherish on alert. One here, one there looked like Abner or Hastings himself.

Great, now I'm hallucinating.

Maybe the Gang hadn't notice she was gone. She walked into and joined groups of people, ignoring their pointed looks, her head down. What was it called? Hiding in plain sight. That's what she was doing.

Rachel would never believe she was being chased by murderous crooks Her sister didn't know she was in Chicago, even. A lump rose in her throat thinking of Rachel, what she meant to her, that she might not see her again.

Sirens blared by and lights flashed. Did it mean anything? Had someone been shot? Was it Gray or one of his brothers?

She stopped in the middle of the sidewalk, and people thronged around as if she were a rock in a river. That kind of thinking was not helping. She stomped her foot. "I'm so sick of being helpless," she declared to no one in particular.

"What miss? Are you okay?" asked a passing man. The only person who noticed her.

She smiled. "Yes, thank you for asking."

He frowned and continued his path.

She got in step with a group of three women chattering brightly. Her eyes straightforward, she pulled into herself. Walking, walking, for her life, that's all her mind would focus on.

Suddenly, she gasped. She saw him. Hastings. He was coming in her direction. She pivoted and headed to the first open business she saw. She stood still, staring at the reflection in the large window of the scene behind her. Her breath came in short pulls. Despite summer heat, her fingers turned icy. Twisting to check on Hastings was the last thing she should do. She knew that. But her nerves stretched too thin strings, ready to snap.

Quickly, she glanced in the direction she had first seen him. Her eyes darted around the crowds. Maybe he hadn't seen her and just walked by. It was possible she'd missed him.

Then he was there, mere yards away and his eyes were on her.

Darting inside the gallery, Cherish threaded through the main exhibit, almost running but not so it would attract attention. The space was scented with spicy candles and they sucked the air out of the room.

She spied a large, stone sculpture that took up an entire corner of the room. That might work. She slid behind the piece and pulled her cell to her lips. She pressed Gray's number and prayed. *Please answer, Gray.* Her heart pounded so loudly in her ears she could hardly hear herself breathe.

"Cherish?"

"Oh, God. Yes, it's me," she whispered. "Hastings found me."

"**W**here are you?"

If Gray himself couldn't be at her side right now, at least she had his soothing voice. "I'm inside an art gallery east of the station."

Footsteps slowly drew closer and she held her breath. It could be anybody, somebody shopping for art. Or it could be Hastings.

"Cherish, what's the name of the gallery? Is someone close?"

She nodded her head.

"You can't talk. I get it. I'll wait."

"Come here," a woman said. "I want you to see this painting."

The footsteps moved away from her, and Cherish let out her breath. "I don't know the name. It has an awning and big windows. It's east of the station. Oh, I wish I could tell you." She closed her eyes tightly. "I think I ran past a Starbucks."

"Stay put if you can. I'll find you. Be right there."

Cherish thought he'd disconnected. "Gray, Gray are you there?" There were things to say.

"Yes, I'm here."

"I want to tell you—"

"It's okay. We'll talk later. It's going to be okay."

"Right."

Silence rang in her ear. This was torture. Voices and approaching and retreating footsteps were pins and needles pricking her skin. Everything ached in the scrunched position she sat in behind the sculpture.

Dared she peek? Maybe she could make a run for the door.

"Are you sure you saw her? Maybe you saw someone who looked like her."

Cherish shrunk into a ball. Harvey Smith. Two of the gang were close by now, were the others nearby too?

Hastings coughed. "It was her. And she's in here somewhere. We need to sneak in the back rooms. We haven't checked there yet."

There was no mistaking Hastings' distinctive croak.

Damn it. So much for running out the door. This cat and mouse game was not what she had imagined for her trip to Chicago. How could she take control of the situation? Maybe she could create a diversion.

"We're wasting time," Harvey said. "Either we get back on the street or see if we can get into the back. Maybe she's hiding in a storeroom."

"You're right," Hastings said. "Let's go."

Footsteps walking away were her cue. Her heart fluttering in her throat, she slowly peered from behind the sculpture in time to watch the two men slip down a hall.

Casually, she stepped into the main gallery space, as though death was not on her heels, and fast-walked out the door.

After hiding in the shadows, she squinted in the bright sunlight outside the gallery. Immediately, she fell in step with a small group of women shoppers, but scanned frantically for signs of Gray. Lost in the city of Chicago was not her most pressing problem. She was a needle in a haystack. All she could do was keep searching for Gray and hoping her bright copper hair stood out.

Cherish slowed her pace to fall back and veered toward a receded door. She slipped into the darkness and hugged the wall, peering out. Gray, where you are, she called in her head.

A cab pulling up across the street to park outside the gallery grabbed her attention. Could it be Gray?

Then her heart stopped. She spotted Hastings's head above other pedestrians about a block down from the gallery. And at the same time Gray slid out of the cab and sent the cab away.

The moment froze in front of her, as the good and the bad approached a deadly collision.

She leaped from the small stoop inside the doorway and wove through traffic as fast as she could run. Her gaze riveted on Gray, she stretched her stride to reach him before Hastings did.

Mere seconds from him, Gray spied her. He headed toward her. She shook her head vigorously, and mouthed. No! No!

He shot her a quizzical look. Her insides wanted to explode. Hastings picked up his pace, marching directly for Gray.

Frantic, she pointed him out to Gray. Her sneakers pounded on the hot pavement; she stumbled into Gray's arms.

"Hastings," she breathed, "and Smith. Maybe more."

"I got you. Let's get to the L."

Gray grasped her hand and pulled her along. Her hand in his gave her feet a lilt, and she matched his pace. She dared a glance back. Hastings and Smith drove through other pedestrians, knocking them aside.

"Don't turn around, Cherish. Focus on Damen Station. It's not far now."

She put everything she had into running faster, faster. Finally, Cherish climbed the stairs with Gray just as a train was preparing to leave. He brandished his pass and quickly paid her fare, then held her hand tightly. She boarded with him just as the doors closed.

Hastings slammed his hand against the moving L. "Steele! This isn't over."

Gray, still holding her hand, led the way to a pair of seats. Cherish sat beside him, catching her breath. He wrapped his arm around her shoulders and she collapsed into him. "That was so close. I thought one of those men was going to get to you before I could."

"We got so lucky with the timing." He swept his finger down her nose. "You amaze me. I'm so glad you found a way to get free. You can tell me all about it later. Right now, I just want to keep you close and breathe."

"That sounds good to me." She jostled in his arms with the L's jerky movements. Her lids shut, Cherish savored Gray's nearness. Against his solid chest, her heartbeat relaxed to match his and her breathing slowed.

The train pulled up to the Sedgwick stop and Gray pulled her to her feet. "This is where we get off."

His muscles tensed and Cherish noticed his eyes narrow. He was on alert.

"The walk to the hotel isn't long. We need to keep our eyes open." He put his hands on her shoulders and looked down into her face. "Don't be afraid. I'm not, and I'm not going to let anyone hurt you."

She took courage from his steady gaze. He meant it. She could take care of herself, but sometimes, with a man like Gray, it was comforting to know she wasn't alone.

She stood on tiptoes and lifted her lips to his. He brushed hers softly, lingering. One kiss turned into two, then he pressed a hard, demanding kiss to her mouth and the world fell away.

"Cherish," he whispered against her lips.

"Yes?"

"We better get going."

She pulled away, collecting herself. "Oh yeah, let's get out of here."

"STAY CLOSE TO ME. I don't want to be caught unaware."

Cherish had been such a trooper, even after being held captive and barely escaping on the L. The hotel wasn't safe, but knowing she was quietly walking behind him lent him a sense of control.

Gray was surprised the Gang had given up so easily. But the situation wasn't over. He hadn't let go of Cherish's hand at any point in their sprint back to the hotel. Finally inside, he crept through the hall on the tenth floor, his nerves ready for anything.

He unlocked the room door and heaved a sigh of relief with the door locked and latched. Cherish perched on the edge of the bed, her hair tousled, her eyes wide, and her shoulders straight.

"How are you? Really?"

She slanted her head and pursed her lips. Silence ticked by, but he waited.

"I'm fine."

"Fine? How could you be fine?" He tried to be gentle, but maybe she was in some kind of shock. "But if you don't want to talk, that's okay."

"I really want to shower and put on some clean clothes. Brush my teeth." Her eyes dropped, even as she gave him a smile.

"They didn't hurt you, I mean viola..." Gray wasn't sure how to say what he wanted to say in a delicate way. Shit, there was no delicate way to ask if she had been raped.

"No Gray, nothing like that."

He sat down on the bed beside her and folded a stray lock of her hair behind her ear. "My brothers went looking for Hastings and his men at the location you gave us. With any luck, they'll have those creeps in the hands of the FBI at some point. But right now we need to move to another hotel in case the Gang comes back here. I'm sorry, showering will have to wait."

Her shoulders slumped. "Of course."

Minutes later, Gray hailed a cab out front and they climbed in with their things. "The Regency Hotel on North Wacker."

Gray twisted in his seat to keep an eye on Cherish and the traffic. Hastings or his men could have seen them leaving the Lincoln. He didn't want to be caught unaware.

He rubbed Cherish's arm. "We're okay."

"You're worried we're being followed."

"I'm not worried, just vigilant. I don't see anyone. Just to make sure, we're going to make a move in another mile or so."

She nodded. Her brow knitted, and she turned to look out her window.

He had to believe what he'd told her, that things were going to be fine. It was the only thing keeping him going because nothing, he vowed, would hurt Cherish.

The cab weaved through traffic and the blocks passed. Gray's body perched for danger. They drove south on Lake Park Avenue a few blocks until he leaned toward the driver. "Change of plans. Could you let us out here?"

The cab driver pulled to the curb and he and Cherish climbed out. He handed the fare to the driver. "Thanks!"

"What now?" Cherish asked, surveying the sidewalk.

"Let's get off this street and hail another cab." Gray took her hand and led her around a corner on another bustling street. He sighed with relief when another cab stopped within seconds.

He helped Cherish climb in and followed her. "Take us to the Fairmont Hotel on North Columbus."

"You got it," the cab driver said.

"It won't take long to get to our new place. We'll be safe there." Again, he sat so that he could watch traffic and Cherish. Adrenaline made him jittery, but he couldn't lose focus.

"I'm fine, Gray. Don't worry about me." She gave him a tight smile.

Yeah, I can see that. He didn't respond but he could see she was not so fine. She rested her head on the seat and watched out the side window, watchful.

"You guys on vacation?" the cab driver asked.

Oh swell, the driver is chatty. Gray squelched a sharp thought. "Yes. We're here to see sights. We're not sure where to start."

"You're starting with a great location. You're not far from Millennium Park, the Magnificent Mile, or Navy Pier." The driver adjusted his cap and laughed. "And don't forget to take in a ball game. Are you a Socks fan or Cubs fan?"

Cherish kept her eyes looking out the window, but chuckled. "Neither."

"Oh, you're in Chicago, you got to watch a Chicago team," the driver teased.

"You're right," Gray said. Anything to keep the driver quiet. "I let Rachel know what happened to you," he said under his breath. "I thought she should know. You have time to call her before we get to the hotel. I'm sure she's worried."

"Thank you. She's been on my mind." Cherish tried, but didn't reach Rachel and left a voicemail. "I'll call again at the hotel."

The driver pulled into the hotel's drive and stopped at the entrance. "You guys have fun."

Gray paid and ushered Cherish inside. He couldn't get her to the room fast enough.

Fifteen minutes later they took the elevator to the second floor and found their room. Inside, he breathed a sigh of relief. He dropped their bags and rested his hands on her shoulders. "Cherish, the shower's all yours. I'll give you your privacy for as long as you want it."

"Thank you. Now that I'm sitting still," she ran her gaze around the room, "and kind of safe behind a locked door, fatigue is settling in."

"Maybe a nap? But you should call Rachel. I told her what happened and she will be worried sick."

"Oh, poor Rachel. Yes, I will. But I need to clean up first."

"Of course. I know you're starving. I am too. I'm not going to leave you to get food. But I'll work something out when you're ready to eat."

"I'm not hungry. Maybe later some coffee? We could go together."

He chuckled. "You're falling asleep sitting up and talking, sweetheart."

"You're right." She carried her bag into the bathroom and a few minutes later Gray heard water running.

Thoughts picked up where he left off working on his article. He sat down at his laptop and started pounding out the rest of the story. It was easier to concentrate now with Cherish close by and safe. Still, it was five o'clock and his mind wouldn't stop interrupting with questions: where are Rhys and Jasper? Are they all right? Why hadn't they contacted him? Hell, he shouldn't but he picked up his phone and called Rhys. He needed to tell them his new location anyway.

Gray blew out a long breath waiting as the phone rang, rang, rang, then went to voicemail.

"Hey, what's happening? Call me."

His muscles tightened. What could he do if his brothers had gotten captured by Hastings' goons? Who could he call for help?

There was no one and nothing more to do but wait to hear from Rhys and Jasper. He brushed aside his annoyance and forced himself to focus.

The Gang of Four — Abner and Brock Cross, Harvey Smith, and Kane Hastings — did the dirty work, led by Hastings. But the duration and extent of their criminal behavior was possible because high-level officials participated, according to Judge Jeffrey Tessler. Tessler claims an investigator working in CPD Internal Affairs took a bribe to keep quiet.

"If Internal Affairs had done its job, those criminals within the district would never have gotten away with coercing and lying," Judge Tessler said.

He quickly answered when his phone rang.

"Gray, it's Rachel. I tried calling Cherish but she didn't answer. Is she okay, really?" Her voice trembled.

His heart went out to her. "She is okay. She was going to call you, but wanted wash up first. I'll remind her. As soon as she comes out of her bath. I'll tell her you called. I know she wants to talk to you."

"Okay. I'll be waiting to hear from her. And Gray, thank you so much for taking care of her," Rachel said between small sobs.

"You don't have to thank me." *Besides, her kidnapping was my fault.*

He returned to writing. The story needed completion so he and all involved could move on. He centered his attention and the words flowed.

But the corruption went further up in command.

The system had moving parts that all worked together. Internal Affairs couldn't have been so successful at hiding the crimes without the cooperation of Brady Paul, the district's commander. Lawrence Pasely, a dirty lawyer paid to go along with the deadly scam made another link in the chain.

Gray paused in his writing when he heard Cherish turn off the shower. A warm feeling spread in his belly, knowing she was safe, at least for now. Her well being meant as much to him as breaking the story. The two were intertwined.

She walked out of the bathroom, her hair wet and her face shiny. Dressed in a pair of tattered denim shorts and a pale blue shirt that read 'Coffee First,' she looked refreshed. "That was wonderful. I see you're working. Do you mind if I take a short nap?"

"Please do. After what you've been through, you need the rest. But Rachel called."

"Oh, I'll call her right now."

CHERISH PICKED up her cell and punched in Rachel's number.

"Cherish!" Her sister's sobs came over the phone and suddenly her own tears released. "I'm so glad to hear from you. Are you okay?"

Cherish walked into the bathroom and closed the door for privacy. "I was afraid, Rachel. I was afraid I wouldn't see you again. But I'm fine. I'm at the hotel now with Gray."

"Do you want me to come to Chicago?"

"Aww...you're the best sister. No. I have to stick around. I—" her thoughts were hard to put to words, "I need to talk with Gray. He's been so wonderful with so many things. I came to talk to him about Devin. Before he left for Chicago I told him I was going back with Devin. I had to come here and tell him the truth about Devin and the blog post and Mom and Dad. He's easy to talk to and he's been a good friend."

"So much has happened. Are you sure it's over with Devin?"

"Absolutely sure. I don't know how I didn't see him for what he was."

"I do. Dad and Mom took you over." Rachel blew her nose. "Now that you're getting your freedom, you need to trust yourself. You'll figure it out, sis."

Cherish let out a breath. "Thanks for the support. I have to talk to Dad and Mom. And I have cases waiting for me. So much to think about."

"Just think about one thing at a time. Trust your instincts. They are good."

"Maybe. I better let you go."

"I'm so happy you're okay. And actually, you sound better than I think I've heard in a while. Love you."

"Love you." Cherish hung up feeling stronger. Her sister gave her things to hold on to, to think about. She now had actual choices, and she intended to make them deliberately.

Feeling more relaxed, she walked into the room and sat on the bed. Gray was busy at his laptop. "Gray, do you mind if I nap now?"

He turned around looking a bit distracted. "No, I'll try to keep it down." He turned back to his story.

"Thank you. I'm so tired I don't think I'll hear anything." She climbed in and slipped off her shorts under the blanket, nestling in. She watched Gray at work, warmth spreading throughout her body. It comforted her to hear his fingers hit the keys and see his solid body not far away. He'd been such a rock and she didn't know how she'd have gotten through the ordeal with Hastings if Gray hadn't been the strong man he was.

Her lids fluttered, but she kept her gaze on Gray. Completely unaware that she was watching, he ran his fingers through his hair and muttered to himself.

Her eyes closed, but she heard his words.

"No, that's not right. Geez."

She smiled to herself at his frustration. She knew from his blogging that the article he was working on would be elegant and moving. How would a love letter from him read? It wouldn't be clichéd or trite. She pulled in a deep breath, words of love he might write drifting through her mind.

. . .

GRAY CHECKED THE TIME, wondering what Rhys and Jasper were doing. Frustration balled in his chest. He was in the dark and he had no way to know if his brothers were okay. All he could do was write.

The story was laying out blow by blow. Emotions stirred for the judge. He felt bad that his family would learn about the man they thought they knew. But fact was Tessler had made terrible choices and innocent people were sentenced to prison in his court. The truth needed to come out for Chicago area residents to be able to trust their police department and justice system.

He continued where he'd left off, writing to the backdrop of Cherish's soft breathing. It had taken only minutes for her to crash.

But Tessler admitted, he too was involved in carrying out the final step. He cooperated by accepting manufactured evidence, false confessions, and false witnesses' testimony.

"I regret my part in the machine that hurt many lives," Tessler said.

He believes the former detectives are no longer active.

"All that business is over. I'm not involved in any criminal activity now, and those cops are gone," he said.

But as new evidence has surfaced that the corruption continues under the influence of the Gang of Four, Tessler said he is willing to do what he can to see justice prevail. He said the early release from prison of the head of the gang, Kane Hastings, suggests an under the table deal should be investigated.

Gray jumped when his phone jangled. It was Rhys. "Hey." He kept his voice low so not to disturb Cherish. Stretched out on the bed, she looked sound asleep.

"We got the bastards." Rhys was breathless. "I'll tell you about it when I see you."

Relief sighed through Gray. "I can't wait. I moved to another hotel. I'm at the Fairmont Hotel on North Columbus."

"We're on our way."

"Hey, Rhys?"

"Yeah?"

"Are you and Jas all right?"

"We're fine. No worries. How's Cherish doing?"

"I don't know yet. Not really. We haven't talked much. She called her sister and now she's lying down."

"Good. Those things will help her recover."

Gray disconnected and twiddled his thumbs, his brain firing off impatience. Waiting, waiting, waiting. He'd put his life on hold to escape the threat of death in Chicago, and the daily wait began for danger to show up. Waiting even a little longer for his brothers to get to the hotel, for Cherish to tell him everything she needed to about her ordeal, to see Hastings and the Gang meet up with justice stretched too long.

Still, he had no choice but to wait more.

He ran his gaze over Cherish's body covered with a blanket and his thoughts took solace in her presence. He started imagining climbing under the covers with her and running his hands over her slim curves, and his pulse jumped. He breathed in slowly to calm himself, but his mind took him to her side, in his thoughts, nuzzling into her neck, savoring its warmth and softness, savoring her soapy scent.

Oh boy. Simmer Gray. These are not just-friends thoughts. No, they weren't. But his attraction was genuine, he'd simply kept it below the radar. Now, with the danger Cherish had suffered and the possibility of losing her had been brought up close, his heart wanted to hang on tight and reach for more.

He ran his hand over his mouth and dragged his gaze away, refocusing on the text of his article on the screen. He stared at it unseeing. Softly behind him he heard Cherish breath in and out in her sleep. The steady rhythm punctuated the reality of her nearby presence, safe and sound. A smile lifted his lips.

A soft rap at the door stopped him mid-thought. Cherish stirred, so he went to the door to check it out before she awakened.

His tension dropped, and he opened the door, shushing Rhys and Jasper. "Cherish is sleeping," he said, and stepped into the hall, holding the door ajar a crack. "I'm so glad to see you. I'm glad you found the hotel all right."

"Man, do we have a story to tell you," Jasper said. His face was smudged with dirt, but his grin was full and satisfied.

"You're both okay?"

"Yup." Rhys lifted his cap and peeked around Gray. "Our job is done. Are you going to let us in?"

"Yes, but would you do me a huge favor first?"

"Another one?" Jasper lifted his brows. "Don't you think taking care of your thugs was huge enough for one day?"

Gray chuckled at the teasing and pulled his card from his wallet. "I'll buy you food. Cherish hasn't eaten at all today, and I haven't eaten in a while. I've lost track of time. Pick up something for us, please, and whatever you two want."

"So you'll let us in when we come back with food?" Jasper grinned. "That's the price of admission?"

Gray ruffled his hair. "Cherish will probably be awake then, so of course you can come in."

Weariness dragged on his bones, but determination to finish his story took him back to his laptop. Everything but the story receded. He wanted to know what Rhys and Jasper had worked out to corral the Gang, but he didn't need to know now. He just needed to tell the story of the crimes, the criminals, and the need for constant oversight of the justice system.

Finally, Gray felt the charge of the story inside him begin to relax as he proofed the text and sent the final version to Eric.

He stretched his arms over his head and yawned.

"Did I hear your brothers arrive?"

The sound of Cherish's voice elicited a smile. "Hi, sleepyhead. Feeling better?"

"I'm starving." Her eyes sparkled, provoking his heart to do flip-flops.

"Rhys and Jasper have gone to fetch food." He checked the time. "It may take them some time, depending on where they decide to go."

Cherish smiled wide and her eyes sparkled with mischief. "Join me?"

The unexpected invitation surprised him. "Really?" Excitement stuttered his heart.

She lifted the covers off exposing her bare legs and underwear. She grinned. "Please."

It was heady stuff, and Gray didn't waste any time weighing shoulds and should nots. He slipped off his shorts and slipped beside her. The touch of her skin against his sent his heart racing. But he held back, cautious. Were they truly going to move past friendship into *this*?

Cherish rolled closer to him and laid her head on his chest. "This is nice. I feel so comfortable beside you. After all the drama of the last few days and the fear of what could happen, it feels right to lie here just being alive and safe. With you." She lifted her head and grazed his heart with her beautiful green eyes full of tenderness. No matter what happened next, even if nothing, this moment would always remain in his heart.

He smoothed her copper curls away from her face. "You're really something."

"What do you mean?"

"It's so easy to be with you. It was from the beginning. And what you said, well, I feel the same." His voice got hoarse for some reason, and the space between their eyes got electric.

Cherish lifted off his shirt, then wriggled out of her top, exposing her sweet breasts.

God, this was definitely more than friend behavior. He couldn't take his eyes off her, as she pressed her body against him and brought her mouth to within nanobreaths of his.

"Did you lock the door?" she asked, a twinkle in her eyes.

"It locks automatically."

"Good."

He placed his hands on both sides of her head and drew her closer. Her felt her breasts lying intimately against his chest and his insides yearned for more. His lips met her lips and he kissed her gently, once, twice, then he pressed a hard kiss to her mouth, his tongue diving in to taste of her and she reciprocated.

When she pulled back, he swallowed hard, not quite believing what was happening. This was Cherish in his arms, half-naked. The Cherish he'd been keeping himself in check around, always refraining from letting his mind wander too far from strictly friendship, strictly platonic imaginings.

"That was nice," she said. "Let's do it again."

He laughed, then rolled her over onto her back and began showering kisses to her head, her neck, her nipples.

"Come back," she pleaded.

He kissed her lips hard again, unleashing his pent up longing. Hers was the most delicious mouth he could ever dream of, and if he only ever kissed her lips this once, he would die a happy man, he was certain.

She sighed and rolled onto her back. "I'm sorry. I have to stop."

"Is something wrong? Did I do something wrong?" He must have for her to withdraw so abruptly.

"No, not at all. It was very nice. I probably shouldn't have asked you to get in bed with me. We have things to talk about, don't we?"

"That sounds ominous."

"I don't know what I'm feeling right now, Gray. So much has happened so quickly."

His gut contracted. She was right. "Are you having second thoughts about what we just did? I'm not going to pressure you for anything you're not interested in." Those words were required, he knew that. He meant them. But he did not feel them in his heart.

"I don't want to blindly move from one relationship to another." Her eyes pleaded with him. "I've taken steps to create my own life, and I don't want to follow my old patterns into a relationship with you if it's not right."

"I don't want you to do that either," he said, dressing. "You did come all the way to Chicago to talk to me. So let's talk. Put our cards on the table and see what we have." Deflated, that's what he was, but she had the need so he would respect it.

"Thank you. I think I need that."

He held up his fist. "Friends?"

She knocked her fist against his, smiling. "Friends."

Cherish watched Gray roll away, her heart swirling like a revolving door. Did she want in or out? She hadn't missed the dispirited droop in his eyes and parts of her wanted to get over her fear of being lost again and pull him back to her side.

But not all of her was willing. He'd seen her need to know for certain she could make her own way, and that was so what she wanted. It was the only way she could truly be whole and in a meaningful relationship. Being an individual was precious. Gray had helped her learn that.

She pulled on her clothes and she relaxed into watching him check his email, admiring him for the special man he was. He was strength, he was courage, and he was compassion and insight. Her heart throbbed, aching to tell him all that was in her heart. Just not until she knew for certain it wasn't a passing passion or reflex action to lean on him.

Without turning around, he read her the email from Eric.

"'Great story. It's going in today's evening edition. It's going to grab attention. I hope you're prepared.'"

"Congratulations. I'm proud of you, Gray. Do you need to be worried about ramifications?"

He turned his chair to face her. "I don't think there will be any death threats this time. This story reveals all parties involved, and hopefully will prevent officers like Austin from getting deeply involved. At least I've done my part."

"Your work is so important. I don't believe I've thought too much about the importance of the press before." Admiration for him bubbled out of her spontaneously. She could get used to having a close friend who didn't commit crimes.

"Thank you." He turned back to his laptop. "I have to respond to Eric. There are other factors now he needs to know for a follow-up."

"What factors?"

"I'm going to find out more as soon as Rhys and Jasper get back."

From the other side of the door, she heard familiar voices. They made her smile, and she opened the door to find Jasper, Rhys, and Gray all talking at the same time.

"Do I smell food?" she asked. "Where's mine?"

"You're up. Does that mean we can enter your domain?" Jasper teased.

"As long as you have food for me."

Cherish chomped on the deli sandwich and sweet potato fries Gray's brothers had brought her, quietly listening to Rhys and Jasper's account of securing the Gang. Like Gray, they seemed so self-assured. The way the three men interacted awed her. It was like they had such a brotherly connection that they could read each other's minds, completing one another's sentences, and filling in pauses.

"Cherish, your directions were spot on and it didn't take us long to find the vacant building." Rhys took a bite of his sandwich and Jasper took over the story.

"The problem was getting inside. But the building was old and deteriorating. We shoved hard against a door at the back of the building. It was in bad shape and just gave in."

"Nobody heard you break down the door?" Gray rubbed his chin, thoughtful.

"Nobody came running." Jasper walked in exaggerated tiptoe.

"We were stealthy. We walked around until we found a basement door that wasn't locked."

Gray smiled. "Very funny. I told you these men were dangerous. I hope you didn't get overconfident."

"No worries." Jasper gave him a dismissive wave. "We were very careful. Besides, you're interrupting the story."

"The unlocked door to their hiding spot was odd, so we were very vigilant. We didn't want any surprise." Rhys took a sip of his bottled water. "In fact, we could hear the men arguing through the door."

"It makes me cringe just hearing how close you got to them." Cherish shivered. "When I was there, they were very volatile. I couldn't see it because my eyes were blindfolded, but it sounded like one man was whooping another guy for stealing an extra beer."

"I don't doubt it. They were some rough men. So that was the point when we called the lawyer you told us about, Gray. You were right. When we talked to him before we went in, he hooked us up with a contact at the FBI." Rhys talked through a bite of food. "He got there just minutes before the agents, thankfully. But some cops showed up too. One of the cops, a young guy, tried to interfere."

"Yeah, four squad cars and four officers showed up, including the young guy named Austin." Jasper took a bite of his sandwich.

"Austin's uncle is one of the original Gang of Four," Cherish added.

Rhys nodded. "Yes, we learned that Austin was not on the up and up when he tried to get the FBI agents to leave and let him handle the scene. The lawyer dealt with his lack of cooperation, demanding to speak with Austin's sergeant. So the Gang is in jail. Austin wasn't arrested but he was suspended and is under investigation. And you two need to give your statements."

Cherish glanced at Gray, noting his eyes flashing and knew why.

"You didn't give the CPD our location, did you?" he asked.

Rhys shook his head. "Give us some credit, bro. Of course not. That's why you have to contact the agency as soon as possible."

"The lawyer, Orlando, promised to make sure you follow through," Jasper added. "He made the case that you've already been followed, threatened, and kidnapped, so it was prudent to keep your location secret."

Cherish exchanged a glance with Gray, looking for assurance. Did he understand it had been a couple of scary days? The idea of going to the FBI at this hour made her skin crawl.

Without breaking eye contact, Gray smiled. "I'll call Orlando and make arrangements to meet him there tomorrow."

Cherish blew out a quiet breath. "That sounds very right to me. Having representation with us would be reassuring." She pulled her knees up to her chest. "I don't know how to thank you two. You put your lives at risk."

Jasper rubbed the back of his neck. "He is our brother. And he seems to like you, so you're as good as family. Besides, those guys are a menace and we didn't do very much."

"Wish we could take down all those crooked cops," Rhys said. "Michigan has their fair share too, but nothing like what Gray has unearthed here — nice job bro."

Jasper shot them a snarky grin. "Of course, we helped, right? Gray, Cherish, you can thank us later."

Cherish couldn't breathe. Although he said it in jest, Jasper was right about the size of the deadly problem they encountered in Chicago.

Gray lunged at Jasper and got him in a chokehold. "Don't listen to this guy, Cherish. He has picked a really inappropriate way to joke."

"Sorry." Jasper said as Gray let go. "I didn't mean that at all," he said, directing a sheepish look at Cherish. "I was trying to get a rise out of Gray."

"So you're stressed. I get it." Gray wrapped his arm around Jasper again and they tousled some more for a couple seconds.

Rhys sighed heavily and turned his attention on Cherish. "I'm happy you're safe. You handled yourself very well. You probably saved your own life and Gray's, as well as helped put the Gang in jail."

Unease wriggled through her. She wasn't used to such high praise, especially one free of a 'but, you could have done better'."

Being around the Steeles Cherish was realizing how much

Devin's off putting remarks affected her. These men reminded her of who she was, who she's always been. She needed that and was thankful for it.

"Thank you. I'm so relieved to be here, alive."

Gray sat beside her, about a foot away. He gave a half-grin. It triggered confusion in her for a split second. Then she realized he wasn't distancing from her, he was complying with her wishes for space. Instinctively, she reached for his hand. "Thank you."

Gray relaxed. "We need to talk."

"Well, Jasper, that is our cue to take off." Rhys clapped his hand on his brother's knee.

"Yup, let's get going."

Not a whisper of awkwardness between them. But warmth still spread up Cherish's neck.

"You don't have to leave. I wasn't suggesting anything. It's going to be late when you get back to Dunes Bay."

"I know, but we can handle it. My adrenaline is still high." Rhys nodded. "Our work is done here."

"Really, why are you still here?" Gray teased. He slapped a hug on each brother. "I hate to admit it, but you guys are the best."

Jasper's expression sobered. Cherish stood apart to give Gray and his brothers a moment of privacy.

"When are you coming home?" Jasper asked. "There's a boat waiting for you to finish. Mom and Dad are happiest when the whole family is near."

"Jasper, stop pressuring," Rhys said. "Gray, you do what's right for you. That is what Mom and Dad would want."

Gray tapped his shoe against the desk legs and stared at the floor. "I don't know." He lifted his gaze. "I'll be in touch when I know what's happening next."

Jasper grimaced. "I understand. The big city offers you more opportunities as a journalist. I just miss you."

The moment between Gray, Jasper, and Rhys touched her heart like a mini-tsunami. Their relationship was clean, supportive, even sacrificial. Did she have that with her family? With Rachel, yes. But their family framework was based on demanding and oppressive love.

It had always been that way, but recently she'd allowed it to change, to get the best of her and she wasn't sure when that happened...maybe it was when she started dating Devin. She'd been blind to the man he really was.

"Bye Cherish, see you back in Dunes Bay, I hope." Jasper waved walking out the door with Rhys behind him.

"See you." Rhys tipped his cap. "Have a safe trip home."

Alone in the room with Gray, Cherish collapsed on the bed. "Ugh, that was hard."

"Jasper wasn't trying to make me feel bad. He was simply expressing himself. We both understand that."

Gray's point streamed through her, awakening new possibilities in relationships. "Right. I have to let that sink in."

"And he and Rhys were expressing their interest in being your friends. You don't owe them anything. They like you, that's all. There is no pressure to befriend them." His voice dropped. "Or me."

Her heart expanded. How could she not want his friendship? "We are friends, in my mind." She walked to the couch and motioned him to sit with her.

"We started out as strangers that day at the restaurant. We both were tied up with reasons that, for me, meant that encounter was a one-time thing." He slanted his head. "But I was drawn to you. I wanted to help you and support you. Then I wanted to be with you. Be more than simply friends, but you were still involved in many things that presented obstacles. But we can still be friends, Cherish, and only friends. Maybe best friends. Enjoy your freedom fully. I am happy for you."

His gleaming blue eyes held genuine and unselfish joy.

"I've never known anyone like you. I'm amazingly lucky you're my friend." A sob caught in her throat.

"I feel the same way." He nodded. "I'll call the lawyer, get the scoop from him and schedule a time we can give our statements. Then I'll take you home."

"I can take the train. You can stay ... here." She cleared her throat, covering for a lump.

"No, I'll take you. It will make a nice drive and give us both time to let go of the chaos that happened here."

$\mathscr{B}$ehind him Gray heard Cherish flip through television channels. He stared out the window at the Chicago skyline, his thoughts drifting from one topic to another, but fell under the same category–what do I do with my life now? His mind sounded like a line in the movie *Rainman*—"Stay with Charlie Babbett, go back to Wallbrook"—only his line was *Go back to Dunes Bay. Stay in Chicago.*

Getting in stride with the pace of the city and the all-in of investigative reporting had been like getting back on a bicycle. He loved writing. He loved the thrill of reporting. But it hadn't possessed him as it had before he left. This time it was more about not dying and protecting Cherish than the thrill of investigating and writing.

He turned back and watched Cherish. Her long legs stretched out bare and silky. Inviting. But his feelings for her went so much deeper than appreciation for her physical appearance. Despite the hard cards she'd been dealt, she had persevered, come alive in her own right, and for all that, she'd brought out the best in him. He ran his fingers through his hair, wondering, what did that mean in the big picture of his life?

"Gray, why are you staring at me?" Cherish asked.

"Oh, I was lost in thought. I didn't realize I was staring." Sort of true.

She arched her eyebrows. "What were you thinking?"

He gave her a sheepish look. "Honestly, you."

"Me? What about me?"

"How you changed my life so much and I'm not sure what to do about it, if anything." Now that was honest. Maybe a little too honest.

"You know that's true for me too. You've changed my life in ways I never could have seen coming." She pouted her lips just a tad.

She didn't mean anything sexual by it, he knew she was just thinking. But all he could think of suddenly was those lips. Adrenalin pushed reason aside, and he strode to her and pulled her to her feet.

"GRAY?" was all she got out.

He grabbed her face and swept her up in a hard, demanding kiss. Passion overwhelmed her senses and all she knew was his touch, his lips, his warmth, and that she wanted more.

He pulled away, his eyes steamy, looked over her face, her hair, into her eyes. "You're so beautiful. How did I keep my hands off you before?"

She nuzzled into the nook under his chin and breathed in his scent. It was fresh air and summer, and she couldn't get enough of it. "You smell so good."

Gray lifted her into his arms and carried her to the bed. It was already rumpled. He laid her down among the folds of sheets and blankets and his scent surrounded. Her breaths deepened, and all of her body's senses heightened.

"This is okay?" he whispered and slipped one hand over her bra.

She reacted, twisting under his caresses. "Uh huh."

He tore her shirt over her head and make quick work of removing her bra. Everything in her tingled, writhing under the touch of his mouth on her breasts, her stomach, her thighs. Oh my God. She moaned, unwilling to tap down her body's responses.

"Take off your clothes." She wanted to watch him reveal every portion of his body.

He stood and swiftly unbuckled his belt and started shoving down his pants toward his hips.

"No, slowly." She ran her tongue over her lips, craving to kiss the bow of his hips, the bulge of his muscled thighs. His bare chest was broad and solid. She ran her hand over the taut muscles of his chest and midriff.

"Okay, your turn." He stared at her, swiping the back of his hand over his mouth.

She wriggled out of her Bermuda shorts and let them drop to the floor.

"Wait." Gray stood and pressed his naked body against hers, fingering the edges of her underwear and slowly, achingly slowly, he inched it down and she kicked it off.

She gasped, standing skin to skin, all her nerves firing. He pulled her down on top of him, pushing his face between her breasts. He took one nipple in his mouth, then the other, driving her insane with desire.

But he didn't stop. He trailed kisses down, down until he reached between her legs and pleasure sparked like fireworks. She raked her fingers through his thick hair and inched away from him to kiss his hardness.

Her eyes met his. Glazed, with wide pupils, his eyes closed and he groaned. He grabbed her ankles and yanked her beneath him. She couldn't lie still, and moved under him, wanting to feel every bit of him. From their first meeting, Gray had accepted everything she truly was. *This.* This unabashed expression of her desire was truly alive. No shyness or sense of propriety came between her and what she wanted. *Him.*

Luckily, she planned ahead when she left Dunes Bay, and she motioned to her purse.

"Protection?" He smiled, and handed her the purse.

The wait was seconds but she wanted to tear at the sheets until he was back with her.

He moved against her, pressing himself to her thigh, then teasing her intimately. She wiggled under him and rose to pull him close.

Gray kissed her hard, darting his tongue deep into her mouth. He thrust inside her and she wrapped tightly around him.

His movements caught Cherish's breath. Her thoughts silenced. She arched to meet him, body to body, taking everything he had while giving all that she was.

Frantic, she heard herself whimper as though from a different place. "Gray, I'm going to explode," she whispered.

He groaned, low, tender, thrusting faster, faster, harder, harder.

Her body trembled as he quivered inside her. She was helpless under his touch. Ecstatic pulsing streamed through her, connecting her with Gray in the most intimate way. Climax against climax burst between her and him.

"Oh God," Gray breathed.

Cherish kissed his glistening cheek, entirely relaxed. His breath still heavy in her ear made soothing music. She wanted his body completely spent and heavy on top of her, to just stay. In this moment she was fulfilled. She had everything she could ever want.

Gray looked down at her through strands of his hair fallen in his face. "Cherish, Cherish."

"Yes?"

He kissed her as though in worship. "There are no words for what just happened."

She smiled at him not responding verbally.

"Okay, that might sound weird." Gray thought of taking back his comment, maybe it was just him who felt the earth move.

Her eyes misted. "No, not weird at all. It was that way for me too." She closed her eyes, stirred in a way she'd never been before.

Gray didn't say anything, but he nodded, knowing.

He eased off her and cocooned them together in a rumpled sheet. Cherish rested her head on his outstretched arm and traced the lines of his taut muscles. "Can we stay here, just the two of us? There's nothing outside this room I need." She waited for him to laugh, but right now here was enough.

"That sounds perfect. He sighed and kissed her forehead. "Things are so easy here with you."

Cherish didn't say anything. She just lay still beside him, listening to his heart beat. Thud, thud, thud thud. The sound made her happy in a way she couldn't remember. Lovemaking had happened so effortlessly, so naturally. It had to be right. Maybe their timing was now.

34
_____

Gray didn't know how long he and Cherish had been lying still just resting and absorbing the moment, but a pounding on the door elicited his reflex reaction. He jumped out of bed and grabbed his clothes.

Her eyes wide, she whispered. "I wonder who that is?"

Another short rap. "Gray, it's me, Eric."

"Coming." Sheepish, he dressed while Cherish picked up her things and hurriedly pulled them on. "Sorry. I overreacted I guess I'm still a little jumpy."

She laughed, the tinkling bells sound that made him happy inside. "So did I."

Gray opened the door. "Eric, come in. Cherish, this is my editor Eric Lee, Eric, this is Cherish Moss."

He shook Cherish's hand. "Nice to meet you, alive and well?"

"Definitely alive, and very well."

Eric unfolded a newspaper and slapped it on the desk. "There it is, front page, lead story."

Gray looked at the large type of the headline. It blared like an announcement from a circus ringmaster. "Chicago Police Corruption of the Past Spawns a New Generation," he read. "I thought you'd rewrite my headline."

"Nope. You did sort of bury the lede, but I liked how you handled the story. You told the hard facts but you didn't crucify the whole CPD. Great job."

"Thanks. I try."

Eric rolled his eyes. He glanced at Cherish, then back at Gray. "You're my top reporter. Would you consider coming back to *The Daily Banner*? The death threats are eliminated."

He had given it a thought. But now, after what he and Cherish shared things were different for him. "I'll consider it. I want to go back to Dunes Bay and see my family, get out of the city and ponder."

"Is this going to be a 'random ponder' or a specific, do-you-want-to-take-my-job-offer ponder?"

Gray looked at Cherish, sitting huddled in a chair reading the newspaper. Clearly she was opting to stay out of the conversation, feigning being absorbed by a story.

"Well?" Eric prodded. "Why do you keep looking at Cherish? Does she have something to do with your decision?"

Cherish kept her eyes down, as though she hadn't heard what Eric said.

"Man, that was rude. I looked at her because we're standing here talking work right in front of her as though she is invisible. That too is rude. Can't this conversation wait?"

Eric shoved a hand in his pants pocket and gave him a weak smile. "Sorry." He moved toward Cherish and got her attention. "I'm sorry for ignoring you. If you know Gray very well, you know us newspaper reporters can be quite insistent."

"Don't worry about me. I'm just reading Gray's article. You're right. He's a good writer." She looked at Gray and surprised him with what appeared to be admiration, tinged in sorrow.

"Okay, I'm going to take off," Eric said. "When I get back to the office I'm going to email you a list of broadcast reporters interested in a follow-up to your story. This story is big, and national network news want interviews. Do what you want, but I would think you should at least talk to some of them. The story and the way you've been treated, as well as her treatment," he motioned toward Cherish, "is a first-hand account of policing gone bad."

"Send me the list, but I don't know if it will work out. The FBI may want to keep a lid on the case, you know, not taint the jury pool. But I could ignore their wishes. People have the right to know what's been going on."

"Don't worry. I'll square it with the FBI just to let them know you're going to give pertinent details in the interview but with descresion."

Gray gave him the thumbs up. "Sounds good. Oh, and thank you for the paper and letting me complete my series. It means a lot to me."

"I'm the grateful one. Chicagoans owe you, Gray." He headed out into the hall. "Don't forget me."

Gray latched the door and turned around to almost run into Cherish.

"He's right, you know. You're very talented. You don't belong in little Dunes Bay." Her voice caught. "You should be changing the world for the better here in the big city."

Her words landed hard in his gut. "You don't want me in Dunes Bay?"

"That is not what I meant. Friends don't hold each other back." She glared at him through misty eyes.

"There are good writers everywhere. But thank you for your support. Let's do this: I'll trust you to know what's best for you, and you trust me to decide what works for me." He hadn't meant it to come out curt, but he let it ride. He meant what he'd said.

She nodded and pivoted to the couch. "Good advice."

His heart pounded as he checked his email. Hell, he didn't know what he should do. He knew what he wanted, but Cherish once again had made it clear friendship was all they had. He respected that. But more than that, maybe it was too soon for her to think of getting involved with him so quickly after breaking up with Devin. If she wasn't truly ready, he would have to accept it. After all, he didn't want to be simply her rebound guy.

"I've got a list of calls to make," he said over his shoulder. "We talked about meeting with Orlando tomorrow at the FBI Chicago main field office and giving our statements. Is morning okay with you, say nine-thirty?"

"Yes, the earlier the better. I want to get it over with." She scrolled her phone, engrossed with what she found there. "So much for managing client and employee expectations. I'm supposed to be on vacation, but I have a million messages."

He turned to face her. "I hope you'll be willing to do one interview with a reporter before we leave. From my perspective, the purpose of the interview is to inform, not take credit. I'd like us to give an exclusive, rather than sit down with a bunch of reporters. Stations can pick up the story from the wire service."

"I understand. Informing is what you do as a reporter. I'm open to any time tomorrow after we're done with the FBI."

Her voice was clipped, business-like. Gray let acceptance filter through him. Cherish was in business mode.

He called Orlando, and across the room he heard Cherish hash out legal things with Pansy. It seemed so long ago since she announced she was on her way to see him to talk about their relationship. And yet, the touch of her skin, the heat of her passion, the serenity of her soft breathing beside him remained as keen in his body and soul as if it just happened.

Cherish wrapped her hands around the cup an assistant something or other handed her in the green room at the television station. The hot coffee helped. The studio was so frigid Cherish's teeth verged on chattering.

"We're almost ready, so let's get you both settled at the host desk, okay?" the same young assistant said.

Gray took her hand. His touch was almost as warm as the coffee. "Let's get this over with," he said.

"I've never been on television before," she whispered.

"You've never been kidnapped before either, right?" His smile reassured her nerves.

The morning host nodded and the camera's rolled as she welcomed viewers. Cherish shivered. It was all so surreal.

Her eyes pinned on Gray, admiring the smooth way he delivered his answers to the reporter's questions.

"Your article in *The Chicago Daily Banner* asserts that the Gang of Four, as you named the crooked group of detectives, has left a legacy of corruption at the CPD that continues. What does that mean to Chicago-area residents?"

"I believe the majority of the Chicago police force are admirable, honest individuals dedicated to the law and keeping the city safe." Gray's words sounded velvety, believable. Cherish hung on them. "My job as a reporter is to inform. It's up to Chicago citizens to demand vigilance against any corruption that persists. And to hold their elected officials accountable."

The reporter addressed her. "Cherish, your ordeal was harrowing. What does it feel like to know first-hand that the very people we need to protect us tried to hurt you and Gray? Do you feel safe in Chicago?"

Cherish strained to focus on the reporter's questions, resisting replaying what happened to her. "I was terrified, I admit, to encounter such ruthless individuals." She glanced at Gray. His

face was all business, but his blue eyes shone warmly, encouraging her. "It's sad to discover their terrible influence on younger officers exists. But I believe in Chicago and its people to address the problem effectively."

Ms. Reporter narrowed her eyes. "So do you feel safe in Chicago?"

Cherish hashed her answer in her head, on the one hand, on the other hand, and dug deep

into herself to answer true to her beliefs. "No. Chicago is a complex city. There are scary

elements in the city that no one should take lightly. It requires paying attention and avoiding dangerous situations. But I love Chicago and all the wonderful things it offers, including a

professional police force."

"Thank you for your candor, Ms. Moss." Ms. Reporter dismissed Cherish with a drop of

her gaze, and a big smile for Gray. "Thank you, Mr. Steele, for your excellent article and your

bravery. You've done more than your part in exposing corruption and making Chicago safer."

"Thank you, but I just wrote a story. The real heroes are the officers who uphold the law and the fine lawyers and honest judges who champion justice."

Cherish beamed inside. Gray's words were thoughtful and humble, perfect in fact.

The reporter ended the interview, but not her attention on Gray. As he stood to go, Ms. Reporter ran her fingers down his arm and complimented him again.

Cherish had to get out or lose her blueberry pancakes on the floor. An overreaction to be sure, she knew. Hadn't she told Gray she needed space and time with no expectations of a romantic relationship?

Cherish blew out a long breath, realizing she had been sighing a lot lately. She couldn't be jealous. But she was. She had to get over it.

She strode out of the building beside Gray. "You did a great job in the interview. Very insightful, and you controlled your part of the interview," she said.

"Thank you. I'm very proud of how you handled the interview." He stopped and took hold of her shoulders. "Are you upset about something? Have I done something wrong?"

Her shoulders drooped. "No, you haven't. You were smooth, articulate, and very authoritative."

"Thanks." He rested one hand on his hip and scratched his head. "You seem abrupt."

"You know that sometimes I make a big deal of things that aren't rightly so."

His eyes warmed. He slanted his head and peered at her. "No, you don't do that, Cherish. People have told you that, but you don't. What's bothering you?"

This was Gray. He didn't disregard her, even when she felt petty and small. "Could we walk? I don't like standing here in the middle of the sidewalk."

"Of course." He strolled away from the television station at an easy pace.

She gazed upward into a mostly clear sky above skyscrapers. Fluffy white clouds drifted casually above the bustle at the street level, soothing her nerves. And Gray remained quiet. Finally, after several blocks, her thoughts congealed. "I didn't like the way the reporter was coming on to you. In fact, I didn't like it at all. It was very unprofessional."

"If it makes any difference to you, I wasn't even close to being interested in her." He continued to saunter.

"It doesn't matter. You have the right to be interested in anyone you feel like. I know that," she declared. Her voice got tiny. "I should be unaffected by her flirting."

"You think she was flirting?" His smile creased the corners of his eyes.

"Yes!" She wanted to disappear into one of those white clouds.

"I know she was flirting, but I was oblivious. I had one reason for being there and that was because my editor asked me to at least do one follow-up interview to promote the newspaper. Honestly, I was glad you were sitting with me going through that. Your part was important."

Cherish humphed. "Imagine the hard-press she might have given you if I hadn't been there." The words tumbled out unrestrained, and it felt good to have an audience of one that didn't judge.

"The bitch." He grinned.

She had to laugh.

"We can go back to the hotel to get our things and check out. What do you think about getting lunch on the way out of town?"

"Sounds good. I'm more than ready to get back home." Home was where she would be most comfortable, but her shoulders tightened as all the things on her to-do list lined up in her mind.

35

———

Gray left behind the bumper-to-bumper traffic around Chicago at one and settled into less hectic driving on the interstate that would take him home. Chicago might be the place to expand his career, but it didn't call to him as it used to.

He glanced at Cherish in the passenger seat of his truck, and smiled to himself at the way she held her mouth as she poured over the Decidedly Laboratories file. Her mind was nowhere inside the car, it was in the courtroom.

He kept quiet, letting her concentrate on her work for more than a hundred miles. The only sound was traffic noise, but it gave him time to think about family, writing, and his blog.

The landscape around the highway changed from city to rural, to more city as they drove along. At three he rubbed his eyes and yawned.

Without lifting her eyes, Cherish startled him. "What did you decide about Eric's job offer?"

His breath paused, surprised she interrupted her work. "I haven't decided anything."

She chewed on the end of her pen. "Oh."

He drove another thirty minutes in silence before she spoke again.

"You wrote about my case with the drug company on your blog." She looked at him, her head slanted. "Why?"

"I don't have a simple answer." He shifted in his seat.

"Good. Shoot."

"I've written stories about new drugs and the process they go through before being released to the public. I've interviewed drug company executives. Drug research is big money, and those who own the companies are not always the most altruistic or honest. Their priority is making money, and sometimes corners are cut during drug trials, and sometimes participants endure effects that are covered up and compensation is not given."

She nodded. "I see." She looked out the windshield, twirling her pen.

The sweet sweep of her pert nose sent his heart stuttering. Her long lashes fringed her eyes in copper the color of her gleaming hair. Maybe he couldn't be just friends with her after all.

He kept his eyes on the road and let that thought sift through him. Not talk with her, not watch her argue with him? No, he didn't want her out of his life completely. But he had to accept it was a possibility.

"Do you know that I am not a lawyer because I want an income that would support a lavish life?" She rushed on before he could answer. "I believe in justice. So the implication in your blog post about me hurt."

"The post was not personal. I stated my concerns that by hiring your firm, Decidedly Laboratories stacked all the cards in their favor. The plaintiff suffered real and unfair consequences and does not have the means to hire a flashy expensive lawyer."

"Excuse me. I am not flashy and the money doesn't make a difference in the quality of representation. I volunteer for a charity organization. I give my all to those cases, just as I do those who can pay well."

Gray knew he should just stop talking. Cherish's face was turning pink, verging on crimson.

"I believe you." He eyed her and kept quiet. They had only another forty two miles to go until they reached Dunes Bay. He didn't want to have a knockdown drag-out with Cherish. Still, it was fun to debate her.

Quietly she cleared her throat. "I'm afraid you may be right."

Gray did a double take. Okay, that was unexpected. "I didn't mean I believe all drug research companies misrepresent the safety of their trials."

"I know what you meant. You have reason to believe Decidedly Laboratories is unscrupulous. I understand now why the post about me wasn't aimed at me."

"All the same, I'm sorry it hurt you."

She just smiled, a sweet sincere smile. And sent his pulse racing again.

Gray cracked his window and pulled in a deep breath of fresh air. "We're almost to Dunes Bay. I can smell the lake already." No matter what the future held for his relationship with Cherish, they would always have their times at Lake Michigan.

Cherish started packing away her files in her briefcase. "I'm glad we're here, but I have so many things waiting for me. I almost feel like staying on the interstate and pushing through to wherever we decide to go."

His heart reached out to her. But he had learned things about Cherish while in Chicago together, and he was certain she would get through the tough conversations and the trial without the need of rescue by him or any interference from meddlesome people, such as her parents and Devin.

"You're right, the scent of lake water is in the air. I love it."

Gray took the next exit, relieved his long ordeal with Hastings and his men was behind him. His stomach growled. "It's been a long time since lunch. Would you want to stop up ahead at Dunes Bay Indian Restaurant before I take you home?"

"No, I just want to get home."

"Are you sure? You need to eat anyway."

"I know, but—"

The driver's side of the windshield shattered and Gray slumped forward against the steering wheel.

"Gray," she screamed.

Searing pain exploded in his chest. He fought blacking out, and reached out. "Cherish." He could barely speak, but he needed to know if she was okay.

"I'm here," she said.

He let go and everything went dark.

The truck swung hard to the right, throwing Cherish against the passenger door. Panic screeched in her mind, and she grabbed the steering wheel. "Gray, Gray," she hollered, but his body slumped against the door, out cold.

The truck streamed toward a ditch and she pulled at his right leg to dislodge his foot from the accelerator. She had to reach the pedal before the truck hit the ditch and rolled over.

She shoved her foot over Gray's legs and pressed down slowly on the brake. Steering to the side of the road, she brought the truck to a stop just seconds from the ditch.

But there was no time for relief. Blood streamed from Gray's chest. Adrenalin rushed through her body, and she scanned the rode for a shooter, knowing she had to stop the bleeding. She scrambled through her tote bag at her feet and yanked out her hoodie.

"Gray, Gray, you're going to be all right." She had to believe it was true, she just had to. "You're bleeding, so I'm going to press on your wound."

Gently, she pulled him back against the seat. She suppressed a gasp. If he could hear her, she didn't want to alarm him. But the wound was bleeding badly. Her fingers trembled as she unbuttoned his shirt and pressed her hoodie against a small hole in his upper chest.

She flipped on the four-ways, hoping to get a passerby's attention. She couldn't leave Gray, not the way he was bleeding and unconscious. Her phone was in her tote bag, but it was out of reach. Damn it! She had to let up on Gray's wound in order to get it. Everything was happening so fast, while time stood still.

"Gray, stay with me, Gray." Her fingers fumbled through her bag. "Come on, come on, where are you?" Panic fired her nerves. Finally, she touched the shape that was her phone. With it in her hands, she slid back to Gray's side.

"Miss, please step out of the car."

Her heart jolted. A cop stood at her window, his hat pulled low. "Officer, can you help me? Please, he's been shot." Thank God a passing driver must have called the police.

Nothing was happening. She looked back at her window and into the barrel of a rifle.

"Out of the car."

"But Officer, this man is hurt."

"I know. I shot him. And if you don't get out, I'll do the same to you, Cherish."

Her heart dropped. He knew her. The voice, she should know it. "All right, I'm coming out." Her heart aching for Gray, Cherish got out and stood before the officer.

He shoved back his hat and laughed at her reaction. "Hello, Cherish. I bet you didn't expect to see me again."

"Austin," she breathed. "You shot Gray. You shot Gray. How is this possible?" She fisted her hands, wanting so much to pound his chest silly. It dawned her how, remembering he hadn't been arrested. "You weren't in enough trouble? You had to follow us to Dunes Bay?" Her mind a flurry, her breaths were shallow and quick.

"No, I got here before you. I've been waiting. I knew I'd run into you two eventually."

Keep him talking, Cherish. "You're not going to get away with this. You're in Dunes Bay jurisdiction, remember. No one is going to help you evade justice." She traced her fingers over her phone in her pocket. All she had to do was hold the side button and volume at the same time, and cross her fingers that her pocket would muffle the alert.

"Excuse me, I have accomplished my goal. I shot your boyfriend." He pulled zip ties from his pocket.

"Help! Help!" Cherish hollered with all her breath and kicked him. She screamed like she'd never screamed before.

He clapped his hand over her mouth and dragged her to the ground. "Keep your mouth shut, or I'll silence you for good."

He tightened the ties around her wrists. What did he have in store for her? "Why wait? If you're so hot to kill me and Gray, what are you waiting for? Why tie me up?"

"I'm going to make good on the promise Hastings made to kill Gray." His eyes darkened. "People like you and Gray shouldn't meddle in police business. Gray is done for. He's written his last exposé. But you, you may be worth keeping alive for a while."

"Are you talking hostage?" Lights went off in her head. He knew who her parents were and that they had money.

Austin ran his fingers over her cheek. "I'm sure Mommy and Daddy don't want something terrible to happen to their perfect daughter."

His voice slithered through her and she shuddered. She stared him in the face. "Did Hastings or your Uncle Smith put you up to this? You don't have to do their beckoning. If you let me go there's still a chance Gray will survive. That would put you in good standing with the district attorney. That's your only way out of a long prison sentence."

"You're so naive. I'm doing this because you and Gray need to pay for sending my uncle and his friends to prison. Like I said, you shouldn't meddle in police business. We protect our own."

From a distance, the sound of a car approaching penetrated her hearing. No, she heard several cars and sirens.

"It's not too late, Austin. You can save yourself."

"Shut up, can you do that?" He pulled her to her feet and started running toward a group of trees.

"No!" Cherish fought to get out of his hold on her, praying the police would get to her before he dragged her away.

He shoved the rifle into her side. "Settle down or I'll pull the trigger." His eyes were wild and his breathing was rapid.

"No." She twisted to face him and landed a hard kick to his groin. Caught totally off guard, Austin instantly dropped, moaning.

"You bitch!" he yelled between gritted teeth.

She sprinted toward the road without a backward glance. Her feet flew, and she didn't stop until she ran into a Dunes Bay officer.

"Okay, you're okay. I've got you."

Shouting and hollering rolled from where she had left Austin on the ground. But there was no time for relief.

"He shot Grayson Steele. Please help. He's bleeding."

"Are you hurt, miss?"

"No. Don't worry about me. Please, please check on Gray."

"The EMTs are on their way. One of them will be his brother Jasper."

36

Cherish chewed on her fingernails, watching Jasper and the other EMTs remove Gray from the truck and lay him on the ground, wasting no time. They took Gray's blood pressure and pulse then put a tube down his throat. Tears threatened but she didn't want to cry. *He's going to be fine.*

The crew worked fast, like a small symphony playing a song in allegro. And she watched, helpless.

Gray lay so still. It chilled her. Jasper and the others transferred him to a gurney and loaded him into the back of the ambulance.

Her muscles stiff and tight, Cherish didn't move. But as Jasper walked her way she braced for news.

"Cherish. Sorry I couldn't speak to you sooner." His voice was firm, clipped. "He's lost a lot of blood. He needed help getting air, so that's why we intubated him. I don't have time to go into details. Do you want to ride with him to the hospital?"

The air around her got thin and his voice sounded distance. She couldn't speak, but she would not faint. She nodded emphatically.

Jasper put his hand to her shoulder. "You've been through a lot, Cherish. Come on. Let's get in the ambulance. I'll wrap a blanket around you. I don't want you to go into shock."

Sounds and activities buzzed around her. The sirens blared as the ambulance wove through traffic. Cherish was aware of all of it, but only on the periphery of her mind. Her attention was for Gray only. She sat at his side, caressing his brow.

"You're going to be fine," she murmured, over and over, convincing herself as much as assuring Gray.

Within minutes the ambulance pulled up to the hospital emergency room and everyone inside went into action.

"I'll help you out, Cherish," Jasper said, directing her to the back of the vehicle. "I'll find you a place to wait. You won't be able to go with Gray."

Then she was alone in the waiting room surrounded by a roomful of people. Was she making a big deal about Gray's condition? Was he seriously wounded or was he not? Her brain wouldn't resolve the question. She let out a breath and called Rachel.

"Rachel? I'm at the hospital. Gray has been shot. Please come."

"Oh no! What happened?"

"One of the men who want Gray dead shot him on our way into town." Her breath caught. "Doctors are examining him right now."

"That's terrible. I'll be right there."

Cherish closed her eyes and snuggled deeper into the blanket around her. She should have slept in the truck on the way back home. Maybe she wouldn't be so dead on her feet if she had napped. Her mind turned like gears that needed greasing. Gray had been so close to losing the dark cloud that followed him for a year. Her heart wrenched. And now he struggled for his life. It couldn't be.

Oh my gosh, oh my gosh, oh my gosh. Helplessness fogged her thoughts. Would she talk to Gray again? *Stop it. Think positive. He'll be fine.* He had to be. She couldn't make her hands stop shaking.

A touch on her shoulder made her jump.

"Oh, I'm sorry. I didn't mean to startle you." Rachel wrapped her in a hug. "You're so pale. Are you all right?"

Her sister's presence brought her down to earth. She found her voice. "I'm fine. Don't worry about me. The EMTs checked me over." Her chin quivered. "Thanks for coming so quickly."

"Oh, I'm so glad you called. I didn't even know you were back. What happened?"

"I gave my testimony at the FBI Chicago field office. It was a different experience. I've sat in many times with a client, perps, and victims. But this time, I was the victim."

Rachel gave her a quizzical look. "I meant do you want to tell me about what happened to Gray and to you on the road?"

"I know. But Rachel, sitting at the table giving my testimony, I was afraid. I knew the procedure very well, and yet I felt overwhelmed and scared. What if the corrupt cops came and hurt us? What if the agent taking our testimonies was corrupt? Those thoughts dominated my brain."

Rachel slanted her head. "It must have been awful. I can't imagine going through that. God, I'm sorry you had to."

"It was. But I'm glad it happened. It has changed me, and my perspective of the law. I don't know if I can do it anymore."

"Do what? I don't understand, sis."

"I don't know if I can continue to work in Mom and Dad's firm and practice law as they want me to."

"Oh, sweetheart. Give yourself some time to process what's happened. You don't want to make rash decisions in your present condition."

Cherish's heart slowed. "I love you, Rachel." She did, with all her heart. But Rachel didn't get it. She didn't realize that much had changed for her and she wouldn't go back to living her life as others believed she should. She couldn't just fall back into blindness and insecurity. She was no longer that person. She had to try to help her understand. "I know we said we would deal with that situation together. But I have to talk to them as soon as the moment is right. I have to stand up to them."

"It's okay. You need to fight your own battles and you don't need my help or permission." Rachel wrung her hands. "Now that we know Mom and Dad have done things we don't condone, it's challenging every day to look them in the eye."

"Cherish." It was Gray's mother. She rushed in with his father and

Rhys. "What do you know about Gray's condition? Is he all right?" Her voice cracked.

"I don't know anything yet. He went right to surgery. I wish I could tell you more."

His father nodded. "It's okay. Jasper told us someone shot him. It's hard to believe anyone would do that to our son."

"I'm just glad he told us about the danger he was in. Otherwise this shooting would be inconceivable," Rhys said.

The worry visible on his parents' faces pained her. She wished she could make it go away and fast forward to when Gray would be smiling and joking again.

"Have you been checked out? You don't look so good." Rhys scowled. "Did Jasper take your vitals?"

"An EMT took them in the ambulance, but I'm fine, really. I'm just tired and cold, hence the blanket he gave him." She gestured to Rachel and made introductions.

"We're glad you're okay and that you're here," Gray's father said. His expression was kind but worry furrowed his brow.

The three of them took seats down at the end of the row.

"They seem like nice people," Rachel said.

"They are. Their family is so different, mainly because Gray's parents aren't overbearing like Dad and Mom."

"Mom and Dad are tough, I'll give you that. Our business can do that to a person, but they've always been very scrappy."

"I love them to death, but Rachel, Gray and his family have opened my eyes to how a family can be very loving and supportive."

A doctor came in, scanning the room. Jasper stepped up beside him and pointed at her and his family. Nerves jittered in her gut. The Steeles gathered around her.

"I'm Doctor Peters. I can update you on Grayson's condition. The bullet hit his right upper chest. It hit a rib and the upper lobe of his right lung. The EMTs intubated him at the scene because his right upper lobe collapsed. During surgery we inserted a chest tube so we could inflate his lung, remove the bullet, and repair the damage. He lost a lot of blood, so we gave him a transfusion. We're giving him IV fluids because he will be dehydrated from the blood loss."

Rhys crossed his arms over his chest and leaned closer. "Is he going to be okay?"

"He is in recovery now. He's still on the ventilator. He'll probably be in recovery for another four hours. Then I expect him to go to ICU. We'll keep track of any bleeding and at some point try to wean him off the ventilator. Do you have any questions?"

"Why was he unconscious?" His mother wiped at her eyes.

"The trauma to his body was severe. When the lung collapsed it diminished his breathing and the flow of oxygen to his brain. That's why the EMTs immediately put him on oxygen. They were trying to control his breathing and ventilate him as best they could on his way to the hospital."

His mother nodded, still wiping at tears on her cheeks. "Does that mean he may have brain damage?"

"We haven't seen any signs of that, but we'll know more when he wakes up. I wish I could tell you everything is going to be all right, but right now, it's more of a wait and see."

"When can we see him?" Gray's dad shifted his weight on his feet, then shifted back. He appeared calm and collected, except for his tell. The shifting was a giveaway, but of course he was scared, and she hated that he was going through this terrible experience.

"If he does well in recovery, probably in two to three hours. But not all of you will be able to go in at once. He needs calm and time to rest. The anesthesia will affect him too for a while."

"You've already been here a long time, Cherish. I'll take you home. You won't do Gray any good if you get exhausted," Rachel said.

Rhys pointed at Rachel. "She is giving you good advice. Listen to your sister. Gray would want you to take care of yourself."

Sure he would. That's the way Gray was. Tears misted her eyes. Would she ever see him alive again?

CHERISH STARED at the calendar hanging on her kitchen wall, heavy hearted. The three days that had passed since Gray was shot went by in a fog for Cherish. She'd divided her time between the hospital and work, but every time she left Gray lying silently in the hospital bed, her heart ached until she returned. Rachel, God bless her, had been ready to help at a moments notice. And this morning, like the last few mornings, she'd arrived at Cherish's house early to make sure she ate before leaving again.

Cherish's kitchen smelled like oranges and coffee, but she wasn't interested in the fruit or the beverage. "Thank you for fixing this for me."

"No problem." Rachel planted a hand to her hip. "I hate to bring this up, but what should I tell Mom and Dad?"

"I'll tell them, don't worry about it."

Rachel scowled. "When? They should know what happened to you, how you were almost killed, shouldn't they?"

"I guess. I didn't tell anybody I was going to Chicago. I just left, before anyone tried to talk me out of it." She rubbed her forehead. "I hurried to Chicago, then I got kidnapped, and Gray got shot. It's just been a lot. Honestly, I haven't given any thought to Dad and Mom. The only thing they will want to know is have I been working on the Decidedly Laboratories case."

"I understand. So let me tell them. I'll tell them what you just said," Rachel said. "And, I can help you with the case."

Cherish almost broke down in tears. What a relief. "Thank you. I know you're busy with your own caseload."

"Well, I'm not taking it on, but I can help."

"I appreciate it. I'll talk with Pansy if you want."

"I will. Listen, I'm going to take off. Just call me if you need anything. I wish you would stay with me tonight."

"I'm okay, really. Austin and all his cohorts are in jail. Gray is under doctor's care. And I'm fine. Go."

"Yes, you're always fine." Rachel shot her a wry smile.

Cherish eyed her. "You know, I'm not always fine. I get angry. I get hungry and sleepy. I even get horny, thanks to Gray." She smiled, "I'm making changes and there are more to come."

Suddenly the tears she'd been holding back spilled and she couldn't stem them.

"This is fine?"

"No. I don't know if I'll see Gray again. And I want to."

"Then go to him. I see your droopy eyes and shoulders and I want to take care of you. But Cherish, you're stronger than I've ever seen you. I'm proud of who you are and how you're grabbing hold of life and living it."

Cherish grabbed her up tight. "You're the best sister."

"I love you." Rachel blew her a kiss on her way out the door.

Showering and dressing in clean clothes revived her. She felt almost normal. Her brain started working again, and she assessed her priorities from the list of things she needed to do. Each one clambered for attention. But all of her heart ached to see Gray.

She nuked a cup of the coffee Rachel had brewed and grabbed her briefcase and purse. She wouldn't be able to sit still until she returned to the hospital.

The drive to the hospital helped settle anxiety churning in her body. The streets, the businesses, and restaurants were a part of her hometown. Their familiarity wrapped around her like Aunt Patty's warm arms, and she felt safe. The harrowing experience in Chicago flashed into her thoughts and she shivered. It would take time to recover from the trauma, she knew, but it wasn't going to ruin her life.

At the front desk in the lobby she learned Gray was still in recovery, but enough time had passed that she would be allowed to see him.

She took the elevator, hoping he would be awake, but it didn't matter if he wasn't. Seeing his face and that he was doing all right would calm her racing pulse.

The nurse at the floor nursing station looked up from her work. "Can I help you?"

"I'm here to see Grayson Steele. I'm a ... friend."

The nurse directed her to his room. The flop, flop of her sandals joined the choir of chirps, bleeps, and swishes filling the hospital hallways.

The door to his room was cracked open, so she pushed it a little, just enough to be able to see Gray. On reflex, her hand popped to her chest. *Oh Gray.*

"Come on in," Rhys said. "He hasn't come around yet. Mom and Dad went home to catch some rest."

"You stayed."

"Right. Someone should be here when he wakes up." Rhys rubbed his eyes. "I'll give you some privacy. I could use some coffee," he said.

"You can go home too. I'll stay until one of you returns."

"You sure?" He tilted his head in question.

"Yes," she nodded. "I want to stay with him."

"Okay, I understand. Thank you. I think I will get a shower and some shut eye." He turned to leave, then turned back abruptly. "I'll give you my number. Don't hesitate to call."

"Good idea." She added him to her contacts and gave him her number.

Rhys gave Gray a long look, then left.

Cherish couldn't take her eyes off Gray. Tubes were coming out of his mouth, his chest, and an IV was inserted in his arm. Blood was dripping from the chest tube into some kind of drainage system near his bed.

His skin was pale and his eyes were closed. An overwhelming urge to check his pulse, his breathing for herself surged.

Instead, she leaned close to his face. "Gray, this is Cherish. I'm here."

Gray moaned quietly, and she jerked back. When no bells went off and Gray quieted, she pulled a chair up to his bedside and, gingerly, she took his hand. "Gray, you're in recovery and you're doing really well. I wish you would open your eyes. I love your eyes."

She touched his face, afraid to disturb him, but needing to feel his skin and know he it was warm, that he was alive.

Which of course he was. The machines near his bed told her his pulse was a little weak, but his heart was beating a steady line of hills and valleys. His blood pressure was low, but she deduced that was probably better than high blood pressure.

A nurse walked in and smiled at her. "Hi, I'm Karyn. I'm just going to check some things. You're fine. I'm glad you're keeping him company."

"I'm Cherish. How much longer will he be in recovery, do you know?"

The nurse checked the time. "Well, that's kind of up to Gray. He needs to wake up. We may try to wean him off the ventilator, but that's iffy right now."

Cherish's breath caught.

"Oh don't worry. We want to make sure he can breathe on his own. He may go to ICU before we remove the tube."

"I see he is still bleeding." Cherish pointed to the chest tube. "Why is that?"

"The bullet hit some large blood vessels in his chest. We took care of all that damage while he was in surgery, but sometimes it takes time for the bleeding to stop. That's another reason we're paying close attention to him."

"Thank you. I'm sorry I have all these questions."

"Don't be. It's totally understandable. I'll be back later to check again. I'll let you know when he's ready to go to the ICU. Do you want to give me your phone number in case you have to leave?"

"Yes," Cherish gushed. "I would appreciate that."

"His parents and Jasper were here earlier. I'm not going to kick you out until they come back, because we can only allow one or two of you in at a time. So keep talking to him. It helps. Or read to him. I can get you something to read if you want."

"No, I'm okay. Thank you."

The room got relatively quiet with the nurse's departure, allowing Cherish time to process Gray's condition. She didn't want to. "Gray, let's go. I want you and I to walk out of this room right this minute. You've had enough troubles, it's time for carefree and fun times." Her eyes glued to his face, she swore he opened his eye. Just one. But she must have been seeing things.

"Great, Cherish. You're having hallucinations and you're talking to yourself. Did you hear that Gray? I'm losing my mind. You have to wake up."

Nothing. Not even a twitch.

"You know, you owe me at least a tiny smile. You did break up my wedding. It was you and the way you paid attention to me at the restaurant that day we met that made me question Devin — made me question everything."

Tears welled in her eyes, remembering the banter that day, and the way he had helped her escape from the chaos in the aftermath of ditching her wedding. It was the beginning of finding herself, and it was Gray who had set her on her path to freedom.

She traced his fingers, willing them to move, even jerk.

She rose and bent close to him. "Thank you for breaking up my wedding," she whispered in his ear. "Thank you for believing me and accepting me for myself. I can never repay you, but if you just damn wake up, I will try, Gray. I will try so hard. I love you."

37

"Cherish, it's time to leave."

The voice in her ear was soft. Why was the voice in her bedroom?

She jolted awake. "Oh, sorry. I fell asleep."

The same nurse, Karyn, looked down at her with a smile. "It's okay. It's time to take Gray to ICU. It's morning. You stayed here all night. No one wanted to disturb you and you weren't doing any harm. But you couldn't have been comfortable."

Cherish couldn't believe she'd fallen asleep with her head against Gray's leg. She rubbed her eyes and pulled herself together. "Actually, I don't recall waking up even once." She stretched and yawned. "Okay, I'll go to the floor waiting room."

"Why don't you go get something to eat, maybe go home and sleep for real? Come back later."

"Okay." She grabbed her briefcase, which she had not opened once, and purse and walked to the elevator, still a little wobbly.

Leaving Gray made her skin itch. Knowing he was in good care didn't ease the itch to stay by his side. But the forced break would give her time to go into the office and get some work done. It wasn't sleep that was on her mind; it was her parents, her house with Devin, and wedding gifts to return. And the court date for the Decidedly Laboratories case loomed, but at least Rachel was helping with that. Pansy would have files of information for her to catch up. Etcetera, etcetera, etcetera.

She drove to her office, still dressed in a sundress and sandals. She could at least hit two birds with one stone. Ick, what a terrible thought.

In the elevator she punched in her parents' floor, absolutely ready to have a talk.

Her mother's office door was open so she walked right in. "Hi Mom. Busy? Did Rachel talk to you last night?"

"No. We were out late. Why?"

So her mother didn't yet know she'd been in Chicago or that she and Gray had almost been killed. But she wasn't going to find out now, either. Cherish had to confront her about other things before all that came out.

Her mother smiled. "Come give me a hug. I haven't seen you in days."

"Yeah, I've been busy." Cherish eased into a chair across from her mother.

"Busy doing what?"

"Sorting things out. I want to talk to you and Dad about it. Could you ask him to join us?"

Her mother frowned but called her dad's office number. "Cherish is here in my office. She would like to talk to us. Can you come over?" she asked. She hung up the phone. "He'll be right here. Is this something serious?"

"Yes."

Her mother rolled her eyes. "Oh Cherish, honey. What is it now?"

Cherish's heart winced, but she kept quiet. She chewed on the inside of her cheek.

Her father walked in briskly. "Hello, sweetie. So glad to see you. I've missed you. What have you been up to?" He sat beside her and patted her arm.

"She's been sorting things out, Adrian. She wants to talk about it."

"Let's hear it."

The new, regal décor and furniture from her mother's recent update to her office surrounded her. It was tempting to distract from her topic, maybe ask for new furniture and paint for her office. They would be happy to give her a thumbs-up about that.

No. She was not going to flinch from her plan. "I can't do your style of lawyering anymore."

Both of her parents snapped to attention.

Her mother glared at her. "What do you mean, our style?"

"You told me certain things have to be done in order to serve our clients. Well, I don't want to do those *certain* things, the things that walk a narrow line between legal and illegal, and even cross to the wrong side of the line."

"What are you accusing us of, Cherish?" Her dad's expression was so sober. It gave her chills.

She leaned toward her mother's massive desk. "You told me it wasn't wrong for Devin to doctor evidence and bribe the investigator. You said it takes doing things like that to win cases. I don't agree. Do you know that Devin told me you two have done things, things that would get you disbarred, even arrested?"

"Devin is lying to get you to stay with him. He's desperate because he loves you." Her mother pursed her lips.

"No, that's not love. He bargained with me to lie for him during the bar's investigation and he promised he wouldn't bring your activities to the authorities' attention."

"He did that?" Her mother's voice remained steady, eerily so.

"Yes. He's been pressuring me to marry him for the same reason. To avoid you both being disbarred. I checked for myself and found the truth, so I know all about the special things you do for Tantorum and other clients, including money laundering." She left out Rachel's part in the situation. It wasn't her place to tell on her sister.

Her dad let out a long breath. "What do you want from us?"

She didn't know if she respected him for his tacit admission to wrongdoing or if it broke her heart. The white horse she had always seen him on disappeared, and reality might not be so mesmerizing. But at least it was real.

"I'm asking you to change your ways. I don't want anything bad to happen to you, but our firm cannot serve justice and commit unethical practices. I won't tolerate it. Do you understand what I'm saying?"

"You're holding the law over our heads," her mother said through clenched teeth. "We do things your way or you'll report us."

"I don't want anything bad to happen to you. I'm not going to talk to anyone about it." Cherish skewered them with her gaze, as much as she could. "But you must stop. The best thing would be to report your activities yourselves before they come to light."

Her mother ignored her demand. "You said you weren't going to practice law in the way we do. What exactly are your plans?"

"I'd like to continue working for the firm."

"Why, so you can spy on us?"

"No Mom. I haven't stopped loving you or loving the law. But I am going to do more work for Lawyers Can Help. I want to help people, not just corporations. And I want the firm to start doing pro bono work for individuals who are in need of representation but have limited resources. I want to be in charge of a new department here to meet the needs of those kinds of clients." She pursed her lips. "And I want you to check on Uncle Peter to see what you can do to help him."

Her father just stared at her and her mother glared.

"You don't know what you're talking about with Peter. He is a bum. You don't know the whole story," her mother charged. "He can't be helped."

But Cherish wasn't done. "You must close the off-shore accounts and stop laundering money. No more illegal services for clients who ask for "special" favors, such as pay-offs to protect them or creative financing. Those things are wrong and you are putting the firm, my career, Rachel's career in jeopardy."

Her mother lifted her chin and skewered Cherish right back with her intense stare. "I don't like your tone. Your father and I have built a solid and extremely profitable firm, for you and your sister. How dare you try to shame us and make demands?"

Cherish jumped out of her chair and leaned on her hands over her mother's desk. "How dare you, Mom, take such cavalier moves with my career? I'm giving you a chance to be the kind of attorneys I've always believed you to be: Strong, powerful, pillars of the law."

Her dad cleared his throat. "Are you threatening us, daughter? Is this about that Gray guy, Grayson Steele? Devin told us all about him. Has he turned you against us?"

"Dad, no... I've just grown up a bit more. It was high time I became myself, and not always live in your shadow, needing guidance and protection. I couldn't respect myself if I didn't learn to live my own life. Just as you and Mom do. These changes are for the good of the firm, can't you see that?"

"We've always been so close. I miss that," her mother said, pulling on her heartstrings. "You're putting a wedge between us and you're asking too much."

She didn't have the heart to let her mom know she didn't feel the closeness, she felt smothered, squashed, disempowered. Hope for real love and acceptance faded. Her mother was unwilling to see that she had some good ideas for the firm and for them. "It's too much to want my parents to respect good values? It's more than you can manage to practice law guided by ethics and honor?"

"You don't understand. What we've done is not beyond standards of practice in our field," her mother said. A muscle in her cheek ticked.

"Your mother's right. As we told you before, we're not the only lawyers who participate in supplement services appropriate for our clients. You'll learn. There is no distinct line between right and wrong."

Emma Moss turned her attention to her computer and Adrian Moss slapped his hands on the desk. "Well, thank you for talking to us, Cherish. This is strictly a family matter, so I expect you'll keep our business private."

Her heart plunged. Meeting was over. She was dismissed, along with everything she asked for.

"My statements and requests stand. Your choices will lead somewhere, but I hope you know what you're doing," she said, straightening her shoulders and striding out.

On her way to her office, Cherish relished in the concept of speaking directly and unflinchingly with her parents. It had come easier than she had expected. She at least had that, even though nothing was going to change on their part. Not yet.

Inside her office she found boxes and boxes. "Pansy, can you come in here?"

"I bet you're wondering about the boxes," Pansy followed her inside. "This is information I've gathered about the case between Decidedly Laboratories and Henry Pole. It's fascinating stuff."

Cherish opened one box and flipped through a file on top. It was a photograph of Pole before the study and after. It took her breath away. "So do you have an opinion about the plaintiff's assertion?"

"I wish I didn't. I love your Mom and Dad and I know Decidedly Laboratories is an important client and I know what your job is, in fact, the job of the firm. It's to take care of clients." Pansy's words flew out of her mouth and she gestured with both hands, adding emphasis to her love.

"So what do you know that I need to know?" Cherish asked, knowing Pansy always talked fast when she was nervous or had bad news. "Give it to me straight."

"Decidedly Laboratories denied Mr. Pole's symptoms were a result of the drug being tested, but he is not the only one who had problems."

"I see. I don't like that, but I appreciate your input. You're right about the company being an important client. But please, don't ever hesitate to give me bad news. I value truth over billing."

Pansy sighed. "Okay. Well, the truth is in the investigation."

"Absolutely. Thank you for all your hard work. I'm sorry I bailed on you for a few days. We need to go through what you've found.

Could we do that another day? A good friend is in the hospital and I want to go back there."

"Oh, oh, of course. Whenever you're ready, I will be too."

"Could you shut the door when you leave, please?"

Cherish sat at her desk and dialed Devin. She tapped a pencil on her desk, counting the rings until he answered.

"Cherish? Hey, it's good to hear from you."

His voice was a little too cheery, a little too forced.

"We need to list the house for sale. I can take care of that."

"What? Why?"

Cherish gritted her teeth. "We're not going to live there. Do you plan to? If so, you need to buy out my share."

"Well, this is a surprise. I thought we had a deal."

"No, we don't. I'm not at all interested in marrying you. I'm especially not going to marry into a deal."

"Go ahead and try to sell it. I won't agree to it."

"You know that won't work. I'll simply sue you and win."

Silence stretched. This was the man she was going to spend her life with? What had she seen in him? He was arrogant, self-centered, and unreasonable. Had she really changed so much since her nonwedding day eight days ago?

"I've been put on leave from my firm. The Bar Association has censured me."

"When did all this happen?" she asked.

"It went fast. It turns out the anonymous tip came weeks ago. The Bar Association had been collecting information before their official announcement of an investigation. The fire investigator was subpoenaed. During the hearing he pointed a finger at me for intimidation. Said I threatened to report him for drinking on the job if he didn't submit a report favorable to Dunes Bay Property Management."

"You can't get away with a crime when you're supposed to be upholding the law," Cherish said.

"It's all garbage, you've got to know that. You know I'm innocent."

"I wish I did. I'll be petitioning for a new trial." Cherish couldn't let her guard down or she might feel sorry for him and lose her way again.

"I'd expect nothing less." He got quiet, and she twirled her pen, waiting. "The firm is going to settle and I'm to make an official apology. My boss will be in touch with you."

"I see." Cherish shook her head. "You must know, I'm not happy about any of this. I don't take any pleasure from your censure."

"I would still appreciate it if you would talk to the senior partner in my firm." Devin arched his brows. "It would help my position if you could give me a good word."

Her heart went out to him. But she couldn't save him from the trouble he'd gotten into. "I'm sorry, I can't do that. It wouldn't be ethical. But I wish you well."

He expelled a loud sigh into the phone. "So we're really over." He sounded pitiful, and Cherish almost felt guilty. "You don't deserve to be with me."

Here was his edge. The anger in his voice made a good defense against her rejection. But it also confirmed she was doing the right thing.

"So what about the house?"

"Fine, I'll buy your half of the mortgage. I'll have a check sent this week. The house will make a wonderful home for me and Alicia."

"You're back with Alicia." Her brain stuttered. Deep down, she knew this, especially since he slipped up after she'd left him at the alter and brought up Alicia randomly. Not so random, after all. The woman had never completely left his life. "Did you ever truly love me?" She had her suspicions all along and that he was merely using her to make useful connections to the infamous Adrian and Emmy Moss. Not that any of that mattered today.

His voice rose. "Don't you do that. I did not walk out on you."

"No, you didn't. I'll return your ring. And I want half of the purchase price of the house from you. I'll write up a purchase contract and get it to you tomorrow. The money from the house will make a good contribution to the Standishes needs."

"What? You're going to give away the money? You're insane."

"I don't want anything from our wedding or the life we intended to live."

"You really hate me, don't you?"

"No, Devin. I don't. This is all just a business transaction, nothing personal. I hope you and Alicia have a very nice life." His change of heart from trying to get her back to telling her he was going to live with Alicia made her head spin. Crazy. But it was him, not her. She'd dodged the bullet on him for sure.

She disconnected and enjoyed the sense of completion of tying up ends with him. She hadn't known how he would take the news, and his mean spirit had taken her aback. But she hadn't faltered. She stood her ground and said entirely sensible things. A thrilling sense of invigoration raced through her.

Joy spread throughout her, a joy she couldn't remember ever experiencing before. *So this is what living from my core values as an individual is like. I could take a lot of this.* "My work here is done for now." The only place she wanted to be was Gray's hospital room.

"You can't stay long," the nurse in the ICU, Melanie, cautioned Cherish. "He's not awake, but you can go in. Down the hall and on the right."

Cherish made a straight path to Gray's room.

She had raced to arrive at the hospital quickly after leaving her parents in shock. Still, she tiptoed in. Except for the sounds of monitors, the room was hushed and Gray lay still in bed, unconscious. She stood above him, breathing shallow breaths. His hair was mussed, and she wanted to smooth it for him, but didn't want to disturb him. What was his mind doing? Did he know she was there?

She sat in a chair beside his bed. "The nurse said to talk to you. She said it would be good for you. So I'm going to read you a poem. Here it goes. 'Delight me with mystical rhythms,'" she read.

'Whisper my name
Stroke my fancy

I'm so parched.

LIGHT THE STARS with sweet melodies
    Drench my skin in iridescent drops
    Converging into unimaginable temples
    I'll enter inside.

TOSS eloquent fragrances upon the breeze
    Drizzle tangy potions down my forehead
    I'll taste of worlds echoing silently
    Deafening me to all things lifeless.'"

SHE GAZED at his peaceful expression. "Did you hear me? Do you like my poem? Wake up, Gray."

Her eyes closed and she envisioned him dreaming, a smile on his face. "Is that it, are you dreaming? Where are you in your dream? Are you at the beach, maybe the cove, is that where you are, enjoying the sun and water?"

She opened her eyes, and dared to caress his cheek. His skin was warm, just like normal. She bent her face close to his and breathed in his scent, savoring it, letting it close the space between them. "Wake up. I want to hear your voice."

Gray stirred, and she jolted back in her chair. "Did I hurt you? I'm sorry."

He lay still again, then moaned.

Her hand flew to her lips. "Gray, I'm here with you."

She watched his face for signs of consciousness. She stared. "This is silly," she said, chuckling a little. "You wake up when you're ready. I'll be here."

Gray muttered something she couldn't understand.

"What? What did you say?" Her voice rose in volume. "Can you hear me?"

His lids fluttered. His face contorted, as though he couldn't quite make things happen. Oh, no! Does he have brain damage?

She whispered in his ear. "Take your time. This is Cherish. Just open your eyes." Under her breath, she cheered him on. "You can do it, just open your eyes and you'll see me."

"I'm tired. Is that you Cherish? My tongue is huge." His words were slurred. He slowly, deliberately moved his jaw up and down and sideways.

He reached for her, and she grasped his hand. "That's right. I'm here."

His lids opened, slowly, deliberately. He gave her a weak smile. "Hi. I...know...you."

Laughter bubbled out. "Yes you do." She pressed his hand to her lips. "I've been waiting for you."

Melanie hurried in. "What's going on in here? Oh. You're awake. That explains the raise in your pulse. Welcome back. I'm going to let your doctor know you're awake. Don't go away. I'll be right back."

Gray lifted his head a little. "Have I been gone somewhere? I don't remember much."

"Maybe you should take it easy. You've been unconscious for three days. We were driving home from Chicago—"

"I remember Chicago. You were there. Oh, oh, and I got you kidnapped." He started to move around in his bed.

She put her hand on his arm and tried to calm him. "You remember. That's good, but you didn't get me kidnapped. Gray, you need to lie still. Do you remember getting shot?"

His breathing slowed and he closed his eyes again while he thought.

"That's why you're in the hospital," she said, smoothing his hair, gently, savoring the soft feel of it. The doctor would come and Gray would be all right.

"Hastings." Gray's eyes widened. "This is all his doing. I remember driving home and talking about us. Then things go black. And here I am, in a hospital bed."

"Hastings didn't shoot you. Austin did. When the FBI arrested

Hastings and the Gang, Austin left Chicago, he told me. He was holing up in Dunes Bay, just waiting for our return." Cherish kept watch on how the facts were affecting him. She didn't want him to become overwhelmed.

The doctor and nurse walked swiftly into the room and up to Gray. "Hello, I'm your surgeon." He shook Gray's hand gently. "My name is Dr. Jon Bryan. I'm going to ask your friend to leave so I can check you out. Okay? We're so happy to meet you and glad you're back with us."

"Never trust a man with two first names," Gray teased. The doctor chuckled, obviously pleased at Gray's remark.

Cherish patted his hand. "Doctor, he might be under the influence of anesthesia," she said. "Bye Gray. I'll be back." She kissed his cheek as she left.

38

Gray's mouth was dry, his brain was foggy, and moving his upper body took almost too much energy than Gray could muster. He winced, trying to lift his arm. "Oh, that hurt."

But the kiss Cherish left on his cheek lingered. She didn't know it yet, but she was the woman he'd come to love. At least he didn't remember telling her.

"You're going to have pain in your upper body. You're on a morphine drip so your pain should be manageable."

He wanted to ask the doctor to define manageable, because deep pain throbbed in his body. "How do I look, doctor?" he asked, while the doctor shined a light in his eyes. "Do my eyes still work?"

"If by still work you mean they can track and your pupils react within normal range, yes. Tell me your name, birthday, and occupation."

Gray squinted. His brain trudged along slowly. "Umm, Grayson Steele, October twenty-six, Boatwright. Did I pass?"

"Your brain wasn't completely deprived of oxygen when you got shot, but the oxygen level dropped," he said. "Your memory may give you problems initially, but that should clear up. It's too soon to know for sure, but you appear to be normal."

"I feel very groggy." Gray fought the sleepiness that wanted to take over.

"That's to be expected. You lost a lot of blood, you're dehydrated, and you just sustained trauma. You need to be patient with your recovery." Dr. Bryan smiled. "You are a very fit guy and you're in excellent health. Those factors are in your favor. Your body is resilient, therefore your recovery will be speedy. But you need to let your body heal."

"When can I go home?" Laid-up in bed was the last thing he wanted. He needed to talk to Cherish, spend time with Cherish, and figure out what would happen next with his life.

The doctor glared at him. "I'm not even going to discuss a release date. You are still in ICU. Now, Melanie here will make sure you're comfortable. If your pain increases, let her know immediately. I'll see you again."

The nurse logged her notes in a computer and Gray tried to think through the fog. "There, that's done. Your family has been called, so when they arrive they'll be allowed to see you one or two at a time."

"I'll be here." He had questions but he would wait to ask. But there was one he wouldn't wait for. "Do you know where Cherish went?"

"The pretty woman with the red hair? No, but I'm sure she'll be back soon. She has stayed with you almost all the time since you got out of surgery," Melanie said. "Between your family and Cherish, you haven't been alone. I'll see you later. Call if you need something."

Alone now, Gray lay listened to the quiet. Hospital sounds drifted into his room, but everything sounded muted. Bandaging around his shoulder and upper body squeezed him snuggly.

So this is how the danger driving his life for more than a year comes to an end? Hastings and his Gang of Four in custody. His family safe. His life opened with opportunities available.

The need to stay alert, on guard was over. But it wasn't sinking in. Vigilance spun in his gut. He needed to see Cherish and touch her, verify she was okay.

He started to drift into sleep, and his brain replayed bits and pieces of the nightmare in Chicago. Finding Cherish gone from the hotel room. Her desperate phone call. Hastings bearing down on them.

Gray, run!

Cherish's warning jerked him awake. His breaths came fast, constrained by the pain and the bandage. He was back in bed in a hospital room. Cherish was safe.

It took a few minutes for him to feel completely present, not caught in the trauma of the memory.

His throat was parched, and he reached for water. It was just out of reach. Awkward and weak, he scooched closer to the bedside table and grabbed for the plastic container, but knocked it over instead.

"Crap!" He stretched farther and managed to pick it up before much water spilled out.

He leaned back against his pillow and had to summon energy to sip his water. This being a patient stuff was too much work and absolutely no fun.

"Gray?" Cherish stood at the door, a question in her eyes. "Are you all right?"

～

"Cherish, come here." Gray motioned to her, sending her heartbeat tripping.

"Hi." Words, where were they? She ran her gaze over his face, his chest. Seeing him again lying on his back under a hospital blanket reminded her how close he came to dying. Just thinking the word made her want to hold him tight and pretend none of it had happened. Not the death threats. Not the shooting. "Is it silly to ask how you're feeling?"

He chuckled, then stopped. "Oh, oh. I'm okay. Laughing isn't good, though. Not yet."

"Describe okay."

"I hurt. My strength is zapped. But I'm alive. That's good enough for me." He lifted his head and tried to sit up more, then winced.

"Yes, that's a very good thing." She laid her hand on his shoulder. "Do you need help from the nurse to get more comfortable?"

"No. I have a button if I need to call her. Comfortable might be a way off. I don't know. The doctor said I have to be patient." He lifted his hand. "This IV is giving me morphine, so I don't have a lot of pain."

Despite his summer tan, Gray's skin was ashen. Bandages covered his shoulder and chest. When he spoke he struggled to breathe.

She pulled a chair up beside his bed. "I'm glad you're not in terrible pain. That's good to hear. You look like shit, you know."

"Don't make me laugh. And please, don't hold back. Tell me the truth."

He gave her a smile that grounded her to the earth. She eyed the drain beside his bed, and chewed on her lower lip. More blood than yesterday flowed.

"Has the nurse or aide checked the drain lately?" She tried to sound nonchalant. "It looks different today."

"Were you here before? When?" He rested his head against the pillow and his lids dropped.

"I was with you in the ambulance and I visited you in recovery. This is the fourth day you've been in the hospital." She refused to get emotional over those memories.

He opened his eyes and met her gaze. "Thank you. I wish all this hadn't happened. There are things I want to say, but probably not right now."

"You can say anything, Gray. I'm here for you."

His eyes drifted closed and his head rolled to one side.

"Gray, are you awake?"

Suddenly a machine started beeping loudly. A nurse flew into the room and Cherish stepped back. "Oh my God, Gray. What's happening, tell me, is something happening?"

"His blood pressure is dropping and he's bleeding more."

"What does that mean?" Cherish grasped her throat. Her pulse surged.

"I'm sorry. I need to attend to Gray. Could you please step out of the room? Someone will talk to you in a minute."

A doctor and another nurse passed without noticing her as she walked out the room. She couldn't make her feet take her away. There was nothing she could do, but it was unthinkable to do anything but watch and wait.

What felt like forever ticked by, but it was only minutes before Gray was wheeled out of his room.

"He's going back into surgery. He appears to be hemorrhaging. Go to the waiting room and I'll find you as soon as he's out of surgery."

Then the nurse marched in the direction Gray had been taken and Cherish watched until he and his team were out of sight.

She slipped into the first bathroom she found and leaned on the sink, slapping down her trembling hands and the emotions ready to spill. She raised her hands upward. "Gray." She said his name as prayer. "Don't leave me."

39

"Oh, oh, remember the time when Gray ran away and you and I went after him?" Jasper asked.

Rhys laughed. "Yeah, he was only about ten. I don't remember why he left."

She could hear the smile in Rhys' voice, and was grateful for being able to listen to his family's stories rather than go to the dark place her mind wanted to be.

"What matters is we went after him and he got over his hurt feelings," Jasper added.

"You guys made fun of a story he'd written." Gray's mom said, then sniffed.

Gray's dad chuckled. "He did like to write little stories back then. I guess we didn't appreciate them enough." His voice drew down.

"He is going to be all right, Dad." Leave it to Jasper to be optimistic. "It's been an hour. We'll hear something soon."

Cherish put her mind on following his example. She opened her eyes and slid into a chair closer to the family. "I'm grateful you've allowed me to be here with you, even though you don't know me very well."

"We're glad you're here with us." His mom gave her a weak smile. "I know he cares for you."

Cherish suddenly starting crying. Drat! She didn't want to fall apart.

"Oh, don't worry." His mom draped an arm over her shoulders. "He made it through the hard part."

Footsteps in the doorway got Cherish's attention and she turned to see the surgeon come toward them. She couldn't read his expression and she couldn't stop herself from gripping Rhys' arm.

"Gray is back in recovery. He's going to be fine. In his first surgery we took pains to make sure we'd repaired all blood vessels. But there are large vessels in the chest. We repaired them, but we missed a small leak. The leak grew. That is why his blood pressure dropped and he went unconscious. We'll monitor him closely while he's in recovery. As long as the bleeding stops, he'll go in a room within a couple hours."

"Why did he have a leaky vessel?" Rhys asked.

"Trauma like a bullet wound can damage a lot of things. Sometimes we don't catch a leak until it gets worse. We thoroughly explored for any more risks of hemorrhaging and feel confident he's fine. He's a strong, healthy man with a lot going for him."

Cherish's rigid muscles relaxed. Could she believe the worst was behind them?

"Thank you, Doctor," his mother said. "When can we see him?"

"I'd like you wait until he's in a room. But even then, just one or two at a time, please. He needs rest."

Cherish watched the doctor leave and decided the right thing to do was leave the family to visit. She was jumping-up-and-down-inside impatient to see him, but his family deserved time alone with him.

She told them all goodbye, butn her way to her car she fought the urge to ran back to Gray and confirm all was well. Though the hospital staff wouldn't allow her back in this soon and besides, she couldn't let down her sister, her parents, or her client.

She grabbed a quick sandwich at a drive-through to take to her office and tried to bring everything she had emotionally and mentally to her work.

~

CHERISH CHECKED her phone for messages from Gray's family. No update yet. She and Pansy had been working for three hours on documents for the Decidedly Labs' case and viewing depositions Rachel had done. It was becoming clearer and clearer to her that there was a problem. A big problem.

She stretched the stiffness out of her body. "Thank you for coming in on Saturday, Pansy. I'm nervous."

Pansy turned away from her computer. "I am too. I can't believe the plaintiff's lawyer was able to convince the judge to jet the court date Tuesday," she said.

"It's a tough break for us, but considering the patient's health, it's understandable. Of course I knew when my parents assigned this case to me it would take at least a month and probably longer to build a defense," Cherish said. They'd done that to her, knowing her wedding was planned and she would be gone on her honeymoon for two weeks. "But I took it, believing I had to."

"I get that," Pansy said, nodding. "Your parents are dynamos and they think everyone in the firm should also be dynamos."

"Yes, they do. I really appreciate you helping me gather information and talk to experts. I would never be ready for this week if it weren't for the work you've done."

"I'm happy to help. Besides, assisting you is my job. But Rachel helped a lot."

"Time isn't the biggest problem, though. It's the facts." Cherish's throat was dry. A different truth than what Decidedly Laboratories had told was coming out of the depositions.

Pansy clicked on another recorded interview. "This is one of the most important pieces of evidence."

Cherish listened as a young man recounted for Rachel the events of his sister's death.

"My sister died two weeks into the drug trial for Ceedadelphine62. The company running the trial said no one else had had side effects. They said it was a freak accident."

Cherish looked at Pansy. "So there have been patients with dire side effects. Good job finding this one. Why haven't we found any others?"

Pansy pointed to a blank document on her screen. "My research turned up only one because the files of other cases of side effects have been destroyed."

"What?" Cherish wanted to sling things. "How do you know that? Do we have a witness?"

"I talked to a former employee. He worked in records, and he claims he erased some of the files, as per instructions."

"I had a feeling we might find something like this. But we are defending Decidedly Laboratories." She chewed on the end of her pen.

"I know. You'd just be doing your job to ignore this person's claim or discredit him. I found him. The defense did not give us this information."

"If I let this case absolve Decidedly, I would not be serving the law. That is my job." Cherish thought for a few minutes, tapping her foot against her desk. "Could you set up an appointment with Henry Pole for as soon as he's available? I'll visit his home if that's okay with him." Cherish was running on adrenaline as it was. But finding the truth was important enough to keep dragging a little longer.

"I'll go call right now."

There was no doubt in her mind about what she had to do, and actually she was so darn ready for it, it was silly to put it off.

She checked the time, wondering, wondering. Was Gray out of the woods? But she couldn't just mess up in court, she had to be fully prepared. She had to be the perfect lawyer.

"Mr. Pole and his lawyer are available this afternoon. What do you want me to do?"

"Tell him I'll be right over."

. . . .

With Pansy at her side to take notes for the deposition, Cherish sat across the kitchen table from Henry Pole and his lawyer, letting his story sink in as he told it. The idea of what happened to him fumed inside her. His eyes drooped, as though he had missed a few nights of quality sleep.

"I responded to an ad about joining a drug study for a cholesterol lowering drug. I had been trying to lower my cholesterol, the bad kind, so it seemed like a good opportunity. Besides, I needed the money."

"So you were in it for the money?" She attempted to keep any judgment from her voice. Needing money wasn't a crime.

"Look, I give blood to the blood bank. I donate to the Humane Society. I'm not a bad person. But I did need money. My daughter was in a bad car accident and my insurance didn't cover all of her hospital expenses. I thought earning some extra money while helping find a more effective way to lower cholesterol was a decent idea."

Cherish shook her head. Talk about a run of bad luck. Her heart went out to him. "I'm sorry, Henry. Is your daughter all right now?"

"Yes, thank God." He drew in a deep breath and leaned against the table on one elbow.

"It was a thirty-day study. Everything seemed to go well. But about a month after it ended, I got what I thought was the flu, you know, nausea, vomiting, fatigue. I didn't think anything of it."

"How long did that go on?"

"It didn't go away, I just got worse. At two months after the study I called the company. I was told side effects were normal, but typically they happened during the trial, not months after a patient stops taking the medication."

"So you didn't know what was happening to you."

"No, but I believed the company."

"I understand. Did you go to your doctor?"

"No. I called Decidedly Laboratories around four months later. I was tired all the time and lost all my energy. They gave me an appointment at their clinic. They drew blood and gave me a vitamin B shot. Said it was a bad case of flu."

She nodded, trying to stay out of his story as much as possible. The facts had to come from him.

"At six months, my skin and the white parts of eyes were yellow. My belly was big and hard. My wife took me to the emergency room and that's when I learned I was in liver failure. Failure." He slammed his hand on the table. "I need a new liver. I didn't do this. Decidedly Laboratories did. And they need to be held accountable."

"You know I represent the company, Mr. Pole." She nodded toward his lawyer. "But I assure you, I am subject to laws just like everyone else. I will talk to my client about what you've told me."

"I don't want to settle unless that company admits wrong doing and pays a pretty sum."

If what Henry told her was true, he had every reason to be angry. "I'll note that when I talk to my client."

What she'd learned about the drug trial from Henry and other sources pounded in her head on the way out of the man's home and behind the wheel of her car. She had choices to make, and it wasn't as simple as just pretending she didn't know of wrong doing.

Her phone chirped that she had a text. It was from Rhys.

Gray's out of recovery in room 226. He's doing well. Jasper left and me, Mom and Dad are leaving now. Gray's asking for you.

40

Cherish pulled out of the Pole driveway and shoved her foot to the gas pedal. With five o'clock traffic to face, she wanted to beat the rush. She charged through open lanes and around pokey drivers, impatience building until she reached the parking deck at the hospital.

She thanked her lucky stars when she found a parking spot in the crowded garage and rushed inside, her heels clicking on the tiled floor. Only one elevator was going up, and she darted inside just before the door closed, breathless.

After visiting with his family, Gray was probably worn out. At his new room, she peeked inside, cautious of waking him if he was sleeping.

Monitors and machines surrounded him, but there were fewer than when he was in ICU. It was less intimidating. His eyes closed, he lay quietly, his chest rising and dropping. Apprehension subsided in her heart. He must have been breathing easier, she surmised. Maybe this time he was on his way to healing. She stood at the door, grateful he looked peaceful, and sighed.

Gray's lids fluttered open. "Hey there," he said, his voice sounded hoarse.

She went to his side. "It's good to see you looking better. Do you feel better?" A kiss was right on the edge of her lips, but she didn't give in to it.

"I've been awake for a few hours, I guess," he said. "I don't have good memory of anything, but I remember you telling me you'd be back."

"I did come back. Then you crashed. You've had quite a week." Please tell me you want me here. The shot had interrupted their relationship discussion. Had she really told him she was unsure of him?

"I'm sorry for all you've been through. But I'm glad you're here." He reached for her hand and wrapped his fingers around it.

She gripped his lightly. "I wouldn't want to be anywhere else. I can't stay long. You need rest." She pulled a copy of *The Chicago Daily Banner* from her tote bag. "I brought you something to read, when you feel up to it."

"That's great," he said. "Would you feel like reading to me?" He smiled sheepishly. "You know what I like."

"You don't think it's too dry and boring?" Cherish asked.

"No, news is never boring."

She sat beside him and started with headlines. "'Two Charged with Shooting Death in Oak Park. Man and Woman Claim Innocence in Stabbing of Elderly Man and His Grandson. Police Task Force Accountable Chairs Named.'"

"Oh boy, Chicago," Gray said. "That's enough dark and dreary headlines. I'd like to know more about the Task Force, though.

"Me too." Cherish didn't rush through the story. The morphine was again dripping into Gray's arm and probably making his mind unclear. She wasn't expecting him to remember the articles, she was just entertaining him.

When she finished the first story, she found another, and another. Gray started to nod off a couple times and the nurse came in to say his dinner would be coming soon.

The evening settled in around Cherish like the mellow sounds of the tide going out on Lake Michigan. It was comforting to sit with

Gray and get quiet. But her time was up and the nurse would be kicking her out very soon.

"Gray, I'm going to go home. I'll see you tomorrow."

He looked tenderly at her, and her pulse skittered.

"Thank you for staying with me. I know you're busy, so you don't have to come back. I'd understand," he said.

"Maybe we can talk about my work. I could toss around ideas with you, if you're up to it."

"That would be something different. But I enjoyed listening to you read." He yawned. "So I'll see you tomorrow?"

"I'll be here," she promised. Before leaving just as Gray was nodding off she brushed his cheek with a kiss.

THE NEXT MORNING Cherish liked the brightness in Gray's eyes and that he could sit up by himself. She brought him the Dunes Bay community newspaper, and he asked her to read headlines again.

"Sure," she said. "Let's see what's happening. Construction Starts on Car Dealership's New Location. Solar Farm Proposal Moves to County Board. Water Park to Get a New Face."

Gray chuckled. "There's a lot going on in Dunes Bay, but entirely different activities. That's interesting. How about read me the piece about the solar farm proposal? There might be a bit of controversy there." He gave her a thumbs-up and sighed. "I'm so glad you're here."

"One of these days you'll go home," she said, then wondered why. She hadn't meant to be pushy. "But this is the right place for you now."

"You know, my dose of morphine is down. I feel the wound, but it's manageable. And I'm not so groggy. I can't wait to be up and about," he said.

She nodded. "It will happen soon.

ON HER WAY to the hospital the next morning Cherish picked up Gray's laptop from Jasper. Butterflies danced in her stomach, thinking how he might react. She got to his room and startled.

"You're up. Are you supposed to be sitting in a chair?" She had her doubts.

"Melanie helped me. The doctor wants me moving around."

"That's quite an improvement over yesterday. I brought you a surprise," she said, and drew out his laptop from her bag.

"Yes, thank you. I have been itching to write." He set it on bedside table and booted it up. "This is so perfect."

"Are you thinking of another story for Eric?" Her heart sunk asking. Maybe he would go back to live in Chicago.

"No, I'm going to blog." He lifted his gaze from his computer. "I'll show you when I'm done."

The nurse told Cherish she could stay longer, so she sat reading a book while listening to Gray's fingers tap around the keyboard and him talking to himself. Even though they hadn't talked much while he was under the weather, she had let down her guard and enjoyed a sense of togetherness.

He stopped typing. "My memory." He shook his head. "You were going to tell me about your court case. The one with Decidedly Laboratories, right?"

She nodded. "Yes. I am as ready as I can be. I didn't have a lot of time to prepare, but I'm confident."

"Good."

"Did I tell you Decidedly is one of the firm's most important clients?"

"I know it is. There's big money there. I bet your parents want you to win for a lot of reasons."

"Yeah."

"I'm not going to lecture you," Gray said quietly. "You know how I feel about drug companies that put sales above patient health. But if the truth is the plaintiff is wrong, then so be it. That's still justice. I would never ask you to do less than your best for a client, and your best is very good."

"Thank you." She rubbed her finger across her mouth, thinking. "The truth is, I may have to make compromises. The question is, does the end justify the means?"

Gray's eyes glistened. "Hm. That question is always up for interpretation. And in this case, only you know.

"Did I tell you I'll be in court tomorrow with the case?"

"You did." He reached his hand to her and she grasped his. Her heart fluttered. If she'd needed his approval, she couldn't have gotten it in any better way.

$\mathcal{C}$herish sifted through trial notes spread in front of her on the defense table. As her the CEO from Decidedly Laboratories, Dennis Brewer, slid into the seat beside, she turned to the opposing lawyer, Paul Striker, and smiled.

Brewer leaned close. "I have an appointment at eleven o'clock, so I'm hoping we can get this over with quickly." He pulled at his tie.

"I'll do my best." She shrugged, mainly to release a teensy bit of guilt rattling around in her chest. She didn't want to bushwhack him, but she had no choice.

"All rise," the court officer directed. "The Court of Dunes Bay County is now in session, the Honorable Judge Georgana York presiding.

The judge greeted the room, then called the case, while Cherish's heart thundered in her ears.

"Are both sides ready?" the judge asked. "I see a motion to dismiss from the defendant."

"Yes your honor," Cherish began, "We move for non-suit. The plaintiff has failed to provide sufficient evidence to support his claim that the defendant violated any laws or caused harm due to negligence."

Striker jumped to his feet. "Your Honor, counsel for the plaintiff is prepared to mount our case. We have witnesses and documents that elucidate sufficient reason for judgment against Decidedly Laboratories for serious neglect and attempt to suppress evidence. I have files here from the company I submit into evidence that will prove beyond a shadow of doubt the company's intention to evade regulations meant to protect drug trial participants."

"I object. The defense has not been made privy to such files, your Honor." Cherish frowned, marshaling indignation.

"All right, all right. Save your arguments for trial. I see no reason to dismiss. Mr. Striker, call your first witness."

Cherish crossed her legs and bounced one vigorously as Striker's first witness took the stand and was sworn in. Her mind tuned tightly on the questioning and answering. She couldn't miss a thing.

"Mr. Long, can you tell the jury the name of your former employer and the length of your employment," Striker asked.

"I worked for Decidedly Laboratories for two years."

"And what did you do at the company?" Striker faced the jury box. "Please speak up so the jury can hear you."

"I was a database technician. I kept track of critical documents pertaining to the various studies. The FDA requires companies to maintain meticulous information on every participant during the study. Everything is documented."

"So blood tests, x-rays, urine analysis, all of these things are monitored for each patient and you make sure the information is entered into the patient's records."

"Yes. We have to have the information in order to continue studies."

"Your honor," Cherish stood, annoyance dripping, "could you please ask Mr. Striker if there is a point coming any time in our near future?"

Striker turned to Cherish and exchanged a solemn look. She swallowed hard. He looked back at the judge. "Your Honor, I'm laying background."

"Get to the point, Counselor."

"At any point during the Ceedadelphine62 study did you see information on a patient named Beatrice Noble?"

"Yes I did."

Cherish's heart almost beat out of her chest.

"Terrance Muelle?"

"Yes I did."

"Henry Pole?"

"Yes sir."

Striker handed a file to the witness. "Would you please read from the top where it lists Ms. Noble?"

"Beatrice Noble, Ceedadelphine62, dropped from study."

Striker handed another file to Darnell. "Please read from this file what is written about Beatrice."

"Beatrice Noble, Liver Screening: ALT 62 units per liter; AST 66 units per liter; Coagulation panel: 22.4 seconds; Albumin 2.1 g/dl; Bilirubin: 3.0 mg/dl. yellowing of the sclera and skin."

"To me, those are numbers. Can you interpret in layman's terms?"

"In a nutshell, those tests indicate enzyme levels in the blood. Numbers that are higher than normal in some enzymes indicate liver problems, and some numbers that low indicate damage. Ms. Noble's numbers are such that the patient should be seen by a physician. Her bilirubin levels are elevated. The documentation lists physical symptoms that are the result of a compromised liver."

"Thank you. Now, please read from these two files where it mentions Henry Pole." Striker passed the folder to Darnell.

"Henry Pole, Ceedadelphine62, drug interaction, dismissed from study for lack of compliance."

Cherish stared ahead, watching Striker control the courtroom like a pro. It was a beautiful thing.

Dennis leaned close. "What is happening? How did the plaintiff's attorney find this worker?" He gritted his teeth.

"He probably did a search of former employees, just like I did. Mr. Muelle was a wealth of information, it turns out."

"What did you do?"

"I had to give the plaintiff's counsel our discovery materials. Mr. Muelle was on the list of our depositions."

"I'll have you fired." Dennis's eyes flamed. "How dare you."

"Do you really think my father would fire me?" She took quiet satisfaction in serving the law, even if it made her client blow steam from his ears.

"Henry Pole, Ceedadelphine62, Liver Screening, oh, I can tell you his Bilirubin levels are very high, which is why notes in the file tell us he had dry, itchy skin, yellowing of the sclera and skin, hard, distended abdomen, and fatigue."

"What does that tell you about his liver?"

"He was in liver failure and should have been in the care of a doctor."

Cherish popped up. "Objection. Speculation, your honor."

"Sustained." The judge eyed Striker, her face blank.

Chatter rose in the courtroom and the judge pounded her gavel. "Quiet everyone, court is still in session. Proceed, Counselor."

"How do you account for the two files, the different information?"

Darnell sucked in a deep breath and blew it out. "I was instructed to erase the original file on patients who suffered side effects during the study, and replace them with the whitewashed information."

"Do you know why?" Striker stared at Dennis. "I mean, side effects are not unusual in a drug study. Patients are monitored so closely to learn the right dosage and the safety of the drug, right?"

"Yes. The company knew the drug in that particular study wasn't panning out. It was causing severe, irreversible side effects. If that had gotten out, the drug would not receive approval and the company would face large legal problems."

"Who instructed you to erase the files?"

A collective pause hung in the air.

"The clinical supervising RN."

"Did you object at all?"

Darnell's muscled tightened and a small muscle in his cheek began twitching. "I certainly did. But the clinical supervisor said the order came from Mr. Brewer and she didn't want to lose her job."

Cherish stood. "I object. This is hearsay, your Honor."

Judge York leaned on her elbows, eyeing Brewer. "Sustained. I'll allow."

She knew the routine so well, the process of getting a witness to reveal information in an authentic and effective way. For her part, all she had to do today was object a few times and let Striker present the facts. But the charade was about over.

Dennis spit a whisper in her ear, "Stop this. Undermine the witness.

"Okay, I'll stop this." She stood again. "Your honor, could I approach the bench?"

The judge motioned her forward and Striker joined her.

"I believe at this point my client may be persuaded to agree to a settlement."

"We want this trial to go to the jury for a judgment, your honor."

"Looking at the evidence I can understand that, Mr. Striker. We'll recess for twenty minutes for you both to speak with your clients. Meet me in my chambers."

Minutes later, Dennis slammed his hand on the table in a conference room. "I will not settle. I will not admit to any wrongdoing. It would ruin my company."

"Mr. Brewer, the solvency of your company is the least of your worries now. What you've done will be reported to the FDA, and the FDA will take away your license and close all current studies. There will be no more studies for Decidedly Laboratories. You may face criminal charges. The best thing for you to do to help yourself under these circumstance is to take responsibility and to give the patients fitting restitution."

"How can you say such miserable things to me?"

"I'm your lawyer. It's my job."

CHERISH LEFT the judge's chambers and went directly to Henry and his family. Gratefulness spread through her that he hadn't had to take the stand. He didn't have to go through grilling and replaying his terrible ordeal. She waited with him to hear from Striker what settlement was offered.

"I'm glad you're sitting down, Henry." Striker chuckled. "Decidedly Laboratories agreed to pay you five-hundred million dollars. There is no amount that would be enough for losing your liver. But I think that should more than cover your medical bills."

"I can't believe it. Thank you so much. It will be a big help." Henry frowned. "I did want an admission of guilt."

"You got it. Decidedly was ordered to release a public statement claiming its responsibility and pledging to create a resource group for individuals they have harmed." Striker wrapped an arm around Cherish's shoulder. "You need to know, Cherish made all this happen. Suffice to say, she's a genius. A truly great litigator who I am proud to call a colleague."

Warmth crept up Cherish's neck. "Stop it. You won the case."

Her thoughts pivoted to her parents and she frowned. They wouldn't be pleased with her performance. She nearly shivered thinking of their cold shoulder and dreading having to remind them she wasn't going to wait long for them to address their legal problems.

Her phone chirped in her purse and she grimaced. "I have to take this." She turned aside. "Hi Dad."

"I heard from Dennis Brewer. He's not at all happy with you. He said you lost the case."

"I did, but justice won. I know that sounds clichéd but it's true." She would not apologize or offer an explanation.

He cleared his throat and she waited for what was coming, knowing whatever he said, she could take it.

He cleared his throat again. "I've been thinking about what you said. That you want certain things from your mom and me. I'm going to make those changes. Your mother is not agreeable to that, but she'll come around. You made a very sound case."

"That means a lot to me." Cherish stood surrounded by good news, but the person she wanted most to share it with wasn't present.

42

Gray had been IV-free for days. He'd strolled around floor, his legs steady and his breathing easy countless times. His pace was slow and deliberate, but he was on his feet and walking without help. If he wasn't well enough to go home he didn't know what it would take.

His stomach clenched watching Dr. Two-First-Names look at the computer screen in his room, evaluating the latest tests. "How do I look, doctor? Are you ready to release me?"

The doctor sighed. "Gray, you've had some very fine doctoring, if I do say so myself. How do you feel this morning?"

"Like if I have to spend one more day, no, one more hour in this hospital I'll die of—"

The doctor held up his hands. "Whoah, whoah. I get the picture. You'll die of boredom. That's a good sign. You're ready to exchange those pajamas for street clothes. I'll sign your release and the nurse will be in to get you on your way."

"Thank you. You don't know how glad I am to hear that." Gray offered him his hand and they exchanged a hearty shake.

"I think I do."

Gray started gathering his things, excitement fluttering in his gut.

He had plans in the works and really hoped to be able to follow through. He had so much to be happy about.

Every day Cherish had visited him she brought him hope. She encouraged him to get his strength back and expect to heal. He smiled at the realization that she had really stepped away from her parents' dictatorship and into a life of her own creation.

Vitality streamed through him. His freedom of movement was invigorating and his brain was completely clear. No more pain meds making him foggy. He lifted his laptop from the bedside table and laid it on the bed. He stared at it and his other possessions going home, twirling his thumbs. Gratitude for being alive flowed in his blood vessels, practically singing.

Boy, that sounded good. Going home.

"Knock, knock. Are you decent?" Cherish stood at the door and peeked inside. "Good morning. I brought you coffee from your favorite coffee shop. I snuck it by the nurses' station because I didn't know if you were allowed outside food."

He took the cup and sipped. "Ahh, that's great coffee. Thank you. Come sit with me." He patted the bed, a secret smile glowing his heart.

She slid into a spot beside him, sipping her coffee. Her scent wafted around her. He breathed in the delicate peach and relaxed deeply.

"I want to show you something," he said, and opened his laptop. "I finished my blog post. Go ahead, read it out loud."

"Oh cool. I have no idea what your topic was." She looked into his face. "Is it live?"

"No, you're the first person to see it. I wanted it that way." His pulse raced and she began reading.

"Well, the title is Things Change. Hmm, interesting. *'Today's post is a little different than my usual posts. Rather than lay out details for an injustice or dire situation going on in the world, I want to share a personal experience in the hopes you faithful readers find something you can take away.*

"*Like Martin Luther King Jr., I had a dream. I came out of college with a strong drive to make the world a better place with my writing.*"

Cherish paused and sipped from her water bottle. "This has my attention," she said.

"Good." Gray couldn't take his eyes off her. She transfixed him with her tone and deep engagement as she read. But would she understand the point of his piece?

"'*Investigative journalism was my vehicle. I dreamed of writing for a top newspaper in a big city, fighting hypocrisy, corruption, and greed with my keyboard. When I realized that dream, I thought I had conquered the world.*

"'*But things change. Begrudgingly, I left my great life in the big city and moved to a mid-size town along Lake Michigan. It was in that place that I discovered that accepting change and focusing down on my true values was where I would find peace and true love, the kind that sits beside you when you're sick in the hospital. The kind of love that brings you exactly what you needed but didn't know. And makes no demands other than to find your way. It's the kind of thing that can be missed in a pursuit of adrenaline and winning. There is nothing wrong with those pursuits. But for me, I've found they are underpinned by a foundation of courage, insight, and living according to my values.*

"'*I will always love the big city and investigative reporting. But the mid-size town and what lives there is now, more than ever, my home. My dream changed, it expanded as a result of dark and scary circumstances and the faith of a best friend. I want to remind you faithful readers that there is always hope, but it is found in a bigger picture, a bigger sense of self, and a bigger dream.*'"

"Thoughts?"

Cherish closed her eyes and he watched her chest rise and fall as she said nothing. Chatter outside his room contrasted sharply with the hush he sat in with Cherish.

She leaned her head against his shoulder and sighed. "Gray, your writing is so eloquent. I'm moved. Your premise is striking and simple and so important."

He pulled her chin up to face him. He wanted to see her eyes. "You like it?"

Her eyes misted and her lips quivered. "Of course. But you didn't write it for me. It's for your followers. They benefit from your thoughts."

"Yes, it's for the public." His heart pounded in his chest. "But it's for you. I'm not going to take Eric's job offer. I'm going to see if the Dunes Bay newspaper could use a reporter."

She gasped. "What? You'll get bored, you know you will. There's no fire and fury to write about in Dunes Bay."

"Oh, I may write as a contributor for *The Chicago Daily Banner*, but I discovered while listening to you read the news to me that I'm more interested in the Dunes Bay community. Maybe the *Banner* would consider using me for the digital version of the news."

She let loose a burst of laughter and climbed out of bed. "I'm sorry, I'm not laughing at you, I'm laughing in delight. You're staying."

"I'm staying." She made his heart sing.

"This news is my kind of news," she said, beaming. "I have other news."

"Oh, your court case. I'm sorry. I dominated the conversation with my silly blog post. I am interested in your work." He sighed, annoyed with himself. It wasn't that he'd forgotten it was more that he was distracted by Cherish and his thoughts about his plan. "Tell me what happened."

"I lost." She beamed and especially sparkly smile.

He shot her a quizzical look. "And that makes you happy?"

"So happy. I was representing a reprehensible client. He is a criminal. He hurt people. I served the law. That just happened not to give him a free ticket to commit crimes."

"Oh I bet it was spectacular. I wish I could have been there. Congratulations!" He high-fived her. "We need to celebrate. It will be one of the first things on the list when I get out of here."

Melanie walked in to check Gray's vitals, and he and Cherish sat quietly waiting.

"Oh, Gray, your blood pressure is up a tad." She glanced knowing at Cherish. "You mustn't make him too excited, you know. He's recovering." She exaggerated the last word and laughed. "Just kidding."

She headed out of the room, still chuckling at herself.

"Now what we were talking about," Cherish asked.

"We were discussing your failure," he teased. "Congratulations, you lost. But you did win for the client and for justice."

"Exactly why I'm happy, in addition to seeing you looking better. You're making progress." Her eyes softened. "I can't wait until you're out of here and life can get back to normal, whatever that might be."

"Me either. In fact, the doctor is releasing me today."

Her eyes flashed wide. "What? He told you that?"

"Yes, just a few minutes ago. Can you stick around until it's official and take me home?"

Cherish threw her arms around his neck and nuzzled under his chin. Her breaths came hard and fast.

He pulled her back and peered into her misty eyes. "What's this? I just gave you good news."

"I'm so relieved. I'm so happy. These are tears of joy, Gray. Tears of joy." She stepped away and spun in circles. "Where are your things? Where's your bag? Let's get you packed."

He laughed, enjoying every second of pain-free hearty laughter. "I'm with you. The sooner I put this all behind me the better."

He went into the bathroom and closed the door to dress. He pulled on his pants and shirt, socks and shoes, then stood in front of the mirror. He was thinner than before the bullet put him in the hospital. But his color, his eyes, everything looked normal. It was hard to believe he'd almost died, but here he was, going home with Cherish by his side and plans in his back pocket.

43

Sitting in the front seat in Cherish's car, Gray took in the familiar passing scenery and sucked in the moist summer air streaming in the open window.

"Mmm, it is good to be alive," he marveled. "I never want to spend time in the hospital again. It is good to be on my way home."

Cherish laughed. "Yes it is. Are you sure you're going to be all right alone? I would be happy to stay with you, just to be sure."

He reached across the seat and fondled a lock of her copper hair. It glistened in the sunshine slanting through the window. "You're too good to me."

"Well, enjoy it while it lasts. As soon as you're perfectly fine, it all ends and you will owe me." She flashed him a broad smile, then turned her attention back to driving. "I can go to the store and get you some groceries after I get you settled in. But I bet your mom already has done that. She's so excited to have you back home. Everyone is, Gray." Her expression sobered.

"What? Why the gloom suddenly?"

"Your family loves you. Your brush with death really affected them. There is a new sense of how fragile life is and how precious loved ones are."

"I get that." He kept quiet for a few miles and so did she. It was a comfortable quiet, but it reminded him of their drive home from Chicago. His insides squirmed remembering that Cherish had voiced second thoughts about them that day. He scratched his head absently, rehashing his thoughts from the hospital.

"Here's our turn," she said, heading the car down his road. "I bet your beach house is going to look great to you."

Peace was close. He saw his house and the lake spread out before him as she pulled up to his property. Peace was so close, but not quite in place yet.

He climbed out of the car, taking in everything: the scent of the lake, the solid feel of the ground beneath his feet; the wind coming off the lake blowing in his face. He unlocked his front door and turned to Cherish. "Come on in."

She followed him and went right to his kitchen. "Do you mind if I look around?"

"Not at all." Tension tightened his muscles. He knew what he wanted but the timing had to be perfect. He hesitated.

"Yup, just as I suspected. Your cupboards are full and so is the frig. Your mom took care of you," Cherish said. "She's so great." Her eyes held a far off look and he could guess what she was thinking.

"I know she is." He walked to her and pulled her into his arms. "But have I told you today how great you are?"

"No, but then, you don't need to." She molded her body to his and he felt her heart pulse against him. Could she feel his pulse race?

"Hey, mind if I intrude?" Jasper stuck his head inside the front door, Rhys behind him.

Cherish pulled away, laughing, and Gray's nerves jumped. How long would it take to settle into a new normal where danger wasn't lurking he wondered.

"You already have, Jas. Come on in."

"It's good to see you back home," Rhys said, grabbing him in a hug.

"I'll say," Jasper added, making it group hug.

A dog barked outside, startling Cherish. "Aww, whose dog is that?"

The dog barked again and scratched at the door. "What is he doing here?" Gray asked.

"Well, you see, bro," Jasper began and opened the door. A German shepherd loped inside. "He's yours."

"Mine?"

"A little welcome home gift," Rys said, grinning. "Hey boy, meet your new daddy."

"Oh, you shouldn't have. What's up with this?" Gray had to admit the dog was full of life and probably would make a good excuse to run the beach.

"His name is Koda. He's a retired police dog. Well trained, protective. Perfect for you." Jasper said, grabbing a ball from the basket at the door and rolling it acro" Call him your guard dog slash playmate,"

"Yeah, that's what he is. Here, my turn." Rhys tried to snatch the ball from the dog.

Cherish got in on the fun, stooping low. "C'mere boy." The dog dashed over to her and nearly knocked her over. She collapsed in laughter. "He is playful."

"Playful is good," Gray said.

Cherish got to her feet and brushed herself off. "I think I'll let you boys have fun. Gray, call if you need anything."

She headed to the door and Gray grabbed her hand in his. He brought it up to his lips and kissed it. "Thank you again for all you've done. You don't have to go."

"Yes, yes I do." She ran her hand gently over his cheek. "I'll see you soon. Don't over do it."

Koda and Gray's brothers were raising a ruckus behind them, but all his attention was absorbed by Cherish, standing in the doorway saying good bye. A shiver went through him. Nothing was certain, he knew that more than ever. But there wasn't anything to do about it.

Except wait.

44

Cherish sped away from Gray's beach house, questions weighing heavy on heart. Why oh why did she always react to things so largely? Gray was in the clear. He was home, healthy, playing with a new dog, for Christ's sake. Why was she glum?

The breeze from the window filled her head with the scent of the lake. It felt like it had been forever since she'd been to the beach, her favorite place. The place where she could always find peace.

She turned her car down the lane that led to the parking lot of 'her' beach, the sound of the waves lapping up onto shore drawing her in. After all the danger, angst, changes, and drama of the last few weeks, this was what she needed. A place where she didn't need to think, she could just be. Nature would do its magic.

She parked and took off her shoes. She stood in the warm sand with the sun overhead and savored the sheer bliss of sensations all around. Gulls overhead cried, punctuating the sense of spacious freedom that enveloped her.

She headed down to the shore and walked barefooted into the surf. It splashed against her and she couldn't help but smile. So many moments of her life had come together along this beach. She'd laughed here in happy times and cried and yelled at the wind when things were tough. Standing ankle deep in the cool water, she tried to sort the strange mixture of feelings circling in her brain. *What did she want?*

Suddenly a dog splashed into the water and chased the waves, barking. It startled and her she looked around. Wasn't the dog Gray's?

"Sorry Cherish. He got away from me. I don't know if he's ever seen a lake before." It was Gray, walking up the beach, laughing into the wind.

Her heart skipped a beat. "This is unexpected. What are you doing out here?"

He waded to her side and took her hands, while Koda played in the waves. "Oh, I had to meet a girl," he said softly. "I hope you don't mind."

Something let loose in her chest and tears meandered down her cheeks. He wiped them away. "Why the tears?"

"I don't know. I was feeling let down, for some reason, I think. I came here to collect my thoughts."

"Just as you did a few weeks ago and we met right here." He caressed her cheek and she leaned into it. "Why were you let down?"

"Well, so much has happened. So much of what has happened has been intense. It seemed like there should be something to show for it. To substantiate that a lot has changed. But I just walked away from you and that was that."

"You wanted more?"

"I want something."

"I want to tell you something. Can you bear with me?"

"Uh huh."

Gray struggled to suppress a smile. "I had a dream a few days ago. I was lying in bed in the hospital and I couldn't wake up. You were there, talking to me. I couldn't understand everything you said." He dared to look deeply into her eyes. "But I heard one small sentence. You said, I love you Gray."

Her eyes widened and she inhaled sharply. "You heard me say it in your dream?" Her eyelids fluttered.

"Yes, and I tried to say something, but I couldn't. I opened my mouth but nothing came out."

Cherish looked down and chewed on her lower lip.

"I'm sorry if I've made you uncomfortable. Just forget about my dream. I didn't mean anything by it."

"No. I won't forget it. I did say it. You were unconscious, but I needed to tell you."

"I understand needing to express something deep. Something you're not sure makes sense." His heart pounded and his grip on his nerves was tenuous. "I love you Cherish. I've wanted to tell you but I didn't think the timing was going to work for us."

She leaned closer. "I love you. I've been so wishy-washy, fickle, really. I wanted you in my life, but I was afraid of losing my way again and turning over my life to another person—you. When you got shot and almost died, I realized I wasn't afraid anymore, except for one thing. Losing you forever." Her shoulders shook as tears streamed.

"No more tears." His heart opened wide, wider than ever before. He pulled her close, hugging her until it hurt. "Cherish, Cherish. I love you. I love you so much. I don't want to ever lose you."

He lifted her chin and pressed a kiss to her silken lips. It was the kiss he had been longing to give her, the kind of kiss that asked for a promise.

He got lost in the kiss, and felt his heart sing.

Cherish started laughing and he pulled back, laughing. "You're laughing while I'm kissing you?"

"I'm so happy."

He held her hands in his and slowly walked onto the beach. Then he lowered to one knee.

"Grayson, what are you doing? Get up. You're going to get wet." She tried to pull him up, but he remained rooted to the ground.

"Cherish Elena Moss, will you marry me?" He held up one finger to silence her. "And, would you promise not to marry me until you are completely and irrevocably ready to share the rest of your life with me?"

"Yes!"

Her eyes sparkled for him like stars in the sky. He pulled a small velvet box from his back pocket and opened it to reveal a ring. The diamond the color of butter sparkled in the sunlight. He slipped it onto her left ring finger, and the complete peace he'd been waiting for filled him. He picked her up off her feet and slowly twirled in place around and around, his eyes pinned to hers. As he twirled her, dark lonely nights, sadness, and the troubles they had been through together, all of it faded away.

He set her feet back to the ground, but didn't let her go. He brushed a tear from her cheeks. "You're still crying."

"Happy tears, Gray. Happy tears."

EPILOGUE

The day Cherish felt completely and irrevocably ready to share the rest of your life with Gray

CHERISH LAY IN BED, savoring the soft touch of her sheets and stretching her limbs. Sunshine slanted into her bedroom from tall windows on the east wall.

"It's my wedding day." Musical notes danced in her belly to the melody of "Here Comes the Bride." "Dum dum da dum. Dum dum da dum." She thanked her lucky stars she'd woken up in time to recognize the fiasco-in-the-making by intending to marry Devin, and on this day, she had no misgivings, no hestitations, no second thoughts, and definitely no jitters. Knowing in every nook and cranny of her soul that she was completely and truly in love with Gray made all the difference.

The oval diamond Gray gave her sparkled on her finger. Her phone interrupted her reflection. Her heart leapt as though she were in high school. "Hi Gray."

His baritone voice flowed over the phone, so familiar and so loved. "Happy wedding day, my love. Are you out of bed yet? It's beautiful outside."

"I'm almost up. I've just been lying here thinking."

"Really?" Gray sounded startled.

"No second thoughts, just warm memories. I'm excited to become Cherish Elena Moss Steele."

"And live together for as long as we both shall live?"

"Exactly. Thank you for making this day so perfect."

"It's perfect for me too."

"I would never have been able to imagine a wedding like the one my family planned before I met you. The cove will be so private. And I like that we invited just a few special people other than our families."

"Me too. It won't take long to get them all to the cove and back to the reception at my house. I mean, our house."

"I better go. Rachel and Mom will be here soon."

"All right," he moaned. "I'll see you at the end of the aisle."

"I'll be the one in white."

"Cherish, are you up? You better be," her mother called from the bottom of the stairs.

"I hope you're decent." Rachel laughed. "We're coming up."

Cherish jumped out of bed and darted into the shower. "I'm showering." Talking to Gray on the morning of her wedding made a great start to her day.

"Hurry up."

Her mother's push didn't even register with Cherish. It was her day, truly her day. She wasn't going to think about what her father was doing to set things right with the law or that her mother had still not changed her ways. Emma Moss was giving her more space to be herself and that was more than she had expected. It was hard to say what gave her more satisfaction, that her parents had rectified their abuse of Uncle Peter by offering him financial support, that Devin was fighting the legal system for his freedom, or that Hastings and the Gang of Four, Austin, and the crooked lawyer and judge were doing their time. But none of it weighed her down today.

A few minutes later Rachel went to work on her hair. It would be a simple style. Everything she and Gray planned was simple, so they could engage fully with each other and their guests. No worrying about place settings, parking for hundreds of cars, paying for an expensive orchestra.

Her mother wandered around her room, picking up knick-knacks and books from her bookshelves as if she was seeing the room for the first time. "The poem on your wedding invitation is very beautiful," she said, holding it up. "'I am not afraid of ships, for I am learning to sail my own ship. Louisa May Alcott,'" she read. "Interesting but fitting for a wedding, I think. What with Gray's boat business and all."

Cherish exchanged a look with Rachel. They each knew the meaning behind the verse she and Gray had selected had nothing to do with Gray's boating business.

Hair and make-up done, Cherish held her arms up for her mother to lower the dress over her. She loved the feel of the lace bodice that gathered at her waist, and the tulle elbow-length sleeves and skirt. Its simple lines made her comfortable, as though she could glide.

"The circle of curls around your head holds the white roses really well and really enhances the copper color of your hair." Rachel stood back to admire her work. "I hope it's not windy at the cove." She bit her lower lip and Cherish laughed.

"Did you use lots of pins?"

"Lots."

Her mother stood a few steps away, eyes misting. She came over and hugged her. Cherish didn't so much care about the hair and make-up messing up, she wanted to show her love. "Mom, you make a beautiful mother-of-the-bride. I'm so glad to share this day with you. Your dress is gorgeous. I know this isn't the wedding you imagined for me, but I am happy. I love you."

Her mother put her hand to her heart. "You look so pretty. You made good choices, sweetheart. I love you."

Rachel started flaying her arms. "Okay, no more tears. Let's get to the wedding."

. . .

Small groups chatted on the dock at Gray's business while waiting their turn to catch a ride to the cove in one of the boats with Jasper or Rhys at the helm. She waved at her soon to be brothers-in-law, laughing lightly. "You both look so dashing in your tuxes."

Jasper pulled playfully at his bow tie. "You're beautiful." Then left for the cove.

The lake rolled calmly in a soft breeze. The water glistened in the sunlight. Peace welled in Cherish.

"May I escort you to your ride, ladies?" Rhys bowed and gestured to Gray's sailboat. She climbed in with his help and took a seat along the side.

"Is this safe?" Her mother squinted.

"Oh, Mother." Rachel patted her mother's arm. "Of course it is. Rhys knows what he's doing, right?"

Rhys's smiled wide and warm. "Trust me." His eyes lingered a brief moment on Rachel. "I'll get you there safely, Mrs. Moss."

Cherish kept her hands in her lap and her eyes pinned in the direction of the cove. Her heart beat fast, thinking of standing alone with Gray under the trellis trimmed in white roses and lilies of the valley.

Finally, they entered the cove, her nature cathedral. The sound of breezes and lapping water were hushed by the half-moon of trees enclosing the grassy area. Gray was nowhere in sight, but it only made the moment more mysterious and just for her.

Rhys helped them into a small boat to reach the cove, where the sounds of a singer and small ensemble of stringed and wind instruments floated in the air. The lyrics and music of "Call it Dreaming" made her smile. The singer's voice was sweet and the ensemble played beautifully. Knowing the musicians were playing as a way to pay their legal bill made one more thing perfect.

All the guests—Henry Pole and his wife and children, Sam and Lucy Standish, Eric Lee and his girlfriend, attorneys Nathan Orlando and Paul Striker, Aunt Patsy, and Pansy—were all seated in wooden folding chairs on both sides of an aisle of white cloth.

Rachel stood at the end of the white runner. She turned around and smiled wide at Cherish, then walked toward the trellis. Cherish loved her so much and was so grateful to share her day, the day she wanted, with her.

The musicians starting playing Wagner's Bridal Song and Gray stepped under the trellis, Rhys at his side. He looked at her as she took her father's arm and moved down the aisle. Each step was a step closer to him and the life she had chosen, and his eyes held her the whole way. Surrounded by family and other people she valued, she felt warmed and assured.

Her father kissed her cheek at the end of the aisle. "I love you, Cherish." He joined her mother, while nodding to Thomas and Susan Steele and Jasper.

Gray held tight to her hand and they stepped up to the minister.

"Friends, we have joined here today to share with Cherish Elena Moss and Grayson Thomas Steele an important moment in their lives. In their time together, they have seen their love and under-standing of each other grow and blossom, and now they have decided to live out the rest of their lives together as husband and wife. Gray and Cherish have written their own vows and will recite them now to each other.

Gray slipped her wedding ring on her finger. The band of glit-tering green tourmaline and sparkling diamonds glinted in the sunlight, capturing her breath.

"Cherish, I give you this ring as a token of my vow to you. A vow is a promise."

Cherish took his words in and saw only his clear blue eyes and his lips as he spoke only to her.

"I promise to always be fascinated by you, to always be your soft spot to land, to walk beside you through whatever life brings to us. I promise to care for you in meaningful ways. And I promise to always, always love you."

Cherish slid Gray's wedding band on his finger, and admired his manly hand. It was steady and calloused.

"Gray, I give you this ring as a promise that, like the circle of the ring, my love will never end." She looked up into his face and a tear meandered down her cheek. "I stand here with you on the edge of a marvelous adventure that we will create together. You've brought me so many opportunities to be set free, and I will always love you for that. I promise to always be in awe of you and all that you are, to grow alongside you as your partner throughout our life. I promise I'll be your biggest fan and love you forever."

The minister continued, "As we've witnessed the coming together of Grayson Thomas Steele and Cherish Elena Moss, we are all blessed with their love. By the power vested in me by the state of Michigan, I now pronounce you husband and wife. You may now— oh, you beat me to the moment." The pastor chuckled as Gray pulled her into a kiss. Gray's lips moved over hers, sweeping her into a private place where she could go only with him.

She pulled away and looked into Gray's eyes with the crinkles in the corners and saw a lifetime. It was just beginning.

ABOUT THE AUTHOR

After cutting her writing teeth as a feature writer for commercial and trade magazines, a reporter for newspapers and radio, and an executive editor for a communications company, award-winning author Lynn Crandall tuned her voracious appetite for stories to writing contemporary and paranormal romance, women's fiction, and romantic suspense. In her books, she enjoys taking readers on emotional journeys with relatable characters who refuse to back down, and face challenges and tribulations with heart and soul. She believes every love has a story, and hers is with one handsome husband and a large, beautiful circle of family, including her cat Winter.

For more from Lynn Crandall, visit lynn-crandall.com . Stay up to date with releases, including Dark Sides books two and three, *Hear Me, See Me*, by subscribing to her newsletter.

ALSO BY LYNN CRANDALL

Touch Me, Dark Sides Book One

Love, Forever (sampler anthology)

Touch of Breeze: The Common Elements Project

Snowbound (audible)

Nutcracker Sweet (short)

Two Days Until Midnight (novella)

At Midnight (anthology)

Captured by Christmas (anthology)

Fierce Hearts series

Secrets

Cravings

Heartfelt

Probabilities

Unstoppable

Finding Finn

Aegar Investigations series

Dancing with Detective Danger

Always and Forever Love

Chapter 1

Rachel Moss sat beside her parents, Adrian and Emma Moss, at the counsel table in the Dunes Bay Michigan County Court House and readied herself for their probation status hearing. Nerves jangled inside like they never had with any other court case. As their daughter and a lawyer, she was expected to ensure they'd be released from probation just as one year ago they'd demanded she keep them out of prison to continue with the family law firm, Moss Attorneys at Law.

Rachel tried not to think about the day she and her sister Cherish discovered their parents were money laundering. It still made her livid. Adrian and Emma hadn't cared that they were not only putting themselves in jeopardy, but also her and Cherish as members of the law firm, as well as the whole staff. The situation could have fallen on all of them, though they were innocent of any wrong doing.

Noticing her mother's fidgeting, Rachel followed her gaze as she turned around, and in the process knocked her phone to the carpeted floor. It made a thud sound that barely registered in Rachel's mind as she scanned the rows of people behind them, pausing on someone in a black suit two rows back. Rachel quickly checked over her shoulder and collided gazes with a man in a black suit. His hair was neatly trimmed into a close cut and his eyes peered at her through slits. She shuddered and turned forward. Was it a mere coincidence that her mother appeared to have sought him out? It was hard to think so, but knowing her mother Rachel suspected something devious was going on.

Rachel eyed her mother. She was furtively texting under the table. Another of her suspicious phone exchanges, Rachel was sure. They'd been happening a lot lately and her mother kept them secret.

Emma leaned closer. "Don't be nervous. Your father and I have done everything right over the past year. All you have to do is make sure the judge sees we're completely in compliance."

Rachel listened to her mother but couldn't help wonder if she was telling the truth. It had been a long year since her parents' money laundering had come to light and she'd represented them in court when Cherish's jilted fiancé, Devin Raye, tried to parlay information. A disgraced lawyer, he had been dealing with legal problems over evidence tampering and witness intimidation in a trial a year ago. As a friend of Emma and Adrian, he'd also been a confidant to their criminal behavior, and tried to use what he knew to lessen his own sentence. The media had a heyday with the story at the time, and it felt like everywhere she went people were looking at her suspiciously. But it had died down after just a few news cycles passed when reporting turned to a lake-shore company dumping chemicals into the environment and a town board member's extra-marital affair had taken over the headlines.

Rachel shivered. It had all been such a terrific mess. "You were lucky you were put on probation and only for two years. You better be telling me the truth."

Her mother pulled back. "You think I would lie to you? That's insulting."

Her father whispered from the other side of her mother. "Now, Emma. Don't make a scene. You know as well as I do that Rachel has reason to doubt us. Let's just get through this, we need her help."

"All rise. This court is now in session," the bailiff said. He announced Judge Georgana York and Rachel breathed a sigh of relief that the court proceedings were moving forward. *Let's put this behind us.*

"In the case of Emma Moss, is the defense ready?"

Rachel stood. "We are, your Honor. Adrian Moss is also here for his hearing."

"Noted, but we're starting with her."

Rachel prompted her mother to stand, and stared straight ahead. Muscles from her neck to her legs were rigid and tense. She supposed it was natural for her to be worried about her parents. They never really seemed to appreciate the trouble they were in. They didn't suffer from remorse, they simply were eager to be done with their probation.

"Mrs. Moss, this hearing is to decide whether you're eligible for early release from probation. I have your file and I see you have paid all your fines and haven't missed a single check-in with your probation officer. Is that correct?"

"Yes, your Honor," her mother answered. Thankfully she sounded humble and sincere, all of which Rachel doubted was real.

"Good. I have a few questions to ask you. Along with the fines and probation, you were to perform community service. Do you feel you learned anything from your community service that could translate to your law practice?"

Emma stared at the judge, pursing her lips.

Rachel's nerves twitched. Emma should have prepared a statement.

"Mrs. Moss. Answer the question," the judge ordered.

Her mother drew in a breath. "Your honor, I'm grateful for the terms of my probation that required me to volunteer. Being up close and personal with the indigent individuals at the legal clinic where I volunteered made me realize how lucky I am just to be able to help them. They deserve the justice we all expect, no matter their income status. Thank you for helping open my eyes."

Realization dawned in Rachel. The reason Emma paused before answering was to add drama. Her mother was a world class drama queen. No, she didn't just breed drama, she lived for it.

"Very nice to hear. Now, I have another question. Do you regret what you did?"

"Oh yes. I was wrong to do business with a criminal organization. At the time I didn't feel I had a choice, but I now see I did and I made the wrong one." Her mother's voice quivered just enough to give her answer a hint of truth.

Rachel held her breath. The judge would see through the charade but would it make her continue probation for another year?

"Mr. and Mrs. Moss, I hope you both have learned that the only just way to practice law is to follow the law. You both are prominent lawyers, and as that, I feel you have an obligation to stand for truth and model integrity. Despite the crimes you've committed, you did not do jail time. You did not lose your law licenses. You're being given a second chance to lead a good life. I don't want to see you back in court ever again. The court agrees to release you, Mrs. Moss, from probation."

Her parents turned to her and each one hugged her in turn. Her mother whispered in her ear. "I'm going to do the best to restore your faith in me," she said.

The judge pounded the gavel. "Order. Now, we proceed with the case of Adrian Moss," she said, and proceeded to ask her father the same questions and dismissed his probation, too.

They walked out of the courtroom together and headed out into the sunshine.

"See, this is why we wanted you to represent us," her dad said, beaming from ear to ear. "You're a damn good attorney."

"Thanks, Dad." She warmed under his praise, she couldn't help it. But something about their demeanor made her skin prickle. They looked a little too smug, a little too happy with themselves.

"You don't seem surprised, Mom, that your probation was dismissed. Did you have a good feeling about it?"

"I did." Her mother smiled.

Rachel's stomach churned. Her mother's smile reminded her of a Cheshire cat's. What wasn't she saying? And why, why was it up to her to keep them in line?

"It's Thursday, a good day to have dinner together. Do you want to come to dinner tonight, sweetheart? I can make something special to celebrate," her mother said.

"Umm, no." She checked her pockets in her suit pants for her cell-phone. "I'll see you at the office. I think I left my phone in the courtroom."

Court was in recess, so she hunted down the bailiff. She found him just down the hall a ways. "Excuse me, John," she called. "Can you let me into Judge York's courtroom? I forgot something."

"Of course, Rachel," he said. "Come with me."

John led her to a side door and unlocked it. "Here you go," he said, following close behind her.

She almost ran into the tall, slim man in a black suit she'd seen in the courtroom earlier coming out of the hallway to the judge's chambers. She got a whiff of his scent and recognized it as Jo Malone's unique Oud & Bergamot. He dropped a brief gaze on her, then looked away and made a bee line for the open door. His eyes meant as much business as his suit, and he gave her the chills. She didn't like seeing him exiting the judge's chambers, and couldn't help but read into it something illicit connected to her parents.

Rachel went to the defendant's table and saw her phone lying on the floor under it. She had been so eager to get out of the room she must have knocked it off the table without noticing.

"Thanks," she said to the bailiff, and walked out the door, trying to shake off the suspicions in her mind and get to her office with a clear head.

"Rachel you've got to help me. Soren is going to hurt my babies. He's going to steal them from me. You can't let that happen."

Rachel reached across her desk and touched Shaylahna Lucia's hand. Her heart squeezed for her best friend. Soren, her husband, had shown his hot temper soon after he'd married Shay, and their four years together had been rocky. Now it sounded like their four months separation was also rocky.

Tears streamed down Shaylahna's cheeks and her body trembled. Shay was having a meltdown and everything in Rachel wanted to make it stop. "I want to help. But I'm not a divorce or custody lawyer."

"What do you mean?" Shay shook her head. "They belong to me. There is no custody to work out. Besides, you're an attorney, aren't you? Taking care of problems is what you do."

Rachel winced internally. Was it that obvious that her job in life, especially with family and friends, seemed to be keeping everyone going, attending to their latest drama. *What? So now you're going to turn selfish, on your best friend?*

Shay sniffed, and Rachel offered her a tissue. She strategized in her head, while Shay blew her nose. Of course she could help her friend. She was right to tell her she wasn't a divorce lawyer, but there were other things she could do. Things that now splashed around in her head like Lake Michigan waves slamming against a rocky shoreline.

She swallowed hard. Her parents wouldn't be pleased if she took on Shay's case. It would be different from their typical corporate cases, and there wouldn't be a big pay out, because she wouldn't invoice her friend full civil lawyer's fees. Was she honestly going to let fear of her parents' stop her from helping?

No. She was not. Rachel straightened her spine and smiled at Shay. She and her sister stood up to their parents all the time, it was just a regular part of life for them. Prime example, her last case.

"Yes I am a lawyer. This law firm specializes in representing corporations. I don't have family law training, and you need a lawyer with that kind of experience." Her heart sunk when Shay's face crumpled. At thirty-three, she and Rachel were the same age and had gone through many things, both fun and some hardships too, but always supported one another as good friends do.

"But I trust you. You're brilliant. I don't know anyone else like you." She dropped her head in to her hands.

Wheels spun in Rachel's mind. She couldn't see Shay getting through the day, much less the weeks or months dealing with this pressure.

She shrugged. "I can't represent you in court but I can damn well consult and be by your side in all this mess," she said, and savored the sweet moment of bringing a relieved smile to Shay's face.

"Oh, thank you, thank you. You're the best," Shay gushed. "I can't imagine a life without my rescue Greyhounds in it. I know you'll keep them safe from my soon-to-be ex-husband," she said, emphasis on soon-to-be *ex*.

"I'm so sorry this is happening." Rachel really was sorry for her friend. She suspected there was more to the story than Shay's husband threatening to separate her from her dogs. At least she has them now. "Has he truly been abusive to Wendy and Rocket?"

Shay's face scrunched and new tears brimmed her eyes. "He

didn't start out that way, but he is determined to hurt me for divorcing him. He thinks if he threatens to take the dogs from me I'll reconsider. But I won't, no matter what, no way. He's involved in some surly things associated with his real estate development business, he's mean, and I can't be with him anymore. And he can't have the dogs." She dipped her gaze.

Rachel shivered at the unthinkable possibility that popped into her head. "Has Soren hit you? I've seen his quick temper."

"Well, he is fiery. That was one thing that attracted me to him. His passion. He claims it's the Italian in him, but that doesn't have anything to do with his temper. No. The only way I could get away was to leave behind my kids, but I got out the day he promised he'd hurt me before giving me a divorce. He still won't relinquish my kids. When he lets me visit them, they behave as if they're on alert. I'm afraid for them, and I think they're skittish because he's hurt them." Sobs took her over. "I didn't know. I just didn't suspect he'd be like this."

"*This* meaning spiteful, rageful, and downright mean? I wish I could tell you it never happens, but," Rachel frowned. "It happens more than most people realize." Disappointment sickened her heart. "People can really let one another down, even though they once proclaimed love."

Her thoughts drifted to Emma and Adrian Moss. She'd never forget how the truth from her mother smacked her hard in her heart. It splintered and still hadn't mended from learning about a year ago that her parents had put up a good façade of marital bliss. They had married each other to create a power couple, not because they loved one another. It wasn't love that kept them together, it was the wealth and status they'd acquired. Loss of hope in her parents and humanity in general set in and she couldn't imagine how to find it again.

"Well, that is a depressing thought." Shay grabbed Rachel's hand. "You're a great friend. If you can prevent Soren from taking away my babies, I'll be forever grateful."

Rachel grabbed Shay in a big hug. "Don't worry about anything. I'm here for you."

Shay gave her a weak smile. "Wendy and Rocket are out in my car. Soren left them with me today and said he'd pick them up later. I think he just wants a reason to see me. Soren 'allows' me to have them for short periods of time when he feels like it. This morning he felt like letting me take them to an open house for one of my clients. They lend a homey touch to my real estate transactions, and they love the attention. But for Soren, he probably saw something in it for him, like me making money so he can squirm out of paying me alimony, not that I want his money anyway."

"Oh, bring them in. I haven't seen the puppies in weeks."

"Okay, I'll be right back with them." The sounds of Shay's shoes against the hall carpeting were a brisk swish, swish, swish, that came to an abrupt stop.

"Well, hi Shay," Rachel heard her mother say. "I haven't seen you in so long. How are you and that handsome Italian husband of yours?"

Rachel pulled in a long breath. She couldn't hear Shay's response, but Emma Moss was a force of nature. If Shay didn't waver in front of her mother she'd be doing much better than she was a few seconds ago. That was unlikely.

A pendulum inside Rachel swung from one position to another; she could go to Shay's rescue and interrupt her mother's probe-in-progress or she could trust Shay to manage the situation herself.

"Well, I'm sorry to learn about your divorce. I always thought you and Soren made such an adorable couple." A long sigh came from her mother. "But relationships falling apart seems to be the trend these days. You probably heard that Cherish, Rachel's sister, dumped poor Devin Raye at the altar. It was a sad day."

Rachel popped to her feet. "Cherish took exactly a year to get to know Gray and take care of critical business before they married, and now they are very happily on their honeymoon in Paris. So I guess all said and done, things worked out," she hollered as she stepped out into the hall. "Not so much for Devin. His disbarment put a real damper on his career and he's still got legal problems, despite reporting you and Dad to the feds. So I'd say Cherish did pretty well with her choices." She didn't try very hard to keep sarcasm out of her voice, and pivoted back into her office. Boy it made her boil when her mother distorted the truth.

"Oh, well, surely that could be the case." Rachel heard her mother's fluster in her voice. She wasn't accustomed to people disagreeing, but Rachel simply had to from time to time. If she didn't, her mother would plough over her, and that would be intolerable.

Rachel's heart swelled with pride in her younger sister for taking control of her life. It had taken her most of her life to learn that acquiescing to their parents wasn't any way to live. Cherish was a drill sergeant in the courtroom, but when it came to her parents, she'd complied with what they told her to do ninety percent of the time. Her heart warmed remembering her sister coming into her own over the year that passed following the breakup with her fiancé. Case in point, she ran away from the marriage made in Emma and Adrian's concept of heaven, and found the man of her dreams in Grayson Steele.

Riveted to her office floor, she held her breath, waiting for the other shoe to drop. Then she heard Shay say good bye and Rachel relaxed into her desk chair. She propped her head on her hands and breathed in and out slowly to clear her mind. Relief shuddered through her for Shay, who had just barely escaped the lecture Emma was about to deliver detailing how other people should live their lives. She did it whenever she caught someone standing still. *Yeah, Mom has problems.*

Rachel sorted through her brain finding it hard to free her mind. She'd known Shay since grade school. As her best friend, Shay stood a single notch below Cherish as a confidant.

Breathe. Breathe.

Funny she had to coach herself to keep breathing. So much was happening this week following Cherish's wedding, and it was only Thursday. Two weeks, Cherish would be on her honeymoon for two weeks, while things at home would weigh heavily on Rachel's shoulders. She wished she could talk to her sister. With Cherish gone and

Shay in deep chaos, Rachel had no one to turn to. She'd just have to sort this through herself.

She stared at her desk, her head still resting on her hands. The weightier topic, the one taking up most of her mind, was a question that needed an answer pronto: Were she and Cherish safe from her parents continuing on their criminal path. Yes, her parents had gotten off easy with the Michigan State Bar Association and federal prosecutors a year ago when Devin let it be known they were laundering money for "special" wealthy clients. Such were the privileges of the rich and connected, but not legal all the same. Rachel was grateful for the leniency the courts offered, but still, their crimes loomed large, right under her skin, scratching like sandpaper. She and her sister didn't trust their parents anymore.

Rachel's mind filled with memories of discovering the truth about her parents and her world crashing when she and Cherish overheard them discussing illegal activities with Devin It was also the beginning of the end of Cherish and Devin's relationship. Cherish demanded they change their ways, and they agreed, Emma reluctantly. But it was too late. Devin was as guilty as they were and handed over her parents to the authorities in hopes of getting off easy for his crimes. Their parents' crimes and lies were a hard truth to face. She and Cherish got through by leaning on each other, and Shay had also been there for Rachel. It had taken a good piece of lawyering on Rachel's part with Cherish's help to prevent their parents' disbarment. They agreed they'd give their parents the benefit of the doubt for one year, believing they could stay true to their word to go straight, but she and Cherish had to remain watchful. If their parents dipped their fingers back into the wrong pot, they would have to take steps to protect themselves and their careers. Keeping an eagle eye on their parents was exhausting, but necessary. She had to accept she didn't have Ozzie and Harriet for parents. No, more like Bonnie and Clyde in designer clothing. Another gloomy thought that dropped her heart into her gut.

"Oh, Cherish, I need you," she mumbled to herself.